SHADOW OF EMPIRE

ALSO BY JAY ALLAN

FAR STARS

Shadow of Empire
Enemy in the Dark (**December 2015**)
Funeral Games (**January 2016**)

CRIMSON WORLDS

Marines
The Cost of Victory
A Little Rebellion
The First Imperium
The Line Must Hold
To Hell's Heart
The Shadow Legions
Even Legends Die
The Fall
War Stories (**Crimson Worlds Prequels**)
MERCS (**Crimson Worlds Successors I**)

PORTAL WARS

Gehenna Dawn
The Ten Thousand

PENDRAGON CHRONICLES

The Dragon's Banner

SHADOW OF EMPIRE

FAR STARS BOOK ONE

JAY ALLAN

HARPER Voyager

An Imprint of HarperCollins*Publishers*

SHADOW OF EMPIRE. Copyright © 2015 by Jay Allan Books. All rights reserved. Printed in the United States of America. No part of this book may be used or reproduced in any manner whatsoever without written permission except in the case of brief quotations embodied in critical articles and reviews. For information address HarperCollins Publishers, 195 Broadway, New York, NY 10007.

HarperCollins books may be purchased for educational, business, or sales promotional use. For information please e-mail the Special Markets Department at SPsales@harpercollins.com.

FIRST EDITION

Harper Voyager and design is a trademark of HarperCollins Publishers L.L.C.

Designed by Shannon Nicole Plunkett

Library of Congress Cataloging-in-Publication Data has been applied for.

ISBN 978-0-06-238890-2

15 16 17 18 19   OV/RRD   10 9 8 7 6 5 4 3 2 1

SHADOW OF EMPIRE

CHAPTER 1

ARKARIN BLACKHAWK STOOD BAREFOOT IN THE HOT, BLOOD-stained sand of the battle pit, Kalishar's noon sun searing into his back like a blowtorch. He could feel the burning sweat pouring down his neck, hear the lusty shouts of the crowd calling for his blood.

None of it mattered.

He stared straight ahead, toward the black iron bars of the gate fifteen meters from where he stood. Whoever—whatever—came charging out of there in the next few seconds, that was all that mattered. The battles in the pit were to the finish, and Blackhawk knew he had been sent there to die. Which meant that the opponent he was about to face was one his captors were sure could defeat him. He was certain of that. But they underestimated him.

They always underestimated him.

They'd stripped him down and dressed him in the traditional loincloth for the fight. The accused was allowed no armor or other protection in judicial combat. Blackhawk was extremely fit, muscular without an ounce of fat on his two-meter frame. His chest and back were covered with scars, the markings of a life spent in battle. He looked to be in his midthirties, but that was an illusion, a side effect of his superior genetics. As it was, he was well past fifty, though no one would have guessed it watching him stand there, half naked in the blazing Kalishari sun.

They'd left him his own blade. That was something, at least. Tradition demanded even a condemned man face his adversary armed, but they could have given him a stick and upheld the letter of the law. Blackhawk held the shortsword tightly, the familiar smoothness of its worn leather grip a source of calm. It was an anchor to cling on to, to center himself for the contest he knew would begin any second. He'd killed before with that sword, more times than he could easily recount, and he knew it would find its mark again. It wasn't the battle Blackhawk was worried about. He knew he could handle anything that came out of that gate. What would happen after he won . . . that was the problem.

Whatever happened to him, at least his people would be safe. He'd ordered *Wolf's Claw* to blast off and get back to Celtiboria as quickly as possible. The mission would be completed and the crew would escape, though his hastily issued command had cost him all hope of rescue. Fact was, Blackhawk didn't fear his own death. Indeed, in many ways it would be a mercy. He had too many memories, images he longed to forget, ghosts that haunted him from the edges of consciousness. It was always there, the remorse for the things he'd done, the crimes he'd committed. More than a decade had done nothing to reduce the intensity of his guilt or wash away the regret and pain. Perhaps death would be his escape.

Blackhawk had the same thoughts every time he faced danger, a strange melancholy, almost an indifference to his own survival. But there was always something in him that fought back, that refused to give up. It was a force of will he couldn't resist, one that demanded he fight to survive with every bit of the considerable strength he could muster. Yet, while he'd fight until his last breath, he wouldn't needlessly endanger his crew, not even for his own survival. The thought of bearing more guilt was the one thing he couldn't accept. That's why he was here alone, ready to face whatever stormed out of the ominous gate. Ready to deal with whatever happened after he dispatched his foe. Alone.

And what a place to be alone. Kalishar was a pestilential hole—a miserable, useless world—save only for its good fortune to lie close to the richest trade routes in the Far Stars. The place was an ideal pirate refuge, and in every way it lived up to that image. The planet was a sunbaked rock, its most habitable areas vast sandy deserts where, at least, the deadly pathogens and aggressive carnivores that infested its steaming jungles and tropical swamps were less of a threat. Kalishar had no resources to speak of, no fertile farmlands, no productive mines, no modern industry. But it had built substantial wealth as a sanctuary where—as long as they left their guns in their ships and didn't cause too much trouble—the most notorious pirates, thieves, and killers in the Far Stars could come to rest, drink, lie low, and spend their ill-gotten gains.

Blackhawk had chased one of those pirates halfway across the Far Stars to Kalishar, grimly pursuing his target and resisting every effort the fleeing rogue made to evade him. Cyrus Mondran had proven to be an elusive enemy, one who'd almost shaken Blackhawk and his crew more than once. But the fleeing pirate had kidnapped the daughter of Marshal Lucerne of Celtiboria, and Lucerne was one of Blackhawk's few friends. The marshal hired him and his crew to get her back, offering a king's ransom despite Blackhawk's offer to do it for nothing. And Arkarin Blackhawk always completed his mission. Always.

When he finally caught his prey and rescued the marshal's daughter, Blackhawk thrust the very blade he now held through Mondran's black heart. It was common enough for pirates to kill each other on Kalishar, and the authorities, such as they were, didn't much care. As long as the prohibition against firearms was obeyed, rival buccaneers were welcome to have at each other—provided they didn't do too much damage or interfere with local business. Contests between pirates and other scoundrels fighting over loot were one of the planet's minor attractions, and crowds quickly gathered around any street fight that seemed worth watching or gambling on.

On this occasion, though, Mondran had been under the protection of the ka'al, Tarn Belgaren, and the ka'al ruled Kalishar. Killing someone in service to the ka'al was a bad idea; taking out five of the dictator's men when they came to arrest you was downright insane. But Blackhawk did just that . . . and almost fought his way back to the ship before they finally brought him down fifty meters short of his destination with three blasts from a stun cannon.

Blackhawk's crime warranted death, at least on Kalishar. Offending the ka'al in any way was a capital offense, but attacking and killing his men all but guaranteed an unpleasant end. Blackhawk knew Kalishar's laws and customs well, though, and he had loudly demanded a trial by combat as they were hauling him away. He knew the ka'al would have preferred to give him a long and painful death in the catacombs beneath his stronghold, but the whole thing had become too public for that. The crowds loved nothing as much as watching an off-worlder die in the pit, and Belgaren knew keeping the mob amused was the key to retaining his power, and failing to provide sufficient spectacles was a good way to lose his head.

The mob roared as the gate swung open and slammed into the stone wall of the arena with a loud crash, rousing Blackhawk from his thoughts. His eyes focused like two lasers, and he could feel himself slip into the strange battle trance that always took him in combat. He felt a rush of adrenaline, and his genetically engineered muscles tensed, his body readying itself for the fight that was about to begin. It felt instinctive, almost automatic. Effortless. There was no fear, no panic. He approached combat like a surgeon: meticulous, methodical. It was time to kill.

He moved instinctively to the left, taking himself out of the direct path of anything charging through the gate. He listened carefully, focusing on every sound, every clue. The sooner he knew what he faced, the better prepared he would be. Even fractions of a second counted.

Sound analysis suggests a large quadruped with a humanoid rider.

Blackhawk heard the familiar voice in his head. It wasn't a voice, really, not a sound at all. He'd never been able to characterize exactly how the artificial intelligence implanted in his brain communicated with him. It interfaced with his thoughts somehow, but it was a feeling like nothing else he'd experienced. The AI had been installed against his will, and he'd mistrusted it for years. But the thing had saved his life more than once, and he'd gradually begun to accept it, eventually learning to rely on it. It was part of him, just like an arm or a leg.

He was about to flash a thought back to the AI, but just then his enemy burst out into the blazing sunlight. It was indeed a quadruped—a big one—with two horns and a spiky ridge just above its eyes. Two long appendages protruded from behind the creature's thick neck, swaying back and forth in front of its head.

A stegaroid. From the Kalishari jungle zone.

Blackhawk nodded, a useless gesture to an AI implanted in his head, perhaps, but a habit nonetheless. The creature was over three meters at the shoulders and covered from head to toe in armored plates. There was a rider on its back, a huge man wearing a leather breastplate and wielding a long spear. His face was hard to see under the shadow of his helmet, but there was something familiar about him.

Beware the creature's tentacles. They are highly toxic. One sting is sufficient to kill a normal human.

Blackhawk nodded again. It was useful information, no question, but sometimes he wondered how it would feel not having a voice in your head telling you things were worse than you thought. He'd been like that once, like everyone else, but that was years ago.

His eyes locked on the creature's flailing appendages. They were at least two meters long, and they moved with surprising speed. That was going to be a problem since his sword was barely fifty centimeters. He figured he could survive a sting, maybe two. Blackhawk was the genetically engineered product of a centuries-long breeding program, and his constitution was vastly stronger than a normal man's. But he didn't like to advertise his abilities, and surviving a sting from the stegaroid in front of two thousand screaming people wasn't the best way to play the part of a common pirate.

The creature reared back its head and let out a deep roar. Then it charged. Blackhawk's eyes remained fixed on the tentacles reaching out ahead of the beast, following their every move. He dug his feet into the sand, standing firm, sword at the ready. He waited until the last possible second before lunging down and to the side, his blade whipping through the air, slicing through one of the gruesome appendages.

The beast howled in rage and agony, thick green blood spraying from the severed tentacle. Blackhawk rolled forward, sliding underneath the stegaroid. He thrust his blade up and into the creature's unarmored belly, stabbing with all his genetically enhanced strength. He almost lost his hold on the sword as the beast bucked wildly and staggered away, squealing hideously and leaving a trail of viscous blood behind it.

Blackhawk pivoted as quickly as he could, but he still took a partial blow from one of the stegaroid's back legs. He sucked in a deep breath and pulled himself back up, ignoring the pain in his side and turning to face his wounded enemy. He knew the fight wasn't over yet, not even close.

"Let's move it. We've got to get this tub in the air now!" Jason "Ace" Graythorn stood on the cramped bridge of *Wolf's Claw*, shouting at the ship's pilot. Graythorn was one of Blackhawk's oldest companions, and he wasn't about to let the boss get scragged by some jacked-up dictator of an armpit planet. And the fact that Blackhawk himself had ordered them to make a run for it didn't change a thing. No fucking way. He wasn't leaving without Blackhawk. None of them were.

"I'm powering up the launch system as fast as I can." Lucas Lancaster was frantically working the ship's main control board as he snapped back his response. His voice was tense, bordering on panic. For all any of them knew, Blackhawk was already dead. Lancaster knew as well as Ace—as well as anyone on *Wolf's Claw*—just how urgent seconds were. But an emergency start of the ship's engines was no joke. "We're not gonna save the skipper if I blow the damned ship up, are we?"

Lancaster worked frantically. He couldn't let his shipmates down, but most of all, he would not allow himself to fail Blackhawk.

The *Claw*'s captain had saved his life.

Lancaster had been the black sheep of one of the wealthiest families in the Far Stars, expelled from the Antilles Naval Academy despite posting the highest flight aptitude scores in its long and storied history. His natural piloting skill had bought him second and third chances, but eventually gambling, drinking, fighting, and—ultimately—seducing the commandant's daughter, sealed his fate. He was sent back to his family estates in disgrace, where he buried his sorrows by going on an epic binge, one that put his earlier debauchery to shame. His father pulled him out of one mess after another, but eventually Lucas had bedded too many important men's wives and trashed too many bars in drunken, drug-addled rages. The elder Lancaster's patience was finally exhausted.

Expelled from the family, Lucas fell deeper into an epic downward spiral of depravity and self-destruction. And until

Arkarin Blackhawk found him, he'd been half a minute from getting into a fight that would probably have been his last. Lancaster was too drunk to stand and had enough pharmaceuticals in his blood to stock a midsize hospital, but Blackhawk saw something worth saving.

And that was something no one else ever had ever done.

Blackhawk had extricated the kid from the situation and taken him back to *Wolf's Claw* . . . where he proceeded to beat him within an inch of his life in the empty cargo hold. He told Lancaster with each blow that he'd get the same every time he took a drink or popped a pill. It took a while—and a lot of beatings and sleepless nights—but Blackhawk's firm discipline and intense focus did the job. The *Claw*'s new pilot had been stone-cold sober ever since, and he hadn't ingested so much as an aspirin as far back as any of the crew could remember. Lancaster may not have been with Blackhawk as long as Ace had, but he was at least as determined as anyone on the *Claw* to pull the skipper from the mess he'd gotten himself into. Lucas Lancaster couldn't imagine losing Blackhawk. The captain was like a father to him.

"Just get us in the air." Ace knew Lancaster was doing the best he could, but gambler, womanizer, and shameless rake that he was, Ace thrived working under the maximum possible pressure, and he assumed everyone else did, too. He knew Blackhawk could take care of himself—better than any man he'd ever known. But this time the skipper had gotten himself in deep. If they didn't get there in time . . . he didn't want to think about it. He'd seen Blackhawk in a hundred fights, and he knew better than most just how good he was, how much stronger and faster than other men. But the ka'al had no intention of letting Arkarin Blackhawk live, whether or not he won in the arena.

No, Ace knew Blackhawk was as good as dead. Unless *Wolf's Claw* got there in time. "Get us in the air now. Damn the risk."

Lancaster glanced down at the gauges. He needed at least another five minutes for the engines to warm up to optimum levels. But he knew the skipper might not have that five minutes. He took a deep breath and gripped the throttle. "Hang on to something. This could get rough." The warning was for Ace. Everyone else was strapped in below, but Graythorn had insisted on breathing down Lancaster's neck, and if he ended up on his ass on the middle of the bridge, it would serve him right. Lancaster activated the thrust controls and pulled back on the stick. The ship lurched upward, its belly thrusters lifting it roughly from the rocky sand.

Wolf's Claw was an old ship and, to the untrained eye, she looked like a pile of junk, the battered wreck of a marginal smuggler. But Blackhawk had upgraded her power plant and weapons systems with state-of-the-art equipment. The old girl had almost-new engines that could put out three times the thrust of her original ones, and her stealth technology was first rate. She packed a potent punch in a fight, too, and if things went wrong, she was fast enough to make a hell of a run for it. The only thing her captain hadn't touched was her exterior, not so much as a new paint job. Being underestimated by an enemy was a huge step toward victory, or escape if necessary. Just like with himself, Blackhawk saw no point in advertising his ship's true capabilities.

The *Claw* moved upward with a violent jerk and pitched to the side. Ace was almost thrown across the bridge, but he managed to get a hand on Lancaster's chair and hold on as the pilot pulled the ship around in a tight circle and accelerated toward the arena.

Lancaster pushed the throttle forward, sending more of the output from the ship's reactor to her engines. It was delicate work feeding power to the cold drives, but he had a light touch. He could almost feel the engines, tell by intuition just how much raw power they could take before blowing themselves— and everyone on the ship—to plasma.

He hoped.

The arena wasn't far from the desert valley where they'd stashed the *Claw*, and it was only a few minutes before he could see it up ahead. "I've got this," Lancaster said. "You better get on the needle beam, Ace. We may have some fighting to do before we get the skipper out." It was almost showtime.

Ace nodded and grunted his assent. He tapped the small communicator clipped to his collar as he worked his way across the bridge to the weapons console. "Shira, Tarq, Tarnan: you guys better suit up and get ready for a fight. We don't know what shape the cap's in."

"We're already on it, Ace." The voice on the comm was like ice. Shira Tarkus had been with Blackhawk as long as Graythorn, and no one on the *Claw* had any doubt she'd do whatever it took to get the captain back. They'd all seen her in action. Tarkus was cold and remorseless in combat, as skilled a killer as anyone on *Wolf's Claw* except Blackhawk himself . . . Like Lancaster, she owed her life to Arkarin Blackhawk . . . He'd saved her from execution on some backwater planet for a crime he thought sounded a lot like self-defense. He had busted her out of her death cell, and the two of them shot and sliced their way back to the *Claw*, leaving a trail of burned and gutted corpses behind them. She'd been with him ever since.

"All right, everybody"—Ace's voice blared through the ship's speakers— "we're one minute from the arena." He paused for an instant, then added, "Remember, we're only gonna get one chance to get the captain out. No fuckups, you hear me?"

Blackhawk leaned forward, gasping in Kalishar's thin, oxygen-poor air. It was a charade, a performance directed at his enemy, and at the screaming crowd. Blackhawk's lung capacity was better than half again that of a normal human, and he wasn't feeling any real fatigue. The stegaroid was lying on its side, howling its death agonies as the last of its syrupy blood oozed slowly from the meter-long gash Blackhawk had sliced through its abdomen. The beast was done—he knew that. But its rider was still very much alive. He'd dismounted before the stegaroid collapsed, and now he raised his arms, playing to the crowd, working them into a near hysteria of bloodlust. He held a long spear in one hand, and with the other he pulled off his helmet and threw it to the ground. He stood there, 120 kilos of pure muscle, waving the spear above his head. The cheering grew even louder, and the crowd jumped to its feet, screaming a name again and again. "Ajax, Ajax, Ajax . . ." Blackhawk knew the face. He'd seen it before.

Ajax Tragan. The ka'al's top henchman. He is said to be the best fighter on Kalishar.

Great, Blackhawk thought. He still wasn't worried about the combat itself, but killing Belgaren's number two wasn't going to make things any easier after the battle. Kalishar's ruler was already angry and lusting for his head. Killing his right-hand man was going to send him over the edge. Blackhawk wouldn't be surprised if the ka'al ordered his men to gun him down right in the pit, despite the onlooking crowd and the fact that Kalishari law was clear that a victory absolved him of any wrongdoing and entitled him to immediate release. He sighed. Of course the only option to killing Tragan was letting the bastard scrag him. *No good choices,* he thought grimly. As usual.

The massive warrior let out a primal scream and charged, holding his spear out in front of him as he did. Blackhawk felt his instincts take over and direct his actions. He spun to the side, almost too swiftly for the eye to follow, moving out of the path of Tragan's oncoming spear. He continued around in a full circle, his sword slicing into his enemy's shoulder as he did. The crowd screamed wildly at the spray of blood. They were pirates and cutthroats, mostly, and they respected nothing as much as strength. They'd come here to watch Blackhawk die, but now they were cheering for him. *That's just great,* he thought. *One more thing to piss off the ka'al.*

Tragan turned, quivering with pain and rage as he faced Blackhawk again. Blackhawk knew the ka'al's champion had expected to dispatch him easily, as he had every adversary he'd fought before. But Tragan had never faced a foe as capable, as cold-blooded and deadly, as Arkarin Blackhawk.

Blackhawk could smell his opponent's fear, his astonishment at facing a foe he couldn't defeat . . . Tragan was a bully by nature, used to facing terrified and overmatched opponents. But now, Blackhawk knew the ka'al's hired thug was realizing he faced his own death. He paused, staring at Blackhawk, his arm covered with the bright red blood still pumping from his wound.

The captain watched his enemy approach, taking more care than he had on the first pass, holding the long spear in front of him, ready to strike at the first opening. Blackhawk's eyes were on his foe. He saw Tragan's chest expand, taking in the deep breath he knew would come before his adversary charged.

Blackhawk stood ready, his gaze fixed on the giant, probing for weaknesses. He waited, his body tingling with anticipation, ready to lunge at just the right moment. He saw Tragan's muscles tense, and Blackhawk reacted instinctively, parrying the incoming spear thrust and swinging around quickly, stepping forward and shoving his blade hard into his foe's chest.

The crowd went silent as Tragan stood transfixed, his already lifeless body standing in place for an instant before sliding off Blackhawk's sword and falling to the ground.

Blackhawk stood still, his enemy's blood dripping from the tip of his blade. *That was stupid,* he thought, *much too quick.* He knew he should have played for time, but that wasn't how he fought. It wasn't how any veteran warrior fought. In a battle to the death, when you have an opening, you take your man down. Period. Ajax Tragan had been a dangerous opponent, one Blackhawk knew could have killed him given the chance.

More to the point: What the hell was time going to change anyway? Whenever he finally dropped the bastard, he was still going to have to find a way out of this mess. Dancing Tragan around the pit for ten minutes wasn't going to make a difference.

Blackhawk's eyes snapped upward, fixating on the ka'al. Kalishar's pirate king was staring out at the sands of the battle pit from his royal box, as stunned and silent as the thousands in the crowd. Tarn Belgaren had been one of the more ruthless and successful pirates to plague the Far Stars a generation past, before a freak series of events allowed him to seize control of Kalishar's throne. He'd been a feared warrior in his pirate days, but he had become sodded and drunk on power. His once muscular frame had gone to fat, and his initially skillful rule had become ever more brutal and arbitrary.

"Seize him!" The ka'al's sudden roar stunned even his own

guards, who paused for an instant before drawing their weapons and rushing out onto the sand.

Blackhawk tensed, preparing for the fight he knew would be his last. He was good, better than any of the ka'al's men, and he could take more punishment than any normal human. But there were at least a dozen guards, and they had guns as well as swords. They would obey Belgaren's orders to try to capture him, but after Blackhawk dropped a few, he had no doubt the guns would start blazing. He might get a handful of them before they riddled him with bullets and took him down. Maybe. Only one thing was certain: he wasn't getting out of the arena alive.

Then he heard something in the distance: a low-pitched whine—and it was coming closer. He felt a rush of excitement, and he let his sword hand relax, bringing the blade down from its ready position. He needed to play for time again.

Wolf's Claw is approaching.

Yes. He flashed the thought back to the AI. *I'd know that sound anywhere, my helpful little friend.* He frowned for an instant. He'd told Ace to get the hell off Kalishar and take the *Claw* back to Celtiboria. Apparently his number two didn't take orders any better than he did. A feral smile replaced the grimace as the sound grew louder. Orders or no orders, it was time to get off this shithole.

The crowd's eyes moved upward as *Wolf's Claw* came right over the ancient, crumbling stone of the arena. The ka'al's men, who had been moving toward Blackhawk, stopped and stared up at the incoming vessel . . . then one of them was torn apart, his half-roasted body falling in two sections to the sand.

Then another.

And another.

The crowd began screaming and rushing for the exits. The slower and weaker fell—or were pushed—to the ground and were trampled by the rest of the panicking mob. In the ka'al's booth, his guards were lifting his great bulk from his chair, pulling him toward the exit.

Blackhawk saw it out of the corner of his eye. And then he saw something else: Tragan's spear, lying in the sand a meter from the big man's body. His eyes flashed to the guards—they were all staring at the fast-approaching *Claw*—and back to the forgotten weapon. He lunged forward in a textbook combat roll, grabbing the abandoned spear, and he fixed his eyes on his target. He loosed the weapon in a fluid motion, just as he rose to his feet. The heavy spear wasn't built for throwing, but Blackhawk put all his strength behind the herculean toss. The weapon ripped through the air, heading right for the fleeing ka'al.

The guards were pushing their screaming ruler toward the box's door. One of the men in the pit had seen Blackhawk grab the weapon and shouted a warning. The bodyguards responded, trying to push the ka'al down, but they were too late. The spear hit Kalishar's ruler in the thigh, slicing through the layers of fat and embedding itself deep in the muscle below. Belgaren shrieked in pain, but the guards ignored it and pulled his enormous body through the door and out of the arena.

Blackhawk didn't care if the ka'al lived or died—he had more pressing things to worry about. *Wolf's Claw* was hovering just above the battle pit, its needle gun firing at any of the ka'al's people brave—or stupid—enough to show themselves. The lower hatch was open, and a series of lines dropped to the ground. Several black, shadowy figures slid down the nylon ropes, dropping into combat positions and pulling heavy assault rifles off their backs. Blackhawk recognized the Twins immediately. The brothers were just about the biggest men he'd ever seen, two giants standing half a meter above his own considerable height. They opened fire, shooting at the guards, but hitting more than one of the crowd as well. The Twins were killing machines: deadly, relentless, and totally loyal to Blackhawk. But no one ever called them discriminating. They were sledgehammers, not scalpels.

"Let's go, Cap." The voice was low pitched but identifiably female. Shira Tarkus was hanging about halfway down one of the lines, firing her trademark pistol over Blackhawk's shoulder. She was the deadliest shot he'd ever met—except for himself, of course. "This place is crawling with unfriendlies." Tarkus shared seniority with Ace as Blackhawk's oldest companion. She was a cold fish, but her loyalty to the captain was absolute.

Blackhawk jogged forward, reaching out and grabbing one of the lines. He began climbing and turned his head to look down at the Twins. "Let's go, you big oafs! Time to get the fuck out of here." He maintained his gaze until both of the Twins had grabbed hold of a rope and begun climbing. Then he hauled himself up and into the lower airlock of the *Claw*. He reached down, helping Shira, and then the Twins, into the ship. "*Claw,* close the hatch," he shouted at the ship's AI as he pushed himself up and onto his feet. "Now!" He stumbled over to the wall and slapped his hand on the intraship commlink. "Lucas, my man. Get us the hell out of here.

"Fast."

CHAPTER 2

BLACKHAWK FELT HIS BODY PRESSED HARD INTO THE THICK cushioning of his command chair as *Wolf's Claw* blasted into the upper atmosphere of Kalishar. *Good riddance,* he thought bitterly. *There's a shithole I could live the rest of my life without seeing again.* He was a little annoyed with Graythorn and Lancaster and the others for ignoring his orders to leave him behind and escape, but he couldn't get too upset with them. They were misfits, all of them—outcasts of one kind or another he'd gathered on his journeys—but he wouldn't trade them for a crack legion of the Imperial Black Guard.

What he might trade them for was a pair of pants.

He was still wearing the loincloth from the arena. He felt ridiculous, sitting in the *Claw*'s command chair wearing what looked like a big diaper, but running off to his quarters to change clothes wasn't priority number one right now. Not until the *Claw* and all his people were safely out of this godforsaken system.

"How's she handling, Lucas?" He could feel the vibrations under his feet, a lot heavier than normal. The engines were running a little rough.

"She's fine, Skip." Lancaster didn't sound too concerned. "I had to rush the liftoff sequence so we could get to you in time, and I'm bringing the core temps up slowly. She might shake and rattle a little, but no big deal." He paused. "It was the original liftoff that was a gamble, but I managed to massage her through it."

"That's why I told you to leave me and get the hell out of here." There wasn't any real edge to his voice. He wanted to be angry his crew disobeyed his orders, but it was hard to get mad at loyalty. There was little enough of it in the galaxy, and his people had more than their share.

"We couldn't leave you behind, Skipper." Lancaster's voice was earnest, sincere. "No way."

Blackhawk hid a smile. He was proud of his crew. More so than he'd ever let them see. They'd be insufferable if they knew how good he really thought they were, and how much they meant to him. Blackhawk's people were all extraordinarily talented individuals, despite their personal—and societal—flaws. Alone they were lost, but together under his leadership they became a formidable force. Anywhere else, they'd be at one another's throats—or in the local prison—but on *Wolf's Claw* with Blackhawk, they were a unit, a tightly knit family.

"Well, I can't say I'm not happier on this bridge than in that stinking pit." That was the most Blackhawk was going to say about the whole episode. "Time to orbit?"

"Orbit in forty-five seconds, sir."

"Very well. Plot a jump to Ingara." They were going to return Astra Lucerne to her father, but Celtiboria was too far for a single jump. Ingara was a stable, united planet with rigidly enforced laws and a strong system patrol. It was the kind of place the crew of *Wolf's Claw* usually avoided, but it was ideal for a quick refueling stop or a refuge when being chased by pirates . . .

"Already done, Skip. Locked into the computer." Ingara was the logical choice, and Lancaster obviously knew it as well as his commander.

Blackhawk forced back another smile. His people were good, really good. "Nice guess, Lucas."

"It was Ingara or Gordion." He turned and glanced back at Blackhawk. "And I don't think they're too anxious to see us back at Gordion any time soon."

Blackhawk nodded. "Probably not." They'd gotten off Gordion by the slimmest of margins last time. The whole thing had been a misunderstanding, really, Blackhawk thought, recalling the blood-soaked finale of the *Claw*'s previous visit. But it was way too soon to go back.

A misunderstanding resulting from your crew shooting their way out of the main government building with a data crystal full of military secrets.

No one asked for your opinion, Hans, he thought back at the AI. The computer's full name was HANDAIS—an acronym for "heuristic algorithmic nanotech dynamic artificial intelligence system"—but Blackhawk had shortened it years before. He'd have forgotten the words behind the acronym long ago if the blasted thing would have let him. But, among other effects, the mysterious presence in his head gave him perfect recall. Blackhawk remembered everything he'd seen, everything he'd done. Everything. It was a useful ability, and it had probably saved his life more than once. But there was a dark side to it too, especially when you'd done some of the things Blackhawk had, been some of the dark places he'd been. Forgetfulness was a mercy sometimes, one he had long been denied.

"I think we've got trouble, Skip." There was concern in Lancaster's voice.

"What's happening?" He shot back the response, but he was already staring at his own screen. There they were: three ships, coming up through the atmosphere, hot on their tail. *Fuck,* he thought angrily. The ka'al's really got a bug up his ass about this.

> It is unlikely you helped the matter by wounding him with his dead friend's weapon. I suggest you consider exercising more caution and a better analysis of human psychology and emotional responses the next time you find yourself in a similar circumstance.

You might have said something at the time, he thought back at the AI. The damned thing had a tendency to make annoying and pointless observations.

> An analysis of your mental state and bodily responses suggested a warning would have been ineffective in preventing you from making the attack. You frequently ignore my counsel. I elected not to provide pointless distraction during a period of extreme physical danger.

Blackhawk sighed, trying to ignore the AI. He didn't have time to get into a pointless exchange. He turned his attention back to Lancaster. "Let's see if we can outrun the bastards, Lucas."

"My thought, exactly." Lancaster grabbed the throttle and pulled it back. "Hang on. This might get a little rough."

"Ace, we've got more company. I need you and Shira in the turrets now." Blackhawk's voice was crisp as he spoke into the comm unit, as it always was in combat situations. Whether in a battle pit or fleeing a pirate king, he kept his unique calm, setting aside excitement and fear, and focusing on the battle. "We may have some fighting to do."

"We're on the way, Ark." Ace, on the other hand, tended to be informal, even in battle. Blackhawk had never imposed a rigid hierarchy on his people; he didn't need one. He didn't doubt for an instant they all knew he was in charge—or that they'd get the job done. If anything, the lack of military formality was a relief, allowing him to avoid painful reminders of a troubled past. Hans made sure Blackhawk never forgot any of the things he'd done, but still, anything helped.

Blackhawk flipped on the shipwide comm. "All right, everybody, it looks like we've got some fighting to do before we get the hell out of this shithole system." He was staring at his screen, watching the enemy ships approaching as he spoke. "So the rest of you stay strapped in unless we need you on damage control." His finger went to the button to close the connection, but he paused. "Tarq, go check on Miss Lucerne and make sure she's strapped in."

"Got it, boss." Tarq and his twin brother, Tarnan, spoke with the slow drawl typical of their home world, a steaming primitive shithole where rice was the main product and most of the people were virtual slaves, bonded to the service of the ruling families. The brothers would still be working twelve-hour days in the rice paddies if it hadn't been for Blackhawk's intervention. They weren't the smartest of crew members on the *Claw*, but brains weren't everything.

"The rest of you get ready to do damage control in case we take a hit." Blackhawk cut the connection and turned to look over at Lucas. "What's our status?" The pilot had been staring at his screens while Blackhawk was on the comm, and from the grunts and sighs coming from the helm, he knew the news wasn't going to be good.

"Our status is shit, Skipper." Lucas's voice was tense, distracted. Blackhawk could see him working furiously, calculating potential course plots to keep the *Claw* out of range of the enemy ships while the hyperdrive charged for a jump. "We've got six bogies hot on our tail, and two more groups of three coming in on different vectors."

Fuck, Blackhawk thought. *Wolf's Claw* could beat any one of those ships, even two or three. But a dozen bracketing them from all directions? There was no way. "Time until we can jump?"

"Ten minutes. And that's cutting it to the bone." Lancaster's voice was grim, serious. "Jumping with a half-warmed-up hyperdrive and a hastily calculated plot is fucking crazy to begin with, Skip . . ."

Blackhawk agreed, but he didn't think it would do anyone any good for him to say it out loud. Besides, he knew it would take everything Lucas had to keep the ship from disintegrating or getting lost in hyperspace.

The captain opened his mouth then closed it again. There was no point in driving his pilot any harder. Ten minutes was tight. Pushing him for a better time was pointless. "Time until nearest enemy force is in range?"

"Less than ten minutes, Skip." Lancaster was poking at his workstation's keyboard, entering his sixth course change in as many minutes. "A lot less. Four minutes, maybe six."

Blackhawk knew it depended on how quickly the enemy could respond to Lancaster's evasive maneuvers. But those captains and crews out there were pirates—their success depended on thwarting a target's attempts to escape. He bet it would be closer to four.

He flipped on the comm again. "Ace, Shira, get those guns warmed up and ready. We're gonna have to take on one of these enemy groups." He stared at the screen and added, "Maybe two."

"Don't worry, Ark." Ace's voice was cocky, almost unconcerned. "We'll blow 'em to hell."

Blackhawk knew his oldest companion well, and he was sure the arrogance was a put-on. But it was a good one, and it fooled almost everyone else into thinking Ace was fearless. Blackhawk used to worry about what looked like overconfidence, but he'd long ago realized what came out of Ace's mouth and what was going on in his head were two completely different things. There was no one he'd rather have at his back than Jason Graythorn. Except maybe Shira.

And he had both of them in the turrets right now.

Shira Tarkus was the polar opposite of Graythorn's loud, theatrical personality. Grim, quiet, quick to anger, she disliked most people and didn't make any effort to hide her disdain. She'd followed Blackhawk first out of gratitude for rescuing her from the executioner. But it soon became apparent she'd found a kindred spirit in her new commander. There was a darkness to her, one that ran deep like his own. Shira was a hard-core cynic, as misanthropic as he was, at least outside their chosen inner circles. They even liked the same kind of women—pretty, not too smart, and completely replaceable. Tarkus enjoyed her diversions as much as anyone, but when she was done, she was done. She was a loner at heart, and she had no use for clinging creatures expecting her attention around the clock.

For all her aloofness, Blackhawk knew she'd found a home on the *Claw*. He was sure she'd never admit it, but he realized how attached she'd become to everyone on board. Even Ace.

Blackhawk focused on the task at hand. "It's my job to worry, Ace. You just make sure you blast these bogies as they come into range."

"We're on it, Ark." Graythorn's voice was calm, serious. "You can count on us."

"Here they come." Lucas's voice pulled Blackhawk's attention from the comm. "Three coming in now. Sending targeting data down to the turrets."

"Okay, let's do the work and take these fuckers out." As always, Blackhawk sounded confident, but his eyes were focused on the screen, and he could see that yet another of the enemy groups was going to get a pass before *Wolf's Claw* could jump. *Fuck,* he thought, *this is going to be bad.* "Lucas, if you can shave anything off that ten minutes, I suggest you do it."

Shira Tarkus sat silently in the small compartment of the *Claw*'s starboard turret. She was staring at the bank of screens, watching as the targeting computer's calculations scrolled by. Hitting a ship thirty thousand kilometers away with a five-centimeter-wide laser blast was mostly the computer's work. But initiative played a part too, the mysterious bit of intuition that seemed to come from the human gut. It was hard to quantify, but there was no question it was there. Some people were just good gunners and, with the same targeting systems and training, they could consistently outshoot less gifted adversaries.

Shira was one of the best.

She closed her eyes, letting the neural feed input the enemy vessel's plotting data into her mind. She could see her target; she felt as if she was floating in space, watching it approach. She knew it was all illusion, her mind constructing an image from the computer data flowing through her implants. But it provided a focus for her, a baseline targeting plan she could modify with her thoughts.

Shira was about to fire when her mind hesitated. This wasn't right, the shot was off. *They're accelerating,* she thought, *and they're going to keep increasing their thrust. The plot needs to move ahead, farther along their projected course.* The pirates were going to adjust their heading, angle so they were coming straight at *Wolf's Claw. There is no subtlety here, no caution. They have numbers, and they think that's enough.* She could see the image in her mind change, the perspective moving to reflect her alterations to the firing plan. *Now,* she thought . . .

Fire!

She imagined the shot ripping through the vacuum of space. The laser beams would be invisible during the tenth of a second they took to reach their target, except where they happened to pass through a random cloud of dust or other particulate matter. The triple laser turret was stronger than any armament an enemy would expect the *Claw* to possess, with gigawatts more output than weapons normally found on a smuggler's vessel. They were still at long range, but the pulse was powerful enough to bore through the enemy ship's hull if her aim was true. She was advertising the *Claw*'s true capabilities by firing at this range, but there wasn't any alternative. They were too outnumbered to play it cool, to hold fire until the enemy was closer. Longer range was one of their advantages, and they needed everything they could get now.

Shira saw the laser, visible in her head if not in reality, rip through space—three beams lancing from her triple turret and slamming into the side of the enemy vessel. It was a solid hit, if not a critical one, and she could see the enemy ship bleeding air and fluids from a meter-long gash in the hull. Of course, she didn't actually see it—she was watching a reconstruction, imagery created by the computer based on scanning data that was flowing in. She stared silently, her head nodding in satisfaction as she worked the controls to recharge the laser battery. It took about thirty seconds to build up enough power for a shot, and she figured she just might have time to get another blast in before the enemy came into their own lesser range and it became a two-way battle.

"Eat that, you fuckers!" Ace's voice blared through the ship-wide comm, as his own shot found its mark.

Ace was the complete opposite of Shira: boisterous, dramatic. He made a big deal out of everything he did, and he made sure everyone else knew about it. Shira didn't approve. She thought he looked like a damned fool, and she didn't understand the wisdom behind bragging about accomplishments. She rarely spoke at all beyond the minimum required by the situation. She blended into a room, drifted into the background. She was easy to forget, to ignore. But her enemies usually found that to be a grave mistake. Shira Tarkus wasn't loud or outgoing, but she was always watching, thinking. She stalked her enemies with almost unimaginable patience, waiting for the moment to strike. And when she did, there was no hesitation, no remorse. She killed without pity, without emotion.

Yet for all that she thought Ace was a pompous fool, she didn't doubt his abilities. He was a deadly fighter and a brilliant tactician. Anyone who underestimated him was likely headed for an early grave. Though she'd never admit it to him, she was glad he was part of the team. And they both shared one unwavering trait: total loyalty to Arkarin Blackhawk.

"Weapon will be charged in ten seconds."

The warning from the targeting computer pulled her attention back to the task at hand. Time to line up another shot. She focused on the plot the computer was projecting in her head. She'd been right; the enemy was coming straight at them. The ship she'd hit was lagging behind, its vector off from the other two. A wicked smile crossed her lips. She must have damaged its engines with that hit. With reduced thrust capacity, it would fall behind the others. She had planned to try to finish it off, but now Shira shifted her focus to one of the two fully functional ships. She locked in her shot and watched as the power gauge reached 100 percent. *Fire,* she thought, with the grim finality of a feral warcat charging its prey.

She saw the shot impact the enemy ship dead center. The triple laser blast ripped a huge tear into the hull, She imagined what was happening thousands of kilometers away, the almost unimaginable energy of the laser tearing right through the reinforced armor plating of the target. All around the initial impact points, sections of reinforced hypersteel plating had melted then vaporized, weakening the structural integrity of that section of hull.

She knew the lasers continued through the ship, ripping apart the unarmored interior like a knife slicing through butter. Anyone unlucky enough to be standing in the path of the deadly beams was incinerated, and systems and equipment were blown to bits. She was still watching the projection when a huge plume of fluids and air erupted from the gash in the hull, freezing almost immediately as it was ejected into space.

A smile crept across her lips. Secondary explosions. She'd managed to hit something critical; that much was obvious. Then she saw the projection in her mind erupt into a massive nuclear fireball, as the enemy's power plant lost containment and the controlled fusion reaction in its power core was suddenly released from its magnetic confinement. "Yes!" she whispered to herself.

Even she wasn't immune to a little private gloating.

"Nice shooting there!" Blackhawk's congratulations came through the comm. "She's one up on you, Ace. You gonna sit still for that?" Shira smiled broadly now. She knew the challenge would drive Graythorn more than any promise of reward. Arkarin Blackhawk knew how to squeeze the very best out of his crew.

"How are we on starting that jump?" Blackhawk's voice was calm, but he knew they were almost out of time. Graythorn and Tarkus each had a kill and a cripple to their credit, but that left six enemy ships still engaged with *Wolf's Claw,* and another dozen on the way. They'd gotten off lightly on damage, so far. No one on the enemy ships could match the deadly accuracy of the *Claw*'s expert gunners. The two hits the enemy had managed so far were glancing blows, the damage they inflicted minimal.

But they were getting closer.

Lucas was furiously working his station, trying to plot the jump while he piloted the *Claw* through the battle. Blackhawk could have taken the helm while Lancaster handled the hyperjump prep, but he knew Lucas was the better pilot, and he never let pride interfere with good judgment. Lancaster's evasive maneuvers had given them a big edge in the battle and saved them from at least two hits. So the young pilot wore both hats, and Blackhawk sat in the command chair and let him, and the rest of his people, do their jobs.

"Thirty seconds, Skip." Lucas didn't have Blackhawk's stone-cold calm in battle, but he sounded solid, confident. "My plot's pretty rough. It might be a hard ride."

"Attention." Blackhawk spoke into the shipwide comm. "We will be jumping in thirty seconds. Make sure you're all strapped in. We may have a rough trip through hyperspace." He buckled himself into the command chair, the fabric of the harness cool against his still-bare skin. "All right, Lucas, do your thing."

"Fifteen seconds." Lancaster was focused on the screen, making minor adjustments to the plot.

The 2g pressure everyone had been feeling suddenly stopped, as Lancaster disengaged the engines, rerouting the power to the jump drive. "Ten seconds. Cutting power to weapons systems now." It took an enormous amount of energy to initiate a hyperjump, and Lucas was diverting power from everything but basic life support.

"Prepare for jump . . ."

They all heard a muffled explosion, and the ship pitched hard to the starboard and went into a violent roll. Blackhawk was thrown forward into his harness and then back into the seat cushions as the *Claw* spun around in space. Her engines were off, all their power fed into the jump drive, so there was no way to stop the violent roll. They'd been hit, and Blackhawk knew immediately it was bad.

"I've got multiple system failures, sir." The stress and fear were obvious in Lucas's voice. "What should I do? Abort the jump?"

Blackhawk stared over at the pilot's station. "No. Jump. Now." The jump was a risk, but they were as good as dead if they stayed.

"But, Ark, my plot's no good now. And there's damage to the navcom." Lucas was working his board as he spoke, trying to get a handle on the extent of the damage. "I'd have to navigate through hyperspace myself. I don't even know if the jump system is . . ."

"You can do it, Lucas." Blackhawk's voice was like an anchor, a source of calm in a violent storm. "Do it. Jump. Now!"

Lancaster took a deep breath and flipped the switch.

Wolf's Claw shuddered hard, and the viewscreen went dark. Whatever partially understood forms of matter and energy populated hyperspace, they interfered with normal equipment, rendering all but the most heavily shielded systems useless. As such, only the life-support and jump drive systems functioned. Even the shipwide comm was dead.

Blackhawk felt the familiar headache, the flash of blinding light and then the hard, dull pain. It was the same every time he jumped. Humans had differing reactions to the foreign nature of hyperspace, some more severe than others. About 1 percent of them couldn't handle it at all, and they died the instant they left normal space. There was no known way to test for it, and no shielding ever developed to protect from the effect. It tended to make everyone's first hyperjump a stressful experience, and surviving it was a graduation into the ranks of spacefarers.

"The jump drive's in the red zone, Skipper." Lancaster's voice was near panic. Few things chilled the hearts of veteran spacers like the thought of being trapped in hyperspace, ripping through the universe at a million times the speed of light forever. "It must have taken damage when we got hit."

"Bring us in somewhere now, Lucas." Blackhawk stared grimly toward his pilot. "Anywhere." *It has to be better than where we came from,* he thought. But he wasn't sure he believed it.

CHAPTER 3

THE AIR WAS HEAVY WITH SMOKE AND THE PUTRID SMELLS OF
war. The fortress stood, firm and defiant, rising from the sea
like a great monolith. Its massive bastions and battlements were
images of pure might, spewing death and destruction upon the
armies assailing it from below. This was war, at its grimmest
and ugliest.

Marshal Augustin Lucerne stood in his command post, looking out over the nightmarish scene, watching his soldiers push
courageously forward into the maelstrom. They moved like an
unstoppable force of nature, ignoring their losses, surging irre-
sistibly in the fading twilight, pushing toward the black walls
of the enemy stronghold. Their wild battle cries filled the air,

lustful shouts calling for the blood of their enemies. They knew as well as their leader did that this was the final foe. When the fortress fell, the last of the warlords would be vanquished. All of Celtiboria would be united. The fruits of thirty years of endless war, of death and sacrifice beyond reckoning, were within their grasp. Victory, so long a cherished dream, was at hand. This night they would have vindication for the thousands of comrades they had lost in decades of endless combat. The new dawn would see them triumphant, masters of a world forged together as one nation.

That was the hope, anyway.

Lucerne had spent a lifetime at war, his mind and body devoted to the unification of Celtiboria. He was a grizzled veteran—grim, determined, almost ambivalent to his own pain and hardship. Yet never in those years of endless Arnage—of slaughter and unending savagery—had his heart hardened to the death and suffering of his soldiers. He still mourned each of them lost, cried inside for every fresh recruit who fell to the guns or scarred old sweat who finally met his destiny.

To his soldiers, he was a legendary conqueror. An iron leader. Unbreakable. His men had followed him from one hell to the next, all the while chanting his name with unconditional loyalty. They fought for him, died for him. They followed his orders as if they were holy commandments.

All of which made him wonder why they showed him such devotion and if he truly deserved any of it. As often as not, he gave them nothing but suffering and death in return. But they loved him still. No matter how many took their last painful breaths, lying broken in the mud of one of his bloody battle-fields, his legions still worshipped him.

There would be a celebration when the fortress finally

fell, a joyous salute to a victory long pursued. The soldiers would rejoice, hail the triumph their courage and devotion had secured. How many, Lucerne wondered, would not be there to enjoy the fruits of conquest their blood and sacrifice had bought? How many thousands lay dead in the fields and trenches of three decades of brutal warfare? He didn't know the answer to his own question, and he felt a rush of shame for his lack of knowledge. *Those men followed you, died for you,* he thought, *yet they are only the uncounted dead now, names and faces forgotten, even their numbers no more than a wild guess.*

The marshal was silent as he watched his soldiers launch the final assault. His heavy guns had blown a breach in the fortress's inner defenses, and troops streamed forward now, pouring into the stronghold and throwing themselves at the defenders in a wild frenzy of bloodletting. He had ordered the army to take prisoner any of the enemy who surrendered, but he knew this war too well to expect many captives. Sirion Delacarte was the final holdout, the last of Celtiboria's warlords to stand against Lucerne's army. Delacarte had refused to yield, even when it was clear the war was lost, and his pointless, obstinate defense had cost thousands of lives—his own men and Lucerne's both. His endurance and pride were likely to reap a bitter harvest, as Lucerne's soldiers—enraged at their losses—stormed into his inner sanctum with blood and vengeance in their hearts. The defenders—not to mention their families and dependents cowering within the besieged walls—would pay dearly.

Lucerne mourned for them already, for he detested the pillage and rapine that accompanied a victory, especially such a bloody one. But war was war, and he couldn't deny his soldiers the sack Delacarte's stubbornness had earned. He hated what happened to his veteran troops, the way his normally

disciplined army turned into a brutal, ravaging mob after a
hard-fought victory. Inside the fortress would be brutality he
almost cringed to imagine. He hated it, as he detested almost
every aspect of the many wars he had fought, but he'd been a
soldier for thirty years, and he knew how to lead an army. He
would allow his men their due. Tradition would be obeyed. The
ancient laws of war would trump mercy yet again.

Lucerne watched the unfolding scene with his eyes, but
his mind was elsewhere—on the fringes of the Far Stars, wondering fruitlessly where his daughter was being held captive.
Lucerne had sacrificed virtually all he had to the long struggle
to unite Celtiboria, and scenes from his life danced at the edge
of his thoughts. A home along the beautiful highland coast
he'd left behind to march off to the call of the drum. Parents
and friends he'd virtually abandoned, brothers and sisters long
estranged, a family sacrificed to the demands of war. A wife
he'd neglected, left alone in the cold halls of his stronghold,
though he'd loved her with all his heart. She had died long
before, mad with fever, screaming for him with her last breath
while he was away on campaign. All were gone now, everyone
Augustin Lucerne had ever loved. Save for one.

Astra.

Barely three years old when her mother died, Astra Lucerne
grew up on campaign, as comfortable with her father's grim veterans as she was with her governesses and proper tutors. Stung
by the loss of his wife, the great warrior had refused to leave his
daughter behind in the care of nannies and attendants. Astra
grew up on the fringes of the battlefield, inured to the brutality
of war at an early age. As a young girl, she played quietly on the
floor of her father's headquarters and rode on the shoulders
of his veteran noncoms. As a teenager, she helped in the field

hospitals, awash in blood, as she bandaged wounded warriors and mopped their sweat-soaked brows.

She was a woman now, an unmatched beauty. Her waist-length golden hair reflected the sun as if it had been spun from the precious metal itself. Her tall, sleek frame reminded him of her mother, as did her keen and icy wit. Astra was all he had left, the only thing Augustin Lucerne the man still cared about. Everything else had been sacrificed to the great conqueror he'd become.

But now Astra was gone too, taken by some enemy as a weapon to use against him. For thirty years he had struggled to free Celtiboria from the tyranny of its cruel and corrupt warlords. One by one, he'd destroyed them and freed the downtrodden serfs they'd ruled so harshly, dragging one of the greatest worlds of the Far Stars relentlessly forward from its feudal past. What would he do now if his daughter's life was used to bargain with him? Would he abandon all he'd fought for, all that thousands of his men had died for? Could he surrender the dream that had united a world, even to save his only child?

He prayed he never had to make that choice. There was hope, he reassured himself. Perhaps Blackhawk would rescue her and bring her back to him. The captain was an enigma to most who knew of him, a man of almost unmatched ability who had chosen a life of relative obscurity. Blackhawk wanted the universe to see him as a petty smuggler and freebooter and nothing more, but Lucerne knew the truth: that there was no one in the Far Stars as capable as the captain of *Wolf's Claw,* neither on the battlefield nor on the trail of an enemy. If anyone could bring his daughter back to him, it was Arkarin Blackhawk.

The marshal considered the captain. Blackhawk was an unlikely friend to one of the ruling elite, he knew. The man was a freelance mercenary more accustomed to the dark corners of pirate sanctuaries than the halls of Celtiboria's great cities. But Lucerne had known Blackhawk for many years, and the two were the closest of friends. Lucerne was the one man in all the Far Stars the cynical Blackhawk truly respected as a leader, and Celtiboria's great marshal was the only one in whom the mysterious adventurer had confided the dark secrets of his past. There was no one Lucerne trusted more with such a vital task, no man in the Far Stars he'd rather have in pursuit of Astra's kidnappers.

Still, it was hard for a man of action like Lucerne to rely on anyone else, especially when the life of his daughter was at stake. He longed to take off after her himself, to leave Celtiboria behind and find her, wherever she was. To strike down the villain who'd taken her with his own blade. But Lucerne knew he'd lost the right to follow his own desires. He'd sold it, the price of his army's loyalty, recompense for the thousands dead on his many battlefields. No, he could not leave his men. Not now, not ever. Marshal Lucerne, the soldier, came first, and Augustin, the man, would have to rely on his friend's skill and dedication.

A wild cheer erupted across the field, claiming his attention once again as the shouts worked their way back from the shattered battlements of the besieged fortress across the cratered and blackened field. A thousand voices rose through the night sky, then ten thousand. They screamed in joyful delirium the words they had waited so many years to say. "Delacarte is dead." The sounds from the field were deafening, soldiers shooting their weapons into the night sky as they screamed again and again, "The wars are over! One world, one nation! Long live Marshal Lucerne!"

Lucerne buttoned up his dark charcoal greatcoat as he walked toward the doorway. His attire was plain, barely a uniform at all save for the five platinum stars on each shoulder of the worn and weather-stained coat. The warlords of Celtiboria had fancied elaborate dress, bright and gaudy, announcing to all who saw them their position and power. But Augustin Lucerne wore an enlisted man's coat and plain gray trousers. His knee-high boots were scuffed and mud covered, and his long hair—brown with increasingly large streaks of gray— hung about his face, unfettered by any hat or helmet.

The command post was a small tower, positioned to give a vantage point over the entire field. A ladder led down from the main level to the ground ten meters below. The marshal gripped the handles along the entry hatch and stepped down onto the first metal rung. His heavy boots clanged with each step as he climbed down and hopped onto the black muddy turf. His men had won a historic victory, and it was his duty to walk among them. He owed them nothing less.

He, too, had long dreamed of this day, imagined the pride and satisfaction he would feel when he stood victorious before a united Celtiboria. But now his triumph had lost all its sweetness. A lifetime's goal had been achieved, but all he could think of was Astra. *Is there nothing,* he thought, *no joy at all that I can keep for myself? Is there naught in life but the harsh call of duty? To be a butcher and nothing more?*

He walked slowly across the field, his aides and personal guards falling in behind him. The men swarmed his group as he approached, raising their rifles in the air, chanting his name again and again. He pushed forward, his arms held aloft, a salute to the jubilant soldiers he passed. The sun had set, and the shattered ground was covered in a deep dusk, almost darkness. It was lit in places by the fires that still burned across the shadowy field, the dying remnants of buildings set ablaze by the shelling.

Illuminated by the bleakness of war.

As he moved forward, the crowds became thicker, the multitudes of soldiers rushing to see the great commander, the man they had followed from one end of Celtiboria to the other, the invincible warrior who had led them to victory again and again. The throngs parted as he advanced, opening the way for his party. He reached out to the sides of the corridor his men made for him, touching the hands of those closest, and waving to the multitudes farther back.

Soldiers began grabbing shards of burning wood from the wreckage, holding them aloft, makeshift torches to light the marshal's way. Soon, his path was flanked by the flickering light, his warriors singing and shouting as he passed by. It was a wondrous moment, one he had dreamed of as long as he could remember. He'd imagined the aftermath of the last battle many times, and the reality matched his wildest expectations. But now he had no taste for celebration—only concerns for his daughter's safety. He moved purposefully forward, giving his men the image of their leader they deserved. And on the outside, that's how he appeared . . . Inside, though, he was imagining every horrible fate that might befall his beloved daughter, and it was on his mind constantly, giving him no rest, no peace. He would avenge her if she was slain—he swore that with every fiber of his being. He would hunt down and destroy all those involved. He would see their carcasses rotting on the crosses after he crucified them. But vengeance wouldn't bring Astra back; it wouldn't salve the deep wound her loss would leave on his soul.

Please, he thought desperately, *please, Ark, bring her back to me.*

He forced a smile, empty and hollow as he plunged through the surging masses. He looked into a soldier's eyes—all hope and excitement and admiration—and steeled his resolve. "Victory!" he shouted, thrusting his arms into the air.

"Victory!" they roared in response.

"You have won the victory, my soldiers, as I always knew you would." He turned to the right then back to the left, pumping his fist above his head. "This is the glory that your courage bought, that the sacrifices of our fallen comrades made possible."

He trudged forward, maintaining the charade. His soldiers deserved this from him and whatever his grief, he wouldn't deny them the praise of their commander. Not now, not when their bravery and blood had won the final battle. "Victory!" he yelled again, and he waved his arms toward the cheering soldiers, a cascade of deafening roars returning in answer.

Ark will find her, he thought again, trying hard to believe it. *There is no one more capable, not in all the Far Stars, not even in the empire. Blackhawk will save her.*

He kept up his pace, heading toward the outskirts of the captured fortress. He had come to accept the surrender from whatever subordinate of the slain Delacarte still lived and commanded the remnant of the defeated forces. It would be a great historical moment, the end of centuries of fractured rule by the warlords. For the first time in hundreds of years Celtiboria's power would be focused, targeted to a single goal. Now his legions could take to the stars to unite the sector, to create a confederation strong enough to resist imperial power forever, and to secure the freedom of the Far Stars for all time. It was that goal that had driven him through thirty years of butchery and death. He would see it done, even if it cost him thirty more years of the same.

He took a deep breath and stepped out onto the small causeway his men had built over the water, extending from the rocky shore to the walls of the broken fortress. He stopped before the battlements of the great stronghold, his eyes scanning the wreckage and the detritus of battle. One of Delacarte's officers, a colonel, was already on his knees before Lucerne, head bowed deeply, holding his blade and sidearm before the conqueror in token of surrender.

Lucerne paused for an instant and then took the last few steps. It was something he'd imagined for decades, a dream realized, but now it was just duty, a task he was obliged to perform. When he took the sword and pistol from his prostrate enemy, Marshal Augustin Lucerne would officially become the ruler of the united planet of Celtiboria, the last challenge to his authority crushed. But the only thing he could think of was a young girl years before, playing quietly on the floor behind his desk as he planned a battle won long ago.

Please, Ark, he thought once more, *please bring her back to me.* He swallowed and reached his arms out, taking hold of the vanquished enemy's weapons, lifting them above his head to the deafening roar of his soldiers.

CHAPTER 4

BLACKHAWK WAS THROWN FORWARD HARD, THE RESTRAINTS ON his chair nearly cutting into his flesh as they held him in place. *Wolf's Claw* was rolling wildly, resuming the out-of-control vector it had before entering hyperspace. The wild ride was distracting and uncomfortable, but at least it was verification they'd made it back into normal space. Having the ship careening out of control was a problem, but it was nothing compared to being stuck in hyperspace with a blown drive.

He saw that Lancaster was already at work, his hands moving over the controls, trying to right the ship's course with the positioning drives—the ones that still worked, at least. Blackhawk could feel the shaking as each of the tiny thrusters fired, negating some of the *Claw*'s velocity along a specific vector. Pulling a ship out of a wild roll was a tough enough job with a fully functioning computer and totally operational thrusters. With an AI still scrambled by the effects of hyperspace and a bunch of damaged positioning engines, it was damned near impossible. But Lucas Lancaster was one of the best natural pilots Blackhawk had ever known. Impossible for others was merely difficult for him, and the *Claw*'s captain had complete faith in the man at the helm.

"Everybody okay down there?" Talking to Lancaster would distract the busy pilot, so Blackhawk flipped on the comm to check on the rest of the crew. He wasn't expecting any major problems, but they'd all gotten a good shaking, and he wanted to check up on them.

"We're all good, Ark, but can you tell that cowboy pilot he's not getting any tip for this ride." Ace's voice was a little tinny on the comm, but his cockiness came through loud and clear.

"Just make sure everybody stays strapped in tight down there, Ace." Blackhawk cut the link. He could feel the rolling begin to slow as Lancaster methodically countered the ship's momentum, firing the thrusters that were still responding along carefully selected angles. "You good, Lucas?"

"Wouldn't exactly say 'good,' Skip, but I'll manage it." His tone was clipped, distracted. "Half the damned positioning thrusters are dead. One of the power lines must have been cut."

Few people could have truly appreciated the piloting job Lancaster was doing, but Blackhawk was part of that small group. Lucas was as skilled a pilot as the captain had ever seen, and slowly but surely, the rolling stopped and *Wolf's Claw* stabilized. They still had a lot of forward thrust, and it would take a while to decelerate or change course once the damaged engines were back online, but Blackhawk was grateful for the relative calm. He had a stomach of iron himself, part of his genetically engineered heritage, but he wouldn't be surprised if the lower level was going to need a significant cleanup effort. He suspected that Sarge and his crew, at least, had lost their last meal. They were stalwarts and good friends, but certified ground-pounders, the lot of them. The ex-grunts had been with Blackhawk for years, now, but they'd never gotten used to space travel.

Blackhawk stared down at his screen, looking at the local star chart, trying to get a fix on their position. They'd dropped out of hyperspace almost randomly, without the usual preplotting. Blackhawk knew they could be almost anywhere within ten light-years of Kalishar, probably in the middle of deep space, a hundred years' travel from anywhere at normal thrust. His eyes panned over the scanning reports looking for something, anything but the emptiness of space.

There it is, he thought with a start, as his scanner detected the yellow primary. Not for the first time, he was glad he'd pulled a drunk and high Lucas Lancaster out of that dive bar on Antilles.

They had dropped from hyperspace without any plotting data, but Lancaster still managed to land them close to a system. They were out on the fringe—a good week's journey from any habitable planets—but at least they weren't lost in the nothingness of interstellar space with a wrecked hyperdrive.

Blackhawk sighed softly, still basking in the relief of that star sighting. "Nice job, Lucas, my man." He pumped one of his hands into a fist, an informal salute among the *Claw*'s crew, their own private acknowledgment for a job well done. "How the hell did you latch onto to a star sighting without the computer or any plotting?"

Lancaster looked back at Blackhawk with a sly little smile. "You gotta feel the stars, Skip." He leaned forward and nodded in a slightly exaggerated bow. "It's a gift, I guess. What else can I say?"

Blackhawk returned the smile. "You bet your ass it's a gift." He got up and walked over to Lancaster's station. "Now, what do you say we try to figure out what star that is?"

A few seconds later, the navcom and the AI in Blackhawk's head both recovered from their hyperspace-scrambled state and analyzed the star sightings in an instant. The computer in his brain beat the *Claw*'s system to the punch.

> **We are in the outer reaches of the Saragossa system.**
> **The sole inhabited planet, Saragossa, is third from**
> **the primary. It is currently . . .**

"Redlined." Blackhawk finished the thought. Saragossa had been a moderately productive world by all accounts, a backwater that exported mostly wine and other agricultural products and imported most of its tech. Not the ideal place to find parts for a hyperdrive under the best of conditions, Blackhawk thought grimly, and things were likely to be far worse than that. The planet was redlined—declared off-limits by the combined transport guilds and the Far Stars Bank. That meant no trade with other systems, no embassies or consulates, not even any official communications with the rest of the sector. Saragossa was outcast, cut off from all meaningful contact with other worlds.

Blackhawk had been to the planet once, a long time ago, years before the system had been interdicted. He remembered it as a backward world, mostly agricultural, with a hereditary aristocracy ruling over a vast population of bonded serfs. There was some industry even then, but it was rudimentary, mostly primitive factories processing raw materials. The industrialization had drawn a significant percentage of the peasantry to the cities. They came in search of a better life than they had working twelve-hour days on the huge plantations, but all they found was another version of serfdom toiling in the filthy, smoke-spewing factories.

Blackhawk punched at his keyboard, accessing the *Claw*'s main data banks. Saragossa had been redlined by order of the transport guilds seven years ago due to ongoing revolution and warfare on the planet.

Well, it all made sense, Blackhawk thought. The place was a shithole, and the aristocrats had lived in obscene luxury while most of the people barely had enough to eat, and sometimes not enough. It had been a rebellion waiting to happen even years before, and now his people were heading straight for it.

"Luke, what's the chance of managing some makeshift repairs and pulling off another jump?" He knew the answer, but he asked anyway.

"I'd say none, Skip." Lancaster's voice had calmed down. "I couldn't get this tub back into hyperspace for all the emperor's gold. I think the core's blown. You'll have to check with Sam to be sure, but I'm not getting any power readings from it at all."

Blackhawk leaned back and sighed. A hyperdrive core wasn't going to be easy to find in a place like Saragossa, and trying to do it in the middle of a violent revolution was going to be that much worse. He'd had a bad headache already when his crew pulled him from the arena, but now he felt like his skull was going to crack open like an egg.

"All right, Lucas, I get the point." Blackhawk turned and walked toward the ladder to the lower deck. "If Sam can't patch things up, we'll land on the planet. There's got to be a hyper-drive core somewhere on Saragossa. We may have to steal it, but I'm sure we can track one down." *It's not going to be fun,* he thought to himself, *but everything's relative—a few hours ago you were fighting a steroid-pumped freak riding a dinosaur.*

"Plot us a course toward the planet, Lucas. Bring us right in, shortest possible route." Saragossa didn't have a navy or even satellites, so there was no need for stealth. But Blackhawk was the cautious type; some called it paranoid, he called it smart. "I want full baffles, Lucas. No reason to announce our presence, just in case anybody's watching." He reached out and grabbed one of the rungs and started to climb down.

"You got it, Skip." Apparently Lancaster had already plotted the course, because the pilot punched a single button right before Blackhawk's head disappeared below the floor. "Locked in," he called after the captain. "But we're not actually going anywhere until Sam gets the reactor back online." The positioning jets were capable of limited operation on backup power, but the main engines needed the reactor, and right now *Wolf's Claw*'s nuclear plant was shut down.

Blackhawk shouted up the hatch, "Way ahead of you. I'm on my way down there now."

"So what's it look like, Sam? Is it as bad as Lucas seems to think?" Blackhawk ducked through the door to the *Claw*'s main engineering space. It was a cramped area, tucked under the lower deck. There was maybe two meters of headroom in the center, enough for everyone but the Twins to stand up, but the entry hatch was small, and Blackhawk had to twist his way in.

"It's worse, Cap." Samantha Sparks was the *Claw*'s engineer, the only person who knew the ship and its idiosyncrasies better than her captain did. She was hunched over an open access panel, pulling out chunks of burnt and blackened circuitry, a disgusted look on her face. She wore a pair of heavy insulated gloves, and her long red ponytail was tied into a knot behind her head. "That last hit took out a bank of stabilizers. When the hyperdrive kicked in, it overloaded half the systems on the ship." She shot Blackhawk a quick glance, trying not to react to his standing there almost naked, but she was having a hard time of it. "This was all new equipment a few hours ago." She held up a handful of charred and fused wiring for a second before she dumped it on the floor. "Now it's garbage. Very expensive garbage."

Blackhawk regarded his engineer. Sparks was another of the oddly talented refugees he had picked up in his travels. Like the others, she'd been an outcast . . . Her parents had been killed on the planet Corinthia when she was nine years old, the victims of a feud with a local noble. He didn't know all the details—she never knew them all herself—only that her mother, father, and brother had been killed. She escaped only because she had been outside when the attackers came. By the time she got back, her family was dead. She hid in a crawlspace under the building for two days before hunger and thirst drove her out into the streets.

She grew up a gutter rat in Corinthia City, scavenging for food and a place to sleep for three years, before an engineer at the spaceport found her sleeping in the cargo hold of a grounded spaceship. He felt sorry for her and took her in, letting her sleep in the back room of the repair shop and bringing her food every day. She'd started cleaning up to earn her keep, but soon she was prowling around at nights, teaching herself everything she could about the guts of spaceships. It was complicated stuff for most people, but she turned out to have a great gift for it. Before long her broom and rags were stowed away for good, and she spent her days crawling around the bowels of damaged spaceships, zeroing right in on problems that had the other techs scratching their heads.

She was seventeen when her benefactor was killed in an accident at the shipyard, and she was back on her own again. Blackhawk met her six months later. At the time, he happened to have a price on his head on Corinthia—not the most unique position he'd ever been in. He was trying to quietly repair a damaged *Wolf's Claw,* with limited success until Sam crawled into the guts of the ship and found the problem in a few minutes. He paid her double what he'd promised her and offered her something else. A job and a home. She'd been with him ever since.

He knew he'd rescued her from a difficult situation, but Blackhawk didn't doubt it was he—and the crew—who were lucky to have found her. It didn't change the fact, though, that even her immense skills were being put to the test at the moment.

"Look, Captain, I can jury-rig enough to get a lot of these systems working—or at least sort of working—but we're going to need a new core for the hyperdrive, that's for sure. The old one is completely blown. I tried to cross-wire it, but there's just no way." She turned to face Blackhawk. "And unless we get a new one, we're going be in this system for a long time."

Blackhawk sighed. It wasn't anything he hadn't expected, but he'd held out some hope they might get a break. If something on a ship could be fixed, he knew Sam could do it, and he'd hoped she might pull some miracle out of her pocket. But miracles, as usual, were in short supply.

"What about the distortion field?" Most of the *Claw*'s systems were more or less standard equipment, if better and more powerful versions than those typically found on a smuggler's ship. But the field was something completely different. It was top-grade imperial tech, military and highly classified. Equipment so sophisticated was almost unknown in the Far Stars. Blackhawk had never told anyone where or how he'd gotten it, and the crew knew better than to ask. But he was sure there were no spare parts for that on Saragossa, and that made him nervous.

"It looks okay, Cap." He could hear the wariness in her voice. "But I've only got that thing half figured out, so I'm not certain." Among its other uses, the distortion field rendered *Wolf's Claw* invisible, or at least close to it. It took far too much power to operate when the ship was blasting away on full thrust or fighting a battle, but it was extremely useful for hiding the ship planetside or when it was lurking somewhere in space with the engines off. The field was the only reason the ka'al's people hadn't found the *Claw* on Kalishar. Without it, none of them would have made it off that miserable rock.

"How about the weapons systems?" It was unlikely there'd be any fighting in space near Saragossa, but Blackhawk was still uncomfortable at the thought of his ship blasting around defenseless.

"All offline now, but it's just fried circuitry from the power spike." She looked up at Blackhawk, brushing a tuft of hair out of her face as she did. "I can patch things up pretty quickly." She turned and glanced over at a bank of readouts. "The reactor scragged automatically, but it looks like it's undamaged.

We're on battery power right now, but I can restart the reaction any time." She paused for a few seconds. "I'll be gentle with it, but I should be able to have something close to full power in ninety minutes, at least where the transmission lines aren't fried." Another pause. "Weapons online a couple hours after that."

Blackhawk paused for a few seconds. "All right, let's get the reactor back up as quickly as possible. I don't like operating on backups."

Sparks nodded. "You got it, Cap."

"Get the weapons operational next." He took a deep breath. "We may be alone out here, but I still don't like being helpless."

"I'll see what I can do to expedite things, Cap." Sparks held Blackhawk's gaze for a few seconds, giving the captain a quick smile. Then she buried her head back into the access panel and started ripping out burnt circuitry again.

Blackhawk twisted his way through the entry hatch and back out into the access corridor. He reached up and grabbed a rung to pull himself up the ladder. His muscles rebelled against the exertion, the fatigue of the last few days finally beginning to tell. He ignored the soreness and climbed up to the lower deck.

Most of the crew members were milling around, talking among themselves, but they shut up when Blackhawk stepped out into the middle of the deck. "Looks like we're going to have to land on Saragossa to find a new hyperdrive core." He tried to keep the fatigue out of his voice, but he doubted he was completely successful. "It's not the ideal place, but we'll find something usable. Then we'll get the hell out of here."

"No problem, Cap." Ace had the usual cocky smile on his face. "I'll find whatever you need."

Blackhawk looked back with an expression somewhere between a grin and a frown. "Without shooting the place up this time, okay?" His crew was a capable group—the fact that they were still alive proved that much. But they did have a nasty habit of wearing out welcomes wherever they went. They usually got what they came for, but they tended to leave places in rougher shape than they'd found them, and that didn't endear them to the locals.

"What we need to do is find a ship and grab its hyperdrive core—quick, easy, quiet." He paused. "Maybe we don't even kill anybody this time, what do you think?" He had to fight back his own laugh. He couldn't remember the last job his people pulled where nobody got scragged.

Shira was leaning against a console, looking vaguely amused. But Ace spoke up first. "You know us, Cap. Gentlest souls in the Far Stars."

Blackhawk smiled. "Yeah, that's how I always describe you guys."

He suddenly remembered he was still wearing the loincloth from the arena. "Well, if everything's under control for the moment, I think I'll run down to my quarters and change."

"Don't go to the trouble for me, Ark." It was Astra Lucerne, stepping out from around one of the bulkheads. She wore a wicked grin as she walked into the room, her ice-blue eyes staring at the *Claw*'s almost-naked captain. Her waist-length blond hair was tangled into a riotous mess, and she was still wearing the light gray shift she'd had on when Blackhawk had first found her, though it was now stained with the blood of her kidnapper. He had been thorough in dealing with her abductor, but he wasn't going to get any points for neatness or subtlety. That wasn't really his style, though, and he did his best to live up to his reputation for getting the job done—and for leaving somewhat of a mess behind.

"I think you look good in a diaper." She smiled and winked at him.

Blackhawk felt a rare wave of embarrassment. He'd known Astra Lucerne since she was ten years old, with a long blond ponytail and a precociousness that got her into trouble on a regular basis. But she wasn't ten years old anymore, and the way she was looking at him was enough to rattle him a bit—not that he'd let it show. He forced his own smile and nodded. "I am glad to see you are no worse for your ordeal, Astra."

He turned toward the other side of the room, where most of his crew was fighting the urge to laugh. "Shira, can you set Lady Lucerne up in one of the spare cabins? I'm sure she'd like to get some rest." He flashed his eyes back to Astra as he spoke. "And find her some clothes. I imagine she wouldn't mind getting the stink of Kalishar off her, like I'm going to do myself right now."

"Sure, Cap." Shira suppressed a giggle and nodded to Astra, motioning toward one of the hatches as she did. "Let's get you settled in, shall we?"

Astra nodded. "Thank you, Shira. I am a little tired. Being kidnapped is exhausting, but it's nothing compared to one of Ark's heroic rescues." She shot a last glance back at Blackhawk, smiling again as she did. "See you later, Ark." She tried to hold back a laugh, but she didn't try too hard. Shira walked through one of the hatches, and Astra followed, leaving most of the *Claw*'s crew standing around with a variety of grins on their faces.

"I think you've all got enough work to do to keep busy," Blackhawk snapped, glaring at his grinning crew for a few seconds before he turned and walked down the corridor toward his quarters. *Finally*, he thought, *I've got a few minutes to get cleaned up.* He was still covered in dried stegaroid guts, and it was starting to reek.

He let out a long sigh as he ran his hand over the scanner plate and the door to his quarters slid open. He felt a bit of relief, but it was limited. He'd managed to find Astra and rescue her from the kidnappers, as he'd set out to do. That was a start, and he was glad to see she hadn't been harmed. But he had no idea how he was going to get her back to her father on Celtiboria. The first step was finding a hyperdrive core somewhere in the middle of the Saragossan revolution.

Typical, he thought with another sigh. *Just fucking typical.*

CHAPTER 5

THE IMPERIAL CAPITOL ON GALVANUS PRIME WAS AN AWESOME complex, built to attest to the power and vastness of the empire that claimed suzerainty over the Far Stars. Sprawling over ten square kilometers and built from interlocking blocks of black and white Sytorian marble, it loomed over the capital city, as if daring any other construction to challenge its grandeur, its raw projection of might and greatness.

Yet, for all its majesty, this magnificent compound was a façade, an illusion. The image of imperial power it projected was a fiction.

Galvanus Prime was the imperial sector capital, in theory the center of government and authority in the Far Stars. But most of the worlds outward from the Void had proven to be quite beyond the control of the empire, and few of the sector's one hundred systems obeyed even the barest forms of the emperor's rule. Imperial governors had come and gone, and each had proven as incapable as those who had preceded them at the task of bringing the planets of the sector to heel. The business of the Far Stars went on, as it had for centuries, its worlds busy battling one another or torn by their own internal struggles, quite unconcerned with the edicts of emperors and governors or their empty threats of force.

Kergen Vos intended for that sorry history to end. Vos was the new governor, a man far more capable than any of the others who'd been relegated to this wild backwater on the fringe of human habitation. He was perhaps the first man who had actively pursued the post of governor of the Far Stars. Most of his predecessors had been sent beyond the Void in disgrace and spent the years of their exile sitting ineffectually in their massive headquarters, while the rest of the worlds casually ignored them. Command of the Far Stars was a dreaded assignment, a punishment for imperial courtiers who had fallen into disfavor, and a graveyard for once-promising imperial careers.

Vos was from a different mold than those who had come before him, though. An outsider, without the contacts or patronage usually required to prosper in the imperial bureaucracy, he had risen from the dusty plains of a backwater world up through the ranks of the imperial intelligence service. His ruthless brilliance and moral ambivalence served him well and led him from one successful mission to the next, leaving a trail of bodies behind even as he accumulated favor from a growing list of useful patrons. His career had been an uninterrupted suc-

cess, one that had taken him far from his humble beginnings
and provided him with considerable wealth and an enviable reputation. Yet, despite seemingly better prospects, he'd longed to
take the job so many others viewed as a dead-end posting.

No one in the imperial bureaucracy could remember the
last time anyone had volunteered to take the leadership post
beyond the Void. The unfortunates dispatched to this fringe
on the edge of the empire invariably faded into obscurity and
returned—if they returned at all—to vastly decreased levels
of influence and prestige. Every Far Stars governor quickly
found that the freebooters, warlords, and adventurers who
ran the worlds of the Far Stars simply ignored imperial pretensions, as their fathers and grandfathers had done. They
were as likely to question the governor's intelligence and his
parentage in a single breath as they were to pay the slightest
heed to his directives.

Vos knew it could be the same for him, save for one thing:
he didn't plan to sit in the massive palace and watch the days
slip idly by, enduring the insults of his would-be subjects. He
intended, at long last, to bring the renegade worlds of the Far
Stars firmly under the emperor's control. Kergen Vos was not
afraid of a pack of pirates and mercenaries more accustomed
to fighting each other than facing any real external threats. Vos
was something new, a governor the likes of which the unruly
brigands of the sector had never before seen.

The Far Stars had long been a thorn in the imperial side
and, when Vos delivered it, broken and obedient, into the
emperor's hands after so many others had failed, the rewards
would be immense. He would attain heights he couldn't have
dreamed of before—perhaps even a path to the chancellorship
itself. The man from nowhere, who had reached the pinnacle

of power, who stood at the right hand of the emperor. It was a pleasing image, one he intended to make a reality.

"The earlier reports are now confirmed, Excellency." Mak Wilhelm stood before the governor's chair, his scarlet-and-white uniform spotless and perfectly pressed. The uniform was gaudy and ornate, but it was nothing compared to the hat he held under one arm, black and red with gold lace trim and a ludicrous feather protruding from the top. No one had ever called imperial military uniforms understated.

He bore the rank of general, though he rarely went by it. The imperial military forces stationed in the Far Stars were a joke, a ramshackle fleet of old rust buckets and a minuscule army recruited mostly from rejects and castoffs. All of it together wasn't a force fit for a general to lead, and Wilhelm's other position as an imperial spy was of far greater use to Vos than any halfhearted efforts at military command. The empire had its share of inbred nobles looking for any opportunity to flaunt their pretensions of rank and their ostentatious uniforms, but neither Vos nor Wilhelm had the patience for such fools. They were both manipulators: more than soldiers, meticulously developing plans within plans, weaving a web that would snare those who defied the empire.

It was why the governor kept Wilhelm close. He and his general/spy were similar creatures: calculating, patient, and deadly. Success was all that mattered to them, achieving their goals and advancing their own power. They'd come to the Far Stars together seeking the same thing: a path to the corridors of true power for men born outside the tight fraternity of the imperial nobility. They'd worked together for many years, Wilhelm following in the wake of Vos's brilliant successes and working alongside his mentor. Both knew their victory in the

Far Stars, if they were to achieve it, would be won by stealth and manipulation, not by military power.

And Vos would accept nothing less than total victory.

"It would appear that a group of adventurers has liberated Astra Lucerne from the ka'al's agent and escaped from Kalishar." Wilhelm's voice was strong, clear. "The ringleader was apparently captured in the operation, but it seems he, too, later escaped. They apparently fled in a single vessel, destroying several of Belgaren's warships as they fled. They were able to jump from the system, though there are reports that they sustained heavy damage before they did."

"The damned fool." Vos was seething with anger at the ka'al's failure, though his measured tone betrayed none of his rage. The career bureaucrats in the Capitol were used to bitter and disgraced nobles occupying the governor's chair, and they had been shocked at the restrained temperament of their new master. The previous governor had been prone to throw trays of food across the room when his delicacies were not seasoned to his liking. Vos, by comparison, was quiet, professional. He'd brought a sense of calm to the Capitol that had been long absent.

Vos stared at Wilhelm. "Perhaps the ka'al is not as useful an ally as we had hoped." He paused menacingly. "Nor a fit leader for Kalishar." His mind was weighing various plans and contingencies. There were others on Kalishar who wanted the ka'al's scepter, and some who could manage the deed with enough imperial coin behind them.

"With respect, Excellency, I believe the ka'al may still prove worthy . . . or at least expedient. By all accounts, he was once an exceptionally successful pirate and, in the early years of his rule, an effective monarch. Despite several accounts that he has become sodded and soft, I submit that he still has far more useful off-world contacts than any of the would-be successors currently gathering like carrion birds. And now he's going to be motivated." He locked his eyes on Vos's. "If our plan is to leverage our control of Kalishar to the neighboring systems, a declining monarch with a lingering reputation may be more useful than a younger maverick full of ambition." He paused. "Easier to control as well."

"Perhaps you are correct, General, though I wonder how many of his contacts remain active and useful. He is an old fool now, and his rivals can see that as well as we. Others may pay lip service to ancient commitments at no cost, but does he retain any true power off Kalishar itself? Is he still feared by his neighbors or do they secretly laugh at his weakness and folly, plotting against him, even while making empty promises of continued loyalty?"

Vos wanted to be clear, and his tone conveyed that: he had no faith in the ka'al, and he was reluctant to rely upon an ally who had already failed so spectacularly. "I remind you that he allowed a smuggler with one small vessel and a ragtag crew to sneak through his defenses and steal Astra Lucerne from his grasp. He then failed to prevent their escape from a planet where he is the absolute ruler, where his available resources dwarfed those of his adversary." This time he locked onto Wilhelm with a withering gaze. "Based on what has transpired, I see little reason to continue to rely on the efforts of Tarn Belgaren. Indeed, the stench of his weakness will attract predators without our intervention. The last thing we need is a monarch on Kalishar who is not our creature, one who seizes the throne without our aid and, in so doing, incurs no debt to us. Need I remind you that it was the dire state of economic affairs on

Kalishar that allowed us to gain control over the ka'al in the first place?"

Vos was frustrated. He detested having to rely on allies of dubious capability, but he knew he had no choice. He also knew that if he was going to succeed where his predecessors had failed so miserably, he would have to learn how to manipulate allies with less than optimal abilities. Bringing the Far Stars to heel was going to be vastly more complex an endeavor than dealing with troublesome systems in the rest of the empire. Things were far simpler on the other side of the Void, where imperial power was orders of magnitude greater than that available to Vos. Rebellion and disobedience were easily crushed there, but success in the Far Stars would require a far subtler game, one Vos would have to play carefully.

The governor of the Far Stars lacked the awesome resources of his imperial counterparts in other sectors. Distance from the capital, difficult and unreliable communications with the rest of the empire, and second-rate personnel all weighed against the efforts of even a gifted governor. The empire was ruled by fear and intimidation, maintained by the awesome might of the imperial fleet. But the Far Stars lay beyond the Void, where only the barest fraction of the fleet's power was projected.

None but the greatest navigators could safely jump through the Void, and then only in the swiftest and most maneuverable craft. The crossing was too dangerous for the imperial battleships, great behemoths five kilometers long and bristling with weapons. Those awesome ships of war were too large and too unwieldy to make their way through the great emptiness—at least not without prohibitive losses—and the empire couldn't afford to risk its great battlewagons in the empty depths of the Void. A battleship took twenty years to build, even in the great imperial shipyards at Cestus Magnus, and its cost was almost beyond accounting.

Vos would have no help from the emperor, and that meant he had to make do with what he did have. Even if it meant someone worthless like Tarn Belgaren.

"Nevertheless, General," he continued, "I shall defer to your assessment regarding the ka'al—at least for the time being." There was no enthusiasm in Vos's tone, only the dull acceptance of a lack of better options. "But we will keep a much closer eye on him from now on. Send your best man to Kalishar immediately. He is to advise our esteemed ally, the ka'al, that we remain confident he will recover the hostage and deliver her to Galvanus Prime. And be sure there is no doubt of the manner in which failure will be addressed." Wilhelm's eyes widened slightly, and Vos knew he had made himself clear.

"Yes, Excellency." Wilhelm snapped to attention, slapping his arm across his chest then outward in a textbook imperial salute. "It shall be done as you command."

"Very well." Vos nodded. "You may see to it now, General. Dismissed."

"Sir!" he snapped crisply.

Vos watched as Wilhelm left, his shining black boots echoing loudly on the polished marble floor. At least he had one subordinate in the Far Stars who was competent.

The governor knew Wilhelm was considering which agent to dispatch to Kalishar. It took a special kind of diplomacy, mixed with sadism, to encourage an ally while also subtly threatening death. Vos had a candidate in mind, and he was certain Wilhelm would come to the same conclusion. He was just the man for this job. And the sick bastard would enjoy it.

CHAPTER 6

BLACKHAWK PULLED ON A TUNIC. IT WAS SOFT LINEN, CLEAN AND fresh, and it felt good sliding down his freshly showered torso—his second since the rescue. It wasn't easy getting the smell of stegaroid off his body. He wrapped a plain cloth belt around his waist, tying it snugly and clipping his holstered pistol to one side and a sheath for his well-worn shortsword to the other. He felt naked without his weapons, even in *Wolf's Claw* surrounded by his crew. Blackhawk's life had been one of conflict, of almost constant war and strife, and his sufferings had left their scars, both on his flesh and in the depths of his mind. He passed a weary hand over his eyes—and it wasn't from exhaustion.

He'd managed to get a couple hours of sleep. With Lucas at the helm and Sam crawling around the ship's innards, things were as under control as they were likely to be any time soon. He could go without rest for a long time if he had to, another benefit of the genetic engineering that had produced him, but he was still sharper and more effective when he'd had some sleep. Two hours wouldn't have done much for a normal man after being up for three straight days, but Blackhawk felt refreshed.

The dreams had been there, of course, but they weren't as bad as usual. Blackhawk's past frequently revisited him at night. Even the AI in his brain couldn't stop the nightmares. They were his penance, he knew, and he was sure the dead would haunt him until the day he joined them. Arkarin Blackhawk carried a lot of guilt for the things he had done in his younger days, acts he had told no one about, not Ace or Shira, not any of his crew. No one except Augustin Lucerne. He'd confided in Lucerne long ago, for reasons he still couldn't explain, and his trust in the great marshal had not been misplaced. Lucerne hadn't judged him, and he'd kept his secrets for more than a decade.

Blackhawk had come close to confiding in his people, but in the end it was fear that stopped him, dread over what they would think, of how it might change their attitudes toward him. The loyalty of his people was his most prized possession and, in the end, he didn't have the courage to risk it by telling them who he had been and what he had done years before. So he remained silent, keeping the guilt and the pain to himself.

He could feel the g-forces pressing down on him, pulling him back into the present, and he knew that Sam had gotten the engines back online. Lucas was blasting against the ship's vector, decelerating so he could change course and head for Saragossa. The *Claw* had force dampeners that reduced the g-forces the crew felt, but enough acceleration was still damned uncomfortable. It felt like a little under 2g, which was more than it should be.

Which meant something wasn't quite right.

He walked over toward his workstation and hit the comm unit. "Lucas, what's up with the thrust?"

"You don't miss much, do you, Skip?" Lancaster's voice was hollow on the small speaker. "The dampeners are damaged. I've got 'em up to 60 percent, but I don't think it's a good idea to run them full yet. Not until Sam gets a chance to make sure everything is okay. She was just about to suit up for an EVA to do some diagnostics, but Ace told her to hold off since we're going to be landing anyway." Lucas paused. "We didn't want to wake you, Skip."

"No—that's the right call. I'm with Ace. No sense risking an EVA now." It was dangerous crawling around a ship in the middle of space, and Blackhawk had always been especially protective of Sam. She was quiet and shy, and she gave the impression she needed to be looked after. Intellectually, Blackhawk knew that was nonsense. He'd seen her in action more than once. She wasn't as volatile or quick to violence as Shira or Ace, but when she pulled out that little pistol she carried, someone almost always died.

Guess I'm just old-fashioned, he thought.

"We'll just have a less comfortable ride in, I guess, and she can fix the dampeners after we land," Blackhawk said. *Assuming we land someplace no one's shooting at us,* he thought. "I'll be up in a few minutes. Out." He flipped the comm unit off and walked toward the door, sliding his hand over the sensor. The hatch slid open and he walked out into the corridor and down to the main area of the lower deck.

Ace was sitting at one of the workstations, and he smiled when he saw Blackhawk step out of the corridor. "Well, that's ten platinum crowns for me," he said, chuckling softly. "Shira bet me you'd sleep for three hours, but I told her no way."

"It's too bad she didn't let me in on it." Blackhawk returned the grin. "I'd have rolled over for another forty-five minutes for half that swag." The two shared a short laugh. "What about Astra?" Blackhawk walked across the deck and sat at the workstation next to Ace.

"Shira checked on her about half an hour ago, Ark." Ace turned to face Blackhawk. "She's still asleep. She had quite an ordeal. I'd wager we don't see her for another ten or twelve hours."

"Double or nothing?" Blackhawk smiled. "If you can sucker Shira into another bet." Shira Tarkus was a deadly fighter and an utterly reliable friend, but Blackhawk had seen Ace Graythorn in too many gambling establishments to ever bet against him.

"No, not this time. I knew you, Cap. That was a sure thing. But Lady Lucerne is an unknown. It strikes me there's more to her than just being a great man's daughter. She's got her own strength." Ace was probing gently. Blackhawk knew what he was implying, but he didn't take the bait.

"She's very strong, Ace. She's her father's daughter, that's for sure." Blackhawk smiled briefly. "She's not one to underestimate." He was about to add something else when they both heard heavy footsteps from one of the corridors.

Blackhawk turned his head just in time to see Sarge walk through the door. He looked better than he had when Blackhawk had seen him skulk off to his quarters a few hours earlier, but he was definitely still a little pale. He wasn't a spacer by nature, and the violent rolling of the ship had been a bit more than his otherwise iron-hard constitution could handle.

"Good to see you up and around," Ace said, flashing a smile at the grizzled noncom. "I was just about to raid the food locker. Care to join me?"

Sarge stood in the hatch, staring back at Ace with a look of horror. A queasy expression crossed his face at the mere mention of food. "I'll pass, Ace. But I did manage to keep down some water."

"How are the guys, Sarge?" Blackhawk nodded at the veteran ground-pounder, motioning for him to take a seat. It wasn't often Sarge looked weak, but this was one of those times, and Blackhawk wasn't sure how long the old sweat could stand before he fell over.

"They're all right, sir." Sarge and his people were the only ones on the *Claw* who always addressed the captain formally. Blackhawk had told him a dozen times he could drop the "sirs," but the stalwart old foot soldier was steadfast. Or pigheaded, depending on which member of the crew you asked. "I wouldn't want to take 'em into a fight right now, but they'll sleep it off and be as good as new."

Sergeant Brin Carrock had been a soldier in the wars on Delphi III, a veteran who'd fought long and with great distinction but picked the wrong side to serve. He'd led a platoon during the fateful Battle of the Red Hills and the subsequent brutal retreat through the planet's frigid northern steppes. The defeated army disintegrated, fragmenting into small groups, each struggling to evade the vengeful enemy units pursuing them. The victors in the war had declared the defeated soldiers to be enemies of the state. They were rounded up and put into concentration camps—or simply shot outright.

Sarge's crew held out for longer than most, but he was down to four men and almost no supplies when Blackhawk and his crew stumbled across them, fighting their way back toward *Wolf's Claw* from a mission that had gone terribly wrong. The captain had convinced Sarge that his enemy's enemy was as good a friend as he was likely to find, so he led his people into the battle, saving the day. A grateful Blackhawk agreed to get them all off-planet, away from the vengeful clutches of their enemies. They'd readily agreed.

Carrock and his people had been on the *Claw* for years now, and they were as loyal to Blackhawk as any of the crew. Still, they retained their own unit identity, and they stayed close together, somewhat aloof from the rest of the *Claw*'s complement. Carrock's people never called him anything but Sarge, and after a while, no one else did either.

"Space travel can be unsettling at times." Blackhawk leaned back in his chair. "Still, nothing was quite like the time we were trying to get away from those bounty hunters on Carmellon." He turned toward Graythorn. "Remember that, Ace? It took weeks to clean up the ship."

Ace was about to reply when the 1.8g they'd all been feeling suddenly vanished. There was an instant of 0g, then the artificial gravity generator kicked in.

Blackhawk was the first one out of his seat, racing toward the ladder to the bridge, with Ace close behind. He pulled himself up the ladder in an instant, forgetting to hide his enhanced strength as he usually did when he wasn't fighting.

"What's happening, Lucas?" He bounded onto the bridge, running over to the pilot's station.

"We've got a contact, Captain. A ship inbound to Saragossa." He turned to face Blackhawk. "I cut the engine power and took a chance on activating the field. It seems to be working. I don't think they saw us." With the engines off, the distortion field made the *Claw* nearly undetectable. "Maybe I'm paranoid, but . . ."

"No, you did the right thing, Lucas." Blackhawk was leaning over the pilot, punching keys on the workstation. "Until we know what we're dealing with, better to stay hidden." He hadn't expected any contacts in a redlined system. There was no normal traffic to and from the planet, so whatever it was, it was probably dangerous.

He turned toward Graythorn. "Ace, let's push some power into a long-range scan. I want to know what we're dealing with here."

"You got it, Cap." Ace slid into his seat and flipped on his station. He punched in a code, activating the ship's AI and directing it to scan the contact. *Wolf's Claw* had an exceptional scanner suite, another feature no one would expect to find on a normal smuggler's ship.

"Feed the data over here once you get anything." Blackhawk had moved over to the command chair, and he was activating his own workstation. He was edgy. There was something about that ship contact he didn't like. It was a nagging thought, a familiarity he couldn't confirm, at least not without better scanning data. He was trying not to jump to conclusions when the familiar voice in his head chimed in.

> **The vessel appears to be an imperial special operations ship. Probability 81 percent.**

Yes, I think so, too, he thought back. *But we're taking wild guesses without better imaging.*

> **I do not make "wild guesses." I analyze data and create valid hypotheses based on my observations.**

Blackhawk ignored the AI's banter. He'd learned long ago the voice in his head could wear him down in any exchange. *Still,* he thought, *it does look like an imperial ship.*

"All right, Cap . . . sending you data now." Ace was staring at his scope as he spoke. "I've never seen anything like this thing."

Blackhawk stared at the information coming into his station, and all his doubts were gone, replaced by fear. "I have." He turned to look over at Ace. "That's an imperial Rapier-class special ops ship, used mostly by the intelligence services."

You are correct in your identification.

I know I'm correct, he shot back. *And you only know that because you can read my memory.* Blackhawk knew damned well the AI's original data set did not include classified imperial spy ships.

Ace stared back at Blackhawk, a surprised look momentarily passing over his face. The ship's AI had drawn a blank, declaring that the contact was unidentified. He opened his mouth, but then he closed it again without saying anything.

Blackhawk saw Ace's fleeting expression. He knew his friend had a million questions about his strange bits of knowledge. He was just as sure Graythorn would never ask. "I'm sure, Ace. It's an imperial spy ship." He paused. "You'll just have to trust me."

"I always do. So what does that mean?"

Blackhawk took a deep breath. "I have no idea what that ship could be doing out here in the middle of nowhere, but I'm sure it's nothing good." His frown slowly faded as an odd smile crept across his face.

"But that vessel does have a first-rate hyperdrive core in it . . ."

Ace smiled and nodded. "Sam's got the weapons back online." He started to get up. "I'll warm up the laser turrets."

"No."

Ace froze and looked back at Blackhawk. "No?" There was a confused look on his face. "Don't you want to grab that core?"

"Not that way. That ship packs a hell of a punch." Blackhawk motioned for Ace to sit. "We might win, but it would be a close fight—especially with the *Claw* not at her best." Blackhawk knew his ship at full strength could beat the imperial vessel, but the *Claw* was nowhere near that. "Taking that ship on now would be too big a risk. With our systems jury-rigged like they are, we could lose, too. Besides, even if we won, we'd stand a good chance of frying the core in the battle. We need it intact."

"So what's the plan?" Ace was clearly skeptical. Blackhawk knew his sidekick would prefer a straight-up fight.

"We let the ship land, and we find it on the ground." Blackhawk made it sound like a simple task, locating one small ship on a war-torn planet. He turned toward Lancaster, who'd been silently watching the exchange. "Lucas, can you plot a course to follow that ship in without showing ourselves?"

The pilot turned and looked at the plotting data for a few seconds. "I think so, Skip, but we're going to have to let them get a lot closer to the planet before we slip in behind." He turned back toward Blackhawk. "We can do it, but they'll get there ahead of us."

"How far ahead?" Blackhawk had an idea, but he wanted to hear Lancaster's figure.

"At least a day and a half." Lancaster turned back toward his screen for a few seconds. "Maybe two days. We'll need to have the baffles on full and come in on the right vector. A lot depends on their final course." He looked back toward Ace and Blackhawk. "But we can do it."

"All right, Lucas—do it. Get us in as close as possible without them spotting us. Got it?"

"Got it, Skip." Lancaster spun around and began working on the plot.

Blackhawk turned toward Ace. "You look tired."

"Well, Cap, it's been a busy couple days now, hasn't it?"

"That it has, Ace, but now I want you to get some rest." He motioned toward the ladder to the lower level. "Because we're going to have to get into that ship wherever it lands and steal the core." He forced a weak smile. "And I'd expect a fight . . . 'cause I doubt they're just going to give it to us."

Ace nodded. "Probably not." He got up slowly. "I could use a few hours of sleep, I guess." He yawned and started toward the ladder, but he stopped and turned back toward Blackhawk. "You too, Ark—two hours of sleep isn't gonna cut it."

"I'll get some rest, Ace; don't worry about me."

Ace flashed him a skeptical look, but he turned and headed toward the ladder without another word.

Blackhawk sat in his chair, staring at his screen lost in his own thoughts. Finding the ship on the ground and getting on board to steal the hyperdrive core was a tough enough proposition. But that's not what was really bothering him. *What's going on?* he thought nervously. *What the hell is a first-rate imperial intelligence ship doing out here in a backwater system deep in the Far Stars?*

CHAPTER 7

THE KA'AL'S AUDIENCE HALL WAS A CAVERNOUS ROOM LOCATED exactly in the center of the great palace, between the two massive wings of the structure. The vaulted ceiling rose thirty meters from the polished marble floors, and the glass dome in the center allowed the bright light of Kalishar's sun to stream into every corner of the room. The walls were covered with ancient paintings, the works of long-forgotten masters, now chipped and faded from lack of care. The palace was a magnificent structure, built centuries earlier, when Kalishar's crown had been held by local warrior nobles instead of immigrant pirate kings. The more recent occupants, buccaneers more accustomed to brothels and taverns, had cared less for the splendid art and architecture, and much of it had fallen into disrepair.

SHADOW OF EMPIRE — 75

"You had ten ships to their one, Captain Kharn." The ka'al sat on his throne, his enormous bulk clad in flowing silk robes. His face was red with anger, his hands clenched into shaking fists as he faced the cowering pirate captain. "Ten to one!" he roared, grabbing a golden goblet from the table at his side and throwing it across the room, splashing red wine all over the priceless rugs and tapestries.

To say Kalishar's ruler was outraged that Blackhawk and his people had escaped would have been the grossest understatement. He had summoned the captains of the vessels that been part of the failed effort to intercept *Wolf's Claw*. One by one, the terrified pirate commanders appeared before him to explain the abysmal failure that had allowed a small band of adventurers to steal a valuable hostage and escape from the system. It was an outrage, and he was nearly apoplectic with fury. He swore to himself that Blackhawk would pay. He would see the freebooter nailed to a board, dying slowly as he watched, savoring every moment of his enemy's agony.

Belgaren twisted uncomfortably on his throne, the pain from his wounded leg only increasing his rage. Blackhawk had dared to attack him directly, almost killing him despite the guards deployed throughout the arena. The fools had allowed their ka'al to be injured. Indeed, had his personal bodyguards not intervened, Blackhawk's deadly throw would have killed him. The arena sentries had earned the monarch's wrath, and his anger was fueled by his own pain and humiliation. Those unfortunate enough to survive *Wolf's Claw*'s attack had been impaled, their rotting corpses still hanging from the spikes along the outside of the arena as a grotesque warning to others. They had failed, and they had paid the price of that failure.

Now Captain Kharn knelt before him; the only sound besides

the ka'al's labored breathing was the snarling of his pets. There was a pit left of Kharn, three meters deep, where the ka'al kept his pet carnasoids. The hall echoed as the beasts devoured the last bits of a fresh carcass, becoming more aggressive as they competed for the last morsels. The lizards were two and a half meters long, with ten-centimeter teeth. Their jaws closed with the force of an industrial press, and they could snap any bone in a man's body like a dried twig.

He loved that sound.

There wasn't enough left of their recent meal to identify. But anyone would notice the remnants were covered with scraps of a uniform—the same one Kharn himself wore. The captain was trying to stay calm, but he couldn't keep himself from glancing repeatedly toward the pit.

The ka'al noticed Kharn's distraction. "Ah, I see you have noticed Captain Grax." There was amusement mixed with Belgaren's anger. "He was unable to provide a satisfactory explanation for his failure." He glanced over toward the pit then back to Kharn. "I trust you will fare better than he."

Kharn swallowed hard. "Your Majesty . . ." He paused. He was clearly about to explain his version of events, but something stopped him. Kharn was smarter than most of Kalishar's captains. The ka'al appreciated that and motioned for him to continue. "I deeply regret that I have failed you, my ka'al. I offer no excuses. The enemy simply bested us." He lowered his head in supplication.

There was a long silence, perhaps half a minute. The ka'al's leg throbbed, and the seconds passed slowly—he could imagine how it seemed to the supplicating Kharn. Finally, the ka'al shifted his bulk and stared down at the prostrate captain. "Failure is intolerable, Captain."

He hid his smile as he watched Kharn squirm, making sure to look at the pit often. Out of the corner of his eye, he saw the captain's quick glances, wincing at the slavering crunches emanating from the carnasoids' lair. The ka'al relished his power, and he enjoyed tormenting his subjects. It had been the same with Grax, but this interview would end differently than that one had.

"However, your willingness to admit your own failing is admirable, especially as it appears that your ship acquitted itself better than the others." The ka'al's voice changed slightly, a bit of his fiery rage fading away.

It was true—Kharn's vessel had performed better than those of his colleagues. "It appears from the reports, Captain, that your ship scored a significant hit on the enemy before they were able to transit. If the other ships had performed as well as yours—indeed, if any had performed as well—the enemy vessel might have been disabled and captured." Belgaren paused. "Indeed, it almost certainly would have been. And a very valuable hostage would have been recovered." He stared at Kharn's subservient pose. Sneering, he said, "Rise, Captain Kharn."

Kharn snapped upright, his expression one of shock. "You are the only one of my captains engaged in the pursuit who did not fail utterly." There was still anger in the ka'al's voice, but he had calmed considerably. "I hereby appoint you admiral of my fleet and task you with tracking down the vessel *Wolf's Claw*." He paused. "You are to return the hostage, Astra Lucerne, to Kalishar—alive and unharmed. All raiding activities are hereby suspended. All ships, without exception, will be deployed to the hunt."

"Yes, my lord ka'al." The captain tried to hide his surprise and relief, not entirely successfully. "It shall be done as you command."

"You may go, Admiral Kharn, and carry out your duties." Belgaren stared at him for an instant, then motioned toward the great double doors at the far end of the hall. "Fortune go with you. I shall await news of your triumphant return."

Kharn bowed toward the ka'al. "My thanks, Great Ka'al. I shall do as you command." He turned and walked toward the doors at the end of the hall, trying unsuccessfully to keep his boots from echoing loudly on the hard stone floor.

The ka'al watched his new admiral slip through the massive doors. Kharn had been a good captain, one of the highest producers of all the pirate commanders in his fleet. If anyone could find Arkarin Blackhawk and bring that accursed smuggler back to Kalishar in chains, it was Kharn.

More to the point, it had to be Kharn—the ka'al was running out of time.

He tried to embrace confidence in his new admiral, but all he could feel was fear. The young Tarn Belgaren had been the terror of this corner of the Far Stars, a daring pirate who—it was said—feared nothing. But age and wealth had worn down his courage, and years of too much drink and debauchery had whittled away at his mind. He was a shadow of what he had been, and he was deathly afraid of the imperial agents he knew were watching him. He had taken the governor's coin, but he had not delivered what he promised. He was pompous and full of himself, but he knew the governor's agents were not to be trifled with. They were men like he had been long ago, men of action. And he was afraid of them.

Very, very afraid.

"Get those weapons loaded now, or I will have you whipped to death." Kharn stood on the launch pad shouting at the workers hauling ordnance from the storehouses. *Red Viper* was in the first docking cradle. She was fully loaded with stores and weapons and ready to launch. But Kharn had more to worry about now than his single corsair. There were eighteen ships on Kalishar, and they were all under his command—and a number of them were now missing captains. There was much to do before the fleet would be prepared to launch and little time. Every moment wasted reduced the chances of finding *Wolf's Claw.*

The dockworkers were Kalishari natives, fearful of the ka'al and his pirate followers. They knew Kharn could carry out his threat. He could have them killed for any reason. But laser cannon cartridges and ship-to-ship missiles were delicate mechanisms, and they had to be handled with care.

"Yes, my lord admiral." The leader of the work crew turned toward Kharn and bowed low. "As you command." He bowed again and turned back to face his crews, shouting to them in the native Kalishari tongue.

Kharn watched as a crew pushed a load of torpedoes past him, toward the ships farther down the line. Pirate corsairs rarely carried heavy weapons like that. Their purpose was to disable their prey, mostly lightly armed freighters. But Kharn had seen *Wolf's Claw* in action, and he realized she packed a hell of a punch in battle. Her lasers outranged his own, and her acceleration was like nothing he'd ever seen. He was hoping to find her wounded, limping along in space with half her systems down. But he wasn't about to bet his life on that. And if he found her fully repaired and spoiling for a fight, it was going to take everything he had to disable her.

His eighteen ships could easily overwhelm Blackhawk's vessel, but Kharn wasn't going to have his fleet assembled in one location. He had no idea where to look for *Wolf's Claw,* and he would have to disperse his force to explore as many systems as possible. If one of his search groups found the *Claw,* they would have two, maybe three ships to face her, at least at first. He wanted those ships as heavily armed as possible.

"The whole fleet, Cap— . . . Admiral Kharn? I always knew you were destined for greatness, but this is extraordinary."

Kharn was startled by the deep voice calling from behind, and he turned abruptly to see a hulking figure—two meters tall and heavily muscled—walking briskly toward him. The new arrival wore an ornately decorated captain's uniform, tied in at the waist by a wide black belt and all of it straining against the giant's physique. A pistol hung from one side, in a well-worn holster, and a sword dangled from the other. Many pirates carried a blade, usually just a dagger or a shortsword, but this was a massive cutlass, its hilt covered with jewels. He looked like something pulled from another era, millennia ago, when pirates roved oceans rather than the depths of space.

"Yes, Captain Rhennus, every ship . . . including your own *Black Witch.*" The larger man scowled, but Kharn held his ground. Eventually, though, his serious expression slipped away, replaced by a warm smile. "Rhennus, you old dog! How are you?" Kharn extended his arms and embraced his longtime comrade. "I'm glad you made it in time to join the expedition— Your skills would have been sorely missed, old friend, and I fear I am in need of them as never before."

"I am quite well, my friend. As always." Rhennus returned Kharn's gaze. "Though I'd rather been looking forward to some rest and a drunken binge after a long voyage. The plunder was excellent on this run, and I was expecting to spend a considerable portion at Mirage." Luciana Corelia's Mirage was the most exclusive brothel on Kalishar, a famous establishment, known throughout this section of the Far Stars. It catered to an exclusive clientele, mostly wealthy off-worlders and the ka'al's senior officers and ministers. Kharn was rather inclined to agree with Rhennus, but keeping his head was the priority now.

"Those are worthy pursuits, my friend, but I'm afraid they will have to wait. We launch today."

Rhennus frowned. "Yes, we received the ka'al's orders." There was concern in his face, and confusion. "Why the rush? What is so important?"

"Come," Admiral Kharn said, slapping his friend on the back, "we will discuss it on *Red Viper*. I've got an excellent Antillian brandy in my quarters—the last from a truly memorable raid." He started walking back toward the ship, Rhennus following closely behind. "A weak replacement for the four-alarm binge you were planning, perhaps, but we poor spacers get by as we can, don't we?"

"Indeed we do, my friend." It was obvious the mention of the brandy put a little cheer back into Rhennus. The top vintages from Antilles were some of the best in the Far Stars, almost beyond price, and Kharn knew it would be some solace at least, for the loss of Madame Corelia's ladies.

He hoped it would help soften what he had to tell him next. The two men were walking slowly up the ramp leading to *Red Viper*'s main airlock when Kharn said, "This is serious, Rhennus." All the cheer had left Kharn's voice. "I've never seen the ka'al so angry."

He stepped inside the hatch, turning to face his friend as he entered the ship. "We're looking for a needle in a haystack, my old friend . . . and if we don't find it, I'm afraid we're all in deep trouble."

CHAPTER 8

"THEY'RE MAKING THEIR FINAL APPROACH NOW," LUCAS SAID while bent over his scope, monitoring the imperial ship's heading. The *Claw* had been pursuing the mysterious vessel for seventy-two hours, staying in the target's blind zone to avoid detection. "They should be on the ground within an hour, maybe less." He turned toward Blackhawk, his face twisted into a frown. "I can get us a rough landing location, Skip, maybe a three-hundred- to five-hundred-kilometer radius, but that's the best I can do. Unfortunately, we're too far out for anything more precise than that." His voice was thick with frustration.

Blackhawk nodded, sighing quietly. A thousand-kilometer circle was a hell of a lot of ground to search for one small ship.

Still, he thought, Lucas had done a hell of a job piloting the wounded *Claw,* staying close enough to track the target while still remaining hidden. A five-hundred-kilometer radius was amazing tracking from this range.

Blackhawk knew Sam deserved a lot of credit, too. He had no idea how she'd managed to keep the *Claw*'s damaged engines so close to 100 percent output for as long as she had, but he knew it hadn't been easy. She'd been prowling around the engineering crawlspaces for the last three days without a break, sleep, and with barely any food. He wasn't sure what was keeping her going. Sam was so quiet and soft-spoken, he sometimes forgot she was tough as nails, too.

"Okay, Lucas, get the best read you can, and then bring us in on the most direct route." *Wolf's Claw* was already going to be a day and a half behind the imperial ship, and they had no idea how long their target was staying on Saragossa. Blackhawk didn't plan to waste a second. He wanted to get the *Claw* down to the surface and find the enemy ship as quickly as possible. Then, a quick smash-and-grab job to steal the hyperdrive core, and they'd be off that miserable rock as quickly as Sam could install the stolen system. He was planning for their stay on Saragossa to be short and sweet. The last thing he intended was to get involved in whatever was going on down on the planet. He wasn't interested in wandering around through anyone's civil war, and especially not if there was some kind of imperial involvement. He just wanted to get the *Claw* repaired and back to Celtiboria to return Astra to her father. That was their mission.

That's not the only reason, though, he thought. Because there was more to it than just getting her home. She was too distracting to have on board. His mind kept drifting back to her when he needed to be thinking about other things, and he couldn't allow it to go on.

He wouldn't.

Lucas drew him back to the present. "Got it, Skip. I've got the course already plotted and locked in," the pilot said, slapping his hand on the side of his workstation. "As soon as the imperials land, we don't have to worry about being scanned. We can fire up the engines and revector directly in and save some time." He turned toward Blackhawk. "I think I can get us there in a little over twenty-six hours if Sam can keep the engines going that much longer."

"You hit that time, and you'll earn your pay this month." Blackhawk was surprised at the pilot's claim. He didn't see how he could manage it, but he'd learned not to bet against Lucas Lancaster—not when he was behind the controls of *Wolf's Claw*, at least.

"Sounds great, Skip. Maybe I can send some money home to Mother." It was a joke, one with some edge. Lucas was bitterly estranged from his family after they had exiled him when his drug addiction proved too damaging to the family's standing.

Besides, his mother was one of the wealthiest women in the Far Stars.

"You do that, Lucas." Blackhawk smiled. He was one of the few people who really understood Lucas Lancaster, and he'd recognized the pilot's true quality that day they'd first met, in a dive bar on Antilles. Ace and Shira had been tougher to convince, and both suggested more than once that Blackhawk throw their detoxing passenger out the airlock, or at least drop him on some nearby planet. And their concerns weren't without merit: Lancaster had been a raving lunatic for weeks, a sweating, screaming animal. But gradually, he got clean, and he responded to Blackhawk's mentorship . . . and fists. And the moment he took the controls of *Wolf's Claw,* he truly became one of them.

None of Blackhawk's people had ever seen a pilot as good as Lucas Lancaster. He had all the technical skills, but it was more than that. It was an intuition, a sixth sense that seemed to guide his handling of the ship. The controls were like an extension of his arms, and he coaxed performance out of the ship his crewmates had never thought possible.

"Maybe I'll just hang on to it, Skip. I could use some new boots. Mom will get by." He smiled at Blackhawk. The crew of *Wolf's Claw* followed their captain's lead in maintaining a low profile, but none of them were anxiously awaiting their next payday. Blackhawk was generous with his people, and he always negotiated a heavy purse for the jobs they did. Like *Wolf's Claw* itself—which looked like a struggling smuggler's aging vessel but held a host of surprises for enemies—her crew played the part of wandering adventurers, living from job to job. But that was a fiction. They all had DNA-encoded accounts at the Far Stars Bank, as well as a variety of treasures stashed in hiding places around the sector. They were adventurers and mercenaries certainly, but they were very successful ones. Any of them could retire at any time and live a life of luxury—if any of them had been willing to leave Arkarin Blackhawk's side, that is.

"Good idea," Blackhawk said. "You know I like my crew well turned out." The two shared a laugh, but Blackhawk's mind was wandering down to the lower deck. He couldn't get the image of Astra Lucerne's face out of his head.

And that was a problem.

Because Blackhawk had known Astra for years. He had been her father's friend and ally, and he'd watched her grow up in the shadow of his battlefields. He brought her presents from around the Far Stars whenever the *Claw* returned to Celtiboria, and the young girl's response always warmed his heart.

Then, one time, he returned, and the little girl was gone, a young woman standing in her place.

He couldn't place exactly when he'd noticed she was acting differently around him, but he'd written off her attentions at first as a young girl's infatuation. That worked for a while . . . until he realized he had feelings for her too, much different from those he'd had before.

It wasn't something he would let himself pursue, and he started avoiding Celtiboria, taking jobs farther away and visiting other Prime worlds for repairs and resupply. He hadn't been back in three years when Lucerne's message about Astra's abduction reached him.

If he'd had any doubts about his true feelings, they were washed away during his battle with Cyrus Mondran. His rage had overcome him when he confronted Astra's kidnapper, and his mortal combat with the pirate had landed him in Kalishar's arena and almost cost him his life. He'd been unable to control himself, ignoring Hans's repeated warnings and giving in to pure, elemental fury.

Astra was an amazing woman—strong, beautiful, intelligent. She was like no one else he'd ever known, and just the sight of her distracted him from whatever he was doing. But she was his friend's daughter, and however young Blackhawk may have looked, he was almost twenty-five years older than she was. Worse, he knew she was too good for him. He'd done his best to bury his past, forget the things he'd done, but they were still there. And he knew he could never burden Astra with any of that. She was destined for greatness as Augustin Lucerne's only heir. Blackhawk wouldn't let her waste her life on the likes of him.

No, he thought once again, *I will not drag her into this life of mine. She is destined for much more, and I will not be the cause of her giving up her future. I will take her back to her father, and he will keep her safe. And I will slip back into the darkness.*

"Sorry about the ride in, Skip. The stabilizers must have gotten knocked out of alignment. Sam and I should be able to fix those right away now that we're on the ground." Lucas was leaning back in his seat, exhaling hard. The *Claw* had bucked and kicked coming in, but he'd gotten her down with no further damage. Planetary landings were always tricky, generally the hardest part of piloting a spaceship. Gravity and atmosphere created a lot of complications that simply weren't a factor in the vacuum of space, and bringing in a damaged vessel was not a job for the fainthearted.

"Lucas—you're too hard on yourself." Blackhawk looked over at his pilot. "I suspect anyone else would have smashed us into a hill at 10 kps." He was unhooking his harness with one hand and flipping on the intraship comm with the other. "Everybody okay down there?"

"Yeah, Cap." Ace sounded a little ragged, but Blackhawk knew he'd never admit it. "We got a good shaking, but we're okay."

Ace hadn't shot a barb toward Lucas's piloting. Blackhawk knew his cocky sidekick well enough to realize what that meant. If Ace wasn't giving Lucas a hard time, he was pretty shaken up. "I'm betting Sarge and his guys could use a little time to pull themselves together after that, so you and Shira break out some weapons—I want to go out and have a look around."

Blackhawk had ordered Lucas to bring the ship down in a

sparsely populated area on the very edge of the five-hundred-kilometer zone. That probably meant they'd have some ground to cover, but it also kept them away from prying eyes—both imperials and any factions that were warring one another on this mess of a planet.

"You got it, Ark. We'll meet you at the airlock." Ace sounded a little steadier. Blackhawk didn't know if he was feeling better or just managing to make his bullshit more convincing. He mentally flipped a coin.

"I'll be right down." To Lucas: "Get the field up as soon as you can. I don't know who might have spotted us coming in, but I'd like to keep the number of them actually finding us to a minimum."

Lucas nodded. "I'll have it up in a minute, Skip. Then Sam and I will get up top and take a look at the exterior damage. We might as well deal with that right away. Hopefully, we won't be on the ground too long."

"Exactly," Blackhawk said, walking toward the ladder to the lower level. "Get all the exterior and critical work done as quickly as you can. I want to be ready to get off this rock on a moment's notice." Blackhawk had a bad feeling about Saragossa, even worse than what he might have expected being stuck in the middle of a civil war trying to steal a hyperdrive core from an imperial ship. It was the imperial ship that truly had him nervous, and not just because he had to sneak into it and steal a major piece of equipment. Blackhawk knew an imperial ops ship almost always meant trouble. What he didn't know was why the empire was involving itself in a power struggle on a backwater world. No matter how he thought about it, he couldn't come up with an answer that didn't spell trouble.

And now he was going out of his way to look for trouble.

"We're just going to do a quick reconnoiter and check out the area. Once Sarge and his boys have had a few minutes to pull themselves together, tell them to get suited up and ready for action. And break out the buggy. We've got a long way to go to get to that ship."

"Will do, Skip. Good luck out there. Be careful."

Blackhawk gave Lucas a quick nod then scrambled down the ladder. His mind was still racing when he got to the airlock, coming back again and again to the same question:

Why was the empire here?

"Looks like some nasty shit went down around here, Cap." Ace was a few steps ahead, his eyes panning over the charred ruins ahead of them. It was the third burned-out village they'd come across, and it was just like the others. The stench of death was everywhere.

The buildings had been mostly small huts, but there was little left of them but a few blackened timbers lying in the piles of ash. A long wooden wall was still standing, close to the small square in the village center. It was riddled with bullet holes. In front, there were at least twenty bodies, lying half decomposed, covered with swarms of Saragossa's oversized equivalent of flies.

"There's a reason the guilds redlined Saragossa, Ace." The transport combines were not skittish, nor were they unduly troubled by moral and ethical concerns. They were willing to ply their trade anywhere they could make a profit. The guilds usually stayed above the often cantankerous politics of the Far Stars, happy to deliver supplies of weapons to both sides in a conflict regardless of the ideologies involved. They only redlined a planet when the local situation was too dangerous to their ships and personnel—or when someone paid enough of a bribe. "I don't see anybody caring enough about this shithole to pay off the guilds," Blackhawk said, "so I suspect things got too violent for them. They can make a lot of money running guns into a war zone, so things must be pretty damn bad if they pulled out."

Redlining was a big deal. When the guilds pulled out, the Far Stars Bank almost always followed suit, and whatever other worlds had embassies usually closed them. A redlined planet was on its own, effectively cut off from all interplanetary commerce, even communication. It rarely improved the situation on the world in question, and things often turned more savage and feral once the embargo was put in place.

This village seemed a perfect example.

Blackhawk kept walking, looking past the wreckage and the bodies all around him. The scene was oddly familiar, triggering long-suppressed memories, images of similar atrocities from long ago and far away: destroyed homes, the bodies of helpless villagers—unarmed men and women lying dead in the burnt wreckage. He'd seen it all before, too many times. These simple people were the pawns, the innocents lying in the paths of those who would claim power. And here, as so often before, it was they who paid the price, in pain, suffering, and death.

He pushed the thoughts aside, forcing the anger and guilt back into its place. His rigid discipline slammed down, blocking the distractions. He didn't have time for self-loathing now. He had a job to do. He had to get his people off Saragossa and return Astra Lucerne to her father.

"We're being watched, Ark," Shira said quietly. Unlike Ace, who filled tense moments with his own boasting, Shira preferred to watch and listen, and she was always aware of everything around her. In moments like these, Blackhawk—though he'd never admit it aloud—preferred her on his six. "To the left, just over that ridge. They're trying to hide, but they keep looking over to see what we're doing."

"I see them, Shira." Blackhawk kept walking. "Let's move toward the stone building ahead to the right. There's some cover there." They were out in the open where they were, sitting ducks if their observers were to turn hostile.

"Got it, Ark." Shira's voice betrayed no emotion, no fear, not even stress. Just a cold, relentless calm.

"Ace?"

"With you, Cap." Graythorn's voice was less restrained.

It's never dull going into a fight with Ace, he thought.

They took another few steps. "Now," Blackhawk said quietly. As one, the three of them broke stride and dashed for the cover of the wrecked building. Shira slipped around the end of the half-collapsed stone wall, while Blackhawk and Ace leaped over. The whole thing was over in an instant, and they were crouched behind the wall, weapons drawn.

"Stay cool. We don't want a fight here if we can avoid it." Blackhawk was peering out over the wall, trying to get a read on how many potential enemies they were dealing with. As keen as Shira's observation skills were, he knew his vision was better— another gift from his genetically engineered heritage—and he wanted to get a good look for himself.

"Hello," he called across the narrow plain. Imperial Standard was the primary language used in the Far Stars, but there were various dialects and local tongues, too. Especially on backwaters like Saragossa. "We are not hostile."

"Interesting choice of words, Cap," Ace whispered.

Blackhawk glared at Graythorn, but he knew his lieutenant had a point. If he realized one thing about the crew of *Wolf's Claw*, he knew they were capable of extreme hostility when provoked. They just weren't looking to be hostile at the moment.

"Our ship was damaged, and we landed to make repairs."

He hoped he was getting through to someone over there—he'd spotted at least ten men, and he didn't relish the idea of getting into a firefight outnumbered more than three to one.

"Who are you? What were you doing in this system?" The voice spoke Imperial Standard, but with a heavy local accent. It sounded vaguely familiar, and Blackhawk tried to place it.

It is a Saragossan peasant accent. Ninety-two percent probability the speaker is a factory worker from the industrialized belt in the south ward of the new capital.

Blackhawk nodded, his subconscious acknowledgment of the AI's assist. If the AI was right—and Blackhawk had to admit it was rarely wrong—this peasant would know his way into the capital city . . . and that was the likeliest place to find the core they needed. Saragossa had two capital cities. Old Vostok had been the ancient capital for centuries until New Vostok was constructed in the fair richer northlands of the main continent. The old city had steadily declined in importance until it remained largely a religious center, with only the oldest of the great families maintaining residences there. New Vostok, on the other hand, had expanded rapidly, and it had become the center of the planet's industrial revolution.

They were currently much closer to the new capital than the old. The imperial ship had set down somewhere in or near New Vostok, which was more than thirty-five hundred kilometers from the old city. The *Claw* landed on the outskirts of the thick band of agricultural estates that surrounded the new capital, about four hundred kilometers from the city itself.

Blackhawk stared across the slowly rising ground. Whoever it was they were facing, they weren't great soldiers. They thought they were in cover, but to a trio of killers like Blackhawk, Shira, and Ace, they might as well have been standing in the open. Blackhawk figured his people could have picked off half of them before they even realized what was happening, but a fight hundreds of kilometers away from the core was the last thing he needed now. One of the ways Blackhawk had become such a great warrior was knowing when not to fight.

He just had to hope he could talk them out of this one.

"As I said, our ship was damaged. We had to drop out of hyperspace and land to make repairs." He didn't suspect these peasants knew much about space travel other than how to unload a freighter. They'd probably never been farther off the ground than the second floor of a building.

"So why are you prowling around? Why aren't you fixing your ship and leaving Saragossa?" The voice was suspicious, but Blackhawk could hear confusion as well. He doubted the speaker knew a thing about spacecraft or what it took to repair them.

"Our engineer is working on the ship now. We are just scouting the area."

"We saw a vessel land, but now it is gone." The voice's skepticism was growing. "I will give you one more chance to tell the truth: Were you cast out from your vessel? Did it depart somehow without our notice?"

Blackhawk sighed. The field. They'd probably scouted the area where the *Claw* landed, but the field would make the ship effectively invisible to them. An experienced eye could sometimes detect a distortion field from small inconsistencies in the images projected, but to these peasants, the ship was completely undetectable. He stood up, holding his rifle out to the side as he laid it against the wall. "I am going to come over there." He unbuckled his belt, letting it—along with his pistol and sword—fall to the ground. "I am now unarmed."

"Ark, are you crazy?" Ace had opened his mouth to say much the same thing, but Shira beat him to it. "Get down. We don't know anything about these people."

"I'll be all right, Shira." She looked at him like he was crazy. Shira tended to think the worst of anyone she met, and her primary strategy was to strike first, just in case the other side was hostile. Blackhawk wasn't the most trusting soul, but he tended to be more subtle, to play a situation by intuition as well as intellect. "Trust me, okay? You guys stay put."

Without waiting for their response, he held his arms out to the sides and walked slowly around the end of the stone wall. "We are not hostile. We mean you no harm." He started moving toward the ridge.

"Stop or we'll shoot." The voice was getting shakier.

Blackhawk kept walking. "If you want to shoot me, shoot me. But I think we can help each other, and I'm going to come over there to talk about it." The closer he got, the more he was confident they weren't going to fire. He was alone, clearly unarmed—and they had no way of knowing that even without weapons, he stood a fair chance of taking out all ten of them if he got close enough. If they wanted to shoot him, they would have done so numerous times by now.

Of course, if he was wrong—if they did shoot him—he could imagine what Ace and Shira would do to these peasant soldiers. It wouldn't be a pretty sight. But he was sure that wouldn't happen.

Pretty sure, at least.

CHAPTER 9

"IT IS TIME, MARSHAL LUCERNE." THE CHAMBERLAIN'S VOICE was tentative, nervous. He stood by the door, clearly not wanting to interrupt the pensive military commander.

"I will be there in a moment." He waved his hand, dismissing the timid servant. He frowned. *Is this victory?* Lucerne thought. *To seize power with such brutality and force even my servants to step around me in fear?*

Lucerne was unique among those in history who had marched out to the drum to conquer or die. He did not seek power for himself, nor did he crave the acclamation of those he ruled. Indeed, he considered all of it a burden, one he wished with all his heart he could lay aside. Everything he had truly cared about in his life had been sacrificed to the insatiable demands of war. But he knew his calling: to unite the people of the Far Stars, to make them strong enough to remain free and resist the encroachment of the dark empire that lay across the great Void.

For all its constant warfare and disunity, the Far Stars sector was the only place in man's dominion where the fire of freedom still burned, at least dimly. Lucerne had visited the empire in his youth. He'd seen the terrified and subdued masses, broken to the will of their masters. He remembered the dead look in their vacant eyes.

Men in the Far Stars were different. They fought over gold; they battled for power; they killed for women. They waged war because they felt insulted or to avenge a perceived wrong. They killed and destroyed for a host of terrible reasons—and for one good one. Only in this most remote bastion of human habitation did men still stand up and demand the right to choose their own path, and they defended it with sword and fire. There was plenty of oppression in the sector and untold millions toiling in servitude and serfdom. But the spirit of independence was still alive. Nowhere else in the galaxy had humanity successfully resisted the deadening hand of imperial rule, and Lucerne was determined to ensure that continued. He would destroy the worst of the planetary regimes—freeing their people from the brutality of their oppressors—and he would entice the rest into a confederation, a united front against any future imperial encroachment.

It was a worthy goal, one he prayed would prove to be worth the untold thousands who had died in his wars, and the multitudes that would surely fall as the struggle continued. Worth the parents and siblings he'd left behind, the wife who died alone and abandoned, and the daughter who was now a captive, her life in danger because of who her father was.

He stood up slowly, the ache in his joints reminding him he was no longer the youthful soldier, naive and optimistic, who'd set out after a dream so many years before. Today, a part of that vision would be realized, as he officially became the head of state of the united planet of Celtiboria. It had taken thirty years to achieve that goal. Three decades of blood and death and struggle. After three hundred years of fragmentation, of rule by the warlords, there would again be a Celtiborian Senate, a governing body for a single, unified planet.

Lucerne had begun his quest with the purest intentions, but his youthful fervor had long since faded away, replaced by a pragmatic cynicism forged over years of struggle. He knew that democracy was no magic bullet. There still needed to be good men and women to ensure the government worked. And that's what worried him, that with the warlords gone, the new representatives would simply become the next generation of oppressors. Lucerne didn't know, but he suspected they would. Unless someone was watching them, keeping them from following the path of corruption and madness for power.

The past said yes as well. The dictators Lucerne had spent his life deposing had sprung from the carcass of the old republican system, and most of the warlords were descended from the ancient senatorial families. It had been a gradual evolution from planetwide republic to fractured dictatorships. The same political dynasties had been repeatedly elected by an unfocused and disinterested public, and senatorial families grew more and more entrenched in their power, eventually dispensing with even the form of electorally derived authority to hereditary "representatives," ultimately evolving into the warlords who ruled their domains by force and fear.

Lucerne sighed, pulling himself from his deep introspection. He looked down, smoothing out the bright white pants of his uniform. He'd considered wearing the garb of an old-style senator, but in the end he'd decided against wearing civilian clothes. No one had sacrificed more for victory than his men, and they deserved to see their marshal, dressed as a soldier, climb the steps to the high podium. See their leader accept the appointment as consul, the ancient Celtiborian title for a military commander assuming absolute power in a crisis. The fight would continue, he knew, in space and on other worlds now, and Lucerne would rule with all the absolute power any warlord had wielded.

He felt the hypocrisy, the conflict between his rhetoric and his actions. Even as he decried the oppression of the warlords and sought to overthrow them by force, he pursued his own power as absolute as that of any of his adversaries. But he was true to himself as well. When the confederation was at last a reality, when the Far Stars worlds were prepared to ensure its freedom, Augustin Francois Lucerne would willingly—and gratefully—surrender his powers and retire to private life. Until then, he would do what he had to do, take whatever actions were necessary to see his efforts through to their successful conclusion. Failure to do so would render all the sacrifices already made by so many pointless, and Lucerne couldn't imagine a worse crime.

He stood in front of the mirror, taking a last look at himself. He certainly looked the part of the glorious conqueror, resplendent in the ancient uniform of a Celtiborian consul. His dark blue coat was covered with gold lace, and his chest bore a tangled nest of medals and decorations. His knee-high boots were polished to a glossy sheen, and his white breeches were spotless, almost blindingly bright.

He shifted uncomfortably, the blue uniform jacket, knee-high boots, and all the decorations feeling binding and tight. Not just physically, but also emotionally. Lucerne had always hated ceremony and fancy uniforms, preferring to maintain a low profile and lead his men as one of them, not raised on some pedestal. He had always been known among his soldiers for his simple dress, for his habit of wandering his battlefields wearing a plain enlisted man's coat, the row of bright silver stars on his shoulders the only distinction of his usually mud-splattered uniform.

He was more accustomed to wandering the camps, sharing a simple meal with a random platoon of troopers, than he was to the prattling of insincere courtiers and flatterers crowding the halls of government. He never had been able to tolerate the pandering of those who sought to empower and enrich themselves at the trough of government. Such behavior disgusted him, and thirty years in the mud and blood of the battlefield had done nothing to change that.

But he realized it wasn't just about him now, or his soldiers. He was performing for all the people of Celtiboria and for that audience, trivialities like fancy uniforms and elaborate ceremonies mattered. Hell, he was enough of a politician to realize even his soldiers would expect to see him in his glowing finery, basking in the glory of victory. He knew it was dishonest, but he would play the part, give the war-weary crowds someone to cheer, a larger-than-life figure to follow. Because he would need their enthusiastic support if he was to unite the Far Stars. The wars on Celtiboria paled in comparison to the task that lay ahead.

Even now, the first ships of the fleet were set to launch, to take war to worlds across the Far Stars, planets ruled by petty dictators and brutal monarchs. Their oppressive regimes would be destroyed, their people freed—at least from the sadistic monsters who ruled them now. Lucerne knew he wasn't truly bringing freedom to these worlds, but the leaders he would install would be far preferable to those they replaced.

Lucerne was confident he could win some allies through negotiations as well. Indeed, there were already a dozen worlds ready to join his new confederation. But he knew many worlds would have to be brought in by force, their self-appointed rulers destroyed, totalitarian regimes replaced with new quasi republics. There would be a lot of fighting, and dying, before the Far Stars Confederation became a reality.

He walked through the heavy oaken door and out into the corridor, his boots rapping loudly on the polished stone floor. The walls were lined with guards in dress uniforms, and they snapped to as he walked by, presenting arms to their revered leader. The soldiers were veterans, selected for the duty by their comrades. All his guards had been drawn from the ranks, from among his bravest and longest-serving soldiers.

On the battlefield, Lucerne knew the risks. He could see his enemies clearly. In the political swamp of the capital, conspiracy lurked in every shadowy corner. A knife in the dark or a poisoned drink could end his crusade in its tracks, and the unification bought with three decades of blood and pain would be lost. Lucerne trusted few people, and almost no one outside the ranks of his veteran soldiers. When the time had come to establish a Consular Guard regiment, he'd rejected the insiders and the sycophants flocking around him demanding appointments. He decreed that every member of the unit be drawn from soldiers with five years' experience or more in his army, and that they be named directly by him or nominated by the acclaim of their comrades in arms.

He walked slowly down the hall, turning and nodding to the old sweats standing grimly at attention. Some of them had scarred faces, badges of honor won on the battlefield. Others had grown gray in Lucerne's service, locks of silvery hair protruding from their headgears. All stood rigidly at attention, watching their beloved commander walk slowly by toward his destiny.

Lucerne walked through another set of doors and out into the main hall. He had chosen the location with care. It was the last seat of republican government on the planet. Three centuries before, the Celtiborian Senate had met there for the last time. Once again, the massive structure would become the center of government of the largest, most populous world in the Far Stars. In a few minutes, Augustin Lucerne would address the entire planet, the four hundred million people of Celtiboria watching in rapt attention to see what their new ruler had to say. To many, Lucerne's victory heralded the start of a golden age, bringing freedom from the oppression of the warlords. Others were less sure, wondering if they had simply traded one tyranny for another.

They aren't wrong to doubt, he thought. *There's no way to know how this will turn out. But I swore an oath on the blood of my men, on my family.* So doubt they might, but if they tried to oppose him . . .

A grim determination set in once more.

Lucerne climbed the podium and waited for the transmission to begin. He'd fought brutal enemies in some of the most horrendous battles ever fought. He'd been wounded a dozen times, and he'd lost count of how many friends he'd lost. But Augustin Lucerne had never been as scared as he was now. He'd rather face any enemy on the battlefield than play at politician. For all his republican ideals, he'd become far more comfortable using force to compel rather than persuading with words.

He stood stone still, watching the display count down to zero. He'd written a speech and revised it several times, but he still wasn't sure exactly what he was going to say. He knew the address was superfluous in many ways, that his armies could compel obedience from the people of Celtiboria despite any resistance they might offer. But Lucerne wanted to avoid that road—the path to true tyranny—if he could. He would try to make his case to those he now ruled, attempt to bring them willingly behind the crusade.

Yet even as he tried to focus, all he could think of was Astra. He'd always imagined that when he finally united Celtiboria, his daughter would be there at his side. Now his triumph had finally come, and the one person closest to him was somewhere unknown, possibly suffering, certainly in grave danger.

He tried to put the worries about her out of his mind, but her image was still there, in the forefront of his mind. He told himself to have faith in Blackhawk's loyalty and abilities, that his friend was one of the most formidable and capable men in the Far Stars. And he did have confidence in Blackhawk, but it was becoming harder and harder to rely on that as time passed. Not even Arkarin Blackhawk could succeed on every mission, and searching the entire sector for one person was a monumental task, one possibly beyond even Blackhawk's ability.

But now it was time to address the people of Celtiboria. Lucerne had been a creature of duty his entire life, and that wasn't going to change now, no matter how dead and empty he felt inside. He turned toward the camera, clearing his throat as the clock counted down to zero.

"My fellow Celtiborians, I am here to speak with you on an auspicious occasion." Even from the chamber he could hear the people massed outside cheering. He rallied his discipline, closed his mind to everything but the task at hand. This was a crucial milestone, and Lucerne the soldier, the leader, was firmly in control.

CHAPTER 10

"TO NEW FRIENDS." BLACKHAWK RAISED THE DENTED METAL CUP for an instant before putting it to his lips and taking a tentative sip. The clear drink felt like liquid fire sliding down his throat. It was rakin, a home-brewed whiskey made by the peasant farmers of Saragossa. He was about to pull the cup from his mouth when Hans chimed in.

> You must empty your cup on the first drink. To do
> otherwise is to give grievous insult to your host.

Blackhawk tilted the cup and drained it. He almost gasped for breath as the caustic fluid filled his mouth and poured down his throat, but he fought the impulse, staring back impassively at his hosts.

**Turn your cup upside down, and hold it out in front of
you. Then lay it in front of you upside down. It is the
custom.**

Blackhawk followed the AI's instructions, staring right at the
rebel group's leader as he did. He placed the cup on the ground
in front of him, and he glanced quickly at Ace and Shira, who
were staring at their own drinks with doubtful expressions on
their faces.

As Blackhawk made eye contact with each, they slowly raised
their own cups, mimicking their captain's moves and chugging
down the harsh liquor. Ace was an accomplished drinker who'd
put more than one rival under the table, but Blackhawk could
see him fight back a wince as the fiery liquid slid down his
throat. Shira rarely drank, and when she did, it was invariably
the very best and most expensive wine or brandy she could find.
But she held her emotionless expression better than Ace, her
rigid personal discipline taking control.

The leader raised his own cup, repeating Blackhawk's
motion, then he drained it and held it upside down in front of
him. The rest of his men followed suit.

"We thank you for your hospitality, Arn, and we repeat our
offer of friendship." Blackhawk stared across the crackling fire
at the rebel leader. The hunched figure gazed back at him with
cloudy brown eyes. He looked old, deep lines tracing their way
across his tanned and careworn face. Stringy hanks of greasy
hair, mostly gray, hung about his head. It was obvious to the
captain that years of hardship and war had aged him, and a
lifetime of servitude in appalling conditions before that.

To casual observers, the rebel appeared at least four decades
older than *Wolf's Claw*'s captain, but Blackhawk knew that was

misleading. He himself looked no older than thirty-five, though he was fifty-four—another benefit of the imperial breeding program that had produced him. He guessed Arn wasn't as nearly as old as his battered appearance suggested. He'd have placed a moderate wager that his host was actually younger than he was.

He turned again toward his two companions. "Arn is the leader of the rebel forces in this entire area." Blackhawk had spoken long with the rebel leader and his men before he'd sent for Ace and Shira. "The rebellion on Saragossa is in its seventh year. Arn was one of the original leaders of the peasants' revolt. However, the rebels have since split into two groups that are hostile to each other." He turned toward their host. "Arn, perhaps you would explain to my friends what you told me?"

The rebel commander nodded to Blackhawk. He turned toward Shira and Ace. "When we rose up, we did so to create a new world, one where our children could hope for something more than working the fields or factories every waking hour for the enrichment of their masters. We sought to overthrow the nobility, those who had kept us—and our fathers before us—in servitude and oppression." There was a sadness in his eyes, as though he was remembering some past glory now gone.

"We roused the factory workers and drove the masters from the cities, though it cost us many dead to gain the victory. We liberated many also from the fields, the serfs who had been tied to the land as we had been to the factories." He paused and took a deep breath. "Many others remained in bondage, and we continued to fight to free them.

"There was much death, and vengeance as well. We lost thousands in the fighting, and our hatred was inflamed. Many of the nobles we captured were brutally tortured and slain. Noble women were raped and murdered in the streets, their children beaten to death before their eyes. I do not defend such conduct, yet I would caution those not born into servitude to withhold judgment. My people endured many wrongs and injuries as terrible as these for generations."

Blackhawk nodded slowly, his mind drifting back through the years. "I have seen much war and bloodshed, Arn. I know just what men are capable of when their passions are aroused. I have witnessed the brutality of the oppressor and the hopelessness of those who live under the iron boot. Many times. I've . . . I've even been party to such things. It is not our place to judge you, nor any of your people."

The *Claw* captain went quiet for a moment. Ace and Shira were used to it, and they sat silently, respecting their commander's privacy. Blackhawk wouldn't talk about what he had seen or what he'd done. Someday, maybe. But not now, and certainly not to a complete stranger. He sat up straighter and looked across at Arn.

"So what happened to the revolution?" he asked. "What caused the schism and drove you, one of its leaders, out into the near wilderness?"

Arn was silent for a few seconds before he continued with his story. "It was after our initial successes, when we had driven the nobles from the cities. I pushed to arrange elections, to organize those who'd been freed to choose their leaders. But many of my comrades were against taking hasty action. There were still battles to be fought, they said, more people to free. The war was not over, and the greater good demanded that those of us in positions of power remain there to ensure the revolution was a success." He took a deep breath, his eyes moving between Blackhawk and his two companions as he did.

"I was not comfortable with so few having so much power,

yet I understood the rationale, and I went along. The revolution was still raging. We had the cities, but the nobles most of the countryside—and most of the planet's wealth, which they had carried off. The aristocrats hired off-world mercenaries to bolster their private armies, and everywhere there was war. I led my armies into battle, fighting meter by meter to free each group of serfs, to rally them to the cause and grow our ranks.

"Yet while we struggled on the battlefield, a cancer spread through our ranks. My old comrades had tasted too much power, too much wealth. They took residence in the old villas and began to live as those we had deposed. They gathered more and more power to themselves, and the senior officers in the field were drawn deeper within their web, seeking to attain for themselves positions of wealth and privilege. There were internal struggles, as my comrades began to scheme and fight each other for position." His voice was hoarse and throaty, and his eyes were watery with emotion.

"Then the purges began, and even as we still fought the nobility, we fell upon ourselves like starving dogs. My old comrades, those who had stood with me in the factory where we made our first stand, had become the evil we'd set out to destroy. They were even worse than the hereditary nobility they replaced. Their greed was naked, their lust for power unquenchable. They spoke of freedom, of a workers' paradise, but everywhere there was repression and terror. Those who objected were dragged away in the dead of night, never to be seen again. The evil was cloaked in propaganda. Those who were killed were branded enemies of the revolution, traitors to the new order.

"You have to understand that those of us who started the rebellion were educated, at least somewhat. We had worked on complex machinery in the factory, and we'd been trained so we could perform our duties. But most of the workers were illiterate and without understanding of freedom. Being freed from their former masters, they sought others to follow, as a child searches for a lost parent. They listened to my comrades, and to the commissars appointed to keep them in line, and they obeyed the commands of men no more fit to lead than the nobles we'd deposed." Tears openly slid down Arn's cheek now. He was staring directly at Blackhawk, but the *Claw*'s captain knew he was seeing something else.

That must be how I look to my crew sometimes, he thought.

"I went to my old comrades," Arn was saying, "pled with them not to follow the path they were on, replacing one class of masters with another. I reminded them of why we had begun the revolt, the ideals we had all held dear. But they were comfortable in their new ways and defensive of their new powers and privileges. They ignored me at first, but when I continued my efforts, they turned on me. I was condemned by the Revolutionary Council, sentenced to die as a traitor to the revolution. Many of the soldiers I had led into battle had their minds poisoned against me. They accepted the word of those who used them, who threw their comrades' lives away in pointless battles, who spent the funds they stole on luxuries instead of weapons to arm our soldiers and coats to keep them warm."

Arn paused again. "But I was not without friends and allies. Not all the soldiers of revolution were so easily led by those who would be their new masters. I was able to escape from my prison and gather many to my banner. The rural estate areas were mostly occupied by the old nobles and their mercenary armies, and the cities were held by my former comrades, so we were driven into the undeveloped areas. We struggled with supply and logistics, but still we grew in strength, and we won battles against both our enemies."

His expression darkened. "Then the ships began to arrive. We don't know where they came from, but we soon discovered they brought arms, weapons of a sort we had never seen before. Our forces were swept from the field by our former ally's new firepower, the survivors driven deeper into the wilderness. Their new weapons were superior even to those of the old regime's mercenary forces, guns firing blasts of deadly light that bore right through stone walls and bombs of unprecedented power. Now they are on the verge of total victory against us, and when we are destroyed, they will use their new weapons to crush the nobles and their mercenaries. They will impose a totalitarian regime worse than that of the old nobility, and Saragossans will be slaves forever."

Blackhawk nodded to his host, but inside he felt a knot in his stomach. Arn had described imperial military ordnance, particle accelerator rifles, and other state-of-the-art weapons. Why, he wondered, was the empire sneaking high-tech weaponry to a group of rebels on a backwater world?

Arn stared across the fire at Blackhawk. "When we saw your ship land, we feared it was another of the mysterious vessels bringing even more weapons and supplies to Talin and his people." He gazed at Blackhawk with moist eyes. "With two ships arriving in succession, we feared that the pace of shipments had increased.

"I am pleased we were wrong. We are very near to defeat. We cannot face Talin and the forces of the Revolutionary Army if they become any stronger. Still, even the one ship of weapons is of great concern. I know Talin, how he thinks. His forces will move to finish us first, for he perceives we are a greater danger than the remnants of the nobles. Once we are gone, he will finish off the mercenary armies of the old regime." Hopelessness filled his voice. "Then Saragossa shall know a new level of oppression and despair."

Blackhawk sat quietly for a few seconds, considering Arn's words. He was still troubled at the imperial involvement, but he put that to the side. *I'm not here to get involved in their war,* he thought. *At least not too involved.* He began to realize he'd found an ally, that Arn's soldiers could help his crew get to the imperial ship. A smile crept across Blackhawk's face. "Arn, I think your people and mine can help each other. There is something in that ship we need, a component to repair our vessel. Obviously you want the weapons for yourselves. Or at least destroyed. If we work together, we can penetrate the enemy defenses and get to the ship, then we will take what we need, and your people can have the weapons and ammunition."

Arn looked back across the fire, his eyes taking his measure of Blackhawk. The *Claw*'s captain could tell the rebel leader was slow to offer trust, but he also knew the man had little choice. His people had to have those weapons, and they would never have a better chance to get them than now.

Arn nodded gravely. "I accept your offer of friendship, Captain Blackhawk. We shall go to New Vostok together, and we shall take what we need from this enemy ship." He stood slowly and stepped toward his guest, extending his hand before him.

Blackhawk smiled as he climbed to his feet, extending his own hand. "My thanks to you, friend Arn. May fortune favor us both."

He grasped Arn's firmly, sealing the pact.

CHAPTER 11

"WE HAVE BROUGHT A LARGER SHIPMENT THIS TIME, FIRST COM-rade Talin. New weapons, of even greater power than those we have already provided. Governor Vos is pleased with your progress, and he extends his congratulations on your battle-field successes. There is another shipment three weeks behind us. When it arrives, you will be able to equip a large portion of your army with enhanced weaponry."

Andreus Sand stood before the leader of Saragossa's Revolu-tionary Council, trying to hide his disgust. He was repulsed by this jacked-up Saragossan dictator, but he wouldn't allow that to interfere with his mission. He knew Talin was a schemer of some ability, a man who'd managed to stab enough of his wog comrades in the back to become top dog, but his lack of discipline was offensive to a man with Sand's iron control.

The room was impressive, at least for a frontier world full of former serfs and inbred nobles. The floors were polished granite, inlaid with a fairly intricate design—again, decent work for a world on the extreme frontier. The ceiling soared ten meters above, with a series of frescoes depicting scenes from Saragossan history. The building had been the winter residence of one of the planet's great noble families before the revolution. It was surprisingly opulent, but it was still nothing compared to the Capitol on Galvanus Prime.

Of course, Andreus Sand wouldn't say that to a pretentious factory worker turned freedom-fighting revolutionary turned brutal dictator. Not with the skulls of the former occupants still displayed on spikes outside the main entry hall, including four small ones that had obviously been children. It was apparent to Sand that the Saragossan revolution hadn't discriminated in its murderous vengeance. All the nobles who'd fallen into the hands of the insurgents had been slain, even newborns ripped from their mothers' arms . . . and sometimes babies from their wombs. That was before the revolutionaries turned on themselves and began murdering former allies. What had begun as a war for freedom had become just another series of brutal power struggles.

And it all turned Sand's stomach. But he served the governor, and—for the moment—this savage had a purpose in Vos's grander plans.

"That is excellent news," the monster said. Talin leaned back in his massive chair and stared back at the imperial agent. Sand might have been on orders to aid this man, but there was no way he was going to let him stare him down. Eventually, Talin looked away—feigning indifference, but Sand could tell this Talin was like every other bully he met: all talk until he met his betters. His voice wavering momentarily, Talin finally said, "May I assume you have also brought the . . . ah . . . other items I requested?"

Sand nodded, holding back a sigh. "Yes, your personal goods are here as well." Talin was on the verge of destroying his rivals and seizing total control of the planet, yet his first concern was for the wine and brandy and other delicacies he'd demanded.

Not to mention the hallucinogenics.

How, Sand wondered, did a man who was a bonded serf working in a factory just a few years before become such a useless sybarite so quickly? And that chair—it wasn't a throne exactly, but it was close. What delusions was this puffed-up peasant harboring in that twisted mind of his? Talin was smart, at least in a devious sort of way, but Sand had seen many power struggles. He'd have bet a thousand imperial crowns that half a dozen of Talin's men were scheming against him even now, waiting for the chance to follow his example and climb to the top of the whole foul heap themselves. A knife in the dark was a time-honored political maneuver, one that tended to sidestep the need for endless debate and discussion.

I'd save them all the trouble right now, if I could. His fingers itched for his own knife.

Now wasn't the time, though. His orders were to secure Talin's cooperation—and if Talin were to fall, to do the same with whatever successor managed to seize power. Kergen Vos wanted to secure effective control of Saragossa, and he didn't care what local puppet held titular power. Still, whoever ruled the planet would need a steady stream of supplies to maintain his position, and that ensured future cooperation. And if it didn't, a simple assassination would throw the planet into chaos again and allow Sand to play kingmaker once more to secure the right puppet.

A scenario that becomes more and more tempting . . .

"My people are ready to unload the cargo, First Comrade. Where would you like the weapons delivered?"

Talin looked down from his quasi throne. "I think, Agent Sand, that we will leave the weapons in the secure hold of your ship until the units scheduled to receive them are assembled."

Sand was an experienced imperial agent with years of service and a strong ability to read expressions. Talin was afraid one of his people might make a play for the weapons. That's why he wanted them to stay on board. Sand was sure of it.

"Certainly, First Comrade." Sand nodded respectfully. "I will delay unloading until you instruct otherwise." He disliked Talin, but if one of the bastard's lieutenants got ahold of the weapons—and not from the hands of Sand himself— total chaos would erupt. There were already three sides in this bizarre civil war. The last thing Sand needed was another claimant to power, one equipped with a shipload of first-rate imperial equipment.

He nodded again. "If that's all for now, First Comrade, I believe I will return to my ship until you are ready to receive the cargo." Sand was a veteran agent, and he did whatever duty required, but he had no wish to endure Talin's company any longer than necessary.

"That will be satisfactory, Agent Sand," Talin said imperiously. "However, if it is not too much trouble . . ."

Sand fought back another sigh. "You would like your personal goods offloaded now."

Talin offered the agent a fleeting smile. "Ah, yes, Agent Sand. As I said, if it is not too much trouble. I'm afraid I am down to my last bottle of Antillean brandy."

"It shall be done immediately, First Comrade, as you request." Sand tried to imagine the orgy of looting and drunkenness that must have taken place when these rebelling factory workers first pried their way into the larders and wine cellars of the deposed nobles. Looking at the repulsive Talin and picturing that scene, it was all he could do to keep from shuddering. "Send your men to the docking area in one hour. It will all be ready for you."

"My thanks to you, Agent Sand."

Sand turned and walked slowly toward the door. Once he'd exited the chamber he let his guard down for an instant and shook his head. *This is the material we have to work with out here,* he thought grimly. He'd willingly followed General Wilhelm to his posting in the Far Stars, and he still believed that Governor Vos's plan to subjugate the sector was a brilliant one. Success would enhance the careers of all those involved far more than any routine duty back in civilized space. He knew he'd made the right choice, but sometimes he got exhausted dealing with the wogs out on the frontier. *Just part of the job,* he thought with a sigh. *Just part of the job.*

Kergen Vos stared down at the large screen on the table, his eyes darting over the starmap it displayed. His plans were progressing well. Operations were under way on a dozen worlds, and several more were set to commence shortly. Everything took longer than it should, but that was an unavoidable complication when dealing with the barbarians on the frontier.

The people inhabiting the Far Stars were mostly backward by imperial standards, and they were annoyingly independent.

Even those he'd bribed or coerced into his service constantly asked questions and argued with his directives. More than once, his rigid control over his temper saved him from making foolish emotional decisions. Usually this meant keeping alive a man or woman he'd rather have seen drawn and quartered. He knew there was no point in assassinating someone when the person's replacement was certain to be as bad or worse—he just had to work with what he had.

Especially since he wasn't likely to get a squadron of battleships or a legion of assault troops any time soon.

One of the massive oaken double doors creaked open, and the chamberlain stepped through. "General Wilhelm to see you, Excellency." He bowed nervously as he spoke, awaiting a response.

Vos looked up from his work. "Oh, get up, you old fool." The chamberlain wasn't just old; he was ancient. Vos wasn't sure he'd ever seen a human being so decrepit who could still get around on his own legs. He couldn't imagine how many useless, disgraced nobles the man had served in the decades he'd prowled the halls of the Capitol.

He didn't doubt the inbred fops had enjoyed the bowing and scraping and ludicrous ceremony that had become so ingrained in the daily procedure of the place, but it was starting to drive him crazy. He didn't have time for it, or the patience. He had real work to do. He had real blood on his hands, too, and a fair amount of mud and shit too. He'd fought, suffered, killed, all in the service of empire. He was a man of action and needed men of like mind around him. What he *didn't* need was to have his ego soothed by a bunch of useless sycophants.

"Send him in." Vos waved toward the door, dismissing the chamberlain.

A moment later, Mak Wilhelm entered the room, wearing his general's full dress uniform as always. He stood at attention just inside the room. "Excellency."

"How long have we worked together, Mak?" Vos was still staring at the map on the table.

"Almost ten years, Excellency." Wilhelm sounded a little confused.

Vos looked up from the table. "Wouldn't you say we could all save time and do our work more efficiently if you didn't feel it was necessary to run to your quarters and squeeze yourself into that ridiculous uniform every time you wanted to tell me something?" He ran his eyes up and down Wilhelm's unmoving form. "Those leggings look particularly uncomfortable."

"Indeed they are, Excellency. The whole thing is a twisting, pulling nightmare." Vos was surprised to see the hint of a smile touch Wilhelm's lips. It wasn't quite a laugh, but everyone had to start somewhere.

"Which is exactly how it looks. So let's agree on some ground rules. You will still call me Excellency—I worked hard for the title. But when you need to see me, come however you are already dressed. A civilian suit will certainly do. You are an agent as well as a general, after all."

There was no one more ambitious than Kergen Vos, but he craved real power, not the pandering of terrified subordinates tiptoeing around and kissing his ass. There was too much of that nonsense in the empire already, legions of useless nobles who owed their position to the achievements of grandfathers and great-grandfathers. Besides, Wilhelm was his right hand, the highest ranked of his people, and he needed to have at least one confidant with whom he could converse freely.

"Yes, Excellency. Thank you."

Wilhelm remained at attention.

Vos glanced up again from the map. Wilhelm remained at attention. Vos sighed.

Baby steps, I suppose. "Relax, Mak. You're not on parade." He smiled. "So what have you got for me?"

Wilhelm shifted slightly, his concession to the informality Vos craved. "Sand sent a dispatch as he was entering the Saragossa system. Everything was moving according to plan, and he was about to begin the final approach to the planet. He should have landed by now."

"Very well. I will want his evaluation of the status of the fighting as soon as he leaves Saragossa. We've been pouring very expensive support to the revolutionaries there." He lowered his voice. "Including top-grade weapons we're not really supposed to be distributing to the wogs. I want results. And soon."

"Yes, Excellency. I will advise you as soon as he reports in again."

Vos frowned. "I also want his assessment of this Talin character. He doesn't sound terribly stable to me." He paused, thinking for a few seconds. "If we need to make a move to replace our local surrogate, I want to do it sooner rather than later."

"Understood." Wilhelm nodded. "I will instruct him to provide his complete analysis."

"Anything else?"

"Yes, Excellency. Word from Lucius Vega on Kalishar. The ka'al has suspended all pirating operations and dispatched his entire fleet to search for the enemy vessel. Belgaren assures Vega that his ships seriously damaged the fleeing vessel before it jumped, and he is sure it couldn't have gotten far in hyperspace without stopping somewhere for repairs. His vessels are en route to every system within ten light-years."

"That is good. Of course, it would have been better if he hadn't allowed them to escape from under his nose in the first place, but out here we have to work with what we have." He sat down in one of the chairs at the table, motioning for Wilhelm to do the same. "Anything else?"

"Yes. A name." Wilhelm pulled out a chair and sat down slowly, trying to be inconspicuous as he pawed at the tight pants of his uniform—and failing, Vos noted. "Blackhawk. Arkarin Blackhawk. He was the one who rescued Astra Lucerne. His ship is called *Wolf's Claw*."

"Blackhawk," Vos repeated. "That name is vaguely familiar." He glanced down at the screen on the table. "Display all files involving the individual Arkarin Blackhawk or the starship *Wolf's Claw*." It was nagging at his mind. He knew he'd seen the name somewhere.

The map vanished from the screen, replaced by a series of data entries. Most of them were routine accounts of smuggling and various other mundane offenses, but one in particular caught his eye. It was a report from the agent on Troyus. *Wolf's Claw* had taken Augustin Lucerne to a conference on the planet to negotiate Troyus's participation in his proposed Far Stars Confederation. The whole thing had been handled in great secrecy, and the agent had been unable to get any serious intel on the discussions themselves. The report speculated that Lucerne contracted with *Wolf's Claw* because his forces were still fighting to complete the unification of Celtiboria, and he didn't want it to be widely known he was off-planet.

"Lucerne," Vos whispered. "Lucerne knows Blackhawk." His voice became louder. "So this was more than a dispute among pirates. Lucerne sent this Blackhawk to get his daughter." The implications were racing through his head. Augustin Lucerne was a formidable and enormously capable man who loved his daughter very much. Celtiboria's warrior-ruler wouldn't send just anyone after his precious Astra. There must be more to Blackhawk, he thought, than being a petty smuggler and adventurer.

Vos stared into Wilhelm's eyes with a burning intensity. "I want to know more about this Blackhawk. And I want him found. Dead or alive." He slapped his hand on the table. "Put the word out in every pirate hideout and rogue bar in the Far Stars. A million imperial crowns to anyone who brings me Blackhawk . . . or his head. And another million for Astra Lucerne—alive and unharmed."

Wilhelm nodded, doing a pretty fair job of hiding his surprise. But Vos could see a subtle change in the man's eyes, and he knew he had the general's attention. He expected nothing less: a million crowns was an enormous fortune in the Far Stars, enough for an adventurer to make himself a king on some worlds. Vos's bounty would have the sector in an uproar. Every pirate crew and merc outfit in the Far Stars would be hunting Blackhawk—and fighting one another to get to him.

"Yes, Excellency. I will see to it immediately."

Later that day, Vos sat at the conference table, quietly observing the well-dressed men seated opposite him. Their clothes wouldn't have been fashionable on the other side of the Void, but in the Far Stars they were the ultimate display of wealth and taste. The steward was filling their glasses with a deep red wine. The Finestre vintage was one of the best in all human space, and the bottle would have been welcome on the emperor's table. It had cost a small fortune to get a dozen cases delivered to Galvanus Prime, but Vos knew impressing these men would only make his job easier. They were pompous and haughty, and therein lay their weakness.

The leader of the group took his glass first, holding it up to the light for a few seconds before taking a sip. He looked over at Vos and nodded. "Governor Vos, I must commend you on this extraordinary wine. It is a credit to your cellars."

"Thank you, Chairman Vargus. That is high praise coming from you. Your reputation as one of the sector's leading oenophiles precedes you." He turned toward the steward standing by the door. "Please instruct the captain of the cellar to have a case of the Finestre brought up for Chairman Vargus." He paused, eyes flashing toward Vargus's two companions. "And cases for Directors Allegre and Desimone as well." He glanced back toward the three visitors. "With my compliments, gentlemen."

"You are most generous, Governor Vos." Vargus allowed his normally grim visage to slip into a brief smile—it did nothing to make the man's face any more appealing. "I offer our profound gratitude. Your hospitality has been extraordinary. But we have come a considerable distance at your request, Governor Vos, and I'm sure it wasn't to sample such excellent wine. May I ask that we now proceed to the matter at hand, whatever that may be?"

Vargus was the chairman of the board of the Far Stars Bank and one of the wealthiest and most powerful men in the sector. He wasn't accustomed to traveling great distances to meet with anyone, but Vos had known the chairman would be too curious and greedy to refuse an invitation from the imperial governor. It had been nearly a millennium since the empire and the bank had engaged in any official business, and Vargus had too much ambition to resist the governor's summons.

And for that, Vos was relieved, for he very much needed Vargus and the bank if his plans were to succeed.

The Far Stars Bank was a behemoth, doing business on virtually every world in the sector. The bank and the transport guilds traced their lineage back centuries, to the earliest days of human colonization in the sector. They were interplanetary giants, relics of a time when the worlds of the Far Stars were united, a single province in an empire of man that was young and dynamic—before oppression and tyranny replaced glory and prosperity.

For a thousand years these institutions had maintained trade and communications between the worlds of the sector, and they had helped prevent a dark age when the empire's grasp receded. The guilds maintained contact between disparate worlds, and the Far Stars Bank funded trade and other interplanetary activities. And now they would serve Vos—unknowingly, of course—as his tentacles spread throughout the sector, quietly bringing more and more of the Far Stars under his imperial boot. By the time Vargus or any of his cronies realized what was going on, Vos would control the bank, and through its hundreds of subsidiaries and thousands of stockholdings, half the industry in the sector.

"Certainly, Chairman Vargus. First, I would like to repeat my thanks to you for journeying to Galvanus Prime to meet with me. As to my purposes, I wish to discuss doing some business with the bank. Imperial business."

"I am intrigued, Governor Vos, but also confused. The empire has proscribed the bank and its management . . . numerous times."

"I cannot speak for the folly of my predecessors, but I do not intend to follow their failed example. It is foolish for the empire to pursue its ancient claims to the sector. It is my intention as governor to improve relations between the empire and the worlds of the Far Stars, perhaps leading to a formal recognition of independence, and increased trade and cooperation between the parties."

Vos gauged Vargus's reaction as the chairman leaned back in his seat. All the files on Vargus noted he was an experienced negotiator, a man with an extraordinary poker face, but Vos's words had clearly surprised him.

"May I inquire about your motivations, Governor Vos?" the banker asked. "What you propose is a radical departure from previous imperial policy."

"Previous failed policy, Chairman. It is not my intention to continue foolishness simply because it has gone on for centuries. I intend to take immediate steps toward establishing better relations between the empire and the Far Stars . . . and I intend to begin by making a number of investments in various businesses in the sector, both personally and in my capacity as imperial governor. To that end, I would like to establish several investment accounts at the bank."

This time Vargus didn't even try to hide his surprise—nor his interest in the nature of the imperial investments Vos was suggesting. "May I ask what sort of financial commitment you have in mind, Governor Vos?"

"I was planning an initial deposit of ten billion imperial crowns, Chairman Vargus, in the form of minted rhodium and platinum bars."

Good thing you're not playing poker now, Chairman. Vargus was stunned, as were the two other bankers. Not without reason, either: ten billion imperial crowns was more than the GDP of most of the worlds in the Far Stars. And in precious metals no less. "That is an extraordinarily large sum, Governor Vos," he finally managed to say. "May I ask what type of investments you are planning?"

"Certainly, Chairman Vargus. It is my intention to take minority stakes in a portfolio of major Far Stars firms, with a goal toward promoting trade between the sector and the empire." Vos deliberately avoided saying, "the rest of the empire," as his predecessors would have done. He wanted the bankers to see opportunity, not the beginning of a move against Far Stars independence. Which was, of course, exactly what it was. "I intend to establish a charitable foundation as well, to aid the poor of the sector. The empire has much atoning to do before we can hope to win the friendship and trust of our Far Stars neighbors."

He leaned back slightly in his chair, knowing this next part would shock Vargus yet again. "I also plan to establish a fund to back an insurance concern to offer loss prevention policies and other services to any shippers willing to provide service across the Void."

"You seek to increase trade across the Void?" Vargus was practically out of his seat.

Vos had been right—Vargus was both shocked and, again, intrigued. And, again, not without reason. Trade between the Far Stars and the rest of human space was almost nonexistent. The danger of losing a ship in the crossing was far too great, except when handling the most valuable cargoes. If transport concerns had access to secure insurance to protect their investments in ships, the increase in trade could be enormous.

A frown spread across Vargus's face. "But how can you profitably offer coverage when loss rates are so high? The Void remains a very dangerous crossing."

"The answer to your question is precisely this, Chairman: it is not my intention to earn a profit, at least not at first. Rather, it is my desire to open the flow of trade, and we are prepared to subsidize ship losses to attain this goal. Ultimately, I believe the economic impact of greater and more consistent trade will prove worthwhile, and increased traffic will lead to a reduction in loss rates. I am willing to invest for the long term." Vos could see the board chairman's expression change once more. His greed was affecting his judgment, and he was beginning to accept the explanation Vos was feeding him.

"Your logic is unassailable, Governor Vos. We would be pleased to assist you in such noble efforts." Vos was sure Vargus believed he would be robbing an idealistic governor blind, but that's because Vargus was a Far Stars idiot, and Vos was already six steps ahead of him.

We'll see who's blind in the end, Chairman.

Vos smiled. "That is excellent news, Chairman Vargus. I look forward to doing business with you."

Yes, Vos thought, *you dream about how badly you will take advantage of me, how much money you will steal from these accounts—that is exactly what I want you thinking about.*

Vos didn't care about trade, and he certainly had no interest in helping the poor of the Far Stars. But he did intend to trick the bank into helping him assume control of the major industries of the sector, and ultimately the entire Far Stars Bank and the transport guilds as well.

And I look forward to having you unwittingly sign away control of all the trade in the Far Stars . . . including that of your own bank.

CHAPTER 12

"ARE YOU SURE WE CAN TRUST THESE GUYS, CAPTAIN?" SARGE was standing next to Blackhawk, watching his men load up the buggy. The name was a humorous one, a joke that had stuck. The XL-211 "Warcat" ATV was one of the heaviest armored combat vehicles in the Far Stars. It had eight centimeters of reinforced iridium-faced armor alloy and an array of weaponry that included a 150 mm main gun and four heavy autocannons. Shira, generally regarded as the member of the *Claw*'s crew with the least sense of humor, had inadvertently named the massive war machine Augustin Lucerne had given Blackhawk and his crew two years before.

"Sure, Sarge?" Blackhawk patted the grizzled noncom on the back. "No, I'm not sure. I'm not even sure I can trust *you,*

old friend. But you've never given me a reason to doubt you."
He regretted the comment almost immediately, mostly because
he wasn't sure Sarge realized he was kidding. The ground-
pounder was painfully earnest, a definite challenger for Shira's
title as most humorless member of the crew. "Seriously, though,
I don't think we have a better choice. They know ways to get
into the city that we couldn't find in a month. Besides, it's only
a matter of time before they're wiped out unless they get those
weapons. The mission is as important to them as it is to us, and
that's a pretty good basis for some limited trust."

"I guess so, Captain." He still had a frown on his face. "But
I'm gonna keep a close eye on them anyway." Sarge had seen
most of his friends and allies killed fighting a losing war, one
where their side had been beaten more by treachery than force
of arms. Blackhawk had saved the five survivors of his platoon
from certain death, getting them off-world before their enemies managed to catch up with them. Sergeant Carrock was
cynical and suspicious, but he trusted Blackhawk with his life.

Blackhawk gave Carrock a slap on the shoulder. "You do
that, Sarge—I wouldn't expect anything less. Where would I be
without you watching my back?" He turned to walk back toward
the ship. He'd arranged to meet Arn and his people about five
klicks from the *Claw,* and he was anxious to get started. He
was on his way back to the ship to get his gear when he heard a
commotion. He could see Astra Lucerne standing just outside
the airlock in front of Ace, giving him hell.

Blackhawk tried to remember the last mission they had
where things had gone smoothly. Nothing came to mind.

"You can tell Ark there's no way I'm hiding in this ship while
you all go out prowling around the planet." Astra's voice was
loud and angry, and Blackhawk knew that meant trouble.

"Astra," Blackhawk shouted as he approached the ship, "get over here and talk to me." He wasn't sure scolding her was the best way to get her to comply, but he was going to give it a try. He jogged the rest of the way. "Ace, go get your stuff. We're leaving in a few minutes." Ace nodded gratefully and ducked inside the ship.

Astra Lucerne was fuming, but she was silent, staring at Blackhawk with her arms crossed. "Astra," he said, "I need you to be reasonable. Our mission is to bring you back to your father, and you need to cooperate. I'm asking you. Please."

"But what if you get killed, Ark? I couldn't live with myself if you got yourself blasted to bits while I was cowering in the ship." Her voice was soft, almost pleading. She looked up at him and reached out, putting her hand gently on his face.

The softness of her voice surprised him; the touch of her hand on his cheek distracted him. He pulled back abruptly, and her hand slid off his face. He hadn't wanted to move away, but he'd forced himself anyway. He could see he'd hurt her feelings, but that couldn't be helped. He knew she cared for him, but he'd promised himself he would never let her know he felt the same way.

He decided harshness was the best recourse at the moment. "Do you have any idea how many people have tried to kill me, Astra? After everything I've been through, I'm not going to die on this shithole of a planet." She was staring back at him intently. He could see the hurt in her ice-blue gaze, but also the iron resolve. Astra Lucerne had inherited her father's stubbornness; she was immovable, like a block of granite. And that's when he saw his opening.

Blackhawk put his hand on her arm. "Unless you insist on coming, Astra." He felt bad even as he said it, but he knew guilt was the only chance he had of convincing her. "I need to stay focused, and if I'm worried about you I won't be. You'll only put me—all of us—in greater danger if you come."

"You are a bastard, Arkarin Blackhawk, do you know that?" Her eyes were moist, and Blackhawk could see how hurtful his words had been, though he knew she'd never show the weakness of tears. A lifetime as Marshal Lucerne's daughter had taught her to hide vulnerabilities. She'd grown up in the shadow of the battlefield, amid the horrors of war. Astra's beauty was obvious, but it took a closer eye to see the iron toughness behind it.

"I've been called worse, Astra." He struggled to maintain his discipline, fighting the urge to take her into his arms and apologize for what he had said. There was nothing he wanted more than to touch her, to pull her close to him. But that was a road he wasn't going down.

She stared at him silently for a few seconds, her expression a mix of anger and sadness. Then she sighed softly, and Blackhawk realized he'd won. He didn't feel good about it, and he knew he'd hurt her. But at least Astra would be safe—as safe as she could be on this war-torn planet in a damaged ship without a functioning hyperdrive.

"I'm sorry, Astra, but I need you to stay here with Lucas and the Twins." Blackhawk didn't want the *Claw* completely undefended, so he was leaving the two giants behind. Speed and stealth were going to be as important as strength on this operation. The Twins were like forces of nature in a fight, but they were as quiet as a herd of stampeding bulls.

"Okay." She turned to walk back toward the ship, but she paused and looked back at him. "But don't you expect to pull this shit on me again, Arkarin Blackhawk. You get one 'but you'll distract me and get me killed' piece of crap, and that's all. Next fight, I'm going with you. No matter what."

"Fine." He had a feeling he'd live to regret that one simple word.

He was planning a quick snatch job on the core and then a straight shot back to the ship. As soon as Sam could install the thing, they'd be on their way to Celtiboria. If all went well, there wouldn't be another fight. He tried to draw comfort from that thought, but he didn't feel any.

How often, he wondered, *do things go well?*

"The two of you should have stayed behind." Blackhawk looked around the crowded hold. The Warcat was a hybrid vehicle, half tank, half troop transport. It had room to ferry a squad into battle and strong enough weapons and protection to engage enemy armor.

"And what happens when one of you walks into enemy fire?" Rolf Sandor's voice was low, almost hypnotic. "You guys are not invulnerable"—he paused briefly, looking around the hold— "whatever you may think. Not even you, Ark."

Sandor was a brilliant scholar, one of the senior lecturers at the great academy on Arcturon before he'd been expelled as a result of a scandal he'd never shared with anyone, not even Blackhawk. He'd wandered for years, his academic credentials stripped, earning his way however he could until he came upon a wounded Arkarin Blackhawk.

"And what about you, Doc? What if you run into a bullet? There's not going to be any rear area on this mission." His voice became grimmer. "Or any time to treat the wounded."

The *Claw*'s captain had been lying on a street in Arkon City, almost dead from his wounds when Sandor found him. He managed to treat Blackhawk's injuries and keep him safe until the rest of the crew came looking for him. Though he'd freely admitted that Blackhawk's amazing genetics were as responsible for saving his life as any treatments he had administered, the recovering captain was enormously grateful, and he offered Sandor a place on the crew of *Wolf's Claw.* Ever since, Sandor had served as the ship's resident scholar on a variety of topics. He wasn't an actual physician, but he was the closest thing they had, and from that moment on, he was known among them as "Doc."

"I guess I'll have to take that chance, Ark."

Blackhawk just nodded. Doc wasn't a fighter by nature or training, and the captain hated exposing him on such a dangerous mission. But he couldn't argue with Doc's logic—having him along might very well save one of his people. Or more than one.

He could, however, argue about the other uninvited person in the buggy. "What about you? What are you doing here?" He turned his eyes toward the woman sitting quietly next to Doc. Katarina Venturi was technically a passenger on *Wolf's Claw,* one who had turned down an official spot on the crew and insisted on paying for her ongoing passage.

"I believe my skills may be useful during this operation." Her voice was a slow purr, soft and elegant. She had many talents— stealth, seduction, linguistics—but they were all dedicated to her one true mastery: killing. She wasn't a hardened warrior, a veteran of bloody battles, like most of Blackhawk's people, but she was as deadly as any creature who prowled the Far Stars. Katarina Venturi was a disciple of the Assassins' Guild on the planet Sebastiani, a stone-cold professional who regarded killing as an art. Her targets had been many and varied, including at least one head of state, and few of them had left the universe worse off for their passing. Venturi, like all the guild's students, rose above petty squabbles and disputes, accepting only contracts she considered moral. Those she killed were usually killers themselves, and often mass murderers. She had stopped more than one unjust war with a few drops of poison or a sharp blade in the dark.

And yet for all that, she wasn't crew, and that meant she was risking more than Blackhawk was willing to accept.

Clearly she didn't feel the same way, though, because she simply gazed at the captain seductively and smiled. "Besides—I would say I have the same stake as all of you in securing the hyperdrive core, wouldn't you?"

He looked at her quizzically.

"I don't relish a long and pointless stay on Saragossa," she said. "It is quite a dreadful planet."

"Yes, it certainly is a garbage heap. And I suppose you are in this with us, after all." Blackhawk acquiesced. He'd learned a long time ago that arguing with Katarina was unproductive to say the least.

Venturi had booked passage to the planet Varangia on *Wolf's Claw* two years before. Blackhawk and his crew were heading there to capture or kill a renegade gangster who had made the mistake of stealing a large sum from the Far Stars Bank. The bank didn't take such things lightly, so they'd hired Blackhawk to make an example of the thief . . . and, it turned out, Venturi as well. When he realized she was a guild assassin from Sebastiani, he understood the failure to terminate her target would disgrace her, and he stepped aside, allowing her the kill and forfeiting the bounty.

He sighed softly and leaned back on the hard metal bench.

He'd left the *Claw* in good hands. Lucas and the Twins would keep an eye on Astra, though he felt a twinge of guilt for leaving his young pilot in charge. He'd managed to guilt Astra into staying behind, but that was only going to make her angrier in the long run. He knew just how hard Astra could be to handle, and there was nothing she hated more than being told what to do. Lucas was going to have his hands full if this mission went on too long.

Even the Twins had grumbled at him when he told them to stay.

"We're approaching the rendezvous point, Captain." It was Sarge's voice on the comm. "We should be there in two minutes." They'd been driving for hours, passing one burned-out village and destroyed château after another. They'd stopped a few times to scout, and they'd seen the intensity of Saragossa's revolution up close. There were corpses everywhere, too, mostly on the ground, rotted down to the bones, although plenty were hanging where they were nailed to walls and impaled on stakes months, even years before.

The fighting had moved on, and the devastated area was mostly deserted, its once productive fields fallow and barren. Arn had given them directions through the desolate zone, allowing them to get within forty kilometers of New Vostok without running into any scattered villagers or enemy patrols.

The rebel leader and his people had split off again, riding through the woods along both flanks, mounted on squat and sturdy Saragossan field horses. The stubby little creatures bore little resemblance, Blackhawk thought, to sleek Antillean thoroughbreds or gigantic Delphian Percherons, but unlike those more elite breeds, they could travel vast distances with almost no food or water. All the revolutionary forces on Saragossa had been driven to rely on animal transport due to a shortage of motor vehicles, and Arn's splinter group even more than their better-equipped rivals.

Now it was time for Blackhawk and his people to ditch the buggy and hook up with Arn's men. The road ahead was more hazardous, and the armored bulk of the buggy was too conspicuous. The Warcat was a piece of equipment from Celtiboria's wars, far more advanced and powerful than anything possessed by either side on Saragossa, but it was far from inconspicuous. Blackhawk felt the buggy slow to a crawl, as Sarge navigated the heavy armored vehicle into an area of scrubby trees and thick underbrush. The sparse woods weren't enough to hide the buggy well enough to defeat a strong scouting effort, but it was out of casual sight from the road, and they were still in the deserted zone, where patrols were almost nonexistent.

"All right, people." Blackhawk hauled himself up from the hard bench and climbed toward the rear hatch of the vehicle. "Grab your gear, and let's get going. We've got a lot of ground to cover."

He turned back and watched his crew climb out one by one. "And put on the clothes Arn gave us." The rebel commander had provided them all with bulky Saragossan peasant robes. They weren't perfect disguises, but it was better than his people trying to walk right into New Vostok in their naked body armor, bristling with visible weapons.

"C'mon, Ark. These things stink." Ace was holding his robe in one hand, his arm extended away from his body.

"I don't care if they're covered in pig shit. Put the damned things on!" Ace had a bit of the dandy in him, but Blackhawk had seen him in battle too many times not to want him at his side when walking into trouble.

"That goes for all of you. The closer we can get by stealth, the less fighting we'll have to do." He realized that even in the best scenario he could concoct there would be plenty of fighting, but he was anxious to do whatever he could to keep that to a minimum.

Blackhawk strapped a heavy rifle over one shoulder, and a bandolier full of grenades over the other. Then he pulled the bulky garment over his head. Ace was right; it did stink. But it also covered the heavy battle vest and all his weapons. He wouldn't say he made a terribly convincing Saragossan farmer, but he was certainly a lot less conspicuous than he'd been a moment before.

He looked out over his crew. They were in various stages of strapping on combat gear and crawling into the brown canvas robes.

"Let's go. We're on a schedule here." He reached into one of his pockets and pulled out the map Arn had given him. It was hand drawn on paper. Blackhawk was more accustomed to electronic maps displayed on tablets, and he began to realize just how cut off from modern supplies Arn and his people had been.

He looked around one last time to make sure everyone was ready then he started back toward the battered and pockmarked pavement. "The rendezvous point is about a klick down the road. Remember, we're a group of peasant refugees, so try to act the part. But keep your eyes open, too. These disguises are only going to get us so far."

Blackhawk turned and took a look back toward the buggy. His trained eyes picked it out almost immediately, but he knew it was as well hidden as they were going to get it. The brush was thick right up to the road and the area nearly deserted.

He took a breath and started off down the road. It was time to steal a hyperdrive core.

"I make it three guards, Ark. One in the building, the other two standing just outside." Ace was lying in the heavy brush, looking out over the checkpoint. They'd come about thirty kilometers since hooking up with Arn's people, and they were getting close to the outskirts of the city. These were the first guards they had encountered. "Should we take them out from here?"

Blackhawk was surprised they had made it so far without being challenged. Arn's advice had proven sound. The abandoned areas they had come through were so thoroughly laid to waste, even the crows were running short of provender. The true image of war was always a somber sight, one Blackhawk had seen far too many times.

Blackhawk stared intently at the checkpoint. "No, Ace. We can't be sure there aren't more of them in the building. Or over that hill." He turned toward Arn. "Is this normal, Arn? Only three guards this close in?"

"I expected a stronger force here, but the nobles have launched another offensive to the south, so it is possible they have been forced to divert more troops to meet that threat."

Blackhawk turned toward his own people. "Let's try to do this quietly. We're close in now, and there are probably more pickets ahead. We don't need a lot of gunfire putting them on the alert." He looked at Venturi. "Well, Katarina, you wanted to come. How do you feel about a little knife work?"

"I am ready." The assassin was a master with a blade. She pulled the hood of her robe over her silky black hair. No one was going to buy her as a Saragossan peasant if they got a good look at her.

"Good. The rest of you stay put." Blackhawk walked a few meters, Katarina following right behind. He stepped up from the brush onto the road, just around a small bend from the guard post. The two of them walked forward, slowly, naturally.

"Stop! Hold out your arms." The guard was clearly startled to see anyone coming down the road. His companion had been almost asleep on his feet, but he spun around and leveled his rifle on the two approaching figures.

Blackhawk did as he was ordered, and Katarina followed his lead. He stood stone still, his eyes focused intently on the guards. They had primitive assault rifles—better than the ancient weapons half of Arn's men were carrying, but certainly nothing like modern imperial firearms. He wasn't surprised. Blackhawk hadn't expected to encounter any guards armed with high-tech weapons. Whatever imperial agent was interfering in Saragossa's revolution, he would feed in the equipment slowly. His influence would be based on what the rebels still needed from him, not what he had already given them. From Arn's description of the campaigns the Revolutionary Army had launched against his forces, they'd expended a lot of imperial ordnance. They probably didn't have much left before this new shipment, and they certainly wouldn't have deployed them to sleepy outposts on the edge of nowhere.

"Who are you? Where are you going?" The guard's surprise had passed. Now his voice was harsh, demanding. The third man had come out of the building, and now all three had their weapons out.

"My wife and I are going to New Vostok. Our farm was burned, and I have come to find work in the factories." There was an odd tone to his voice, a perfect Saragossan peasant accent, courtesy of the ever present AI in his head. He glanced back toward Katarina, noticing for the first time that she had a sack tucked under her robe. He fought back a smile. *Not just my wife*, he thought, *but my pregnant wife. Nice touch*. Not for the first time, he was thankful he'd never had to face the beautiful assassin as an enemy.

"Come forward. Slowly."

Blackhawk moved forward tentatively. He felt the adrenaline rush, the beat of his heart loud in his ears. He maintained a calm outer expression, even as his body was preparing for combat. After so many years of battle, it was almost an involuntary response.

His eyes focused on the guard's rifle, waiting for the right moment. The other two sentries were a few paces behind their comrade. They had their weapons in their hands, but they weren't aiming; they were just holding them out in the general direction of the two newcomers. Blackhawk looked up to the small hill behind the guards, and he listened for any sounds from the building. He couldn't be sure, but he didn't think there was anyone else there.

He walked up to the lead guard, stopping when he was about a meter away. He was alert, ready to make his move, but the other two guards were a couple meters behind. Could he kill the first and reach the others before they managed to start shooting? *Maybe*, he thought, *but there's no room for error*. He felt his muscles tense as the guard reached out to search him. There was no more time—he had to go now.

His right hand gripped the well-worn hilt of his short-sword under the robe. He lunged with his left arm, grabbing the guard's rifle and pulling it hard to the side. His opponent managed to hold on, but his finger slipped from the trigger, giving Blackhawk an instant before his enemy could fire. He shoved the sword hard, its razor point slicing through his own robe and just under the guard's ribs. He pushed, jamming the iridium-edged blade deep into his victim's chest cavity.

He yanked hard to free the blade, and his already-dead victim fell hard to the ground. He was about to lunge forward and tackle the two remaining guards . . . but they were already down. His momentum carried him forward a few steps, and he caught himself right in front of the two men. They each had a slender, black-handled throwing knife protruding from their necks. One was dead, the other nearly so, and after a few seconds of gurgling blood, he also expired.

He turned back toward Katarina. She was standing exactly where she had been, but now the canvas sack was lying at her feet. She nodded to Blackhawk and took a few steps forward to retrieve her knives, casually cleaning each of them on her victims' clothing before slipping them under her robe.

Blackhawk just shook his head. Katarina Venturi played the role of a well-bred woman of high birth so well, even he tended to forget just how astonishingly deadly she truly was. Yes, he was definitely glad she was on his side.

CHAPTER 13

"THE OPERATION MUST SUCCEED, GENERAL CARANO. IT IS ESSEN-
tial to our success. Even to our survival." Elisabetta Lementov
sat at the head of the table, an unusual place for a woman on
Saragossa. But Lementov wasn't a normal Saragossan woman.
Eldest daughter of the planet's most powerful noble family, Elisabetta Ataragin had been wed at age fifteen to the patriarch of
the second-strongest family. For centuries, Saragossa's government had been an often unruly oligarchy of the highest-placed
families, but her marriage created a power bloc so untouch-
able, it had allowed Sergei Lementov to rule almost as a monarch. Until the revolution came, at least, and a mob of enraged
peasants massacred him along with his entire escort, parading

their burned and headless bodies through the streets for hours before casting them into the lake.

Elisabetta had taken the news of both revolution and widowhood in stride, assuming immediate control of her family's affairs and ordering the house treasury moved to a secure location. She rallied the guards and the Lementov and Ataragin retainers, and she remained in New Rostov directing the defense of her palace until it was clear the city was lost. She then relocated to one of her country estates, collecting her nieces and nephews along the way and creating a rallying point for the rest of the disordered and terrified Saragossan nobility. Many credited her coolness and courage with saving the cause of the nobility and halting the momentum of the early revolution.

Some also whispered that her calm acceptance of her husband's death had been cold and unfeeling, but none dared say that to her face. She had become the most powerful noble on Saragossa, and the effective leader of the counterrevolution and the effort to reclaim the planet.

In truth, she had mourned her husband, but in her own fashion and not for the eyes and ears of others. The marriage had been a difficult one for her at first. She'd gone to her wedding bed a fifteen-year-old virgin, quite distressed by the rough manner in which her much older—and fatter—husband mounted her, grunting and sweating for the several minutes it took him to finish.

She had been distraught at first, missing her home and dreading the sound of Sergei's footsteps approaching her door. But she matured quickly, and she came to appreciate other aspects of their relationship. Sergei denied her nothing and, as she came to understand the realities of political power, she began to enjoy the status the arranged marriage provided. She was even surprised to discover that Sergei was a pleasant conversationalist, well educated with an amusing sense of humor. She wouldn't say she'd ever truly loved him, but she did come to enjoy his companionship. The sex didn't improve much, but she got used to his visits, which were always short and became less and less frequent as he got older. She compensated for his failings by keeping a whole string of clandestine lovers at her beck and call.

Including the mercenary general she was talking to now.

"It is a difficult operation, Elisa . . . Lady Lementov." General Carano was the leader of the largest mercenary force on Saragossa. Elisabetta had hired his company immediately after the nobles had been driven from New Vostok, and she wasted no time in seducing him when he arrived. She was a resourceful woman, perfectly willing to use sex as a tool to get what she wanted. In Carano's case, it hadn't been entirely unpleasant. The mercenary commander was a little rough around the edges, but he was a magnificent physical specimen, and she found his many battle scars to be strangely appealing.

"We need to break through the enemy's defensive line outside the city and create a significant distraction to allow us to push a picked force through to the spaceport. Even if we succeed, casualties will be enormous."

"Casualties will be enormous, my dear Vladimir, if we allow the enemy to deploy yet another shipment of high-tech weapons." She stood up and ran her hand softly over the rough stubble on his face as she spoke. "I remind you they deployed the bulk of the first two shipments against their rival rebels and not your forces, virtually destroying the splinter group in the process. This latest shipment will almost certainly be used against you and your men." She paused for a few seconds, amused that for all his concern about her plan to raid the shipyard in New Vostok, he still couldn't keep his eyes off her breasts. She had chosen her dress carefully. She needed him at his best, and there was no harm in reminding him of the fruits of victory.

"It will need to be meticulously planned. We have to scout . . ."

"It must be launched immediately. There is no time. While you are scouting and planning, they will be unloading that ship and distributing the weapons. My spies assure me the bulk of the ship's cargo remains aboard. How long will that continue to be the case?"

She knew he'd come to the same realization. Yes, attacking the entrenched lines of the Revolutionary Army was a risky and difficult plan. But allowing the enemy to accumulate more high-tech weapons was suicide. She'd shared the scouting reports from the other front with the general, and the evidence of the weapons' effectiveness was more than apparent. The Revolutionary Army's troops had annihilated the forces of the rebel splinter group, driving the few survivors deep into the wilderness.

Elisabetta was confident that the mercenary forces on Saragossa were more experienced and better equipped than the defeated rebel group had been. They were motivated too, since the guild embargo had stranded them on the planet for the foreseeable future. If their enemies were able to deploy enough superior weapons against them, though . . . no, allowing that to happen was out of the question. Defeat was unthinkable, and it had to be prevented, whatever the cost. Carano was well aware of the fate that awaited his men if the Revolutionary Army won control of the planet. The streets of New Vostok had run red with blood since they had taken control. The nobles who had failed to escape had died first, but since then the revolutionaries had begun killing each other, one purge after another as the leaders struggled for power. He knew his people would be next if they lost the war.

Elisabetta was right, Carano concluded. They had to steal those weapons. Or at least destroy them. "I will have to convince the other mercenary commanders to commit their forces. They will not wish to expose their forces to such heavy losses. They will resist."

"They are in the same situation as the rest of us." She glided around behind him, running a fingernail across the back of his neck. "You will just have to be your usual persuasive self . . . and remind them that if they don't want their heads to end up on pikes in New Vostok Square, they'd better do as they're told."

She could see he was tense, but she also knew she had him. He didn't have any choice.

Elisabetta Lementov was a beautiful and nearly irresistible woman, but there was an icy coldness there too, a grim resolve not evident at first glance. She was fond of Carano, but that wouldn't affect her decisions. Not one bit.

Carano swallowed hard. "We will need the local troops too, the house armies and retainers. You will have to get the other families to consent."

"I will attend to it, my dear Vladimir." She moved her lips closer to his ear, whispering softly, "I will make certain you have everything you need." She paused, holding her mouth close to him for a few seconds.

"And a suitable reward for your success when you return."

"The Tiger Company will attack first." Carano stood in the command post, surrounded by the other mercenary leaders. He was pointing at the map projected on the table. "Here . . .

and here. The Gold Dragons will follow in close support, along with most of my men and the house armies."

He looked up from the map, glancing at the officers clustered around him. He knew they were skittish. Mercenary companies tended to look for relatively easy commissions, fights that were beyond the capabilities of their employers, while remaining easily winnable for a well-trained and equipped force. There was no profit in fighting bloodbaths that got your company shot to hell. They'd all expected the Saragossan job to be an easy one, shooting down a bunch of uppity peasants, but when they got there, they found the peasants were much more formidable than anyone would have thought.

The revolutionaries had taken the cities, along with the armories of the noble families' house retainers. Worse, and even more unexpected, they had able leadership, at least until they splintered into two feuding factions. Carano almost broke his contract and pulled out, but Elisabetta's bed—and then the guild embargo—kept him on Saragossa.

"You are proposing that we mount an all-or-nothing attack, Carano." Colonel Ariano Vulcan was the commander of the Tiger Company. The Tigers were the second-largest group after Carano's own Black Helms, and the only one to deploy a significant force of armored vehicles. "With my Tigers in the forefront."

Carano's command position was informal at best, and he noted Vulcan's use of "propose" in lieu of "order." "Indeed, Colonel, that is precisely what I am proposing." He addressed his colleague again by his rank, though Vulcan hadn't done so when speaking to him. This wasn't the time for a pissing match between the two, and he'd sworn not to let Vulcan provoke him. "And I submit that we have very few options. We cannot penetrate the city's defenses and raid the spaceport without a massive diversion along the front lines, and if we do not seize those weapons—or at least destroy them—we will find ourselves facing total defeat. I placed the Tigers in front because we need your armor to punch a hole through the enemy line as quickly as possible. We must create disorder in their ranks rapidly if we are to succeed." He held Vulcan's eyes with his own. "You are aware of the capabilities of the weaponry the Revolutionary Army employed against the rebel splinter group, are you not?"

Vulcan nodded silently. Carano knew the rival commander resented his position as de facto head of the noble forces, but there was no time for that kind of bullshit now. Vulcan had seen the reports from the scouting parties too, and Carano knew the stubborn pain in the ass had to realize there was no choice.

The Revolutionary Army had been fighting the war with a mix of obsolete weapons—assault rifles, shotguns, homemade bombs. But the new shipments were bringing them some serious tech, ordnance far in advance of anything even the mercenary companies possessed. The revs outnumbered the merc forces and house armies already. If they had particle accelerators and hypervelocity autocannons too, the war on Saragossa wouldn't last another month. "Very well, General, I agree we do not have an alternative. So who do you propose to send to seize the weapons?"

Carano took a breath. "I propose to go myself, Colonel Vulcan. If you feel you can handle overall command along the front, that is." He didn't like leaving most of his men under Vulcan's orders, but he needed the Tigers' commander to be 100 percent on board, and stroking his ego was one way to achieve that. Besides, as much as he disliked the man, Carano had to admit that Vulcan was a strong tactician and a veteran combat commander.

Vulcan was silent for a few seconds, clearly surprised by Carano's words. "Indeed, General Carano, I would be pleased to take command while you lead the mission to capture the weapons cache."

"Thank you, Colonel. I am sure you will execute the attack with your usual skill." *You'll also probably try to recruit as many of my men as you can, if I get myself killed. Go ahead, try.* If he underestimated, Major Zoran, the Helms's second in command, was likely to blow Vulcan's head off, especially if he came sniffing around trying to poach the men. "We need to launch the attack immediately, Colonel. Today."

"That's insane," Vulcan roared. "It will take days just to plan the operation and maneuver the troops into position."

"I'm afraid we don't have days, Colonel. Once that ship is unloaded and the weapons are distributed, it will be too late. You've got to attack with whatever you can get in place, and feed in the rest of the troops as you can move them up."

Vulcan stood silently, staring at the map on the table and shaking his head. He was about to say something when one of the other officers spoke first.

"There is little need for debate, gentlemen." Xavier Garza was the commander of the Silver Swords. His voice was low and gravelly, and he spoke with a heavy Varangian accent. "General Carano is correct. We do not have a choice." He stepped forward from the small cluster of officers standing behind Carano and Vulcan. "I will say what no one else has wanted to say: these are imperial weapons." The room was silent, every eye on Garza. They had all known the source of the sophisticated weaponry, or at least suspected it. But no one wanted to acknowledge that the Revolutionary Army was getting help from the empire.

"These are imperial weapons," he repeated, "and we are trapped here. With the guild embargo in place we have no chance of arranging transport off-world." The commanders of the smaller companies stood behind him nodding. "So we must win this fight, and we must do it soon. Because if the empire is indeed aiding our enemy, this will not be the last shipment. Our superior discipline will be overwhelmed not only by numbers, but also by superior technology."

"Exactly, Xavier." Carano panned his eyes across the assembled officers. "Some of us have been allies before, others enemies. But none of that matters now. Here we are brothers, and we will prevail as one—or we will die as one. We must stand together. I will lead the mission to seize the weapons, but first we must attack the enemy and smash through their lines. We are ill-prepared, but we will have surprise on our side. And I believe we can succeed if we all fight as I know we can." He held his hand out in front of him.

Garza reached out and placed his hand on top of Carano's. "General Carano is right. Will you all stand together?"

One by one, the officers standing along the wall moved forward, placing their hands on top of the others. Finally, Vulcan nodded and thrust his hand forward, slamming his huge palm on top of the pile. "Together!" he roared.

Carano watched the heavy tanks of the Tiger Company crash forward, moving directly for the enemy trenches. They'd covered half the distance to contact before the revolutionaries realized what was happening and opened fire. Their machine guns and small arms were ineffective against the armored war machines, and the defenders, unable to stop or even slow the attacking forces, began to fall back.

It was an orderly retreat at first, but the Revolutionary Army soldiers were poorly trained and only driven by harsh, almost terroristic discipline. Standing up to heavy armor was more than they could handle, even with their officers shouting threats of execution at the men who ran. They had suffered enormous losses in the war, and the Revolutionary Command had squandered its most experienced troops in pointless wave attacks against the superior mercenary forces, thinking they could replace them with fresh drafts, sent to the front after two weeks' rudimentary training. Clearly that wasn't the case, and Carano watched as the entire front line was in a wholesale rout, its soldiers throwing down their weapons and running for their lives.

The autocannons on the tanks opened fire on the fleeing troops, cutting them down in huge swaths, trying to exploit the breakthrough as effectively as possible while they could. Carano knew the easy success wasn't going to last. It was only a matter of time before the enemy got their artillery in action, and that could hurt the tanks. There were heavy batteries dug in all around New Vostok, and Vulcan's tanks would face steadily heavier fire as he pushed them forward. Still, the attack was creating the confusion Carano and his people needed to slip through the battle zone and into the city.

He stared at his handpicked team. He had fifty of his most experienced veterans, men who had been with him for years, through dozens of battles. "All right, we're heading out in five minutes. Once we go, we keep moving, no matter what. There's no turning back, no stopping for the wounded. We must get those weapons."

He could see fear in their eyes, and he wasn't surprised. These were grim warriors, and they knew how dangerous a mission this was likely to be, but that wasn't the only thing on their minds. Carano and his fellow commanders had tried to clamp down on knowledge of the enemy's imperial weapons, but news had spread anyway.

The worlds and people of the Far Stars were mostly open in their defiance of imperial claims to the sector, but there was still an undercurrent of dread. The empire ruled its domains by terror, and no human was without fear of the enormous power it controlled, not even the residents of the Far Stars, protected as they were by the Void from the worst imperial reprisals. Even the grizzled veterans of Carano's battle-tested Black Helms were afraid to see their enemies in league with the massive power of the empire.

Carano couldn't help but agree with them. Unfortunately, they didn't have any choice . . .

"You have all been with the Helms for many years. Together we have been in many fights, faced an array of dangerous enemies. And we have always prevailed. There is nowhere I wouldn't go with men such as you at my back."

He slung a rifle over his shoulder and turned forward, staring out at the gap Vulcan's tanks had torn in the enemy line.

"Now, let's go get those weapons."

CHAPTER 14

BLACKHAWK CROUCHED LOW BEHIND THE WRECKAGE OF THE building. He guessed it had once been a warehouse of some kind. There were a few twisted steel girders still standing and one masonry wall, blackened by fire. The rest of the structure was rubble, piles of broken bricks and mounds of gray ash.

It was past midnight, but both moons were up, and the sky was too bright for Blackhawk's tastes. Lunem Major was just a narrow crescent, but Lunem Minor was waxing, a few days from being full. The moonlight cast an eerie glow over the otherwise dark and deserted streets.

The spaceport was on the outskirts of the city, adjacent to an industrial area that had been hit hard during the initial uprisings. Blackhawk and his people had passed nothing but burned-out hulks and crumbled ruins.

Arn had led them around the main areas of the city, through the nearly abandoned northern sector. They'd run into one small patrol of guards since the first encounter at the checkpoint. Shira had helped Blackhawk take care of that group, leaping out of the darkness to cut the throats of two privates while Blackhawk broke their sergeant's neck. Since then they'd prowled from one blasted neighborhood to another, and they hadn't run into a soul.

They'd been hearing sounds of battle to the south since midafternoon. It had started with an occasional blast, but then the artillery batteries just outside the city opened up. They'd been firing ever since. Blackhawk had no idea what was going on down there, but whatever it was, it could only help their chances of success. If the Revolutionary Army was dealing with some threat to the south, they'd have more on their minds than worrying about an unexpected raid on the spaceport.

It didn't mean they could just walk in, though.

"Stay back," he whispered to Ace, signaling with his hands to the others. He gripped his rifle and crept forward slowly. He thought he could hear something up ahead, but for all he knew it was just a pack of minisauroids digging in the rubble for food.

He pressed his back against the building, sliding forward toward the corner. He stopped. There it was again. Someone was definitely there. He could feel the adrenaline flooding his bloodstream. He breathed slowly, quietly. There were no friendlies out here, so anything he ran into had to be bad news. He stopped just short of the corner, holding his breath as he spun around, rifle held out ahead of him.

His enhanced vision and genetically superior reflexes saved his life. He saw the crouched figure, and his instincts kicked in. He lunged hard to the side as a blinding flash of light ripped by where he had just been standing, lighting up the night sky like dawn for an instant. It was electric blue, and the air crackled around it, leaving a heavy ozone smell behind. He felt the heat of the beam as he swung out of the way, bringing his own rifle to bear as he did and opening fire.

His enemy had been turning too, bringing his deadly weapon around to shoot again, but Blackhawk's fire caught him in the chest and head, slamming the soldier back into the wall. He seemed to stand there for an instant before he slid to the ground, leaving a gruesome red streak on the pockmarked gray concrete.

Blackhawk leaped forward, holding the rifle with one hand and drawing his sword with the other. He crouched next to his victim, holding the blade tightly, ready to strike. But his enemy was dead.

"What the hell was that?" Ace was scrambling up behind Blackhawk.

Imperial particle accelerator rifle. Mark V or Mark VI small-arms model. I will be able to provide specific identification once you examine . . .

Blackhawk ignored the AI. He knew exactly what the rifle was. He'd seen them used far too many times. "Imperial particle accelerator. A pretty modern one. Not what you expect someone to shoot at you on a backwater shithole like this."

Ace moved toward the body, kneeling down. "This is no local, Ark." He pulled open the jacket, revealing a vest made of a strange black material. Blackhawk could see that where his three shots had impacted, the material had hardened and turned gray. Each of the spots was only a little wider than the bullets they'd blocked. "It's a good thing you hit him in the head, Ark. I've never seen body armor like this before, have you?"

Unfortunately, yes, he thought. "Imperial intelligence," he muttered emotionlessly. "That's standard-issue body armor for agents." He shook his head, taking a quick look around. *That particle accelerator shot was visible for kilometers,* he thought. They had to get to the ship. Now.

"Let's get moving." The others had come up behind Ace, and he motioned to the group, pointing his arm forward. "We're running out of time."

Ace stood up. "We're with you, Ark."

Blackhawk noticed Sam standing right behind Ace. "Sam, stay in the middle of the group."

She shot him back a sour look and pulled her tiny pistol from its hidden holster. "I can take care of myself, Ark." A twinge of defensiveness gave her tone an edge.

Blackhawk stared back at her, trying to hold back a laugh. She was twenty-seven years old, but she looked at least five years younger standing there with her coppery-red hair tied back in a ponytail. Blackhawk tended to treat her more like a daughter than a member of the crew at times, but that wasn't the case now. He'd seen her use that stubby little pistol more than once, and he couldn't recall her ever missing with it. It was easy to forget that she'd survived on the streets alone for years. "I know you can, Sam," he shot back with a brief smile. "But you're the only one who can get that core out without blowing us all to hell or giving us a lethal dose of radiation. And that makes you the only one of us not expendable right now."

"Fine, Ark," she said softly as she dropped back between

156 — JAY ALLAN

Sarge and his people. Blackhawk knew she agreed with him, but he also knew she'd never admit it.

"Okay, let's go." Blackhawk turned and moved forward, pausing at the side of the wrecked building to peer off in both directions. There was no room for carelessness. After he looked each way, twice, he jogged out into the rubble-strewn street, staying close to the buildings on one side.

The crew followed him: Ace and Shira first, then Doc and Katarina, and finally Sarge and his men, who were now taking it as their assigned mission to protect Sam—and probably annoying the hell out of her in the process.

Arn and his men followed, and the whole group headed slowly, cautiously toward the spaceport. Blackhawk knew the area was going to be swarming with soldiers soon. But there was no stopping, no turning back for any of them. Whatever happened, however many enemy troops were guarding that ship, this mission would go forward. It was success or death for them all.

"Dealing with these wogs is taking every bit of patience I can muster." Andreus Sand was sitting at a table in *Grenderia*'s small wardroom, his face twisted into a frustrated frown. He had a cup of coffee in front of him, half drunk and stone cold. The steward had warmed it twice for him, but Sand was too distracted to pay any attention.

Gravis Trent sat opposite Sand, taking a bite from a sandwich and laying the rest of it down on a plate in front of him. "You really should eat something, Andreus. I know you're frustrated with Talin, and I don't blame you. He's a pompous ass. But it's just a mission, like any other one. We do our jobs, and sometimes we need to deal with people we'd just as soon throw in a ditch."

It was true; Sand had dealt with fools before and thrown his share of people into ditches too.

Trent had been Sand's senior subordinate for years, and they'd completed missions throughout the empire, moving up steadily in the ranks as they did. They had both worked for Kergen Vos throughout his meteoric rise in imperial intelligence, and when that master agent accepted a posting as governor of the Far Stars, they were both stunned. Shock turned quickly to horror when he asked them to come with him but, despite their initial reservations, both eventually agreed. They knew Kergen Vos didn't do anything without a good reason, so if he saw opportunity out here at the edge of the universe, they figured there must be something they didn't know. In the end, they bet their careers on their brilliant chief, and they weren't going to start doubting his judgment now.

But that didn't mean Sand wasn't going to vent some frustration. He leaned back in his chair and sighed. He was staring right at Trent, but his mind was wandering. "We brought that ungrateful sack of shit enough high-tech weapons to conquer all of Saragossa, and what does he want? Personal luxuries. So we unload crates of brandy and fine wines, and we sit here with a hold full of weapons."

It was clear Sand didn't agree with the directive to aid Talin. If he'd had the authority, he'd have shot the useless son of a bitch and replaced him already. But that was Vos's decision, not his, and the governor was on Galvanus Prime several long hyperjumps away.

"He doesn't trust his people, Andreus." Trent scooped up the sandwich again, taking another bite, chewing quickly and swallowing. "He wants the weapons here because he knows they are safe until he is ready to use them. He's worried one of his subordinates might try to grab them and seize power. Considering what a useless fuckup he is, I wouldn't be surprised if that happened."

"It would have to be an improvement."

"That's not our call, and you know it." Trent's voice was firm. "Vos calls the shots, and we do what he says. And he's never been wrong before, has he?"

"No," Sand admitted grudgingly. "Still, I hate being stuck on this shithole at the whim of a wog commander too afraid of his own people to let us unload the weapons we brought him." *It's a shame*, he thought. By all accounts, Talin had been a capable leader early in the revolution, one of the four or five prime movers who'd helped turn an outbreak of sporadic rioting and violence into a successful revolution. From what he'd heard, Talin had been a tireless dynamo, the primary organizer of what later became the Revolutionary Army. Then the power went to his head, and privilege turned him into a debauched sybarite.

Sand had seen it before, and he'd never known the condition to reverse itself. Capable men could lose their talent and ability as their egos and decadence increased, but he very much doubted anyone who'd gone down that road ever came back. In his experience, ability, once squandered, was gone for good.

He looked over at Trent. "Have the patrols reported in yet?" Sand was suspicious by nature, and he'd sent out half his guards to check out the grounds of the spaceport. If Talin was too afraid to have the weapons in his own storehouses, Sand figured he'd better take some precautions himself, especially with the sudden enemy attacks to the south.

"Not yet, Andreus. But I wouldn't be too worried about that. We'd be more likely to get a report if there was a problem."

"I'm sure that's true, but I'd feel better getting a status update. Run up to the bridge and check in with them, okay?"

Trent nodded and stood up. "Not a bad idea." He was about to turn when Sand stood as well. "Where are you going?"

"I'm going to take a look outside. Just around the ship." He walked over to a small counter where he had set his gun down. It was a small pistol, a high-powered slug thrower with iridium-jacketed bullets. He snapped it open to check the load and shoved it into his belt. "I think I could use a little fresh air."

Trent laughed, and Sand couldn't help but laugh with him. *Fresh air, my ass,* he thought. If there was one thing New Vostok's primitive factories produced, it was industrial stench that hung heavily over the city. "Enjoy the air," Trent said as he made his way to the bridge. "And be careful."

Blackhawk stood outside the metal fencing, looking across the ancient and pockmarked asphalt toward the sleek, white ship. He'd just cut a hole through the fence big enough for them to squeeze through. It had been tough, laborious work with a small pair of snips. They'd brought a plasma torch with them as well, and it would have sliced through the links like a knife through butter. But it was also damned near as bright as the particle accelerators, and they were way too close to be giving away their position now.

They'd encountered a single two-man patrol just before entering the outer perimeter of the spaceport. They were armed with particle accelerators like the previous sentry, but Katarina and Shira dispatched them both quickly and quietly, before either could get off a shot.

He'd been worried that someone would react to the flash when the first guard had fired, but so far they'd been lucky.

Perhaps anyone who was paying attention had written off the single flash as lightning. It wasn't out of the realm of possibility. The air was getting thicker, heavy clouds of a storm front moving slowly across the sky. A storm might be useful when they ran for it with the core. Anything that cut down on visibility or made it harder for pursuers to find them was welcome. *At least,* he thought, *the cloud cover might block that cursed moonlight.*

He turned back toward the group clustered around him. "Everybody has the plan down, right?" He panned his eyes around as everyone nodded . . . then he repeated everything one more time anyway.

"Ace and I will drop the satchel charges in the engine exhaust ports. They won't do massive damage, but they should knock out the power conduits from the main reactor." *At least I hope they will,* he thought. He'd been pretty sure, and Hans had confirmed his analysis, but he still wasn't positive. If he was wrong, it could jeopardize the entire mission.

I do not make mistakes. If the charges are inserted at least three meters into the exhaust ports, the target vessel will suffer a temporary loss of all but emergency power.

Blackhawk frowned. The AI in his head constantly commenting and correcting his analysis was bad enough, but did the damned thing have to be so prickly and defensive?

"Sarge, as soon as the charges blow, you and your men get on board and take out the crew. Be careful if you end up fighting with anyone in the engineering spaces. We didn't come all this way to blast the hyperdrive core into junk."

"Yes, sir." Sarge always stood out among the informality of

the *Claw*'s crew with his rigid military discipline. He snapped a perfect Delphian salute to Blackhawk. "Understood."

"Shira, you steal us a truck or some kind of transport. The fastest thing you can find. We're not going to be carrying the core back on foot, so we need something we can drive back. We're probably going to have to run for it, so try to be quick."

"Got it, Ark. There should be a transport or a hovercraft in here somewhere." She paused and smiled. "I'll find it."

Blackhawk nodded. "Good. When you've got it, bring it around the back of the ship. We'll have to bring the core out through the cargo hold—it won't fit through the airlock."

He turned and looked at Arn and his people. "You guys go with Shira, and get whatever transport you can find. While we're getting the core out, you take as many weapons as you can load." He paused. "Then we'll blow the ship."

Arn winced at the prospect of destroying so much high-tech ordnance, weapons his men needed desperately. But Blackhawk had explained to him earlier that whatever they didn't get now would end up being used against them anyway. "Yes, agreed." He turned toward his men. "You are to disperse throughout the spaceport and commandeer any transports you can find."

Blackhawk turned toward Katarina. "I'd like you to stay back with Sam and Doc. As soon as Sarge's boys secure the ship, bring them forward."

"Do not worry, Arkarin"—she was the only one who called him by his full first name—"I will make sure they are not harmed."

"I don't need a babysitter, Ark. I'm perfectly capable of taking care of . . ."

"Sam—we've been through this before. I need you to get

that core out and then reinstalled in the *Claw*. You're the only one here who can do that, and we can't risk you getting hit on the way in." Blackhawk appreciated the courage and independence of his engineer, but now wasn't the time. "I promise you the most dangerous job next time." He was joking, but it occurred to him she just might try to hold him to it. But that was tomorrow's problem.

She held the stare for a few more seconds, but finally she nodded in acceptance.

"Remember, we're going to get in and out of here as quickly as possible. We don't want to end up stuck in that ship under siege." Blackhawk had considered bringing Lucas along and trying to steal the vessel itself, but he'd scuttled the idea. Imperial spy ships had all sorts of system security. He wasn't sure even Lucas could penetrate all of it in time to get the hell out before they were attacked and overrun on the ground. He didn't like the idea of racing through the abandoned streets trying to outrun any pursuers, but he didn't have a better idea either.

"We go in in two minutes." He took a last look at the group, staring at each of them for a few seconds. "Is everybody ready? Weapons checked and loaded?" There were nods all around. He grabbed the three particle accelerator rifles they'd taken from the dead guards. "You take these, Sarge. You guys are the likeliest to get into a serious firefight."

The noncom reached out and took the weapons, slipping one over his shoulder and handing the others to two of his men. "Thank you, sir. We will put them to good use."

Blackhawk smiled. "Just be careful, and don't blow that ship to pieces before Sam gets the core out." He paused. "And remember, that hold is full of military ordnance—not just guns, but explosives too. You get careless near there with one of those particle accelerators, and you'll blow the whole ship—and all of us—to bits."

"That won't happen," Sarge said.

"That's what I wanted to hear." He looked out across the open ground toward the imperial ship, counting down in his head (with perfect accuracy thanks to Hans). He held up his arm for a few seconds then let it drop. "Go," he said simply. He slipped through the hole he'd cut in the fencing and raced toward the ship, Ace right on his heels.

CHAPTER 15

"LOOKS LIKE ANOTHER DEAD END, CAP— . . . ADMIRAL." HALOS Grindle flashed a nervous look toward Kharn's chair.

Kharn didn't give a shit about his crew stumbling over his new rank, but he was getting tired of Grindle cringing every time he did it. He knew other pirate captains would space a crew member for less, but his people should know him better than that. He wanted to scream at Grindle, but he knew it was a waste of time. He also knew that it never hurt for his crew to think that he might just chuck one of them out of the airlock if they pissed him off enough.

Kharn wasn't a typical pirate leader, though. He was methodical and far less driven by petty emotions and unfocused rage than many of his peers. He was tough when he needed to be, but never pointlessly brutal. He seemed almost like a naval officer at times, though he was as rapacious as any buccaneer when there was loot to be had.

He knew the crew was still getting used to his new rank. They'd watched him leave the ship, answering the ka'al's summons. Kalishar's ruler had become increasingly unpredictable and capricious in recent years, and Kharn imagined there had been some heavy betting on whether he would make it back. But he had not only returned, he'd come back as the commander of the entire fleet.

It didn't help that he was still skippering *Red Viper,* just as he'd always done. It made things seem normal, as if they were just blasting off on another mission rather than serving as a flagship. They'd been calling Kharn captain for five years. Now he sat in the same chair, on the same ship, issuing many of the same orders, but he commanded Tarn Belgaren's entire armada.

"Let's do one more sweep, Halos." He knew it was a waste of time even as he said it, but he wanted to be thorough. He was already looking for a needle in a haystack, and he didn't intend to make it worse by missing anything. If Blackhawk's ship had been here, it would have come through days before, which meant the energy residue from its engines would be nearly gone. But nearly gone wasn't totally gone. It would take a lot of luck, and perfect scanning, to pick up his trail, but it could be done. And if there was one thing his people could do it was track a ship they were after. They were like bloodhounds in space. Hunting down ships was their business, and a pirate who couldn't sniff out an energy trail wasn't very good at his job.

And my men are the best.

"Yes, Admiral." He watched as Grindle turned back to his panel, plotting a new thrust pattern, revectoring the ship and firing the engines to come about and cover the same volume of space again. It was getting harder to screen out their own energy trails, and he knew this was probably the last pass where they would pick up any older signatures. After that, *Red Viper*'s residuals would be too strong, blanketing out any faint, older traces.

Kharn turned his head, looking toward the comm station. "Order all other ships to rescan their assigned areas."

"Yes, Admiral." Jacen Nimbus was manning *Red Viper*'s comm. "Transmitting now."

The rest of Kharn's fleet was dispersed throughout the system, searching for any signs that *Wolf's Claw* had passed through. A solar system was an almost unfathomably large volume to scan. Even with eighteen ships it had taken three days to complete a basic coverage pattern, and that was searching only the inner system, where the *Claw* would have passed if it had landed on either of Karleon's two inhabited planets. A full scan of the outer system would take far longer, at least a month to do a thorough job, and Kharn had other places to search and nowhere near that much time.

At least Karleon's worlds were poor and sparsely populated, he thought. They had no central authority, and certainly no patrol ships that might take exception to nearly twenty pirate vessels bursting into the system. If the search for Blackhawk went on long enough, to enough systems, Kharn knew that luck would change. Some planets on his list had the strength and the resolve to react harshly to any pirate incursions. Whether any of them would be spoiling to pick a fight with a fleet of eighteen ships was another question, one Kharn wasn't anxious to answer. He was in too much of a rush to properly search each system; he certainly didn't have time to fight with local authorities.

"And remind the ship captains. If they discover anything, pull back and report it immediately. No one is to attempt to engage the target vessel until the fleet has concentrated."

"Yes, Admiral."

Kharn was focused on finding his target, but he was also thinking about what to do if he did. *Red Viper* had been in the thick of the battle in Kalishar's system, and he'd seen the enemy vessel in action. *Wolf's Claw* looked like the semiwreck of a marginal smuggler, but Kharn knew that was a façade.

Blackhawk's ship had been far more maneuverable than anything in the ka'al's fleet, and whoever was at the controls was one of the best pilots Kharn had ever seen in action. Its weapons were far more powerful than anything on *Red Viper*, and they outranged all his guns as well. Finding *Wolf's Claw* was only the first of his problems. The enemy vessel was a tough target, and he knew none of his ships had a chance in a one-on-one fight. It wasn't going to be easy to disable or destroy that vessel—and he was going to lose ships doing it. He wasn't about to make it worse by letting his captains get cocky and go after it one at a time.

He sat back in his chair as *Red Viper* doubled back and re-scanned the space it had already covered. Finally, after several hours of fruitless searching, he'd had enough. He sighed softly. "Order all ships to cease scanning operations and assemble at the designated coordinates. It's time to move on."

"Yes, Admiral." Nimbus repeated Kharn's order, transmitting it to the entire fleet. "Message sent, Admiral." The transmission would take a while to reach the vessels searching the far side of the system, and it would be longer still before the ships of the fleet could change course and reach the designated location.

"Set a course for the rally point, Grindle. It's time to get to the next system."

"Yes, Admiral."

Kharn rose slowly out of his chair. "I will be in my quarters." It would be at least twelve hours before the fleet was in position and ready to transit, and Kharn hadn't gotten more than a few hours' sleep in the last week.

He walked toward the hatch at the back of the bridge then stopped. "What system is next on the list, Grindle?"

"Saragossa, Admiral."

Kharn frowned. "Saragossa is under guild embargo, and it was a backwater shithole even before that." He knew the ka'al's patience wouldn't last long, and Kharn didn't have time to waste on too many more fruitless searches. He had to find that ship, and soon. Maybe he would skip Saragossa. "What system is after Saragossa?"

"Rhodia, Admiral. Then Mercuron."

Rhodia, Kharn thought. *Well developed, strong industry, fairly wealthy.* The Rhodians wouldn't stand still for a pirate fleet invading their space and, for that matter, neither would the Mercurians. He was looking at a fight in either system, or at least a need to keep the fleet concentrated. That was going to slow things down. Maybe he should get there as soon as possible.

He stood in front of the hatch and thought for a few seconds. Should he skip Saragossa and head directly to Rhodia? Time was short, and Saragossa seemed an unlikely place to find Blackhawk and his ship. Still, he thought, a backwater world cut off from the rest of the sector wasn't a bad place to hide.

Finally, he sighed and turned toward the navigator. "Plot a hyperjump to Saragossa, Grindle." *Might as well be thorough,* he thought.

CHAPTER 16

"COMRADE TALIN, I AM SORRY TO DISTURB YOU, BUT I MUST speak with you immediately." General Varig stood outside the door, knocking cautiously. Aides had been banging on Talin's door for hours, carrying increasingly urgent dispatches from the front line, but the first comrade's angry shouts had driven them all away in a panic. Talin had become prone to fits of uncontrolled violence and brutality in recent months, and no one on his staff would risk pushing too hard and setting him off.

Now the situation had become critical, and General Varig was doing the knocking. He'd come right from the front, from the thick of the fighting, and he looked like it. His uniform was dirty and disheveled, and he had a small strip of cloth tied around his arm as a makeshift bandage. His boots were caked with partially dried mud. Varig knew it was dangerous to disturb Talin, especially when he was roaring drunk, as the general suspected he was now. But the enemy was breaking through the lines in three places, and the situation at the front was critical. He needed permission to deploy the reserve formations immediately, and Talin was the only one who could release the reinforcements.

Varig was frustrated. He had been a friend of Talin's before the revolution, and the two had served together in the early battles, when laborers armed with metal pipes and knives charged the armed soldiers of the nobles. Thousands died in those fights, but more and more men volunteered, and Saragossa's former masters were driven from the cities one by one.

Varig and Talin, with Arn and a number of other workers turned army commanders, had been instrumental in forging those early rebels into a fighting force capable of defeating the house troops of the noble families—and later battling their hired mercenaries to a standstill. But as Talin gathered more power to himself, he became increasingly distant from his old friends and comrades. Hunger for power overcame cooperation; paranoia poisoned friendships. Since he'd assumed the chairmanship of the revolutionaries' central committee, he had become extremely arrogant—and increasingly irrational and violent.

Varig had heard the grumbling among others high in the Revolutionary Army's ranks, vague calls for the chairman's ouster, but no one dared to move against him. Talin controlled the Red Guards, the secret police unit that ensured loyalty among the soldiers and citizens of the revolution. The Guards were notoriously brutal—and not overly concerned about actually proving guilt before executing those targeted as enemies of the revolution. Talin didn't hesitate to unleash them on anyone he came to perceive as an enemy of the revolution—or just of himself.

Varig stayed above the scheming. Though he loathed what Talin had become, he wasn't ready to do anything about it, at least not yet. And pointless grumbling was a stupid way to get yourself purged. He knocked again.

"Come in, General," Talin barked through the door.

Varig turned the handle and stepped inside. The room was immense, with a vaulted ceiling soaring almost ten meters above the floor. The walls and ceilings were covered with beautifully painted mosaics, now damaged in places from fighting and neglect. It had been the bedchamber of one of New Vostok's greatest noblemen before the revolution, and Talin had claimed it as his own.

Varig felt a twinge of disgust as he saw Talin, lying on one of the priceless silk sofas, disheveled and clearly drunk. The room stank of alcohol and vomit, and there were plates lying everywhere.

He remembered Talin years before, working long into the night, living in a spare cell with just a cot and a small locker. Just as often—he'd be out in the countryside with the soldiers, sleeping on the ground, with nothing but an old tarp to keep the rain off him. He wasn't prone to brutality then either—except with the nobles. It was only later that he'd begun to spy on his allies, and people began to disappear. "What do you need, General?" Talin's speech was slow, his words slurred.

Varig's eyes panned around the room. There were two empty bottles on the floor next to Talin, and a third sitting on a small table, half drained.

"Comrade Chairman, the mercenary forces of the nobility

have launched a major attack against our lines south of the city." He paused, swallowing hard. He wouldn't let fear of Talin rule him, not like so many of the craven sycophants who followed the chairman around. But only a fool could ignore the fact that Talin and his Red Guard cronies were fond of executing generals who displeased them. And Varig had come with bad news. Still, his comrades were dying right now—his men. He wouldn't cower in the face of Talin while his soldiers were charging enemy tanks. "Our forces have been driven back in several places."

Talin stared back at the general, snorting and rubbing his hand across his unshaven face. "Were your soldiers unprepared, General?" There was an ominous tone to Talin's voice. "Perhaps they were poorly deployed or caught napping."

"No, First Comrade." He marshaled his courage and stared back at the chairman of the Revolutionary Council. "The enemy has thrown all its strength against our lines south of New Vostok. Their strategy is unorthodox and very unlike their previous operations. They have concentrated their forces against a narrow frontage and overwhelmed the defenders in that area."

Talin stared at Varig without speaking. He was very drunk, but anger was beginning to focus his mind. "What would you know of military orthodoxy, General?" Talin's voice was caustic. "Seven years ago you were pouring metallic alloys into equipment molds, were you not?"

Varig bit back on his anger. *And you worked in a concrete plant,* he thought but wisely kept to himself. "Comrade Chairman, I have fought in the front lines of the revolution for all of those seven years. I have faced our enemies in battle many times, seen their strategy and tactics in action." He paused, taking a deep breath and trying to remain calm.

"I am telling you, Comrade Chairman, that this is an attack like none they have ever initiated. As you know, the bulk of the nobles' forces are off-world mercenaries. They have always sought to use their superior training and equipment to attack us in hit-and-run battles, engagements designed to minimize their own losses. But now they are attacking us frontally, and they are continuing forward, ignoring their losses." He looked right at Talin. "They are doing this for a reason, Comrade Chairman, though I do not know what it is. I am extremely concerned."

"So what do you want, General?"

"We need the reserve battalions released, Comrade Chairman. As soon as possible." He hesitated. "Including the special companies." Talin had expended most of the army's high-tech weapons in his campaign against the rebel splinter group. His imperial benefactors had provided extremely effective ordnance, but sharply limited supplies of ammunition and equipment to recharge and rearm the weapons. Most of the previous two deliveries had been used up fighting Arn and his people, leaving only a handful of companies still equipped with battle-ready imperial weaponry.

And all of those were currently protecting Talin.

The chairman stared at Varig. "You may have the reserve units, General, but the special companies will remain in the city."

Varig knew Talin had been extremely careful about allocating the imperial weapons only to units loyal directly to him. That was why the newest shipment was still in the hold of the ship that delivered it. Despite his mental and physical deterioration, Talin remained a wily and dangerous operative. Varig knew the chairman's paranoia was becoming ever more dangerous, and he knew he had to tread carefully. "But, Comrade Chairman . . ."

"My decision is final, General. You may have the reserve battalions, but the special units will remain in place." He turned away from Varig. "You may return to the front. You have much work to do."

Blackhawk glanced over at Ace and nodded. "Ready?" They were lying on their stomachs, halfway down the exhaust port of the imperial ship. He could feel the coolness of the metal through his wet jacket and the slickness on the smooth metal from the light rain that had begun to fall.

"Ready, Cap." The two pulled the pins from the small bags they each carried, then shoved them as far down the exhaust tube as they could.

"Let's get the hell out of here." Blackhawk was already crawling backward as he spoke. They'd set the timers for one minute, not much time, but enough to get away if they didn't waste any of it.

The slick wetness of the smooth metal made it even more difficult to climb backward, and it slowed them down. Finally, Blackhawk managed to get a grip on a small ridge around the inside of the exhaust port and pulled himself out, with Ace following just a few seconds behind. They stepped carefully on the small metal ledge leading to the access ladder on the side of the ship. Blackhawk grabbed the slippery metal rung and climbed quickly to the ground six meters below, Ace right behind.

They ran across the wet pavement, putting as much distance between them and the imperial ship as they could before the charges blew. Blackhawk pointed toward a pile of crates stacked up near the fence, and they both ran for it.

"Stop!"

Damn!

The shout had come from behind them, somewhere near the ship. They hadn't seen any guards nearby when they'd first approached. Whoever this was, Blackhawk realized, he must have come from inside the vessel.

"Run, Ace," Blackhawk yelled. "Now!" He spun around, whipping out his pistol as he did. Before he could fire, a blinding beam of light ripped right past his head, and for an instant the spaceport was lit up like day. The beam was so close, he could feel the staticky charge, like hundreds of tiny insects crawling on his face. He fired his pistol, but the shock from the beam's near miss made his arm twitch, and his shot went wide. He was shaken and disoriented, struggling to focus. It had been a long time since he felt so disoriented in combat, but he quickly got himself under control. He was about to fire again when the charges blew.

The rear of the ship erupted into a firestorm, a massive blast of flames blasting out of the exhaust port. A huge plume of smoke billowed out of the stricken vessel, rising quickly into the night sky.

The shock of the explosion hit Blackhawk, throwing him back into a pile of crates. He landed hard, but his combat instincts took over and he slid his arm down, deflecting most of the impact. He rolled around on his back and then up to his feet again, bringing his pistol to bear.

But his adversary was gone.

He whipped his head around, first to the right then the left, scanning the entire area. He could see Sarge's men silhouetted in the fading light from the explosion, moving quickly toward the ship. A few seconds later there was another flash, as they used one of the captured particle accelerators to blast open the door.

Ace came running around from behind the wall of crates. "You okay, Ark?"

"I'm fine, Ace." He took a deep breath. He was still a little disoriented by the near miss, but he ignored it, nodding to his companion. "Now let's get to that ship and give Sarge and his boys a hand."

Ace returned the nod, gripping his rifle tightly. "I'm with you, Ark. Let's go get ourselves a hyperdrive core and get the hell out of here."

"Keep moving, all of you." Carano waved his arm forward, urging his exhausted men onward. Vulcan's tanks had blown a five-kilometer hole in the enemy lines, and the strike force had slipped through, passing one abandoned defensive position after another and meeting almost no resistance.

Carano didn't know how long that would last, so he'd driven his people mercilessly forward. The revolutionaries could bring up reserves and launch a counterattack at any time. Vulcan's men—and the troops from the other companies—were mostly veterans, more than a match for their enemies in an even fight. Hell, he thought, they could handle the revolutionaries out-numbered two to one. But the Saragossan rebels had shown a willingness to sacrifice huge numbers of conscripts, and if they launched enough wave attacks, even the Tiger Company and the Black Helms would be driven back.

And Carano and his team would be trapped behind enemy lines.

They were on the outskirts of the city, working their way around toward the spaceport. The area appeared to have been a once-thriving district of industrial facilities, mostly basic materials plants, but now it was heavily damaged from fighting and mostly abandoned. It didn't look like any of the factories had been active since the revolution began. As such, the infrastructure had begun to decay. In some areas, the street had collapsed and underground pipes and electrical lines lay exposed and crumbling. There was no power or lighting, and from the looks of the shattered but dry conduits, there was no water service either.

Carano pushed his men farther.

They'd run into two patrols and a few groups of civilians, but they'd scragged them all before anyone could call for help. As far as Carano could tell, their secrecy was still intact.

The night had started out brightly lit by the moons, but the weather had begun to cooperate. The storm front that had been threatening all day was finally moving in, and the moonlight had become obscured by the thickening clouds. Carano's force crept forward, quickly but quietly, cloaked in the near darkness.

Suddenly, a bright flash illuminated the night sky. Carano held up his hand, but his people had already stopped. They were looking around, trying to figure out where it had come from.

"What was that? Lightning?" Kal Riktor was one of Carano's oldest veterans, a grizzled sergeant who'd refused every effort to promote him to the commissioned ranks.

Carano hushed him, staring up at the sky. That looked like lightning, but it might be something else too. Unlike the rest of his people, he'd seen imperial troops in action once, and that flash looked a hell of a lot like a particle accelerator.

"Let's be on our guard." Carano started moving again, motioning for the group to follow. "We're getting close. Stay sharp. I want everybody ready for whatever happens."

———————

Sarge burst through the shattered hatch, holding his assault rifle in his hands. It was an old weapon, one he'd carried for years. The grips were worn smooth, and it was notched in a dozen places, including one large gouge where it had blocked the massive stroke of a tribesman's scimitar on Taurus, saving his life. The mission on Taurus had been a difficult one, and the *Claw* and its crew barely escaped from that barbarous world.

The particle accelerator was slung across his back. Its barrel was still hot from the shot that blasted the door, and it stung every time it slapped against his bare neck. Blackhawk had been clear about not shooting the imperial ship to pieces before Sam got the hyperdrive core out, and Sarge took the order seriously, as he did every word the captain uttered. The particle accelerators were indiscriminate weapons, extremely powerful, but also hard to control in close quarters. A shot in the wrong place could have unpredictable results. Sarge opted for the tried and true instead, the weapons that had become almost an extension of his arms during a life spent at war. This was going to be close-quarters work anyway, and he didn't need any fancy imperial weapons to get it done. His trusted rifle would do the job and, if things got really close, he had his knife—thirty centimeters long and razor sharp.

The main lighting was out. Blackhawk and Ace must have successfully severed the main power conduit with their charges, cutting off the flow of energy from the reactor. Sarge had no idea how quickly the enemy could reroute their power grid, and he wasn't about to wait and find out. It was time to take the ship.

He spun around, turning ninety degrees into a corridor. It was dim, lit only by the reddish glow of the emergency lamps, but he caught a glimpse of a figure ducking around the corner at the far end. He fired a burst in the target's direction, but even as he depressed his finger on the trigger, he knew it was too late.

"Ringo, cover us. Then bring up the rear. The rest of you, let's move. The bridge is this way." Blackhawk had given Sarge a detailed description of the ship's interior. Sarge had the usual burst of curiosity about how Blackhawk knew what the inside of an imperial ship looked like, but he'd long ago gotten used to the captain's bizarre storehouse of knowledge. The captain was almost never wrong about this kind of thing, and Sarge took every word from his mouth as an indisputable fact. If he said the bridge was this way, the bridge was this way.

If he'd had a larger force, Sarge would have tried to secure multiple locations simultaneously, but he only had five men, including himself, and he had no idea what was waiting deeper in the ship. Better to be cautious, he thought, than have his men picked off one at a time.

He pressed his back against the far wall of the corridor, presenting as small a silhouette as possible as he advanced. He held his rifle at the ready as he crept down the hall. From the looks of things, the crewman he'd spotted had bolted, but he wasn't going to take any chances. Carelessness got soldiers killed. He took a quick look back.

Ringo was peering around the corner, covering the corridor as the others advanced. He was a massive hulk of a man, almost two meters tall and muscular from head to toe. He had a long scar running from the base of his neck up to the top of his head. The line of whitish skin traced its way across his scalp, leaving a bald line through his otherwise thick brown hair. At first glance, he looked like a bruiser, a strong but stupid ape of a man, deadly in a brawl but useless for anything requiring more sophistication or subtlety. But looks were deceiving, and Ringo was a sly and canny warrior—and the best shot in Sarge's squad.

Sarge wouldn't have wanted anyone else covering his ass. He took a breath and swung around the corner, his rifle at the ready. It was a long hall, and it was totally empty. Whoever he'd seen leaping around the corner was long gone. "C'mon, men. On me."

He moved swiftly down the corridor. He knew there were surveillance cameras everywhere, and he was doing his best to avoid them. If he gave the enemy too long to track his people, they might be able to organize an effective defense. Speed was his ally.

"Von, Drake—cover the door."

"Yes, Sarge." The two men answered as one. They snapped their rifles up, aiming them chest high at the closed hatch.

Sarge pressed the button to open the door, but nothing happened. He worked at it for a few seconds, punching at the small keypad alongside the hatch. "Fuck it," he finally growled. He waved his men back around the corner and took a dozen steps back, sliding the particle accelerator rifle from his back. "Be ready, boys!" he shouted and pulled the trigger.

The flash filled the dim corridor with blinding white light as the shot almost vaporized the door. Sarge slung the heavy weapon over his shoulder again, gritting his teeth as the hot metal of the barrel rubbed against his neck again.

"Let's go." He ran down the hallway, readying his assault rifle as he did. His men were right behind, weapons ready. He ran through the door, ducking to the side and rolling hard, firing as he did.

His men bolted through after him: Buck in the lead, with Von following right behind. Sarge was prone in the corner, his assault rifle now silent, but still at the ready. There were three crewmen on the other side of the room, all dead, riddled with shots from Sarge's rifle.

Ringo ran over and checked the bodies. They all knew the men were dead, but Sarge had beaten it into their heads for years. Carelessness makes dead soldiers. "Yup," he muttered. Then, more loudly, "They're dead, Sarge. Good shooting." A look of concern came over his face.

"You hit, Sarge?" He jumped up and moved toward the injured noncom. The others followed suit, and in a second they were all hovering over their commander, reaching out and trying to help him stand.

"Get off me, you apes." Sarge pushed them all away, wincing slightly as he did it. "It's just a fucking scratch. I've had worse from shaving." He stood up and glared at them, as if daring them to make a fuss over it.

They could see it was a hell of a lot more than a scratch, but they knew Sarge well enough to shut up. They stood a few paces away and watched silently as he slid off his coat slowly, painfully revealing a nasty gunshot wound on his upper arm. His bicep and forearm were covered with blood. He looked up and saw them staring at him.

"You got better things to do than stare at me! Check those doors!" He waved toward the two hatches on the far wall. "And stay ready in case anyone comes in here." He turned back toward his arm, tearing a long strip of cloth from his shirt and wrapping it tightly around the wound to stop the bleeding. In a minute he was done.

His men were all watching the doors with one eye and him with the other. He made a rude gesture, a disgusted look on his face. "I told you powder puffs I'm okay, so quit the bullshit. We've got work to do." He pulled the particle accelerator off his back, gritting his teeth as he extended his wounded arm to hold it. He could have had one of the others blow the door, but he wasn't going to give them the satisfaction.

"You apes ready?" He aimed the heavy rifle toward one of the doors without waiting for an answer. There was no time to waste. They had a ship to take.

CHAPTER 17

THE FANFARE BLARED ACROSS THE OPEN AREAS OF THE SPACE-port. The band had just played "My Celtiboria," the newly designated national anthem of the united planet. Now they were beginning "Glory of Antilles," a show of respect for the delegation now making its way across the field toward the waiting leader of the new Celtiborian Republic. The Antillean officials moved forward slowly, with Celtiborian soldiers standing at attention to either side, swords held up along their sides. Behind the honor guard stood more soldiers, dressed in combat gear and holding back the throngs of cheering Celtiborian citizens.

Lucerne stood at the reception stand, a handpicked detachment from his personal guards standing behind him. They were clad in their ornate new dress uniforms: tight white breeches with knee-high black boots and dark blue jackets covered with a riotous mass of lace and silver. The soldiers were rugged veterans all, men who had served with the marshal for years in the mud and blood of a hundred fields of battle. They looked as out of place in their silver buttons and extravagant finery as their chief did. These were grim men, warriors, and the fuss and bother of diplomacy and politics was alien to them. Still, like their commander, they did what was required of them, and the men standing behind Celtiboria's ruler were as perfectly arrayed as any monarch's guard had ever been.

The Celtiborian Republic, Lucerne thought, with a combination of guilt and disgust. He'd established a reasonable facsimile of republican government in the weeks following his final victory, but he knew it was a charade, a bit of blatant propaganda to soften the image of his regime. The truth was starker, more blatant. Augustin Lucerne commanded two million veteran soldiers—fanatically loyal and the only forces remaining under arms on Celtiboria. He could impose his merest whim on the helpless population, and nothing could stop him. That was the real truth, stripped of the lies and the republican propaganda.

Lucerne did not crave power for its own sake, as most men did. He was tired of war, worn out from the burdens of command. He intended to rule benevolently and step down once he'd forged the Far Stars Confederation, but he knew that was a weak defense of tyranny.

It would take years more of constant warfare, on an interplanetary scale this time, before his dream was realized. And for all those long and deadly years, Lucerne might call himself president or prime minister, or whatever other title he could invent, but he couldn't fool himself. He might deceive the people; they were easily led. And his ministers and officers would obey him no matter what he became, out of loyalty he hoped, but if not, out of fear. But he would always know the truth. He'd fought three decades of war to make himself Celtiboria's military dictator, and that's precisely what he was.

The warlords he had destroyed were despots too, ones far more brutal than he. The people would live better lives under his rule, even as they worked ceaselessly to support war on a dozen planets. They wouldn't be free, not by any reasonable definition of liberty certainly, but their ruler would be more benevolent than those he'd replaced.

Most important, he thought, the dream of the confederation would live on as a result of his triumph, and his iron rule would give the great plan its best chance of success. A weak and fragmented Far Stars would one day fall under the empire's control. And, without his intervention, that day could be years away, perhaps even generations, but Lucerne knew it would come eventually. It might have come already had it not been for the succession of fools and imbeciles banished to the governor's chair on Galvanus Prime. Lucerne's greatest fear was that a capable man would inherit the governor's chair and impose his imperial will on the Far Stars. Such a man would be worse than all the warlords combined, and the people would be bound by the shackles that imprisoned the rest of mankind.

If that dark day arrived, the people on Celtiboria—and one hundred other worlds—would know totalitarian rule at its worst. They would learn to grovel before their emperor, to beg his indulgence for each day of their miserable lives. They would learn to be slaves.

Lucerne wasn't naive enough to believe he waged a war of light against darkness. Life was rarely so starkly simple as that.

But he knew his regime was the lesser of two evils, and he had dedicated his life to ensuring that the Far Stars remained free of imperial domination. If the people cursed his name when he was gone, if they spit on his grave as they walked by, he would consider it worthwhile—as long as they remained free of the dark regime that held the rest of humanity under its bloody boot.

He had taken the first step by conquering Celtiboria. Now he was hoping to take the next step as he received the Antillean emissary.

Lucerne stood rigidly erect as his visitors approached, covering his discomfort with a show of military correctness. His tension and discipline created a reasonable facsimile of respect for the Antillean emissary now making his way forward through the cheering throngs.

He stepped forward as his guest of honor approached, smiling and extending his hand. "Welcome to Celtiboria, Lord Lancaster. We are greatly honored by your presence."

The diplomat wore an exquisitely tailored black suit with a white vest and long tails, the height of Antillean formal fashion. He reached out and clasped Lucerne's hand. "It is my honor, Marshal Lucerne, to finally meet you and to congratulate you on your great victory. I am certain that Celtiboria is at the dawn of a golden age now that she is free of the rule of the vicious warlords."

Lucerne smiled. He felt a rush of cynical amusement. Lancaster was the wealthiest man on Antilles, and possibly in the entirety of the Far Stars. His many industrial concerns had made millions importing weapons and equipment for Celtiboria's "vicious" warlords as well as Lucerne's own forces. He bit back on a surge of anger when he thought of how many of his men had been killed by those imported Antillean—

Lancaster—guns and vehicles. That rage would serve no purpose now, and without Antillean support, the confederation would be stillborn, and the sacrifices of all those who'd fallen would be for naught. He broadened his smile and said, "My humble thanks to you, Lord Lancaster, for your kind words."

He turned to face the pack of dignitaries who flanked Lancaster. "Welcome to all of you, ladies and gentlemen. All of Celtiboria is joyful at your coming." His eyes moved back to Lancaster. Lucerne knew the magnate was more than the leader of the delegation. Although he held few official titles himself, Danellan Lancaster's money exerted tremendous influence on those who did. Lucerne had no doubt the Antillean Senate would follow whatever advice their duly appointed emissary might choose to offer, lest its members risk losing the flow of campaign contributions—and outright bribes—that flowed from Lancaster's coffers like a river of gold.

Lucerne smiled and hid his true feelings. He was new to politics, but wise enough to realize the truth had little place in its practice. *I was willing to kill for the confederation. I can put up with Lancaster too.*

He addressed the emissary again. "We will begin our talks on the confederation tomorrow, but you have come far, and we would be remiss if we did not treat welcome guests as they deserve. We have suitable quarters prepared for all of you. I am sure you would like to rest before tonight's reception." He waved his arm, and an army of stewards in magnificent livery came forward. Each of them was assigned to a different dignitary and knew him by sight. Augustin Lucerne detested the game of diplomacy, but that didn't mean he couldn't play it with the same skill he used to fight his wars.

"I thank you on behalf of the entire delegation, Marshal

188 — JAY ALLAN

Lucerne. Your warm welcome is greatly appreciated." Lancaster motioned to his companions, and they began to follow the stewards away from the reception stand.

"Lord Lancaster, I wonder if I might have a few moments of your time later." Lucerne leaned in, speaking softly to the Antillean industrialist.

"Why, certainly, Marshal Lucerne." He paused, waiting for the rest of his people to trickle off the stand. When the last had left, he asked, "How may I be of help?"

"Well, Your Excellency, if the confederation plan proceeds, we will be bringing a number of worlds into the mainstream economy of the sector, planets that have long been isolated as a result of internal conflicts or totalitarian rulers."

Lancaster nodded. "Indeed, there has long been robust trade between the Primes, but many of the lesser worlds are quite undeveloped." The pitch of his voice changed and Lucerne knew he had piqued his interest.

"As you know, Your Excellency, I am a soldier. Economics and industry are not my areas of expertise. But I consider economic outreach to these worlds an essential component of successfully integrating them into the confederation." Lucerne paused deliberately, taking a moment to gauge Lancaster's reaction. "I was hoping you would be willing to give me some insight in this area—and possibly even help by serving as the leader of the confederation's economic development programs. Assuming, of course, that Antilles chooses to become a part of the confederation. I would never ask you to do anything that ran counter to the interests of your world."

Lancaster nodded. "I would be very pleased to assist in such a capacity. And let's forget the stifling formality. Please call me Danellan. I am not all that tired, Marshal—do you care to speak of it a bit now?"

Lucerne smiled. "Augustin, please. And yes, I would be most interested in hearing your thoughts." He gestured to a set of stairs along the back of the stand. "Perhaps we can go to my office."

"Yes, Augustin, let's go discuss what can be done for some of these backward worlds."

Lucerne was unnerved at the smile on Lancaster's face. He felt a twinge of guilt for offering up the inhabitants of a dozen worlds as bait to the rapacious Antillean robber baron. The Lancaster Consortium would make those worlds into virtual colonies, stripping them of their resources and turning them into closed markets for overpriced Antillean goods.

Still, he realized, even after Lancaster and his cronies looted the economies of those worlds, most of them would be better off than they were now, cut off from the rest of the sector and buried under stifling statist regimes. The rapid development Lancaster would initiate would lift all boats, no matter how much he stole. None of it mattered, though. Lucerne needed Antilles, and he would do whatever he had to in order to get the planet on board. And, in many ways, Danellan Lancaster was Antilles.

Lucerne sat quietly in front of the fire, filling his glass again from the now half-empty decanter. It was extremely expensive cognac, spoils from the sack of the last warlord's stronghold.

He held the snifter in front of him, staring into the amber liquid. He'd never been much of a drinker, not in all his years at war, nor through all the pain and the endless death and Arnage.

He'd lost friends, suffered painful wounds, unleashed death on millions, faced stalemate and even defeat. But it had taken the abduction of his daughter to drive Lucerne to the bottle.

He had continued his schedule, without change, without pause. To do less would be to hand Astra's abductors the victory. And that he would never do. But the pain was there, every moment of every day, wherever he was, however crucial the task at hand.

The loss of his daughter was painful enough. But the guilt was there too, and it tested the limits of his endurance. Astra had been taken because of him, because of the things he had done and the causes he had championed. Her kidnappers had abducted her from right under his nose, through the security he had put in place to protect her. Her guards fought to the death, but they were overwhelmed. If he'd protected her more carefully, he thought, put more men into her security detail . . .

He knew it hadn't been that simple. Astra was temperamental, with a wild and independent streak. She'd resisted every attempt he made to beef up her security, to surround her with bodyguards and keep her in protected strongholds. Anyone who knew Astra Lucerne realized she was uncontrollable. She may have been born the daughter of the man who conquered Celtiboria, but she did what she pleased whenever she wanted. He understood that intellectually, but the pain eating away at his soul wouldn't let him release himself from the blame, not even partially.

He drained his glass in one gulp, feeling the fiery liquid slide down his throat. He didn't particularly enjoy the sensation, but he knew it would dull the pain. If he drank enough, he might even sleep tonight, escape the images of Astra that haunted him in the evening darkness. He'd come to appreciate anything that could provide a few hours of numbness. It was the closest thing he felt to happiness. The rest of his life was duty and pain.

He'd taken another step earlier in the day, one that promised tremendous progress toward achieving his dream of confederation. Antilles, like Celtiboria, was one of the Prime worlds, the six planets in the Far Stars with the longest histories and largest populations. The talks with the Antillean delegation had gone better than he'd dared to hope. He'd bought Danellan Lancaster's support with promises of economic opportunity, and the mogul now clearly supported Antillean membership in the confederation. He'd assured Lucerne he would speak out loudly for a positive vote in the Senate.

A crucial first step. Lucerne knew he needed to secure the cooperation of the other Primes for his plan to succeed. He could invade minor worlds, topple their petty rulers and force them into the confederation, but war with another Prime was unthinkable. It would be a cataclysm for both worlds.

The other Prime worlds would be impressed by early adoption of the Confederation Treaty by the Antillean Senate. The planet had the largest navy of any world in the Far Stars, and the Antilles Naval Academy produced the best pilots in the Far Stars. The alliance between Celtiboria and Antilles would create a power bloc stronger than any in the Far Stars. The others would be spurred to join for fear of their own power and influence waning.

The access to Lancaster funds doesn't hurt, either.

Lucerne reached out and grabbed the decanter, filling his glass again. Yes, the summit with the Antillean delegation had been an enormous success. It was as good a reason as any for a drink, he thought, and he emptied the glass in one gulp.

CHAPTER 18

"HOW DOES IT LOOK, SAM?" BLACKHAWK WAS STANDING BEHIND his engineer, watching her examine the spy ship's hyperdrive core.

"It looks like some kind of damned alien artifact, Captain. This thing is the most advanced piece of machinery I've ever seen." There was frustration in her voice, but excitement as well. Blackhawk did his best not to get impatient with her. He knew there was nothing Sam Sparks loved more than analyzing a sophisticated spaceship system, and if she had her way, she'd sit there all day, puzzling over the sophisticated imperial tech. As far as he could tell, that's exactly what she was doing. She'd removed the access plate and set up two battery-powered lanterns so she could see what she was doing, but since then she'd just been looking at it and poking around at the fiber optic connections surrounding it.

Blackhawk put his hand on her shoulder. "Sam, I know this is a tough job, but we've got a time limit here. We've got to get this thing loaded and out of here before half the revolution-aries in New Vostok show up and blow us away. I can tell it's a complex device, but you're just going to have to go with your gut. We should have been on our way back to the *Claw* by now."

"I understand, Ark." She looked at the toolkit sitting on the floor next to her, retrieving a small power flow scanner. She glanced behind her toward Blackhawk. "I could really use some quiet." She looked at him knowingly.

He held up his hands in surrender. "Okay, Sam—you're the boss." He turned and looked at the others. "Everyone out. Now." They shuffled quickly out of the room, leaving Black-hawk alone with his engineer. He walked to the door himself, pausing and giving her a quick wink as he stood there. "Just do the best you can, Sam. There's no one I trust more than you." He turned and walked through the door, sliding it closed behind him.

He walked down the dimly lit corridor and into the ward-room. Sarge was sitting up on a table with Doc working on his wounded arm. From the haggard look on the noncom's face, Blackhawk guessed it had been an unpleasant experience.

"There." Doc's voice was thick with satisfaction. He pulled out a pair of small forceps and dropped the projectile in his palm. "The damned thing dug its way into the bone. It was a bitch to get out."

"It damned sure was." Sarge's voice was a little thin, which gave Blackhawk an idea just how painful Doc's probing had been. He'd seen Sarge coolly ignore pain that would have reduced most people to sobbing hysterics.

"You're lucky you're going to keep that arm, my friend," Doc said. "You can thank me for that, and not that pathetic dressing you managed yourself." He paused, expecting a comeback, but Sarge was just too spent. Doc picked up the projectile with two fingers and held it up to the portable light he'd placed next to Sarge. It was small, and much flatter than a normal bullet, and the edges were sharp and jagged. "It's so small, yet it caused such massive tissue damage." He looked over at Blackhawk. "I wasn't kidding. He came a hairsbreadth from losing that arm."

"It's an imperial buzz dart, designed for close-in fire, where a particle accelerator or other heavy weapon isn't practical." Blackhawk had barely looked at the thing, but he had no doubt. "It's designed to rotate as it penetrates the target's flesh, causing the nastiest possible wound. A hit anywhere in the torso is probably mortal, so you're lucky it was just an arm shot. It's small so a clip can hold a lot of ammunition.

"Ace, I want you guys to be extracareful. These things are no joke. They're made to kill. They're top-of-the-line imperial weapons, used mostly by Special Forces and intelligence units."

"Yeah, Sarge. Try not to walk into any more enemy fire." Ace was smiling ear to ear as he ribbed the straitlaced noncom. Sarge was as tight and by the book as they came, and Ace enjoyed giving him shit.

Sarge glared back for a few seconds, but he didn't answer. Then Doc got his attention again when he started fusing the wound shut. He'd offered Sarge a painkiller, but the big soldier had refused. Blackhawk knew Sarge well enough to understand. If there was going to be any more fighting, the old veteran wanted to be 100 percent alert and ready.

"Are we covered outside?" Blackhawk spoke softly to Sarge. The fuser was a great piece of medical technology, accomplishing in minutes what nature would need weeks to complete. But he knew from experience, the thing hurt like fucking fire without an anesthetic.

"Yes, sir." Sarge's voice was weak, strained. "Ringo and Von are outside guarding the ship. I sent Buck and Drake to do a patrol sweep around the perimeter." He paused, sucking in a tortured breath. "Everything's quiet so far, Captain."

"Katarina's out taking a look around, too," Ace chimed in, and there was a twinge of irritation in his voice. "I . . . ah . . . suggested that she stay with the ship, but she just nodded and went anyway."

"Of course she did." Blackhawk sighed and looked over at Ace. "Any sign of Shira yet? Or Arn and his people?"

"Nothing from the rebels, but Shira just got back a few minutes ago." Ace was clearly amused about something. "Wait until you see what she got."

"What is it?" Blackhawk wasn't in the mood for Ace's sense of humor. Not right now.

"She's outside pulling it around. Let's go take a look, and you can see for yourself."

Blackhawk sighed. There was no point in arguing. "Okay, let's go." They walked down the corridor toward the airlock. It was closed, and the control plate next to it was dead. With the reactor down, the automated doors were not functioning. Blackhawk grabbed the handholds and slid the hatch open, stepping through and climbing quickly down the ladder.

Ringo was standing guard just below the airlock. He snapped to attention and saluted when Blackhawk walked past. They'd been on the *Claw* for years now, but Sarge and his boys still ignored the informality of the rest of the crew, giving Blackhawk the salutes and ceremony they felt a commanding officer deserved.

Blackhawk returned the salute, feeling a little uncomfortable as he did. In truth, military ceremony made him uncomfortable. It brought back memories he had tried hard to forget. But he understood that Sarge and his people were showing him respect in the only way they knew, and he appreciated the loyalty.

He panned his eyes around the ship, looking for Shira and the vehicle she had commandeered. He stopped abruptly when he saw it: a giant transport of some kind, sitting right behind the ship. It had some kind of scoop on the front, and it looked like it opened from both the top and the back. He walked toward it and stopped in his tracks about five meters away. "What is that smell?" He turned back toward Ace, who was trying—and failing—to suppress a laugh.

"It's garbage, Ark." Ace could barely speak through the laughter forcing its way out. "She got us a garbage transport."

"I'm glad you're so amused, Ace." Shira came walking around from behind the massive truck. "I live to keep you happy." Her voice was biting, dismissive. "But this thing is perfect. It's big, so it can hold the core and all of us too. It's unobtrusive, and its sides are heavy, almost like armor plating, so we'll have some protection."

"It's perfect, Shira." Blackhawk flashed a cold stare at Ace. "Just ignore our friend here." He walked toward the massive truck. The stench was making his eyes water, but he smiled and nodded. "Perfect." He turned back toward Shira. He pointed toward the heavy ramp that led to the spy ship's main hold. "We'll bring the core out that way, so bring it around with the back hatch toward the cargo door."

Of course, it will all be a waste of time unless Sam manages to disconnect the thing, he thought. By rights that job should take a crew of four a full day or more. But if anyone could do it alone and in a couple hours, he knew it was Sam Sparks.

"What are you doing on Saragossa with a shipment of high-tech weapons?" Blackhawk was glaring at the prisoners. There were three survivors from Sarge's attack on the ship, and he'd locked them up in one of the detention cells. Blackhawk had ordered them shackled to the bench as well. These were dangerous men, and no one knew that better than he did.

He'd known the instant he'd laid eyes on them. They were imperial intelligence, all of them. He couldn't quantify the look, but he'd seen it enough times to be sure. There was death in their eyes, the frigid iciness of space itself. These men were soulless killers, among the most brutal and dangerous of the emperor's servants.

They stared back at him silently, their faces hard in defiance. Blackhawk knew he could break them, make them talk—no man was unbreakable. But it would also take time, and he would have to do things he'd sworn long ago he would never do again. Imperial agents were conditioned to resist pain and brainwashing. He would have to torture them to get information from them, break them down into quivering wrecks. He just wasn't sure he could make himself do that, at least not if there was an alternative. He knew he'd break his vow and do whatever he had to if his ship or his crew were at stake, but not to satisfy his curiosity about why the imperial governor was getting involved in a petty revolution in a forgotten corner of the frontier.

No, he couldn't return to what he had been. Not for that.

Still, he was uncomfortable. The more he thought about it, the less sense it made. These weapons were enormously expensive, and their distribution was strictly controlled. He wanted to write it all off as a random incident, but he knew it had to be more than that.

"Astra," Blackhawk muttered inaudibly. Was the empire involved in her abduction too? He hadn't thought about that before. He'd assumed the ka'al had been paid by Lucerne's enemies. The Celtiborian warlords Lucerne had defeated weren't all dead. Some had fled, leaving Celtiboria with shiploads of treasure for a gilded life in exile on some other world. It made sense that the kidnapping had been planned by one of them, seeking revenge on the man who'd toppled their regimes and taken their power. Now, though, he began to wonder if there was more to the whole plot than simple vengeance, and that led him to a question he wasn't sure he wanted to know the answer to: Was the imperial governor involved? The thought sent a chill down his spine. He had to get Astra back to the safety of Celtiboria. Immediately.

"Ark?" Shira was standing outside the door, motioning to Blackhawk.

He stepped out of the room, pushing the normally fully powered door shut and manually locking it. "What is it?"

"Sam's got the core disconnected. Ace, Doc, and Sarge are helping her get it out of the casing now." She spoke softly, even though she knew the closed door was soundproof. Shira Tarkus was suspicious of virtually everything and everyone she encountered. She always acted as if someone else was listening, trying to hurt the crew of the *Claw*—her family. Ace often teased her about it, but the Far Stars was a dangerous place, and she'd been right more often than she'd been wrong.

"Good. We've been here too long already." He glanced back through the reinforced hyperplastic door at the prisoners. "After the core's loaded, I want Sam to rig the reactor fuel lines to blow. Not the reactor itself, of course—I want to destroy this ship so it can't follow us, not vaporize the entire city." He didn't think New Vostok would be much of a loss to the universe, but that was a poor justification of genocide.

"I understand."

Blackhawk inclined his head toward the men in the cell. "When we're ready to go, we'll move these three to a safe distance and leave them. Let the locals deal with them."

Shira nodded. "Understood." Her voice was clipped, businesslike. She clearly thought he was making too much effort to save the prisoners. Blackhawk didn't have a doubt in his mind how Shira would have handled the imperial spies. He understood her; he even agreed, at least theoretically, and he didn't doubt they all deserved death. But as tough as Shira was, she didn't have the kind of blood on her hands Arkarin Blackhawk did. Even the cynical Shira Tarkus might find it difficult to be so coldly efficient if her soul bore the burdens his did.

"Arn's people are back, too," she went on. "They've got half a dozen big transports, and they're starting to load them up." She paused. "It looks like they're planning to get every weapon in the hold onto those ships."

Blackhawk frowned. "Maybe I shouldn't have brought them. They'll be lucky to get a good load of weapons and destroy the rest. If they stay here too long . . ." He let his words trail off. "Hell, we've already been here too long."

Blackhawk turned and checked the lock on the cell door. He wasn't about to underestimate a pack of imperial agents. "Let's go see Arn. Maybe I can talk some sense into him. I want to get that core loaded up and get the hell out of here as soon as we can."

"Arn, listen to me." Blackhawk and the rebel commander were standing next to the ship's access ramp. "We've already had more time than we could have dared to hope for, but it can't last. You've got to wrap things up and get the hell out of here."

The rebels had been working as quickly as they could, but the imperial ship's hold was packed with heavy crates of weapons and ammunition. They'd been working in near darkness, hauling the crates out by hand. Even Arn's overzealous revolutionaries weren't about to broadcast their presence with a bunch of lights.

"Captain Blackhawk, my forces have been virtually destroyed by Revolutionary Army units wielding these weapons. We are near to total defeat, and unless I can arm all my survivors, we still face extermination."

Blackhawk sighed softly. There were times he wondered how people survived anywhere. It was typical, he thought, that two groups of people who began a war together to fight for their freedom became the bitterest of enemies. He shook his head. It didn't surprise him, but he did feel a touch of sadness.

"Arn, you're not going to get anything done for your people if you stay here so long you all get killed and don't get any weapons back."

"You have my thanks, Captain Blackhawk, for your aid in securing this ship. I bid you and your people fortune on your journey, but we must do what we must." Arn had seen thousands of his men massacred, and all he could think about was getting the weapons and evening the score.

"Very well. Good luck to you as well." *You're going to need it,* he left unsaid. Blackhawk sighed and extended his hand. He realized Arn was on the verge of losing his sanity, and he suspected the exhausted revolutionary would be just as content to die here as to continue the fight. He'd seen his dreams for freedom dashed and his men massacred by the thousands. He was broken inside, pushing forward by momentum only. Blackhawk hated leaving him behind, but he had his own people to think about.

He turned and walked toward the transport. Von and Drake were carrying a crate of particle accelerator rifles toward the open hatch. Blackhawk had ordered his people to grab a few boxes of weapons for themselves, and they were carrying the last of it as he approached.

"Get that crate secured and you guys get settled." His eyes scanned the spaceport. "We're getting out of here in a few minutes."

"Yes, sir," they replied, almost in unison. Their voices were a little strained. A crate of particle accelerators was damned heavy.

Blackhawk walked back toward the airlock. Ace was standing there with Sarge. "On the truck, Sarge," Blackhawk said as he approached. "We're pulling out. Von and Drake are loading the last crate. I want you to get Ringo and Buck and get in." He saw the concerned look in the noncom's face. "Don't worry. We're leaving in a couple minutes, and Ace and I can keep watch until then."

"Yes, Captain." Sarge saluted, barely holding back a wince as he did. The fuser had closed up the wound, but there was still a lot of tissue damage that had to heal. He could use the arm, more or less, but it was going to be tender for a while.

Blackhawk watched him walk to the waiting transport, waving for Ringo and Buck to follow. They got there in time to help the others load the last box. He turned toward Ace. "Well, what do you say we get the hell out of . . ."

His head snapped around. His ears caught the sound before anyone else.

Multiple wheeled and tracked vehicles approaching from the south.

No shit, Blackhawk thought. Those were troop transports approaching. A lot of them. "Ace, I want you to get everyone on board that thing, and get the hell back to the *Claw*."

"What?" Ace stared back for a few seconds with a surprised look on his face. Then he heard the trucks. "No . . . Ark. I'm not leaving without you. None of us are."

"There's no time for an argument, Ace. They're too close. We need a diversion so you guys can get away." He pointed over his shoulder with his thumb. "Arn's guys don't have a clue how to use these weapons, but I can show them." He stared into Ace's eyes. "I'm serious. Go. Please."

"Ark . . ."

"Get that core back to the ship, Ace. If I'm not back when it's ready, get the hell out of here and get Astra back to Celtiboria." He reached out and grabbed his friend's shoulder. "I mean it, Ace. Give me your word. When the core's ready, you'll get Astra back to her father. Swear it to me."

He could see Ace wanted to argue, and he could see his friend's desperation about not being able to. *I'm sorry, my friend. But you know this is the right thing to do.*

"I promise, Ark," Ace croaked, his voice a miserable whisper. He returned Blackhawk's gaze. "You have my word."

"Thanks, Ace. I know I can count on you. And don't worry about me—you know I'm a survivor."

"Don't worry about a thing, Ark. I'll get her back home."

"Good. Now go. Get everybody out of here." He turned and spotted Arn standing next to the cargo ramp, looking out at the spaceport's perimeter, rifle in hand.

He began jogging toward the rebel commander. "Arn, get your men to crack open a couple of those crates. I've got about sixty seconds to show you guys how to use these things."

CHAPTER 19

THE TRANSPORT TORE DOWN THE NARROW BACK ROAD IN ALMOST total darkness, Katarina at the controls, pushing the lumbering truck to its limit as she raced back for the ship. Other than Blackhawk, she had the best night vision of anyone on the *Claw*, a virtual prerequisite for a professional assassin. But Blackhawk wasn't with them, of course. They'd all argued about leaving the captain behind, but Ace had shut them all down, repeating Blackhawk's orders and taking control, personally making sure they all got aboard.

All except Shira. She figured if Blackhawk was going to stay behind and create a diversion, he could use some help. The way she saw it, Blackhawk had entrusted Ace to make sure Astra Lucerne got off-planet and back to her father, not her. Blackhawk hadn't given her any orders, and as such, she hadn't made any promises. It might be a technicality, but she was determined to go with it. The captain needed somebody to watch his back.

And she'd be damned if she was going to leave Blackhawk alone with a bunch of half-beaten revolutionaries he'd known for less than three days.

She'd left with the rest of them, hopping onto the transport just before it pulled out. She knew Blackhawk well enough to be sure he'd have picked her up and put her on the truck himself if she'd told him she was staying behind. She ditched about two klicks from the spaceport, hopping out the rear hatch and making her way back to the spaceport.

I hope I make it back in time.

"Take it easy around those curves. This thing is fragile." Sam was shouting from the back of the transport. She was sitting on a pile of putrid garbage, and it looked like she was trying not to vomit as she struggled to hold the stolen core steady. It wasn't helping either goal when Katarina whipped the cumbersome vehicle around the twisting and pockmarked road.

Katarina ignored her and continued on. Ace glanced at her, then went back to scanning the area around them. They'd already had two firefights trying to get clear of the spaceport and the city. He agreed with Sam about Katarina's driving, but he also knew that getting the transport shot to pieces wasn't going to do the core any good either. They'd taken at least a dozen hits already, and if a lucky shot knocked the thing out, they were beyond screwed. The core was far too heavy and cumbersome to carry all the way back to the *Claw,* and the buggy was still kilometers away.

Katarina steered the truck along the dark street at breakneck speed. Ace was pretty sure she'd managed to keep them on the same road they'd taken on foot after hiding the buggy. He suspected she'd been well trained in memory enhancement techniques—as well as aggressive driving—when she was an adept at the Assassins' Guild on Sebastiani, though the regimen there was a closely guarded secret. Whatever the reason, she drove with utter confidence. The transport had headlamps, but she and Ace had agreed it was too risky. If there were patrols out, the lights would be visible for half a kilometer or more.

Ace was in the front cab of the transport next to Katarina. Ringo was sitting next to him, adjusting a bloody bandage wrapped around his leg. The soldier had taken a hit in the last firefight. Fortunately, it was a regular slug, not one of the imperial intelligence projectiles that had almost taken off Sarge's arm. It was a clean wound, but he'd lost a lot of blood. Doc did what he could on the spot then declared the best thing they could do was to get him to the ship as soon as possible.

Ace was quiet, deep in thought. He hated leaving Blackhawk behind, and his promise to do just that was tormenting him. Worse, he'd bullied the rest of the crew into coming back with him. Every one of them had argued against leaving the captain behind, and Ace had practically pushed them all into the transport. He was only doing what Blackhawk had asked, what he'd promised his friend he would do, but it still felt wrong.

I know it makes the most sense, but it still feels like fucking shit.

They drove down the winding road for another twenty minutes without running into any more enemy patrols. The terrain was starting to look familiar to Ace as well, and when they came up over a small rise they saw the guardhouse where they'd had their first encounter with the enemy on the way in.

"We're almost back to where we hid the buggy." Katarina's

voice was cold and unemotional, as usual, but Ace knew she was as troubled as the rest of the crew. She and Blackhawk enjoyed somewhat of a strange kinship. They seemed to understand each other in ways no one else did. Ace had thought the two were more than friends for a while, but it had been quite some time since he'd seen any signs of that, and he'd long assumed he had been wrong. Still, in her own detached way, Katarina was as devoted to Blackhawk as any of the crew. It manifested itself somewhat differently in the lone wolf personality of the professional assassin, but it was there nevertheless.

"Okay, pull off the road, and we'll see if we can find it." He turned back toward the rear compartment and yelled, "Sarge, we're back near the buggy. I'm going to go out and see if I can find it. Send a couple of your boys out to help me look." Ace turned to climb over Ringo toward the door, but he stopped and added, "And that doesn't mean you, Sarge. You stay the hell put." Doc had done a damned good job on the noncom's arm, but as long as they weren't in an emergency situation, Ace wanted him to rest.

He jumped out of the transport and took a look around. It was dark, the moons obscured by the heavy cloud cover. The storm hadn't really started yet, at least no more than some light drizzle, but it was dark as hell now. He had no idea how Katarina had kept the truck on the road, especially at the speed she'd been going.

Von and Drake came walking around from the back of the transport. The two soldiers had oddly amused looks on their faces. Ace caught the expressions and said, "Sarge?"

Von almost laughed, but he caught himself. "Yes, sir. He wasn't too happy about staying inside while we went out." Sarge was a soldier to the core, and he generally thought of Ace as

Blackhawk's second in command, despite the lack of a clear command structure on the *Claw*. He obviously hadn't liked Ace's order, but he obeyed it.

"You guys fan out to the right and the left. The buggy's around here somewhere." He handed each of them a flashlight. "Try not to use these unless you need them to get around. We don't want to advertise our presence any more than we have to."

"Yes, sir." They wandered off into the brush, moving carefully, feeling their way through the darkness. Ace frowned as he listened to each of them pushing forward with the grace of a megasauroid chasing its dinner. He knew they were trying to be quiet, which made it all the more astounding. Their skills were at their best in a firefight, not sneaking around the woods.

Ace took a few steps forward and chanced a quick look around with the flashlight. The ground was familiar—very familiar. The buggy was just a few meters forward, he was sure of it. He took a step forward and froze.

"It's some kind of armored vehicle, Lieutenant. It's bigger than anything I've ever seen."

Ace stood stone still, listening. The voices weren't familiar, and he knew a patrol had found the buggy. He was afraid the enemy soldiers had seen his light, but they continued as they were, clearly unalarmed.

He tried to sneak slowly forward to get an idea how many enemies they were facing when he remembered Von and Drake. He grabbed his small comm unit, pulling it up close to his face. He had to tell them to freeze before . . .

"Over here!" a voice shouted out of the darkness. "There's someone coming."

Fuck!

Ace could hear troops running through the brush and gruff

voices shouting back and forth. They were heading over to Von's position. Ace knew he had to do something, otherwise they'd overwhelm Von and take him out. He pulled the commlink up to his lips and pressed the button connecting to Katarina's unit. "Enemy troopers around the buggy. They heard Von. It's about to hit the fan." He was interrupted by the sounds of fire coming from his right. He could hear the familiar crack of Von's assault rifle and at least a half-dozen guns firing with a different pitch.

"Fuck," he muttered aloud this time. He held his rifle in front of him and pushed through the thick brush, spraying the area around the buggy with fire.

The flash lit the night sky as bright as a summer day. It only lasted an instant, barely long enough for the human brain to perceive it, but it was followed by another flash. Then another. Arn's men were firing away with the particle accelerators, trying to hold off the waves of attackers pushing toward the captured spy ship.

Blackhawk looked across the tarmac toward the approaching forces. He didn't have an accurate feel for what was out there, but he knew for sure it was a hell of a lot more than he had.

He stared at the enemy positions just outside the fence. They were formed up all along the edge of the landing pad, and they were trying to move around the flank of the defenders. The chain-link barrier was torn apart in a half-dozen places, where particle accelerator fire had ripped through. His normally excellent night vision was temporarily diminished by the repeated blinding flashes from the captured imperial weapons, and he was having trouble picking out the formations of enemy troopers. He knew there were a lot of them—the incoming fire alone told him that much.

He saw a vehicle moving slowly forward. It looked like some kind of APC or even a small tank. Whatever it was, it was bad news. It was coming around from his left, on the flank of Arn and his people. He reached down and picked up the particle accelerator rifle lying at his feet, hoisting it into firing position.

He stared across the field, bringing the small targeting screen to bear on the enemy vehicle. He flipped the arming switch, and he could hear the high-pitched whine as power fed into the firing circuits. He adjusted his angle until the armored vehicle was directly in the small crosshairs. He held his breath and tightened his finger slowly on the trigger.

The particle accelerator sent a blast of highly charged protons ripping through the atmosphere at relativistic velocity. The blast smashed into the enemy tank, delivering an enormous amount of energy to the target. The particles ionized the air they passed through, creating a blinding white light lasting the barest fraction of a second but still perceptible.

The shot was a direct hit, and the vehicle was wracked first by a small explosion then—a few seconds later—by a larger blast as its magazine exploded. Its burning remains careened off at an angle away from the ship, still moving but clearly out of control. Blackhawk brought the weapon down slowly and let it slide to the ground as he pulled the assault rifle from his back. Just using the imperial gun made him uncomfortable. Too many bad memories. It had done its job, but now he needed a tool better suited to the task.

The particle accelerators were terror weapons, designed to instill uncontrollable fear in anyone facing troops so armed. On a planet like Saragossa, where many of the soldiers were armed with ancient single-shot breechloaders, the flash of an imperial particle accelerator seemed like the judgment of the gods.

Anyone facing a force armed with such fearsome weapons was immediately demoralized. Imperial-armed troops went into battle against enemies already half defeated by their own fears.

Blackhawk stood under the ship, taking cover behind a heavy structural support. He had his rifle set for single shots, and he was firing steadily. The spaceport was lit by several fires, as warehouses along the perimeter caught fire from poorly aimed shots. Blackhawk's eyes were sharp, and the slightest bit of light was enough for him to focus on a target. He squeezed his finger again and again, and each time he did, one of the attacking soldiers fell to the ground.

He glanced back toward the rear of the ship. Arn's men were having more trouble. Most of them had discarded their shoddy old rifles for particle accelerators, but they had trouble aiming the heavy weapons. Blackhawk had shouted out a few basic instructions just before the fighting started, but they were still struggling. The rate of fire was slow, and half the shots went wildly off-target. Blackhawk would have encouraged them to use their own weapons instead, but most of them had been armed with bolt-action rifles that belonged in a museum, not a battlefield.

The attackers weren't better soldiers than Arn's people, but they were armed with decent rifles they knew how to use—and there were ten times as many of them. They clearly weren't well trained, but they were coming on relentlessly. The position was close to being overrun.

> This is an optimum time to retreat. It appears the southwest approach is undefended. You have a high-probability chance of reaching the perimeter of the spaceport unnoticed.

He'd seen the opening too. But running away and leaving Arn's men to die didn't sit well with him. He'd only known the rebels a short time, but they seemed honorable. They'd done everything he'd asked of them, and he'd enticed them into the raid with the promise of securing advanced weapons for themselves. Fleeing now and leaving them all to the enemy seemed like the basest form of cowardice. He didn't know if he could do anything to save them, but he wouldn't abandon them.

Blackhawk pulled a clip out of the small sack hanging at his waist and snapped it in place. His deadly accurate fire had cleared the area in front of him, and the troops he hadn't hit had steered clear of the death zone, swinging around on wide arcs to both sides.

He spared another look toward Arn and his people. At least a third of them were down, and the rest were trying to take cover behind the trucks lined up next to the ship. He was about to move toward them when he heard a new sound: automatic fire, heavier and faster than an assault rifle.

Arn's men started falling in clumps as the enemy autocannon roared into action. The projectiles tore right through the light metal plate of the civilian transports and into the rebels crouching behind.

The rebels had fought bravely, but now they began to break. One by one they started to run, dropping their weapons and fleeing for their lives. Arn shouted at them, called them back to their positions, but Blackhawk had seen enough broken combat formations to know Arn's men were beyond rallying. It was too late. His men had been battered and demoralized for too long. Their will was spent.

The rebel leader was standing behind one of the partially loaded transports, holding a particle accelerator as he yelled to his fleeing soldiers. Three men stood with him, his staunchest and most dedicated comrades. Unlike their leader, who was still shouting to the fleeing soldiers, the other men had given up on the routers, and they were firing at the attacking forces.

"Arn, you've got to get out of here!" Blackhawk shouted to the rebel commander, turning and making his way toward the rear of the ship as he did. He couldn't help but feel responsible for Arn. The man had made his own decision to stay behind, but Blackhawk hadn't tried too hard to change his mind. He'd used the rebels as a distraction, a diversion to allow his own people to escape. He stayed behind himself, partially to make sure the fight lasted long enough for Ace to get the others safely away from the spaceport. But he'd also felt a responsibility to assist the rebels, to try to help them get away with at least some of the weapons they needed.

Arn turned and looked over at Blackhawk. "We can't leave without the weapons." His voice was raw, frantic. "We have to get the trucks out of here."

Blackhawk could see the rebel commander unraveling quickly. He'd seen it before—more times than he could count— and he knew there was no way to reach him, that rational arguments would be to no avail.

Too stubborn to not try again, though. He could almost hear Ace's voice agreeing with him.

He crouched down and moved back toward the remaining rebels, ducking behind one of the landing gears as a spray of projectiles swept the area. He knew he had to make a break for it soon, whether or not he could get Arn and his people to follow. *Just a minute,* he told himself. *I'll stay just one more minute, and then I'll slip away.*

His head whipped around, back toward the enemy positions.

There was heavy fire, but there was something different about it, a new sound. Arn and his men didn't notice anything, but Blackhawk's acute hearing zeroed right in on it. It was coming from behind the attackers . . . and it wasn't targeted at Blackhawk and Arn's people. Someone was attacking the Revolutionary Army units besieging the spaceport. And they were using high-tech assault rifles, not the archaic things the revolutionaries were firing.

Now's our chance. He had no idea who else would be getting into this fight, and he didn't care. He had a fleeting concern it was his people disobeying his orders, but the sound of the gunfire was different. They were good weapons, but not as good as the extremely high-end stuff he'd bought for his crew. But it didn't really matter. What mattered was that they had the distraction they needed to make an escape.

He leaped forward, scrambling back to where Arn stood behind one of the trucks. "Arn, listen to me. We've got to make a break for it. *Right. Now.*" He gestured off to the southwest. "There's an opening over there. If we can make it across the field, we can slip into the woods outside the city."

Arn's head snapped around. "And leave the weapons? Even the ones we have loaded? That's ridiculous." He was wounded in the shoulder, but he was ignoring it completely. His eyes were wild, almost glazed over, and Blackhawk knew the long-suffering rebel leader had lost his sanity. Arn turned toward his remaining troops. "Each of you get on one of the transports. We'll take what we've got loaded and make a run for it."

Blackhawk exhaled hard and stared at Arn. "You'll never make it out in these things. Hell, I doubt they even run at this point. But if they do, they'll just be rolling targets. On foot, we have a chance to survive—to fight another day."

"We can't leave the weapons!" Arn turned to his men. "Go!"

Blackhawk could only stand there as the rebels ran to the transports, climbing inside the cabs and trying to get them started. He was frustrated, as he so often was when dealing with foolishness. But he would waste no more time with these fools. The sounds of fighting along the enemy line were becoming louder. Something unexpected was going on. He had no idea what it was, but it offered a perfect chance to escape, and Blackhawk was going to take it.

One of the trucks roared to life, its engine miraculously still functional despite the dozens of bullet holes marking its sides. The others were dead, too badly damaged to run, and the men inside raced to join their comrade. Blackhawk almost yelled to them as they ran by, but he stopped himself. It was pointless.

Now it was time to save himself.

"Blackhawk, come on!" Arn yelled from the running transport.

Blackhawk sighed. "I'm going to head out on foot." *Like you should too.*

He turned to slip around behind the ship. He'd originally intended to destroy the vessel, and all the weapons Arn's people hadn't taken, but there was no time now. He had to get moving or he'd never make it. Whatever was going on in the enemy rear, it was the chance he needed.

He heard the roar of the transport's engine as the heavy vehicle began to move across the tarmac toward the access road. It had only traveled a few meters when the enemy concentrated on it, raking it with autocannon and small-arms fire. Blackhawk sighed but continued to move toward the end of the spy ship. He was going to walk around the back of the vessel and slip off into the darkness on the far side.

He'd only taken a few steps when a lucky shot found the transport's fuel tank. The vehicle exploded in a massive fireball, sending chunks of debris flying in all directions.

Blackhawk reacted quickly, ducking down and putting a hand up to protect his face . . . but he was too late; he had stayed too long. A heavy chunk of metal slammed into his head. He staggered back, trying vainly to stay on his feet. He struggled to retain consciousness even as he fell to the ground and the darkness took him.

Ace was spraying the area with automatic fire. To an untrained eye, he was firing wildly, but his shooting was actually quite precise, and he'd taken out at least four of the enemy already. His eyes were darting around, trying to get an idea how big a force he was facing, but it was just too hard to see in the darkness. Maybe it was just a squad, but for all he knew he was up against a battalion.

He stopped firing. He couldn't see any more targets in the immediate area, but he could hear the fighting off to his right. He moved away from the buggy, back the way he'd come. He knew Von was in a nasty firefight, and he didn't intend to get shot by one of his own comrades. It was costing precious seconds, but it was the only way to get to Von without charging through his firing arc.

He could feel the leaves and small branches slapping against him as he raced through the woods in almost total darkness. He glanced down at a small device in his hand, a reader that homed in on Von's comm unit. He winced as he slapped his arm hard into a tree, but he kept going, running to his friend's aid.

He saw a muzzle flash ahead, then another. "Von," he said in a hushed tone. "Is that you?" He knew it was, but he still wanted the verification. Walking into an enemy in the dark would be an embarrassing way to die.

"It's me, boss." The soldier's deep voice was tense, distracted. "There's bogies all around here. They're trying to get behind me."

Ace was close enough to hear Von's heavy breathing. "I'm here," he whispered as he ran up to the hulking warrior. "Swing around. We'll go back to back." Ace turned and faced the opposite direction, leaning back until he felt Von behind him. They were trapped, almost surrounded, but now they covered each other's blind spots. They'd hold out longer this way.

If they'd been by themselves in these woods, Ace knew they'd have been done for. But they weren't alone, and it was only a few seconds before they started hearing gunfire from the direction of the road. It was a familiar sound, the R-111 assault rifles Sarge and his boys carried, the same weapon Von was firing right behind Ace's ear.

"Watch your fire, Von. We've got friendlies out there too." Ace was firing off to his left. He could hear enemy troops moving around the flank, making a lot of noise doing it. He was thankful the Saragossan revolutionaries were such amateur soldiers. If it had been Sarge and his boys sneaking around their flank in these woods—or God forbid, someone like Katarina or Shira—he and Von would already be dead.

He could hear the friendly fire getting closer. It was splitting up, branching to both sides of them. Ace knew Sarge's people had the same scanners he did. It was a damned good thing too, because he couldn't see a thing in the thick blackness, and he knew it was no better for his comrades.

"Von, hold up." Ace pulled back his own rifle. Sarge and his boys had cleared all the enemy in his field of fire, and he and Von were more likely to hit friendlies than anything else now.

He was watching the small monitor as Sarge, Ringo, and Buck slipped around them, hunting the rest of the enemy forces. He could hear more gunfire, a mix of sounds at first, then only the staccato tone of the assault rifles Sarge's crew carried. Then the shooting died completely. After a few minutes, he could hear someone approaching. He snapped up his rifle, but a glance at the scanner confirmed it was a friendly.

"Ace, Von?" It was Sarge's voice calling to them from the darkness.

"Yeah, Sarge," Ace answered, sighing in relief. "And thanks for the assist." He took a step forward and slapped the big man on the shoulder. "Let's get back to the buggy and get the hell out of here." He turned and started to walk toward the armored vehicle.

Sarge paused, looking off into the wood behind where Ace had been standing. "She's still out there, sir."

"Who?" Ace stopped and turned. Then it came to him. "Katarina?"

Sarge nodded. "Yes, sir. A couple of the enemy troopers got away from us. She went after them."

Ace felt a shiver go down his spine. He didn't know anything about the men trying to get away, and they had attacked him, made him an enemy. But he still couldn't help but feel sympathy for two amateur soldiers being stalked in the woods at night by Katarina Venturi. The assassin had been studying the art of tracking and killing since she'd taken her first steps, and she wasn't about to let live enemies escape to warn their comrades. "A couple you say?" He tried to stifle a small laugh. "This won't take long. She'll be back shortly. Let's get the buggy started."

He was right. They'd barely gotten the buggy's hatch open when Katarina glided silently from the densest part of the woods. "Are you ready to leave?" Her voice was calm, as if she'd been sitting under a tree and waiting for them.

"We're ready." Ace turned and looked back at her. "I don't think we should waste time trying to move the core, so you bring the transport back, and I'll drive the buggy."

She nodded silently and slid into the shadows, back toward the heavy vehicle. Ace felt another shiver, a bigger one this time. He was glad he and Katarina were on the same side. Damned glad.

CHAPTER 20

KERGEN VOS STOOD IN FRONT OF A MASSIVE WINDOW, STARING out at the formal gardens behind the Capitol. It was like every other part of the imperial establishment in the Far Stars: all show, no substance. The magnificence of the compound was a show of wealth and opulence, but it was also useless. No one in the sector respected imperial power, and marble halls and fancy gardens weren't effective substitutes for fear and obedience.

Vos had vowed to change all that, but so far his efforts had been frustrated by a lack of reliable subordinates. He tried to imagine himself relying on someone as useless and incompetent as the ka'al back in the empire proper. It was preposterous. But out on the edge of human habitation, there wasn't much to choose from, and he was desperately short of options.

He'd purged the worst of the imperial staffers when he first arrived, but even the ones he'd kept on had proven to be immensely disappointing. Generations of poor leadership had built a culture of failure and entitlement. They demanded the prestige of imperial position, but they lacked the skill and power that gave those trappings any meaning. The miserable sycophants groveled in his presence, but they were insufferably arrogant and officious when dealing with anyone from the independent worlds. Arrogance and incompetence made a poor pairing, and Vos was tired of his own staff making his job harder.

Vos's plans were moving forward, but they'd been slowed by a lack of capable operatives. The team he'd brought with him was performing well, as always. But alone, they were too few to impose imperial control over a hundred fiercely independent worlds, meaning he was forced to rely on a legion of mostly incompetent bureaucrats for much of what had to be done. But it was Tarn Belgaren he was thinking about now. He'd used the petty monarch and his minions to kidnap Astra Lucerne from Celtiboria because none of his imperial assets stationed there were capable of seeing it done. If he'd had a competent intelligence force in place on the planet, she would be on Galvanus Prime already—and he'd have some leverage with Augustin Lucerne. Instead, he didn't have her at all.

In spite of his lack of reliable subordinates, Vos was reasonably content with the progress so far. He had schemes in the works on a dozen worlds, with more in the planning stages. Slowly, but surely, he would undermine the independence of the Far Stars. He knew there would be problems along the way—Augustin Lucerne the one he was most worried about. That's why he'd formulated the abduction plot in the first place.

By all accounts, Astra was the only thing Lucerne cared about other than his quest to unite the Far Stars. Vos had intended to use her as a bargaining chip to control Lucerne, or at least to restrict the brilliant general's influence to his home world. He didn't think Celtiboria's iron marshal would yield to him fully—even to save his only daughter—but if Vos's threats could keep his forces on Celtiboria instead of launching their push for confederation, that would be enough of a victory. If the rest of the sector fell, so too would Celtiboria eventually—even with Augustin Lucerne leading its armies.

An uncontained Lucerne was a grave risk to his plans. Celtiboria was the most populous of the Primes, potentially the strongest planet in the sector, but centuries of disunity and internal conflict had diminished its power and influence with the other worlds. Now that the planet had been forged into a single nation, though—led by perhaps the greatest military commander in the history of the Far Stars—the previously untapped strength of Celtiboria could become a problem. Quickly.

Vos knew, if anyone could unify the Far Stars to resist imperial encroachment, it was Augustin Lucerne. His first thought had been assassination, but Lucerne was constantly surrounded by his soldiers. Besides, the imperial establishment in the Far Stars was far too weak to undertake a mission of that magnitude with any certainty of success. A botched assassination would be a disaster, especially if imperial involvement was discovered. It would do Lucerne's work for him, scaring the other worlds into his fledgling confederation.

Even a successful assassination would leave an uncertain future. Lucerne had many able lieutenants and, if the succession was quick and uncontested, the overall situation might

remain largely the same. The Celtiborian army would go ber-
serk if they thought imperial forces had murdered Lucerne,
and they would demand vengeance for their fallen leader. A
campaign intended to unify the sector might become a crusade instead, targeted not at the neutral worlds, but at Galvanus Prime itself. The imperial capital had been considered
off-limits for centuries. The worlds of the Far Stars laughed at
imperial claims of suzerainty, but none of them wanted to risk
outright provocation of an imperial military response. But Vos
knew Lucerne's men wouldn't care. They would be blinded by
rage, lusting for revenge, and they would come for him, damn
the consequences.

It was a scenario he'd decided he couldn't risk, at least not
until he could beef up imperial military power in the sector.
Besides, controlling Lucerne would be more useful than eliminating him. Celtiborian strength could be used to further
imperial ambitions as well as thwart them if Vos was able to
influence it effectively.

Which came back, once more, to Astra. She was the key to
that plan. He knew Augustin Lucerne was a hard man, not easily broken. But when Vos began sending pieces of his daughter back to him, he would see how tough the old soldier truly
was. By all accounts, Astra Lucerne was a great beauty, but if
her father didn't go along, she wouldn't be for long. Vos wasn't
a sadist by any accounts, but he certainly wouldn't hesitate to
employ whatever brutality furthered his efforts.

Sadist? No. Pragmatist? Definitely.

Of course, that all assumed the ka'al's people recovered
her from her rescuers and delivered her to Galvanus Prime.
Unharmed. Astra's death would only drive Lucerne to his quest
with even more relentless determination than before, making

Vos's plans more difficult. And if the marshal discovered imperial involvement in her death, Vos would find himself in direct conflict with the greatest warrior in the Far Stars. He wasn't ready for military confrontation yet, and certainly not against Lucerne.

No, he needed Astra alive as leverage against her father. He'd already sworn to dismember every crewman in Tarn Belgaren's fleet if the fools ended up killing her instead of grabbing her back. And he'd roast the ka'al himself over a slow fire and see how long it took to melt all that fat off his body.

Vos was willing to admit he'd take a certain sadistic delight in that particular activity.

Suddenly, the doors swung open and the wardens entered, rapping their staffs against the polished stone floor. The chamberlain hobbled in after them, bowing as deeply as his ancient back allowed. "General Wilhelm to see you, Excellency." The voice was old and faltering, but Vos had to admit the ancient functionary could still manage to project it with considerable volume.

"Send him in, you fool." Vos was already walking toward his audience chair. "As I've told you repeatedly, General Wilhelm is to be admitted without delay."

The chamberlain bowed again, so slowly that Vos longed for a weapon so he could put the fool out of his misery.

He sat down with considerable force, watching as Mak Wilhelm walked swiftly into the room.

Wilhelm was a man of action like Vos. The two had served together for many years, and they were as close to friends as two cold-blooded reptiles could become, but Vos's latest promotion had been a significant leap, and it had put added distance between their stations. An imperial governorship was a lofty position, even if it was in the Far Stars. Vos was technically a member of the imperial nobility now, if one with a decidedly uninspiring pedigree.

The general stepped toward the dais and bowed. Vos waited a few seconds, as short a time as propriety allowed. "Rise, General." He spoke clearly, waving his arms to dismiss the door wardens. They rapped their staves on the floor and spun on their heels to leave.

He sat quietly, waiting until he heard the immense double doors slam shut. Finally, he and Wilhelm were alone. The general looked edgy and uncomfortable, even more than he usually did in his dress scarlet and whites.

"What is it, General?" Vos spoke softly now that they were alone.

"Agent Sand's report from Saragossa is overdue, Excellency." There was concern in Wilhelm's voice.

"He cannot be much behind schedule." Vos rubbed his hand across his face. "Agent Sand reported in just before he landed, General. That can't have been a week ago."

"Six days, Excellency. But he was expected to report again yesterday, immediately after lifting off from the planet." Wilhelm paused. "Agent Sand is extremely reliable, Excellency. It is not like him to miss a scheduled report."

"Perhaps he was delayed in transferring the weapons. You know how difficult these wogs can be. His mission also has a diplomatic dimension, as you well know. Maybe the Saragossan revolutionaries were slow to offload his shipment." Vos gazed down at Wilhelm. "I think we can wait another day or two before becoming unduly concerned."

Wilhelm nodded. "Yes, Excellency."

Vos could see Wilhelm was still troubled. "What is it, Mak? We've worked together long enough to cut the foolishness. What is bothering you?"

"It's just a feeling, Excellency." He paused. "Saragossa is quite close to Kalishar . . . forgive me, Excellency. I have nothing specific to report. It is simply my paranoia."

"Your feelings are enough for me to consider, Mak. I have known your paranoia to be correct more often than it is in error, my friend. I ignore it at my own peril. What would you propose we do?"

"Well, Excellency, I don't know what we can do except send another ship to Saragossa to investigate."

Vos sat quietly for a few seconds. He took Wilhelm's concern seriously, but resources were tight. He was hesitant to send another precious spy ship and its crew to the edge of the frontier without something more solid. Anyone he sent all the way to Saragossa would be unavailable if he received word on Blackhawk's location somewhere closer to Celtiboria.

"Let us wait another day, General. If Agent Sand has still not reported, we will send a ship to investigate." He was considering who to dispatch, but he came up blank. All his reliable people were committed to other missions. "However, I'm afraid I am at quite a loss as to whom to send. Our personnel are stretched thin right now, as you know." He had operatives all over the Far Stars, working on a large number of initiatives. Astra Lucerne's abduction was only one plan of many he had in the works.

"With your leave, Excellency, I will go myself. The mission will likely be short, and I will be back in less than three weeks at full thrust each way. In addition, Excellency, I think my presence in the area might be of some use in . . . ah . . . motivating the ka'al's men. With your permission, I will follow up on their search efforts while I am there."

Vos nodded slowly. His first instinct had been to say no. Wilhelm was his most trusted adviser, and he was hesitant to do without the general just to send him on a seemingly routine mission. But Wilhelm was right. Belgaren's people needed closer supervision if they were going to recapture Astra Lucerne. And there was no one better suited to the job than Mak Wilhelm. "Very well, General. You may make your preparations. If we have not heard from Agent Sand by this time tomorrow, you may go to Saragossa."

Wilhelm bowed again. "Thank you, Excellency. If I'm dismissed, I will go and prepare *Garavin* for the journey, in case she is needed." *Garavin* was Wilhelm's personal vessel, an enhanced spy ship with an upgraded weapons suite.

"Very well, General." Vos nodded slowly toward his second in command. He pressed the small button at his side, sending a signal to the chamberlain to open the doors.

Wilhelm turned and marched across the floor as the wardens opened the doors and stood to the side. "And, General?" Vos called to him across the room.

Wilhelm turned to face the governor. "Yes, Excellency?"

"You are authorized to take whatever action is necessary to ensure the maximum effort from Belgaren's people. And I mean *whatever* action you deem fit. If you feel the ka'al is not providing the appropriate level of cooperation in this matter, you are to proceed to Kalishar. You will have the ka'al killed and replace him with his ablest lieutenant."

"Yes, Excellency." Wilhelm spun around on his heels and headed for the door.

CHAPTER 21

SHIRA CROUCHED DOWN ON THE PERIMETER OF THE SPACEPORT, hidden in the overgrown brush, watching as a group of soldiers swarmed into the area. She scanned them with her usual attention to detail. Their uniforms didn't look like the local manner of dress, and they were wearing high-tech body armor, not the kind of thing she imagined was common on Saragossa, even seven years into a bloody revolution. They looked like a professional crew, not the amateur revolutionary soldiers they'd encountered so far.

She'd seen Blackhawk go down, and she'd been ready to bolt across the field to him, when at least fifty men came running across the tarmac toward the spy ship. Her body was tense, her legs ready to spring forward. Every fiber of her being wanted to run to Blackhawk, to see if he was still alive and to help him if he was wounded. But she knew there was no way she'd make it across that open ground. It was too far, and the light from the burning transports destroyed any chance of sneaking up.

Shira was normally focused like a machine on the job at hand, but hiding in the brush while Blackhawk lay wounded—or dead—surrounded by enemies made her feel sick. There was a fearsome rage inside her, struggling to break through the wall of cold discipline she'd so painstakingly erected over the years. Like it usually did for her, though, rationality prevailed. She had to stay alive to help Blackhawk. Running across the tarmac now and probably getting herself killed might feel heroic, but she realized it actually lessened her chances to help the captain. He needed her reasoned calm now, her intelligence, her focus. Which meant waiting for the right opportunity.

The firefight to the south was over. The Revolutionary Army soldiers who had attacked the ship had themselves been taken in the flank. She had no real intel on who these new arrivals were, but it was obvious they were well armed and drilled as well as superbly equipped. Probably some group of mercs working for the nobles. The new attackers had driven off the revolutionaries, and now they were advancing cautiously toward the ship.

Toward Blackhawk.

Shira lay down slowly, moving her rifle out in front of her. It was the same weapon Sarge and his boys used, but hers had a sniper's scope on it. She watched as the soldiers reached the ship, focusing mostly on the area around Blackhawk. If any of those bastards looked like they were going to finish off Blackhawk, she was going to take the fucker down—consequences be damned.

She watched as they set up a cordon around the ship,

posting guards at all the approaches. They were well-trained military; she was sure of that now. Their movements were perfect—quick, smooth, and right out of the tactical manual. She couldn't imagine any of the rebel forces on Saragossa were so well drilled, and she decided it had to be a merc team. *Probably here to grab the weapons for themselves.*

A small squad moved cautiously up the cargo ramp and onto the ship, with more teams deploying around the disabled trucks, searching methodically for any threats. It took them a few minutes to secure the area, and before they were done, one of their team walked out of the ship leading a group of three prisoners.

Shira watched through her scope as a man walked over and spoke to the men guarding the prisoners. For an instant, she wondered if she should put the three imperials down, but she decided it wasn't worth giving herself away. The prisoners didn't know anything except a small group had seized the ship, and they certainly didn't have any specific information on Blackhawk or the *Claw*.

The man facing the imperials began questioning them, and Shira could see he was becoming frustrated. She guessed he was an officer, but his kit looked just like those of the rest of the soldiers, more evidence that this was a crack military unit. Experienced officers knew they were sniper bait, and they tried to blend in with the rest of their forces. Amateur officers tended to advertise their rank to anyone who was looking.

It looked like the officer was about to get aggressive with the prisoners when his head turned in Blackhawk's direction. Shira whipped the gun back toward the captain's position. Two of the soldiers were standing over him, rifles pointed down. They'd been checking to make sure the casualties were all dead, but now they were standing over his motionless body. One of them knelt down and rolled Blackhawk onto his back while the other stood fast, his rifle at the ready.

Shira felt a rush of hope along with the tension. At least Blackhawk was still alive. They wouldn't have paused if he'd just been another dead body. Now she had to make sure he stayed alive. She angled her rifle slightly, settling the sights on the standing man's head. Her finger tensed slightly on the trigger. Another bit of pressure, and the soldier's head would explode—and she would be in the fight of her life . . .

She hesitated, releasing the pressure on the trigger slightly.

The troopers wouldn't have called over the officer if they'd just been indiscriminately killing the wounded. Blackhawk had a better chance as a prisoner than he would if she started a hopeless firefight. She needed to be ready; she wasn't about to let these soldiers finish him off. But she decided to wait and see what happened.

The buggy veered hard off the road, kicking up a huge cloud of dust as it raced overland toward the *Claw*. Ace knew the distortion field would be up, but he had the coordinates, and he knew the ship was just a couple klicks ahead. He was trying to stay focused on the task at hand, but his mind kept drifting back to Blackhawk. Was he on his way back now? Or was he . . .

No, Ace thought, *I need to put that out of my mind now. Ark's a survivor. He'll be fine.*

Katarina was right behind in the giant transport. The stolen truck wasn't as durable or well protected as the buggy, but there hadn't been time to move the core to the armored vehicle. The core was heavy and fragile, and it was absolutely vital they get it back to the *Claw* in one piece. After the firefights they'd had trying to get away from the city, the last thing Ace wanted to do was wait around and see who else showed up.

Ace flipped on the forward lights. It was too damned dark to go racing around off the road. It wouldn't serve any purpose to slam the buggy into a tree or roll it in a ditch. *Besides,* he thought, *it's been three hundred klicks since we've seen any enemy troops, and in a minute we'll be back at the ship.*

He pulled out his comm unit. "Lucas, this is Ace. We've got the core and we're almost back. Get the cargo hatch open." He hadn't risked using the comm unit before. Blackhawk had gotten them sophisticated equipment, and it was unlikely the Saragossans had anything that could zero in on their communications. But he hadn't expected to find imperial weapons here either, so he'd decided not to take any chances.

"Got it, Ace. Dropping the field now." There was relief in Lucas's voice, and excitement at the prospect of getting off Saragossa. "Lowering the hatch."

Ace frowned. The cheerfulness in Lucas's tone ripped at his insides. *He doesn't know yet,* he thought. *He thinks the captain's with us.* He almost said something, but he caught himself. There was time enough to tell him in person. He knew Lucas wouldn't take it any better than the others, but what he really dreaded was telling Astra Lucerne. She wasn't going to want to leave without Blackhawk, he knew that much for sure.

He saw a faint shimmering ahead, the *Claw*'s distortion field deactivating. Lucas had turned on one of the exterior lights, and Ace could see the ship clearly, sitting right there where there had been nothing an instant before. Ace didn't begin to understand the inner workings of the field, but it was damned sure a handy device to have. He had no idea where it had come from, and he'd never seen another one like it. It was just another mysterious thing Blackhawk had managed to turn up.

Ace pulled the buggy up alongside the *Claw*, leaving room for Katarina to back the transport up to the cargo hatch. He climbed out and jumped down to the ground. Lucas was already walking over. Ace felt his stomach tighten. He wasn't going to be able to put off telling him about Blackhawk. It had taken all he had to tell the others and get them loaded up and ready to go. Now he had to deal with Lucas and the Twins.

And Astra Lucerne . . .

"Ace!" Lucas trotted over toward the buggy. "So you guys actually managed to get it?" He had a broad smile on his face. "You just snuck in there and stole their hyperdrive core from under their noses." His eyes caught Ace's and his smile faded away. Katarina was walking over from the other transport, and Sarge alongside her. They all had the same grim expressions.

"What's wrong, Ace?" Lucas looked around, watching everyone pile out of the two vehicles. "Where's the skipper?"

"Don't worry, Lucas," Ace said, even as he struggled to keep his own worries hidden. "He stayed behind with Arn's people, but he should be back any time." He wished he believed that, but after the resistance they'd run into, he couldn't imagine the road was still open. Blackhawk may have escaped on foot, but then he'd have over three hundred kilometers to cover, with no food or water . . . and plenty of adversaries.

Lucas stared at Ace then at Sarge. He didn't look like he was buying it. "There's more to it than that, isn't there." It wasn't a question.

"Ark?" Astra came running out of the airlock. She looked around quickly and raced up to Ace. "Where is Ark?"

"He's still with the rebels, Astra," Ace said. "He'll be here soon. He sent us ahead with the core."

She stared back at him for a second, then she stepped back and frowned. He could tell she was suspicious. "What's going on, Ace?"

"He's with Arn and his people, Astra. He felt responsible for leading them into the operation, and he wanted to make sure they were okay." It wasn't a lie, not strictly speaking. Not that Ace had a problem with lying when he had to. He was the closest thing the *Claw* had to a confidence man, and he'd tricked his way out of more than one tight spot. But he knew Astra Lucerne was smart as hell, and naturally suspicious too. It was going to take everything he had to fool her, but the last thing he needed was for her to march off in search of Blackhawk. He'd have the Twins restrain her if he had to, but he much preferred a little trickery to a lot of brute force. One way or the other, he'd made a promise to Ark, and he was going to see it done.

She gave him a hard stare, but he didn't give out a clue. Ace Graythorn had the best poker face in half the systems in the Far Stars, and he looked back at her with nothing but sincerity in his eyes. "He'll be back soon, Astra. But we've got to get the core installed so we're ready to get the hell out of here when he does."

She nodded. "Okay." She took a shallow breath. "That sounds like something he'd do."

Ace wasn't sure she was completely convinced, but she wasn't going off the rails at least, and he'd take that for the moment. He had work to do. They really needed to get the core installed and get the *Claw* off Saragossa. Then he'd worry about getting Astra to leave without Ark. He suspected he'd need some fresh trickery for that. *Who knows—maybe I won't. Maybe Ark will be back before we're ready to lift off.*

And maybe I'll inherit a diamond mine from my bastard father.

Even if Blackhawk got away clean and somehow made it through the countryside with no supplies, it would take days to reach the Claw's position on foot . . . if he could find it at all. And they didn't have days. They'd kicked a hornet's nest, and the revolutionaries would sooner or later send search parties this way. The *Claw* had to lift off as soon as Sam could install the core, and Ace knew that meant leaving Blackhawk behind.

"If you'll excuse me, Astra, I've got to see to getting the core aboard." He saw the Twins walking down the cargo hatch, and he waved. "I need you guys to help Sam haul the core down to engineering." The thing was heavy, but he was half certain the Twins could carry a small asteroid between them. He waited for them to walk over, then headed toward the big transport.

He almost stopped dead about five meters away. He'd been in the buggy for five hours, and he'd almost forgotten the stench of the transport. He had an impulse to give Shira a hard time again about stealing a garbage truck, and it just reminded him that she wasn't there either. Whatever Blackhawk was going through, Shira was probably in the same boat. Ace and Shira didn't appear to get along very well, but that was all show. The pointed barbs tossed back and forth, the constant petty competitions—none of it meant anything when things got tough. They'd always had each other's backs. He realized he was just as worried about Shira as he was Blackhawk. Unfortunately he didn't have time to think about either of them at the moment. He had a job to do.

"Sam," he shouted. "The Twins are going to carry that thing to engineering and help you get it in place."

She walked around from behind the transport. "It may not be that easy, Ace. That 'thing' is a hell of a lot more advanced than the one we had before."

Ace could tell she was nervous. He tried to think of what Blackhawk would tell her. "Sam, nobody knows their way around the guts of a spaceship like you. And it's damned certain you're the top expert on this miserable rock." He smiled. "I know you can do it. Ark knows you can do it. We all know . . . so now, you've just got to go down there and do it.

"And you've got to do it quickly."

Ace wanted the *Claw* off-planet as quickly as possible. He was concerned about the revolutionaries finding them, but that's not what was worrying him the most. What bothered him the most was Astra Lucerne. He thought he had her under control for the moment, but he knew she was a ticking time bomb. If she figured out Blackhawk wasn't coming with them, he'd never get her to go along, not without shackles. He'd chain her up if he had to, but even Ace Graythorn found that prospect a bit daunting.

"General, we found one still alive." The sergeant's voice was crisp, professional, but there was a hint of surprise there too. "He is dressed differently than the others."

Carano had been standing opposite the prisoners, his frustration growing exponentially as they ignored his questions and stood silently. Carano wasn't in the mood for bullshit. He'd planned a quick snatch-and-grab job, but he found himself facing half a battalion of Revolutionary Army troops instead. The spaceport had been shot to hell before his people arrived, and they'd come upon a firefight already under way. He had no idea what was going on, but he damned sure intended to find out.

One thing was clear: someone had gotten here before his people. The disabled transports were half loaded with high-tech weaponry, and there were crates lying all over the tarmac. He didn't have much hard info, but from the looks of it, the splinter rebels had made their own unsuccessful attempt to grab the imperial weapons.

"Keep them right here." He stared into the eyes of one of the prisoners as he snapped out the order. "I will be back in a minute." He turned toward the sergeant who had called him. "I'll be right there.

"Sergeant Riktor!" He called out to another member of his team. Riktor had been leading the search of the transports.

Riktor leaped out from behind one of the trucks. "Yes, sir," he snapped back, rushing over toward Carano.

"Sergeant, I don't know what the hell happened here, but our plans are fucked." He looked around the tarmac, now a battlefield littered with dead and lit by the scattered fires of burning vehicles. "We beat off those revolutionaries, but they'll be back, with ten times the numbers. We're not going to be able to get these weapons loaded up and out of here." His gaze moved back to Riktor. "Sergeant, I need you to rig this ship and these trucks with explosives." He exhaled loudly. "If we can't have the weapons, I'll be damned if I'm going to let the wogs have them."

"Yes, sir." Riktor followed the Helms's battlefield protocol and didn't salute. It was standard field practice. Identifying officers only made them vulnerable to snipers. "Immediately, General." He turned back toward the vehicles, waving to some of his troopers.

"And, Sergeant . . ."

Riktor spun around on his heels. "Yes, sir?"

"Hurry." Carano stared off in the direction of the city. "I doubt we have much time."

"Yes, General."

Carano turned and walked around the side of the ship. "What is it, Sergeant Lann?

"We found this one still alive, sir," Lann repeated.

Carano sighed. He didn't have time for prisoners. It was going to be hard enough to break the three imperials, and he didn't see the point in dragging along a wounded rebel. He was about to order the sergeant to finish him off when he looked down.

He could tell at once, this was no rebel. The Saragossans all wore uniforms made from the crappy textiles they produced on-planet. The figure lying on the ground was wearing a plain tunic and breeches, and they were of vastly superior quality to anything he'd seen on Saragossa outside a noble's household. The sergeant had told him the man was dressed differently, but he hadn't mentioned the vest he was wearing over the tunic—a suit of first-rate body armor.

He knelt down to take a closer look, reaching out and turning the unconscious man's face toward his. He knew immediately it was familiar, but he couldn't place it at first. Whoever this was, Carano had met him before, years ago. He was sure of it. Images went through his head, acquaintances from three decades of combat. *Who the hell would I know on this shithole planet?*

He looked down again, his eyes panning over Blackhawk's unconscious form. There was a nasty gash on the side of his head but no other injuries he could see. He glanced up at Lann. "No gunshot wounds?"

"No, General. It looks like he got hit on the head and knocked out." The sergeant waved to the soldier standing next to him. "He had these, sir."

Carano looked up. The soldier was holding a rifle and a pistol, both expensive high-tech weapons, not the kind of thing one expected to find on a splinter group rebel. The trooper also held a shortsword in his hand, old but well cared for, made of forged iridium-tipped hypersteel with a worn leather grip. His eyes focused immediately on the sword, and recollection flowed into his mind. He'd definitely seen that blade before. He still had the scar it left.

"Arkarin Blackhawk," he whispered to himself, "what the hell are you doing on Saragossa?"

CHAPTER 22

"YOU CAN'T BE SERIOUS, ACE." LUCAS WAS STANDING OUTSIDE the *Claw*, gesturing wildly. He couldn't believe what Ace was telling him.

"I'm perfectly serious, Lucas." His voice was calm and soft, and he stared right at the angry pilot as he spoke. "And keep your voice down. You want Astra to hear?"

Ace had promised Blackhawk he'd get Astra off-planet and back to her father, but he'd never said anything about going along himself. It was a technicality, he knew, a hair he was splitting, but Ace had never been one to adhere to the letter of the law when he could skirt along the spirit of it. "Look, Lucas, this isn't about singling you out. You're the only one besides the captain who can fly the ship, right?"

Lucas stared back, but he didn't say anything. He'd gone crazy when Ace first told him most of the crew was staying behind. The pilot didn't want to leave at all without Blackhawk and Shira, but running back to Celtiboria while most of his friends and comrades remained behind made him sick to his stomach. His eyes dropped, staring at the dusty ground.

"Lucas, listen to me. Ark wanted Astra safe. He made me promise him we'd get her back to her father as soon as the core was installed." He crouched down, trying to hold Lucas's gaze. "I promised him."

"You did." Lucas looked back up, his eyes wide, staring back into Ace's. "I didn't promise shit, Ace. And I'm not leaving without the skipper."

"You may not have promised him, but it's what he wants. It's the one thing he asked me to do." He paused. "You can see how much he cares about her. More than as a job or an important passenger. More, even, than as the daughter of a friend." Ace was sure Blackhawk loved the girl, but he stopped short of saying it out loud. "Don't you care what he wants? Are you ready to ignore what he asked us to do because you weren't there for him to make you promise? Because you know damned well that's what he wants." *And I know damned well that I'm playing dirty, but I don't have time for this.*

Lucas took a deep breath. "Damn it, Ace." He shook his head. "This is bullshit."

"Of course it is, Lucas. I know you don't want to go, but you have to. It's what the captain wanted." His voice was rougher, more urgent. "What do you want? To ignore the captain's orders? Or for all of us to come along and leave Ark and Shira here alone? Because that's what we'll have to do if you don't go."

Lucas's eyes bored into Ace's. "Fuck you."

242 — JAY ALLAN

"Fine, fuck me. But that doesn't change the reality. The situation sucks, and we've got to do what has to be done, not what we want to do." His voice softened. "Now will you help me, Lucas? Will you take Astra back home while the rest of us go after Ark?"

Lucas stood silently for a few seconds. Finally, he nodded grudgingly. "I'll do it."

"Thank you." He took a deep breath, relieved that Lucas had agreed. "And you won't be going back alone, remember. Sam's got to go too, at least. I know she's a little worried about the way she's getting that core jury-rigged and, besides, the *Claw*'s still not 100 percent repaired. You'll need her on board in case anything fails on the trip." Ace—like the rest of the crew of the *Claw*—had seen Sam Sparks fix so many seemingly hopeless problems, he just assumed she could do anything. But the spy ship's core was vastly more complex than anything she'd worked on before. The *Claw*'s connecting systems would have to be heavily upgraded before the thing could operate optimally, and without her constant attention in the meantime, there was no way the ship was making Celtiboria.

"And the Twins will go with you, too." Ace stared over at the two giants as they walked down the cargo hatch, ducking their heads as they did. He'd asked them to unload some supplies for the force remaining behind. No doubt they thought that included them. In an accounting of the *Claw*'s muscle, the brothers had to be right at the top of the list. But they were pure brute force, absolutely no finesse. And however strong they were, they couldn't take on the armies of the revolutionaries and the nobles all by themselves. Any attempt to find Blackhawk and Shira would rely on stealth and surprise, not brute force, and their adversaries would see and hear the two giants coming from a kilometer away.

Just as important, with the Twins the rump crew of the *Claw* would have some strength in a fight, at least. Ace couldn't be sure the ship would make it all the way back to Celtiboria without having to land somewhere for repairs . . . and there was more than one world where Blackhawk and his band of adventurers were less than welcome. Ace had to admit Lucas could handle himself pretty well in a fight, and he'd seen Sam drop her innocent routine more than once and, in a heartbeat, put a perfect round hole in an enemy's head with that tiny gun she carried everywhere. But neither was comparable to the Twins. The two brothers were like forces of nature in a fight. He remembered the two of them on Argonia, standing alongside the airlock, with assault rifles in both hands, holding off the locals while Lucas fired up the engines for their escape. And they could handle the *Claw*'s guns if needed, too.

"What about Astra, Ace? What do we tell her?" Lucas glanced toward the ship then back at his comrade. "There's no way she's going to go for it."

"That's why we don't tell her anything." Ace instinctively lowered his voice and glanced toward the ship himself. "She's in her quarters, and if you can keep her there while Sam fixes the core and then lift off without her knowing, it will be done. What's she going to do? Walk back from orbit?"

"But I need to warm up the reactor and feed juice into the engine circuits. That all makes noise. The ship shakes; the lights dim. You know that." Lucas couldn't imagine sneaking a liftoff prep past a passenger, especially one as smart and suspicious as Astra Lucerne.

"Sam's been firing every system in the ship trying to test that core she's installing, Lucas. I'll tell Astra that Sam's getting the core ready because Ark will be back soon." He paused. He felt guilty even saying it, but he knew Lucas was right. Astra would refuse to go if they told her the truth. He hated lying to her, especially telling her Ark was safe, but his promise to Blackhawk was the most important thing in his mind. "I'll even ask her to stay put in her cabin because we might have a radiation leak. By the time she realizes I lied to her, you guys will be halfway to low orbit."

And you will have one very pissed-off Astra Lucerne on your hands. She'd make his life miserable, Ace was sure of that, but what could she really do once they were in space?

Lucas still looked uncertain. "She won't be strapped in when we launch."

Ace shrugged. "She might get bounced around a little, but probably nothing worse than a few bruises."

"I guess . . ."

Ace exhaled with relief. Lucas was on board. Maybe reluctantly, but Ace would take it.

"You'd better bring the captain back," Lucas said.

"We'll find Ark while you're gone," he said. "I promise." They both knew he couldn't really promise that—the captain had been going into a losing fight when Ace had last seen him—but neither would consider the possibility that Blackhawk was already dead. Not consciously, at least.

But in the back of Ace's mind, the doubt lurked, along with a dark, dangerous thought. *If Arkarin Blackhawk dies on this miserable dust speck of a planet, I'm going to make them pay. All of them.*

These backwater pukes would find out just how much damage the crew of *Wolf's Claw* could do.

The light of the explosions ripped through the gloom of the dark wet night. The battle was raging to the east, both sides firing their heavy ordnance in support of the troops on the front lines. It was hard to tell what was happening on the ground, but from a few kilometers west of the fighting it had the look of a bloody stalemate. Whether it would stay that way was anyone's guess.

Shira imagined the better-equipped mercenary forces could establish temporary local superiority at any point, but she didn't know if they could hold it against the wave attacks of the revolutionaries. The mercs were mostly veterans, well trained and equipped. They'd been expensive to raise and arm, and they were the best troops on the planet. But with Saragossa's system interdicted, they were stuck. It was impossible for them to reinforce or replace losses, and Shira knew they had to be running low on supplies. She was sure they'd managed to set up some limited local field production, at least to manufacture ammunition. Still, what primitive industry Saragossa possessed was mostly in the hands of the revolutionaries, and she figured the off-world troops had to be having a hard time maintaining combat effectiveness. The troops were professionals, with high standards of élan and unit pride, but they didn't have any real stake in what happened on Saragossa, not past simply surviving until they could arrange transport and get the hell out.

The revolutionaries, on the other hand, were clearly willing to sacrifice massive numbers of half-trained soldiers to win battles. That had been obvious, even with the limited amount Shira had seen of their actions. It was obvious, too, that whoever was running the show didn't care how many people were expended, as long as the revolution was won. Shira felt a wave

of disgust. The revolutionaries styled themselves freedom fight-
ers, but the system they'd established was already as rotten as
the one the nobles had enforced.

Besides, she thought, *the mercenaries aren't trying to break
through.* She'd been surprised as they approached New Vostok
and first realized the nobles' forces were attacking. It hadn't
made any sense then, not based on what she knew of the situation, but now she understood exactly why they had launched an
offensive. It was all cover for the abortive snatch-and-grab job
on the imperial weapons. She figured the mercs would disengage as soon as their raiding force had pulled back behind the
lines, but she had no idea what the revolutionaries would do in
response. They were bound to be upset about the destruction
of the imperial vessel, and if they pushed hard enough, they
might force a climactic battle. Shira sighed. She just wanted to
find Blackhawk and get the hell out of here, not bear witness to
the final fight for control of the planet.

She had been pursuing the raiding party since they fled
from the spy ship and headed off to the south. Once they
had realized their surprise was blown and they didn't have a
chance in hell of getting away with the guns, they had wisely
decided it was a lost cause. So they rigged the ship to blow—at
least denying the weapons to their enemies as well—and
pulled back, taking the three imperial prisoners and Blackhawk along with them.

Shira was a good tracker, and she'd stayed hot on their heels
for a while, but the light from the battlefield explosions had
forced her farther back. She was determined to find out where
they were taking Blackhawk, but she knew if they spotted her
she'd be toast. She figured she could take a bunch of them down,

but there were at least fifty, and no amount of surprise would let her kill fifty men and ensure Blackhawk wasn't harmed. Not fifty trained soldiers. Not with what she had on her.

She'd had no idea who she was following at first, but they headed almost due south around the perimeter of the battle-field. Shira was less interested in Saragossa than in anything else she could think of, but she was stuck there, so she'd learned as much as she could. The areas to the south of New Vostok were held by the planet's nobility, the former rulers who'd been driven from the cities.

It all made perfect sense. The nobles had supplemented their own guards with hired mercenaries from off-world. From what she'd heard, they'd contracted with some of the best companies in the Far Stars.

The mercs and the noble retinues were better equipped than most of the revolutionary forces, but none of them had anything like imperial tech. They had wanted the weapons for the same reason Arn and his people had. The first two ship-loads had been expended hunting down and virtually destroy-ing the splinter rebel groups, but there was little doubt this new shipment would have been deployed against the nobles and their mercenary allies.

The mercs had been moving quickly, without stopping any-where, even for a short rest. She wondered if that meant the bat-tle was going badly for them, and they wanted to get through the gap before it closed. Shira didn't give a shit who ruled Sara-gossa, but the last thing she wanted was for one side to win and take total control while she and her friends were still there. She was sure there would be an orgy of massacres and destruction when there was finally a victor, and she figured she had a much better chance of rescuing Blackhawk and getting away if the stalemate continued.

The mercs kept moving, slipping around the end of the battle line and continuing on to the south. Shira looked up at the sky nervously then glanced down at her chronometer. It would be dawn soon, and she would lose the cover of darkness. She'd have to stay well back from the retreating soldiers to remain hidden, and she was worried she might lose the trail.

They had passed through a section that had once been some sort of farmland, but it was now barren and largely burned out. There were buildings too, shadowy outlines against the dim light of predawn. A few sturdy stone structures were still standing, but others were shattered ruins, charred beams protruding from piles of ash and broken foundations. Like almost every other part of Saragossa she'd seen, there had been fighting here some time ago, or at least heavy shelling.

Shira moved forward slowly, cautiously, using the buildings and wreckage as cover. The ground was treacherous, with large open pits scattered around. She could make one out ahead of her, a massive trench, at least twenty meters long. It looked like it had been about two meters deep before it had been partially filled. It took her eyes a few seconds to focus, but when they did, she knew at once what it was—a mass grave.

There were broken pieces of bone, bleached and weathered, scattered all around. It didn't take her too long to guess what happened. The rural nobles had held this area when the revolution began, and the graves were those of the peasants who had risen. Unlike the factory workers in the cities, the revolutionaries in the countryside had been quickly broken. The retainers of the nobles had done thorough work here, she realized, methodically executing the rebel farmworkers. That had been years before, but the half-buried bodies still lay where they had been placed in the trenches. Nothing was left now but bones; the wild boars and carrion birds had long since devoured the flesh of the dead, and what scraps had remained after their feast had long ago rotted away to nothing.

The place was thick with the pall of death, and she did her best to ignore it all. She was here to save Blackhawk, not to mourn for a bunch of revolutionaries who had made their move and failed. She'd been called cold—dark, cynical—and she was self-aware enough not to dispute those claims. She could find warmth—heat, even, when it came to the *Claw,* her family—but she didn't concern herself with battles that didn't involve her. To her, life was an ongoing struggle, and the only alternative to killing your enemies was dying at their hands. She didn't think of it as sad or tragic—simply a fact. It was just how things worked, how they'd always worked, and there was no point in attaching pointless emotion to it. The only reason she was still on Saragossa was because of Blackhawk, and he was the only thing she cared about right now.

The sky was getting steadily lighter, and Shira knew it wouldn't be long until sunrise. She slipped forward—slowly, cautiously—taking care to use the shattered buildings and debris for cover. She paused and looked ahead, watching the barely visible silhouettes of the retreating soldiers moving across a broad plain.

"Damn," she muttered. The fields ahead were wide open, without a building or structure in sight. Moreover they were fallow, not even a few tufts of young wheat for her to hide behind. She was going to have to let the enemy get even farther ahead, or risk being discovered. But if she allowed them to get completely out of view, would she lose them entirely?

She looked up, her fists balled tightly in frustration. Then she saw it, a shadowy image at first, almost like a mirage, becoming clearer with each second, as the morning light began to spread across the countryside.

A manor house, a huge, hulking château, loomed over the sprawling gray fields.

That's where they are going, she thought, suddenly certain. The building was enormous, vaster even than she'd first thought. It had to belong to one of the greatest of Saragossa's families, one of the leaders of the noble opposition to the revolution.

She sat down behind a pile of stones that had once been a wall, and she pulled out her canteen, taking a small sip. That had to be it, she thought again. And that meant she knew what she had to do. She'd let the soldiers go inside and then, somehow, she would find a way to sneak in.

Hang on, Ark. I'm on my way.

Ace breathed a sigh of relief as he turned away from the *Claw.* He'd lied well to Astra, and the story he'd told her was a plausible one, but he'd still had a knot in his stomach. Astra was smart as hell, something he'd known before but had only recently begun to truly appreciate.

She was stubborn and suspicious, too, and if she'd have caught an inkling of what was truly happening, God only knew what she might have done.

Oh, well . . . what's done is done.

"You ready, sir?" Sarge walked up behind Ace, followed by his men. Buck and Von were carrying a small autocannon. It was a squad support weapon designed to fire from a heavy tripod. Drake was struggling with a heavy rocket launcher, and a sack of reloads he had strapped across his back. Ace had taken the heavy weapons out of the *Claw*'s armory. Once the *Claw* left, they'd be stuck on this shithole planet for close to a month, and there was no telling what they might encounter.

"I still think you should stay with the *Claw*, Sarge." His wound was neatly dressed, but his face was pale and haggard. "Those imperial bullets are no joke."

"Not on your life, sir. Not while the captain's in trouble." Sarge was normally respectful to rank, but Ace could tell from his tone that no orders were going to make him stay behind. Still, he didn't look like he could handle a rifle very well. But he had a big machine pistol in a holster on his belt, and a half-dozen throwing knives hung from his shoulder strap. Ace had watched him use those knives a hundred times, and he'd never seen him miss—right *or* left handed.

"All right, Sarge. But be careful, and don't tear open that shoulder. We're leaving in five minutes, so get your men ready." He looked over the noncom's shoulder toward Ringo, who was limping around on his bandaged leg, carrying one of the heavy particle accelerators. He glanced back toward Sarge. "Are you sure Ringo's up to this?"

Sarge stared back with cold eyes. "He won't stay behind while the captain's in trouble, sir. No more than I would."

Ace frowned. It wasn't really an answer to his question, but he had a pretty good idea it was all he was going to get. He just nodded and turned to head back to get his kit.

Doc Sandor was digging through the pile of supplies. He had his portable medkit strapped across his back, and he was rummaging through the weapons. He already had a holstered pistol on his belt, and a small survival knife. He pulled an assault rifle and a shoulder belt full of fresh clips from the crate.

"I'm still not sure how you convinced me to let you come along, Doc."

"It's easy, Ace: I'm a little older than you, and a whole lot smarter. But even without that, I'm also part of this crew. I owe as much to Arkarin Blackhawk as anyone here, and I'll be damned if I'm going to stay behind while he's in trouble." He whipped the assault rifle around, strapping it across his back. "He may be wounded, or one of you may walk into more enemy fire. Without me what will you do? Tie up your wounds with the filthiest piece of cloth you can find? As much as I enjoy trying to kill every Saragossan microbe that crawls into your bodies, I'd just as soon do it right from the start." He stared at Ace with piercing green eyes. "So let's cut the shit and get moving."

Ace nodded. There was no point in arguing, not with any of them. Not while Blackhawk's life was on the line. He smiled. The captain deserved this kind of loyalty, and Ace was satisfied to see that he had it. Blackhawk had a dark past, one that tormented his dreams, one that he wouldn't discuss with anyone. Ace knew that much. But he knew one more thing. He didn't give a shit. The only thing that mattered was *here* and *now*.

Ace Graythorn was ready to die for Blackhawk. So were Sarge, Buck, Doc, and everyone else who had stayed behind. They weren't going to abandon their captain.

Not ever.

CHAPTER 23

"I HAVE BEEN SENT TO EXPRESS THE DEEPEST DISAPPOINTMENT of Lord Governor Vos, not only in the original failure that allowed Astra Lucerne's rescue, but the subsequent inability to pursue and find this—it was a single ship, was it not?—that escaped from your entire fleet." The speaker was insolent, showing barely any trace of respect in his tone as he addressed the monarch of Kalishar. He knew any local who'd dare to speak to the ka'al in such a manner would have been impaled or crucified, but he had come from the imperial governor, and he knew the ka'al's fear overrode his anger.

Sebastien Alois de Villeroi was the bastard son of an imperial viscount, the product of his father's incestuous liaison with an underage cousin. The notoriety of his birth had compelled him to live a quiet existence out of the public eye—comfortably provisioned, but utterly without influence or power and with no chance of succeeding to his father's titles and estates.

Bored and restless with such a cloistered life, he'd chosen to leave his father's world of Aquillar to seek adventure and fortune as an agent in the imperial intelligence service. His controversial lineage was no bar to success among the cutthroats and schemers engaged in espionage for the empire. Even more important, his work as an imperial spy offered an outlet for his nearly unbridled sadism. Villeroi loved inflicting pain—on his enemies, on innocent bystanders, even on his lovers. He derived pleasure from tormenting his victims the way others did from love or lust or accomplishment.

And the imperial intelligence service offered endless opportunities to profit from his cruelty.

Left to his own desires, Villeroi would already have hoisted the obese Tarn Belgaren onto a spit and roasted his carcass. But General Wilhelm had been clear that the ka'al was not to be harmed or deposed unless Wilhelm specifically ordered it. The agent could verbally torment Kalishar's ruler—he could threaten him and plot with conspirators to prepare a revolt—but he was forbidden to go any further without a direct command.

"Agent Villeroi, the situation is not as simple as you imply." Belgaren was struggling to keep his voice firm, but his fear was apparent to Sebastien. The imperial spy had heard stories, tales of a younger, bolder ka'al from years before, one who would have taken his head for such impudence. But he could see age and decades of comfort had softened the ka'al, draining away his courage and leaving almost no trace of the proud and violent young pirate who had seized Kalishar's throne so many years before.

"And how is that so? Did your man not arrive on Kalishar with Lady Lucerne? Was he not already on your world when this rogue adventurer plucked her from under your nose?" He ignored the ka'al's titles, and his tone continued to drip with disrespect.

Maybe I can provoke him into doing something rash, so I can then fillet the skin off his greasy hide . . .

Regrettably, the ka'al seemed to get his rage under control. "Arkarin Blackhawk is a dangerous man, Agent, and his crew is made up of the worst rogues in the Far Stars. They . . ."

"Yet you were able to capture this Blackhawk before he could escape," Villeroi interrupted, staring into the ka'al's puffy eyes as he did. "And then you lost him, while you—and all your guards—watched."

"That is enough, Agent." The imperial envoy's abrasive manner finally sliced through the ka'al's fear, provoking an angry response. "You misrepresent what occurred. Lady Lucerne had not yet been delivered into my hands. Captain Mondran had just landed, with *Wolf's Claw* in close pursuit. Blackhawk's people intercepted his crew before they could reach my stronghold, and Mondran and his people were all killed in the subsequent battle."

"An entire crew of one of your ships, slain by a small group of smugglers and petty adventurers?" Villeroi ignored the ka'al's mounting anger. He was here to disabuse the monarch of any notions he might have that he was anything but a servant of the governor. He'd been bought and paid for with the imperial gold that saved Kalishar from economic collapse and the revolution that almost certainly would have followed in its wake, and he would have to learn to serve his new master. Villeroi stared hard into the ka'al's wavering eyes. "And how many of the enemy did your men slay while defending themselves against this attack? They would have outnumbered Blackhawk's people by what . . . two to one, three to one?" He paused, savoring Belgaren's anger and discomfort—since he was limited at present to inflicting psychological abuse. "Is it possible that an entire ship's crew of feared pirates could not kill even one of their assailants?"

The ka'al shifted uncomfortably in his seat, the rolls of fat on his enormous bulk jiggling as he did. "You do not understand, Agent Villeroi. Blackhawk's crew is extremely dangerous. Mondran's men fought well, but they were facing two giants along with the others."

"Giants?" Villeroi's tone was thick with mockery. "Perhaps there were gremlins as well . . . or a dragon?" A caustic laugh escaped his lips. "And what of the fleet you sent in pursuit? What news from there? None, I suppose. Just more excuses."

The ka'al twitched angrily on his throne, but he took no action.

"I have dispatched my entire fleet to search every nearby system. They are the best trackers in the Far Stars, the scourge of the entire sector. They will find *Wolf's Claw* and bring Astra Lucerne back to Kalishar."

Villeroi stood unmoving, silently glaring at Belgaren for a few seconds and making no effort to hide his disgust. "Well, I hope they are successful. Because Governor Vos will not be pleased if the Lucerne girl escapes. Or even if she is killed in a botched rescue attempt.

"Do we understand each other?" His voice was like ice.

Villeroi watched as the ka'al struggled with what he was about to say. A promise like the one Sebastien demanded was nonnegotiable. If he or his men broke his word, the ka'al's life would be forfeit . . . after a time at Sebastien's itching hands.

You came here to live out the life of a fat slug, content in your garden of sycophants and false opulence. But now you are Vos's, and he will squash you if you defy him. And I will be the salt that shrivels your soul to nothingness.

"I am confident they will, Agent Villeroi." Belgaren choked on the craven words, but Villeroi knew they were all he had.

"What will you require if we choose to back you to—how shall I put it—facilitate change on Kalishar?" Villeroi spoke softly, glancing back over his shoulder, though he was sure they were alone. Secrecy was crucial, at least for now. His authorization extended only to preparations to overthrow the ka'al, not actually proceeding with his plans. Villeroi considered Kalishar's ruler beneath contempt, but even a coward would fight for his life if no escape was possible. The agent's schemes had to remain confidential or he'd be forced to openly confront the ka'al in direct contradiction of his orders, and that was something he intended to avoid.

Even Sebastien Villeroi knew enough to be afraid of Governor Vos.

But he also knew Vos rewarded initiative. Sebastien had every confidence that the man before him could help ensure he left Kalishar in the good graces of the governor.

Rax Florin didn't look like a pirate. He looked instead like some sort of ancient barbarian: filthy, violent, and stupid, come down from the hills to raid and pillage. He had a jagged crevice down the side of his nightmarish face, a scar from some hideous wound, poorly healed. His hair hung about his face in two greasy hanks, gray and shoulder length. But looks are often deceiving and, after nearly discounting the buccaneer on first sight, Villeroi had been surprised by Florin's intelligence and temperate manner.

"I would ask for imperial troops, Agent Villeroi, if I didn't already know that wasn't a possibility." Florin's voice was calm, measured—also not what one expected after getting a look at him.

"I'm afraid you are correct, Lord Florin." Villeroi wasn't sure what Florin was lord of, but that's how he'd originally introduced himself, and there was no harm in a little flattery. "Unfortunately, imperial military assets in the Far Stars are already stretched thin."

Thin? More like nonexistent. Vos had a lot of coin available to execute his plans, but the emperor had been firm that he would risk none of his crack legions or major warships on treacherous crossings of the Void. The few troops Vos had were mostly local levies, and they were barely enough to defend the handful of worlds the empire truly controlled in the sector.

"In that case, I would say I require funding, Agent. Preferably imperial coin." The worlds of the Far Stars had their own currencies, but they were frequently debased or subject to wildly fluctuating exchange rates. Imperial platinum crowns were the preferred coinage in the sector, despite the fact that they were officially illegal on more than half the worlds. "Without direct military support, I will need considerable financial resources to proceed."

Villeroi knew Florin was a wealthy man, a spectacularly successful pirate who'd retired after a lucrative career of pillaging that spanned decades. The buccaneer was willing to discuss overthrowing the ka'al, tempted by the thought of becoming Kalishar's ruler himself, but he wasn't willing to stake his own fortune on it.

Villeroi knew Florin's adventures had left him few choices on where to settle. With death sentences on his head on most of the worlds in the sector, he'd come to Kalishar, where wealthy ex-pirates—and their gold—were welcomed. But over the years, Kalishar's wealthy pirate lords had become more and more concerned over the ka'al's paranoia. The aging ruler had begun to fear the courtiers around him, especially those he had showered with lordly titles. From what Villeroi had been able to glean, Florin wanted nothing more than to quietly enjoy his fortune and his stable of mistresses, but the old pirate had come to realize he couldn't ignore Belgaren's jealousy and irrational fears any longer. Villeroi realized he'd found the candidate he had been seeking, a man of wealth and power who felt threatened enough by Kalishar's ruler to take action. He approached Florin with his plan, tentatively, at first, well aware he was exceeding the authority Vos had given him.

The pirate lord had been coy, cautious, but Villeroi could tell he was interested. The imperial spy suspected Florin's motivations had more to do with preservation than raw ambition, but that didn't matter. He knew Florin was ready to make a move, but only if he was sure of the right support.

"How would you define considerable, Lord Florin?"

The pirate stared back at Villeroi with cold blue eyes. "Ten million crowns, Agent Villeroi." Florin's tone was serious, emotionless. "Delivered as imperial coins and stamped platinum bars."

Villeroi stood there, speechless for a few seconds. He'd been ready for a large number, but the old buccaneer had taken him by surprise with his audacity. "Ten million? Don't you think that is a bit excessive, Lord Florin?"

"To simply eliminate the ka'al, perhaps. But I must look beyond the simple seizure of power to my own hold on the throne and my continued rule of Kalishar." He shrugged.

"This isn't an arbitrary number, Agent Villeroi—I've given this considerable thought. While it may be difficult to believe, the ka'al has many friends and allies. If I move against him, I must be prepared to deal with all of them as well, either eliminating them or buying them off." He offered Villeroi a cynical smile. "After all, Agent, we wouldn't want me to overthrow the ka'al for you only to be deposed or assassinated shortly afterward, would we? There are many who whisper the empire discards its allies as soon as they are no longer needed. We wouldn't want to lend false credence to these slanderous assertions, would we?"

Villeroi had to fight to suppress a laugh. Quite unexpectedly, he found himself respecting this intriguing pirate and wondering if he'd picked too capable and intelligent a proxy for his own good. "But ten million? Surely, you can neutralize all your rivals with a lesser sum. Perhaps three million? We are talking about imperial crowns after all, not Kalishar's dubious coinage." The planet's sestars had a bad reputation, even among the debased currencies of the Far Stars' lesser worlds. The ka'al had sought once too often to escape his financial woes by debasing the currency, and now even businesses on Kalishar refused to accept the nearly valueless coins

Florin grinned. "Indeed, three million would be sufficient to eliminate Belgaren and his adherents and set me up in his place. But we both know how precarious Kalishar's economy has become under the ka'al's increasingly erratic and ineffective rule. Were I to step into his shoes without sufficient funding to embark on a significant program of economic expansion, I would be little but a puppet, held tightly upon a leash by my imperial paymaster." He shook his head. "Nay, my friend. If I am to leave my comfortable retirement to take on the burdens of the throne, I will rule on my own account, as an ally to Governor Vos and the empire, not a slave." He stared emotionlessly at Villeroi. "Loyalty I offer in return for your friendship and aid, but not servitude."

Villeroi stood silently, wondering again if he'd chosen well or poorly. Florin was capable; of that he had no doubt. But was he controllable? The empire preferred slaves to allies, and mandated obedience over friendly cooperation. Would supporting Florin achieve his goal? Or simply replace the ka'al with someone far more dangerous?

"Very well, Lord Florin." Villeroi sighed and bowed slightly to his companion. "Ten million crowns. I shall notify you as soon as the operation is approved."

Florin returned the bow. "I shall await word, Agent Villeroi. You may find me in my stronghold north of the city."

The imperial agent watched the pirate lord turn and slip quietly out into the street. He was conflicted. If he got the order to launch the operation, it would be a pleasant change to work with someone competent. He couldn't imagine Florin would have allowed Blackhawk to steal an important hostage from under his nose. But he also knew Florin would be harder to control. Possibly much harder.

"Will I be replacing one problem with a more dangerous one?" he whispered to himself. "Or gaining an ally I can rely upon?" He thought about it for a while, but he didn't come to any conclusions.

CHAPTER 24

LUCAS'S HANDS MOVED OVER THE CONTROL BOARD, GUIDING THE ship into a smooth orbit. The takeoff had been a rushed affair once it was time to go, with not enough time for proper planning, and he'd had to manage the ascent with his gut as much as the nav AI. It wasn't easy to pull off a flawless orbital insertion by instinct alone, but Lucas was a natural pilot, and he felt the ship's systems almost like other people did their arms and legs.

He was hunched over his readouts now, plotting out the hyperspace jump. He checked and rechecked his calculations. A jump this close to a planetary body was tricky, and he didn't want to risk a mistake. Not after all they'd gone through to get the new core. But he wasn't going to lose a day or more moving away from Saragossa, either. He was going to get Astra back to

Celtiboria and get back as quickly as possible, and he didn't care how hard he had to push the *Claw* and her battered systems to do it.

He stared down at the hyperdrive panel and frowned. The power readings from the core were spiking every few seconds. It was a strange pattern, something he'd never seen before. Sam was the best ship's engineer he'd ever known, but she'd rushed to install the thing. Maybe she'd missed something.

He flipped on the commlink to engineering. "Sam, are you sure about this thing? My readouts are going crazy up here."

"It's not the core, Lucas. It's the *Claw*'s power conduits and infrastructure." Her tone was a combination of stress and awe. "This hyperdrive core makes every other one I've seen look like a piece of junk. It's vastly more powerful than our old one. When I get time to upgrade the ship's circuits and the main line from the reactor, you're going to be able to move twice as fast in hyperspace and stay there twice as long. The *Claw* will be the fastest thing in the Far Stars!" He could tell her excitement was building. She was an engine junkie, and the imperial core was a work of art to her.

"That's great, Sam, but I've got to fly this thing now, before you do that overhaul."

"No, you don't."

Lucas turned and looked behind him. Astra Lucerne was standing next to the ladder from the lower deck. She was glaring at him . . . and holding a pistol. "Astra . . ." He was surprised, confused. "What are . . ."

"Take the ship down, Lucas." She stared at him. Her voice was calm and even, but the coldness in her ice-blue eyes told him she was deadly serious.

"Astra, the captain gave very clear orders. I am to take you back to your father on Celtiboria." He returned her cold stare. "So put that stupid gun down, and go get strapped in. We're breaking orbit in a few minutes."

"No." She took a step forward, aiming the gun at Lucas's head. "You and Ace managed to trick me into staying in my cabin while you lifted off, but this is where it ends." She looked at him with deadly intensity. "I told Arkarin Blackhawk I wasn't going to sit out the next fight and, by Chrono's filthy beard, I meant it. If he thinks I'm going to let you escort me home like a little girl while he is in danger, he's crazier than I thought he was."

"Astra, we have to follow Ark's orders." He shifted uncomfortably. He wasn't really afraid she'd shoot him, but it was still unpleasant staring down the barrel of a heavy-duty pistol. The gun she was pointing at him held eighteen slugs in the magazine, and it could fire all of them in less than two seconds. And Astra Lucerne had grown up on the battlefield; he suspected she was a crack shot. "He's the captain, and he knows what's best. We have to obey him."

"Follow his orders? I'm not part of his crew. I don't have to obey anything." She laughed. "Or did you mean obey like you did on Kalishar? Like the rest of your crew is doing right now? I'd wager he ordered all of you to take me back to Celtiboria. That's more his way. He'd have wanted everyone safe, and damned the cost to himself. So where is everybody else? Hmm?"

"Astra, I know you're worried about him. I am too. But Ace and Shira and the others stayed behind to help him. They'll rescue him. He's in good hands."

"I'm not leaving him, Lucas." She took another step. "Now take this ship back down."

He could see the emotion behind the calm façade she was

struggling to maintain. He'd known she was fond of Ark, but now he caught a glimpse of just how strong her feelings truly were. She wore a menacing grimace and projected a tough persona, but Lucas could see she was scared to death that Blackhawk might be in danger or pain. Or worse. "Astra . . ."

"Just land the ship, Lucas. You don't want to leave him behind any more than I do. It'll take you weeks to get back here from Celtiboria. Even if Shira and the others find Ark, they'll all be stuck down there in the middle of a full-scale war." Her mask was beginning to fail, and her true feelings were starting to show.

Lucas forced back his own emotions. He didn't want to leave Ark and the others behind any more than Astra did. But he didn't disobey Blackhawk lightly. He'd been mad when Ace first told him to leave Saragossa with Astra, but he realized it was the only thing they could do. They couldn't ignore Blackhawk's orders and expose Astra to more danger . . . but they couldn't leave Shira and him alone either.

Kalishar had been different, or at least that's what he told himself. It had been a matter of imminent life and death. If they hadn't intervened immediately, Blackhawk would never have left that arena alive. This situation was dangerous, certainly, but it wasn't the same. If Blackhawk had been killed in the firefight outside the imperial ship, there was nothing anyone could do, and ignoring his last request to keep Astra safe would be even more unforgivable. If he had survived the fight—and Lucas couldn't let himself seriously consider the alternative— the captain had probably taken refuge in the woods or with the surviving rebels. Either way, most of the crew was still on Saragossa. They'd find Ark if anyone could, and they'd manage to get someplace they could hunker down until Lucas made it back to get them.

He scrounged up all his determination. "Forget it, Astra. Ark wants you back home safely, and that's where we're going." He looked right into her eyes. "We both know you're not going to shoot me with that thing."

She returned his stare, her eyes as cold and defiant as ever. "You're right, Lucas. I won't kill you"—she lowered the pistol—"but I will knock you out and try to land this crate myself if I have to." Her other hand rose slowly, revealing a stun gun aimed at his chest. "I'm not much of a pilot, so I'd really prefer that you do it. Because either way, we're going down there."

Lucas stared back for a few seconds. He had been sure Astra wouldn't murder him in cold blood, but he wasn't so certain she wouldn't disable him and take the controls herself, risk be damned. "Astra . . ." His hand moved slowly toward his console.

"Forget about it, Lucas. The Twins aren't going to help you. I've got them locked up in the cargo hold." A tiny smile crept onto her face. "They're loyal and dependable—and great in a fight, I suspect—but neither one of them is ever going to unravel the secrets of the universe, are they?"

Lucas sighed, a defeated look coming across his face. "But . . ."

"Sam's locked in engineering, too." She held up Blackhawk's key card. "I snatched it when he was trying to convince me to stay behind. I've reprogrammed all the hatches. So all your potential reinforcements are stuck right where they are." She paused and winked at him. "It's just you and me, baby."

He looked back at her and opened his mouth, but no words came. Blackhawk had told them all Astra Lucerne was a handful before they set out to find her, but now he was beginning to truly understand. She was no spoiled daughter of a great conqueror; she was an incredibly capable woman in her own right, and one who had a huge problem with being told what to do.

"We're done talking, Lucas. Are you going to land this thing?" She took another step forward and glared at him. "Or am I?"

He sighed. "Fine, Astra. We'll go back." He nodded. "You better go down and get strapped in."

She suppressed a chuckle. "I don't think so, Lucas. It's not that I don't trust you, it's just . . ." She let her voice trail off. She took another step and backed into the command chair. "I don't think Ark will mind if I borrow his seat, do you?" She smiled and slid into the landing harness, keeping the stun gun aimed at Lucas as she did. "Now, let's go."

The city was burning, great plumes of smoke rising into the darkening sky, a silent pyre to mark a place where millions once lived. Now that place was dying and the terrified survivors of the bombing attack were fleeing to the countryside, away from the fires, from the death. But there was no escape, no refuge.

The soldiers were waiting in a line, weapons ready. The position stretched out of sight to both sides, at least a full legion deployed, and possibly two or three. There was a heavy autocannon positioned between each ten-man squad, fully loaded and targeted on the fleeing civilians. They awaited only the command to fire.

An officer stood behind them, clad in magnificent body armor and a jet black uniform. He stood stone still, without emotion, watching the panicking mobs approaching. They were screaming, crying, the old, the young—all running as quickly as they could, driven by hysterical fear.

The officer watched, his cold eyes focused on the surging mass of humanity as it approached. They were running for their lives, but it would do them no good. They had resisted the emperor's demands, defied an imperial decree. Their lives were forfeit. The officer watched as each second ticked off slowly, awaiting the moment when he would unleash the emperor's retribution. Finally, he flipped on his comm unit and uttered a single word. "Fire."

Blackhawk was staring at a hazy light above him. The battlefield had vanished, the horror of the dying city no longer before him. The dream had been vivid, as always, but now it was gone. His mind was slow, fuzzy, as it always was when visions of the past haunted his sleep. He struggled to focus, to remember where he was.

> You have been unconscious for seven hours, thirty-four minutes. You suffered a cranial injury during the action at the spaceport. You were carried a considerable distance by soldiers in service to the displaced planetary nobility. I would estimate we are twenty-five to thirty kilometers south, southwest from the spaceport.

Blackhawk struggled to understand. It was a voice, but from where? For a few seconds he was confused, uncertain. Then he remembered. The AI in his head. He felt clarity drift back through his mind, and with it there was discomfort, a throbbing pain from the side of his head. His mind was clearing. *That is an imprecise figure for you, my friend,* he thought to the strange intelligence that had shared his consciousness for so long.

> I am limited to your sensory input in my analyses. I am frequently able to access this input with greater clarity and effectiveness than you are, but when you are unconscious, the flow of data is slowed considerably.

Something hit me in the head, he thought.

> You were struck by metallic debris from an explosion.
> You suffered a moderate epidural hematoma,
> however your considerable recuperative capabilities
> appear to have stabilized the wound. I estimate
> your injury would have been fatal in 73 percent of
> instances in humans with genetics more closely
> aligned with the mean. I project no lasting damage
> in your case. Nevertheless, my readings on your pain
> receptors indicate a considerable headache.

No shit, Blackhawk thought. His head was throbbing, the pain seeming to come from everywhere at once. It was distracting, but as he continued to awaken, he clamped down with his usual discipline and ignored it. As much as he could, at least.

He was lying on his back, staring straight up. The light was dim, gauzy. He closed his eyes and reopened them, trying to clear his vision. He started to make out details of the room. It was large, ornate. The ceiling was painted, scenes of puffy clouds on a blue background, and it was edged with gold-colored moldings. He was lying in a bed, a plush one, covered with soft sheets and blankets.

He moved his arm slowly, reaching behind him, trying futilely to push himself up. He was weak, but he could feel his strength returning slowly, so he tried again, struggling to sit up. The pain in his head got worse as he lifted himself, but he took a deep breath and continued.

"I suggest you lie down for a while longer, Captain Blackhawk. You were quite seriously injured."

The voice was female—gentle, soothing, not at all what he'd expected. He felt a small hand on his shoulder, the skin soft, smooth. He turned his head, gritting his teeth against the wave of pain. It was a woman standing next to him, looking down. She was smiling. "What . . ." Blackhawk's throat was dry, his voice a barely audible whisper.

"Please, Captain Blackhawk, do not overtax yourself." The woman leaned down over him. He fingers passed lightly across his forehead, softly brushing back his hair. "Your wound has been treated, but you still require rest."

His eyes finally focused on her. She was wearing a blue dress of a material Blackhawk had never seen. It was clearly an expensive garment, low cut with a series of laces on the bodice, definitely enticing, but hardly normal attire for tending to a wounded prisoner.

"How do you know who I am?" His clarity was returning, and he realized she'd been calling him by his name.

She leaned in closer, her mass of red hair moving softly across his chest. "You were recognized, Captain Blackhawk, by someone in my employ." She smiled. "For which I am truly grateful. Now we can dispense with any, how shall I say, unpleasantness, and move right to how we can help each other." A hint of menace crept into her otherwise seductive tone.

"And how can we do that . . . what shall I call you?"

"I am Elisabetta Ataragin Lementov, Captain Blackhawk. But, please, call me Elisa." She smiled warmly, but there was something else there too. She was a beautiful woman, certainly, but there was danger there, a hardness. Blackhawk's instincts told him to tread cautiously.

He forced his own smile. "And I am Ark." His eyes panned around the room. The fuzziness was dissipating, and his usual sharpness was returning. Cameras were positioned strategically around the room to monitor everything that happened. There were shadows under the door, probably guards standing out in the hallway. Elisabetta was clearly a powerful woman, obviously one of the planet's nobles. She'd never be in here alone with him, not without protection. Blackhawk couldn't find anything, but he suspected there was a sniper watching him even now, perhaps more than one. He didn't doubt that he'd be dead in an instant if he made a hostile move toward her.

So I guess I should see what she wants. He visibly relaxed, but he didn't lower his guard for a second. She was hinting about some sort of partnership right now, but Blackhawk didn't doubt she had harsher means at her disposal as well. He saw a lot of himself in his initial glimpses of her, and that made him edgy. He understood what she was capable of if pressed.

I'll just have to make sure to press very, very lightly.

"It is not often I am saved by a woman of such beauty and charm." He smiled—a genuine smile, since he wasn't lying: she was quite beautiful. "What can I do for you, Elisa?"

Shira knelt down behind a small trailer hitch, piled high with newly reaped hay. The ground was still soft and wet from the previous evening's rain, and her knees were soaked and caked with mud.

She was peering toward the hulking manor house, her eyes scanning it meticulously. She'd been sneaking around all morning, looking for a way to approach the château without being spotted.

These areas to the south were busier than the blasted terrain to the north, and some of the fields were still tended. She'd seen peasant crews being led out at dawn under armed guard.

She wondered if they were prisoners impressed as slave labor or simply farmworkers who had never rebelled. Either way, it was clear the nobles didn't trust them.

She couldn't imagine that agriculture was profitable when you had to have a small army watching over your farmers, and she suspected they were only growing enough for their own needs. With the guild embargo in place, imported food would be nearly impossible to get, and what little they might manage to buy from smugglers would be staggeringly costly.

She'd been pretty sure the mercs had taken Blackhawk into the manor, but she'd scouted to the south just to be sure. None of the tracks continued past the giant structure. This was it, she thought. Ark was alive—at least he had been a few hours before—and he was a prisoner in the castle.

Shira sighed softly, trying to figure out how to get in and rescue him. The building wasn't a fortress, not really, but it wasn't undefended either. She hadn't been able to find any approach that was unguarded. The ground was cleared for two hundred meters in all directions. She could even see where a small orchard had been bulldozed to deny cover to an approaching enemy.

She looked up at the sky. The *Claw* was probably already gone. Blackhawk's orders had been clear. Shira had no idea how long it would take the *Claw*'s engineer to get the stolen equipment in place, but she'd never bet against Sam Sparks getting the job done better and faster than anyone expected.

She glanced down at the small comm unit hanging right behind her pistol. She'd maintained radio silence all night, not wanting to risk detection until she knew where the mercs were taking Blackhawk. Unfortunately, now she knew and the *Claw* was long gone. She'd go in alone if she had to, but she doubted she had much chance of pulling it off by herself. And, if she got herself killed, no one else would have any idea where Blackhawk was being held, even if they were still on Saragossa. Even if they came back.

Reaching down slowly, Shira pulled the unit from the clip that held it in place. *This is foolish,* she thought. *They're gone. You know they're gone. You're just going to get yourself picked off.* Still, she had to try. Maybe Sam was still working on the core, maybe Ace had decided to delay the liftoff, hoping against hope that she and Blackhawk would come marching out of the woods and up to the ship if he waited just a little longer.

She looked around, making sure there was no one nearby. She activated the comm unit, setting it for low power. With any luck, a short burst wouldn't be detected. She held the unit up to her lips and spoke softly. "Attention *Wolf's Claw* . . ."

"We're going to have to leave the buggy soon." Ace was riding up top, manning the heavy autocannon. They'd already run into half a dozen enemy patrols. Ace had scragged them all before they'd had a chance to get out a warning, but they were getting too close to New Vostok, and they were bound to run out of luck soon.

"I do not know, Ace. We do not know where we are going, where the captain is. It is foolish to expect that he is still at the imperial vessel. The fight there would have ended long ago." Katarina's voice was matter of fact, but her tone was exotic, her soft accent almost hypnotic. It didn't matter that they were under combat conditions, the assassin was a natural seductress, and it came out in any situation.

Ace was amazed at her poise and unshakable presence. He knew seduction was one of the assassination tools taught at the guild on Sebastiani, but understanding that and seeing it in action were two different things. He wondered how many targets she'd led to their deaths with nothing more than soft words and tantalizing touches.

He'd never made a move himself on the mysterious Sebastiani passenger who had become a part of their lives on the *Claw*. He'd thought about it a thousand times, but two things had stopped him. First, he suspected Katarina and Blackhawk had been involved and, though he was sure it had long been over, he'd steered clear ever since. And while his restraint had come from loyalty to the captain, it also came from something else: despite his cocky manner, he had the sneaking suspicion that Katarina Venturi was more than a bit out of his league. Ace Graythorn fancied himself quite the ladies' man, but it was said that adepts from the Sebastiani Assassins' Guild could seduce any man—or woman. He'd never admit to being intimidated, but he still indulged his passions elsewhere . . . as often as not in the beds of wealthy men's wives.

Much simpler. And far less dangerous.

"We may need to split up," Katarina said.

Ace knew she was right. Heading straight back to the spy ship was dangerous, but it also might be the only place to pick up Blackhawk's trail. "Fuck! If only we had a lead . . ." He opened the hatch and slid back inside the main cab. "Maybe we should . . ."

The comm unit crackled to life. "Attention *Wolf's Claw*, attention *Wolf's Claw*." It was Shira's voice. The signal was weak, and the interference made it difficult to understand, but there was no doubt it was her. Ace leaned forward and started adjusting the receiver, trying to clean up the signal, but the problem wasn't on their end. She might be at extreme range, but he couldn't guess how she'd gotten that far so quickly. Maybe her radio was damaged. Or was she trying to avoid detection?

"Shira, Ace here." He gripped the comm unit tightly. "What's your status?"

"Ace . . . damn. I didn't think you'd still be here. Listen: Ark's been captured by the nobles' mercenary forces. He's been taken to a manor house about twenty kilometers south of the city." There was a short pause. "I just sent you the coordinates."

"Got them." Ace was shocked. He'd been concerned the revolutionaries had captured Ark, but he hadn't considered anything else. What were the mercs doing so far north anyway? Their forces had launched a major attack the day before, but from everything Ace had been able to see, their advance had been stopped far short of New Vostok. "Is Ark okay?"

"He was when they got him here this morning. I'm just outside the château, but I haven't found a way in yet. I need backup ASAP." She paused. "What the hell are you doing here anyway? I thought you'd be long gone by now."

"Some of us stayed behind to help Ark, but that's not something we need to talk about on an open line." It wasn't often Ace was the voice of cool thinking in an exchange with Shira, but he was determined to save Blackhawk, and he was as focused as he'd ever been.

And he definitely needed focus now. He took a deep breath. Shira was on the other side of a war zone. *How the hell are we going to get through all that and rescue her and the captain?* "Okay, you just stay put. Keep eyes on the target, and make sure they don't take Ark anywhere else." He still wasn't sure how they were going to manage it, but he would find a way, whatever it took. "We're on the way."

"Got it. Tarkus out."

Ace turned. The others were all gathered around, staring at him intently. "Ark's alive." He could feel his own relief again as he said it, and he saw the same reaction in his comrades. "But he's a prisoner, and it's going to be one hell of a job getting to him."

"Whatever it takes, sir," Sarge said, echoing Ace's own thoughts. "Anything for the captain." The soldier's voice was determination itself. He had a savage gleam in his eye, a look that broadcast pure determination.

Ace felt the same way, but he was pretty sure brute force wasn't going to be enough this time.

"We need a plan. A better one than shooting our way through whatever is between us and Ark. As far as I can tell, there are two armies in our way, and I doubt they're going to stop their war and let us pass."

"There are other ways than force to accomplish a goal." Katarina looked right at Ace. "Stealth, for example. Deceit."

Ace smiled. "That is just what I was thinking. We need to blend in, slip right through without arousing suspicion. That's the only way to get through those battle lines and rescue Ark." Ace looked around for a few seconds before he opened the door and jumped out of the buggy. He ran around to the back and popped the main cargo hatch.

The others scrambled out after him. "Ace, what do you have in mind?" Doc stood just behind him as he ransacked the small hold. "What are you looking for?"

"These," Ace answered, the satisfaction in his voice self-evident. "I knew they were in here somewhere. We had a couple left from the op on Betalax." He looked back at Doc then at Katarina. "We need to sneak through the battle zone to get to Ark, and right now, we stand out like a rabid carnasoid. We need to blend in."

Sarge looked confused, but Katarina just nodded. Doc had a puzzled expression on his face, but only for a few seconds before he smiled broadly. "Yes, Ace." He nodded. "Of course."

Ace turned toward Sarge and his men. "Get ready, boys. We need some uniforms." He pulled a lever on one of the two small spheres in his hand. He took a breath and threw it as far as he could. "Get down. And cover your eyes." Ace turned away and crouched down.

"What was that, sir?" Sarge hit the ground instinctively as he was speaking. A few seconds later, the horizon erupted with a blinding white light.

"Plasma flare, Sarge." Ace climbed back to his feet, pulling the lever on the second sphere. "Stay down!" he yelled as he threw it, ducking low and closing his eyes as it detonated. "That should do it." Ace nodded as he looked off into the distance.

"That will do it, all right." Sarge climbed back to his feet, his men following his lead. "We need to get out of here, sir. They'll have seen that for sure."

Ace smiled at the noncom. "I hope so, Sarge. Those plasma flares cost a fortune. I'd hate to see them wasted." He pointed toward a patch of rocky ground. "Get your guys in cover."

"Yes, sir." The noncom was still confused, but Ace knew he wouldn't disobey a command. He trotted off, barking orders to his men.

"I hope this works, Ace."

"It will work." Ace gave Doc a confident smile. He wasn't as sure as he suggested, but that's not what his people needed to hear right now. He wondered how often Blackhawk had hidden his own fears and insecurity in tough situations. Not for the first time in his life, or even the hundredth, he thought how lucky he was to have a leader—and a friend—like Arkarin Blackhawk. He just wished it was the captain here leading the crew, and not him. *That's what we're here for, though. To save the man who's saved our asses so many times I've lost count. We're getting him off Saragossa or none of us are leaving this shithole of a planet.*

Katarina had wandered off into the woods, but now she came back and walked toward Ace. "They are coming, Ace. I was able to identify twelve of them, though there may be more."

Ace nodded. If Katarina said there were twelve, he knew there were twelve. Not eleven, not thirteen. "Okay, let's get ready." He didn't bother to tell her where to go. Katarina needed no assistance from him to get ready to kill.

He jogged over to where Sarge and his men had taken position. "We've got company coming, Sarge. A dozen of 'em." He turned back toward the edge of the forest. He could hear them now himself, crashing through the woods like a pack of wild megasauroids chasing their next meal. *It's a damned good thing for us these revolutionaries are such shitty soldiers,* he thought. "Here they come, Sarge." He was standing right next to the noncom, crouching behind a large boulder.

"Aim for the heads, boys." Ace gripped his rifle tightly, staring into the woods as the enemy moved closer. "We need those uniforms without holes in them."

CHAPTER 25

"CAPTAIN DRAX REPORTS A CONTACT." JACEN NIMBUS WAS hunched down over his scope, relaying the report as quickly as it came in. He turned and looked at Kharn. "He reports a momentary contact with a vessel in orbit around Saragossa, sir. He thought it was lifting off to leave the planet, but then it disappeared from his scanner almost immediately."

"Is it possible they eluded him and slipped through his scanning net?" There was an edge of menace in Kharn's voice. Drax was a capable captain, and the admiral didn't really think he'd let a ship sneak right by him. But he knew how the ka'al would react if he returned without Blackhawk and Astra Lucerne, and it wasn't a pleasant prospect. He was on edge, and it wasn't doing anything for his mood. And if one of his captains did let Blackhawk get away, the fool better step out of his own airlock before Kharn helped him to it.

"No, Admiral. He suspects the vessel reentered the atmosphere and landed almost immediately after liftoff."

"Perhaps they detected Drax's vessel and returned to the surface to avoid interception." But maybe it was Blackhawk's ship, he thought, trying to escape back to the planet after scanning the pirate ship. It made sense, at least as much as any other explanation.

I hope . . .

But there was reason to hope. Kharn hadn't expected to find any ships at all in the system. Saragossa was the only inhabited planet, and it was redlined. The locals didn't have any vessels of their own, so finding anything at all in orbit was a surprise, one that aroused justifiable suspicion.

He sighed. The question was: Did Drax actually spot the *Wolf's Claw*? The logic was sound. He knew he'd hit the *Claw* in the last skirmish, and Saragossa would have been a short jump for a wounded ship to make from Kalishar.

But it still didn't feel right. For one thing, Blackhawk wouldn't have run from a single ship. Indeed, Drax's *Black Lightning* wouldn't stand a chance in a one-on-one battle against *Wolf's Claw*. Kharn knew its capabilities dwarfed those of any one—or even two or three—of his own vessels. If it was indeed the *Claw* that Drax had spotted, why hadn't it simply destroyed him and escaped into hyperspace? There would have been more than enough time.

So why run from one ship he could easily defeat and slip back down to the planet where he would be trapped?

The admiral couldn't be sure. But this was the first real lead they'd found in weeks, and time was running out. It was a risk, but a calculated one. He cued up his comm.

"Order all ships to assemble at"—he paused, looking at the system plot on his workstation—"coordinates 347.652.111." That was far enough from the planet to avoid any surprises. If he was dealing with Arkarin Blackhawk and *Wolf's Claw*, he wanted everything he had concentrated and ready.

Hope gave way to a rush of excitement. He'd had a cold pit in his stomach for days, wondering what fate awaited him if he was unable to find Blackhawk. He had considered his task to be a hopeless one, searching the vastness of space for one of the most elusive smugglers in the Far Stars. Now he began to wonder if luck was finally on his side. Kharn sat and thought. He knew it was still a long shot that Drax had detected the *Claw*. Maybe he'd picked up some kind of natural anomaly. Or maybe the Saragossans did have a ship of their own. Information on backwater worlds like Saragossa was often inaccurate and outdated. It could even have been a smuggler or freighter making a special run. There was always someone willing to carry goods if the price was high enough. Perhaps it was a cargo ship that detected Drax's pirate vessel and rushed back to the relative safety of the planet's surface.

But Kharn had been a pirate a long time, and he had gotten there by instinct as much as skill. Those instincts were telling him now that Drax had found *Wolf's Claw*. Yes, the scanning data was incomplete. But the estimated mass was in the same range as *Wolf's Claw*, and coupled with everything else, Kharn was hopeful this was the break they needed.

He stared over at Nimbus. "Captain Drax is to enter Saragossa orbit and scan for any liftoffs."

"Yes, Admiral."

Entering orbit put Drax in a difficult spot if *Wolf's Claw* did launch from the surface. He might not be able to pull away in time to avoid combat, and a one-on-one fight withBlackhawk's ship was not one Drax was likely to survive. Unless, of course, the *Claw* was still damaged, its weapons systems offline. None of that mattered to Kharn, though. He wasn't about to let Blackhawk escape again, and Drax and his ship were expendable if need be.

Kharn stared down at his screen, at the projected courses of his ships. It would take a little over six hours to concentrate the fleet. Then he would position them to cover every angle of escape from Saragossa. Arkarin Blackhawk had gotten past him once, but not this time. If that had been *Wolf's Claw* Drax detected—and there was less and less doubt it was—its flight back to Celtiboria would end right here, in the empty space around Saragossa.

General Mak Wilhelm hated hyperspace. *Hate* was barely a strong enough word to describe how much he detested every faster-than-light journey he'd ever taken. Many people found the alien nature of the alternate space uncomfortable, with symptoms ranging from headaches to nausea, even death in a small percentage. Most of these effects were physical and, at least in the 99 percent who survived the transition, they were relatively tolerable.

It was different for Wilhelm. He felt the effects in his head, experiencing waking nightmares that tore at his very sanity. He saw strange visions, unimaginable horrors, creatures he could only remember in vague terms afterward, as though they were impossible to perceive or render in normal space. He had never been able to comprehend if he was seeing creations of his own mind or images of something hideous and alien that dwelled in the alternate dimension humans used for faster-than-light travel.

He'd learned to handle the visions, to compartmentalize them to a point, but he still dreaded every jump. He'd gone fearlessly into battle, engaged in life-and-death missions as an imperial spy, fought in hand-to-hand combat with deadly enemies—all without a moment's hesitation. But his hands shook uncontrollably when a jump was imminent. He clamped down on the terror he felt with iron discipline, but it was always there, just below the surface.

"Approaching the Saragossa system, General." The comm officer's voice was crisp, at least by the standards of interdimensional travel. No one performed at their best in hyperspace, not even hard-core spacers.

"I want all weapons stations manned, Lieutenant." Wilhelm didn't expect to encounter any hostiles, but he was a cautious man, one who became downright paranoid when he was fending off the demons that assaulted him in hyperspace.

"Yes, General." The lieutenant leaned forward and flipped on the intraship comm. "All crews, man your turrets." He flipped a switch, and the battle stations' lamps came on, casting a red hue throughout the control room.

One at a time, six indicator lights on his workstation switched from white to red, signaling the readiness of each of the vessel's weapons stations. "All weapon systems report ready, General," the lieutenant said. "Estimated time to transition back to normal space, one minute."

Wilhelm nodded and took a deep breath. One minute. Then he could bid the horrors of hyperspace good-bye, at least for a while. And he would see what was happening on Saragossa— and why his agent had suddenly gone silent.

CHAPTER 26

TALIN STOOD IN THE MIDDLE OF THE GRAND HEADQUARTERS OF the Revolutionary Army, looking out over the officers and soldiers at their various stations. He wore his uniform, but his appearance was messy and disheveled and he stank of brandy. He'd taken a cold shower and downed a pot of coffee, but he could still feel the fuzziness in his head. He'd been on an epic drunk the past few days, and he was still clawing his way back to mental clarity.

He looked up at the ceiling, thirty meters above where he stood. The walls were two meters of reinforced concrete. The structure had been an asphalt plant before the rebellion—a dirty, grimy, cheerless place where serfs like him had worked grueling twelve-hour shifts for their masters. The plant was a good reminder, he thought, of what had precipitated the revolution.

Its thick walls and sturdy construction also made it an ideal choice for its current use, and its location on the southern perimeter of New Vostok facilitated easy communication with the front lines fifteen kilometers to the south. There were other war zones on Saragossa, and other outposts of the Revolutionary Army, but the largest forces and bitterest fighting had been right here, in the vicinity of the capital. Whoever won the final battle here, all sides knew, would win the war.

"First Comrade Talin, General Varig reports that the enemy has begun to withdraw across the entire front line." The communications officer stood at attention as he addressed Talin, a hint of fear in tone. Talin knew that there had been hushed whispers about him, that he had become erratic, violent . . .

He did nothing to dissuade those rumors.

Just as he did nothing to dissuade the use of "first comrade." In fact, Talin had created the new title recently to differentiate himself and the other leaders of the revolution from the rank and file. He'd used men loyal to him to spread the new appellation, and wisely, the soldiers had quickly adopted it.

Which is only right, he thought. *It was my comrades and I who have fought the longest, made the greatest sacrifices. It is only fair and just we be recognized for our efforts. And me most of all.* He was the first comrade, and the others among the inner circle were honored comrades. He'd considered the idea of numbering his senior subordinates as well, but he'd decided a second comrade would be too clearly defined a successor. He didn't want to encourage any unhealthy ambitions among his subordinates, at least no more than he suspected existed already. He'd become more and more paranoid after Arn's betrayal and the schism that divided the revolutionary forces, and he much preferred a murky command structure below him.

"General Varig also reports that he has recovered all the ground lost to the enemy attack, and he is standing in place."

"No." Talin's words echoed off the heavy concrete walls. Every head in the control room turned to look at the leader of the revolution. "General Varig is to pursue and maintain contact with the enemy."

The room was silent, every eye focused on the supreme commander of the Revolutionary Army. Talin turned his head and looked around the cavernous chamber, his eyes wild with fervor. "I issued a command!" he roared. "General Varig is to continue his attack. He is to pursue the enemy wherever they flee, and he is not to stop until they are destroyed utterly." He took a few steps forward, turning to look out over the thirty or more officers present. "It is time. Time at long last for the revolution to achieve its final victory."

"Yes, First Comrade." The communications officer turned and moved quickly back toward his station, putting his headset on and relaying Talin's orders to the field headquarters.

Talin stood in the center of the room, watching the rest of the men and women present scramble back to their workstations. He could tell his presence unnerved them. He knew they were scared of him. That was one of the burdens to be borne by the leader of the revolution. There was no place for pointless mercy, no pity for those unwilling to sacrifice whatever was necessary to secure the victory of the people. He was willing to do all that . . . and more.

The communications officer pulled off his headset and

walked toward Talin. "First Comrade, General Varig advises he has suffered massive casualties in repelling the enemy attack." The communications officer spoke softly, his voice now openly quivering with fear. "He has over one hundred thousand killed and wounded, and he is low on supplies and ammunition." The officer paused and swallowed hard. "He advises that a continued offensive is not possible at this time."

Talin stared back at the cringing officer, his eyes wild with madness. "Contact General Tellurin. He is hereby promoted to field command of the Revolutionary Army. General Varig is to be arrested and summarily executed, and General Tellurin is to lead the offensive as per my previous orders."

He looked around the room. Everywhere, the staff officers gazed back timidly, though Talin was blind to their surprise and revulsion. He saw them as fools, weaklings unwilling to take the steps revolution required. They couldn't understand the burdens he bore, but that didn't matter. None of them dared to oppose him for fear of being the next one purged.

"It is time!" he shouted. "After seven years of stalemate, after hundreds of thousands dead and the lands laid waste, our chance for victory is upon us."

He walked around the room, waving his hands as he spoke. "The enemy suffered mightily to launch their great attack, expending vast quantities of their limited supply of weapons and ammunition. Now is our chance."

He turned back to the communications officer. "All units are to move forward to reinforce our brave men and women at the front. The reserve units, the remnants of the enhanced units. All the training cadres are to advance. Let all who can carry a rifle march to the fight to win the victory for our great revolution. And all who fail in their duty, who falter when they are called to the great struggle, let them be crushed beneath our boots, condemned for all time as traitors and cowards."

He stood for a moment, watching the staff rush to their workstations to carry out his commands. *Yes, they are all afraid of me and they think me mad.* He turned and walked toward the door. *But they will follow my orders,* he thought, *for they fear me— and I am the avatar of revolution.*

"Come now, Captain Blackhawk, surely we can be friends." Elisabetta was sitting on the edge of the bed, her hand on Blackhawk's arm. "It is so much more pleasant than the alternative, wouldn't you say?"

She smiled warmly, but Blackhawk could see through the softness to the iron core below. This was no pampered noblewoman to be bedded and manipulated. She was intelligent, dangerous, a remorseless killer, he imagined, if it served her purposes. He had no doubt being Elisabetta Lementov's ally offered considerable benefits, and he was just as certain crossing her would unleash the feral animal that lay behind the pleasant and seductive façade.

"Elisa, I desire nothing more than your friendship, but I assure you I had nothing to do with bringing those weapons to Saragossa." It was odd, he thought, how often the truth seems so unbelievable while a lie appears extremely plausible. Elisabetta was convinced he was behind the flow of imperial weapons to the revolutionaries, and he had no doubt he'd be just as convinced in her shoes.

He'd been identified by an old adversary now in her pay. She knew he was a smuggler, an adventurer, one with connections all over the Far Stars. Sneaking weapons into a warring, redlined planet was precisely the kind of thing he might have done in other circumstances. The argument that this was a coincidence, that he was only there to steal the imperial ship's hyperdrive core, was hard to believe, and no less far-fetched for its actual truth.

"You make me sad, Arkarin Blackhawk." She gazed down at him, running her fingers across his chest. "We could be quite a team, I am sure. In so many ways." She sighed, and he could hear a subtle change in her tone. "But it seems you turn your back on my offer of friendship." She pulled her hand slowly away. "And you force me to use far less enjoyable methods." She turned toward the door. "Vladimir, Bascilus."

The heavy wooden door swung open, and Vladimir Carano stepped into the room, followed by one of Elisabetta's bodyguards, a muscular man clad in white livery. Carano had shed the plain black fatigues he'd worn for the operation against the spy ship, and he was now clad in the normal field gray uniform of the Black Helms. His heavy boots rapped hard against the oaken floor as he approached Blackhawk's bedside.

"I must thank you, Captain Blackhawk," the veteran mercenary said. "Elisabetta insisted on making an attempt to reason with you, but I told her it would be to no avail. Indeed, I tried to warn her that you are an inherently unreasonable man, intractable to the last, but she insisted on trying to convince you to cooperate."

Blackhawk sighed silently. He recognized the man at once. He and Carano had a past, and their interaction had come to a head with the shedding of blood . . . and that blood had not been Blackhawk's. He hadn't expected to run into any friends on Saragossa, but it was just bad luck to stumble on an old enemy with vendetta on his mind. Carano had probably been dreaming of vengeance since the day Blackhawk had taken a chunk out of his shoulder in a duel, back during the clan wars on Mycenia.

"I will repeat myself again for your benefit—what is it, general now?" The merc had commanded only a few hundred soldiers when he and Blackhawk had last crossed paths, and Carano had styled himself a major at the time. "That ship was not mine. It was an imperial operations vessel, and I was only there to steal parts I needed to repair my own ship. I had nothing to do with bringing that ship to Saragossa, and I have no idea who did."

Carano smiled. "Thank you, Captain Blackhawk. I think part of me was afraid Elisabetta's potent charms and persuasiveness would lure you into cooperation. I am glad to see my assessment of your character was correct."

There was an edge to Carano's voice, something beyond just his hatred of Blackhawk. *Jealousy?* Blackhawk wondered. *Is he Elisa's lover?* The beautiful Saragossan noblewoman had virtually offered herself to Blackhawk in return for his cooperation. He suspected that didn't sit well with Carano, and that would only make things more difficult.

Carano took another step forward. "As I was saying, I was worried Elisabetta might have denied me the pleasure of obtaining the information by, ah . . . other means." The commander of the Black Helms had a caustic smile on his face, an expression of pure menace.

Blackhawk wondered at the strange nature of the universe, its ability to override the laws of probability to create one difficult situation after another for him to endure. "Well, General Carano, I guess we're both in for a long day." He sighed. "Because I don't know a fucking thing about those weapons or how they got here."

Ace moved forward deliberately, naturally, with the rest of the crew following behind. He avoided large groups of soldiers, but he didn't do it obviously, nor did he turn away from every trooper in his path. He knew any suspicious move could give them all away and leave Blackhawk and Shira stranded.

They were wearing coarse brown uniforms, poorly made garments that matched those of the troops moving all around them. The clothing had been stripped from the corpses of the patrol they had slaughtered, and they carried their enemies' weapons as well, having discarded any of their own gear they couldn't hide under their coats or stash in their packs. They looked just like the various groups of Revolutionary Army soldiers marching up toward the front.

"There appears to be a considerable movement of troops toward the front lines, Ace. It is a reasonable assumption that the intensity of the conflict has increased." Katarina was walking behind him, and she spoke softly, for his ears only. "We may have great difficulty crossing between the two armies, especially if they're heavily engaged."

Ace nodded. "According to the coordinates Shira sent us, the manor house is behind the extreme left of the nobles' battle line, just southeast of the primary combat zone. It looks like the troop densities are lower in that area." He was walking forward, trying not to look out of place as he spoke softly. "If we continue to move west now instead of south toward the front, we may find an easier location to cross."

"I agree, Ace, though we should be prepared in the event we are questioned about our destination." She was right behind him, speaking softly into his ear. "Virtually all troop movements are to the south, and we may draw attention to ourselves by marching west."

He hadn't thought of that. "We'll just have to deal with that if it happens." He took a quick look around. No one seemed to be paying them any undue attention, at least not yet. Ace knew all his people would fight if they had to, but they were in the middle of an enemy army. If their cover was blown, he knew they were well and truly screwed.

Katarina slipped back to a more normal interval for marching soldiers. She had her hair tied up tightly under her hat, and her face was crusted with dried red mud. Her perfectly manicured fingers were hidden inside coarse woolen gloves, and she walked like a lumbering farmhand, with none of the graceful elegance with which she typically carried herself. She looked more like a Saragossan peasant woman conscripted into the army than Ace or any of the crew would have thought possible. It was easy to write her off as a woman of noble birth and few skills, since that was how she usually presented herself. But Ace was once again reminded that Katarina Venturi was enormously skilled and as deadly dangerous as a Delphian sand viper.

"Assuming we make it through and rescue the captain, have you thought about how we're going to make it back?" Doc was walking next to Katarina, right behind Ace, looking uncomfortable in his brown fatigues. The *Claw*'s resident scholar tended to look more like a professor at an archaeological dig than a soldier, and he didn't make a very convincing peasant-conscript on close inspection. "Do we even try? Or do we head off to the south, and find a place to hide until the *Claw* gets back?"

Ace hadn't thought of that, either. He'd been focused on rescuing Blackhawk, and he realized he didn't have a plan for what to do if the mission was a success. It would take Lucas at least three weeks to get to Celtiboria and back, maybe four. The small supply dump they'd hidden near the *Claw*'s landing area was hundreds of kilometers away, and on the other side of the two warring armies. The buggy was almost certainly in enemy hands by now. They had no supplies in place, no food but what they had in their packs, no camping gear. So even if they managed to link up with Shira, and by some miracle they got Blackhawk out, they'd be on the run, with no place to go and almost a month before they had any hope of rescue.

He sighed. There was no point in worrying about what he couldn't change. There hadn't been time to make better arrangements, and even if there had been, they had no way to get supplies across the battlefield. Ace had hoped to find Blackhawk hiding somewhere near the spaceport, not clear across no-man's-land in some Saragossan noble's château, but the gods of fortune were playing with them all. Getting Blackhawk out of that place, that was job one. He'd worry about what to do after that if they survived that.

"I've got a plan," Ace said without hesitation, moving steadily forward to cut off any more questions from Doc.

He wasn't the *Claw*'s resident con man for nothing.

"Shira?" Ace was creeping forward through the ruined farmland, the rest of the crew following in single file. They had been marching for hours, struggling to remain hidden as they slipped through the lines of both armies. He moved slowly, cautiously. They'd come too far to be careless now.

Ace and Sarge were in the lead, wearing gray-and-black camo fatigues, uniforms stripped from two dead mercenaries. They hadn't had time to ambush an entire patrol as they had before, so the others still wore their Revolutionary Army garb. Ace had tied them all up—loosely—and they slipped through the nobles' lines masquerading as two soldiers escorting a group of prisoners to the rear.

They'd been questioned by one suspicious officer along the way, wondering why they had taken captives when the orders were to shoot any revolutionaries who surrendered. Ace had been quick in telling the inquisitive captain they'd been sent out to bring back prisoners for questioning. He wasn't sure the officer was buying it until he mentioned they were heading for the château and gave him the coordinates. Ace wasn't sure why, but the officer accepted that right away and let them pass. *Who else is at that château?* he thought. *What the hell have we stepped in?*

Nothing seemed out of the ordinary, at least by the standards of prowling around behind enemy lines. The grounds of the château were quiet. They'd seen two guard patrols in the distance, but they hadn't had any trouble eluding them. They'd seen a column of fieldworkers walking back from the field south of the manor, but they turned off and headed toward a cluster of outbuildings.

He stopped every few meters and looked around. It was almost dusk, and a heavy fog was settling in. The reduced visibility was helpful for stealth, but it wasn't making it any easier to find Shira. He took another dozen steps and stopped again. "Shira?"

"Ace, over here." The soft voice came from inside a small building, probably an old well house or storeroom.

He turned and moved quickly to the building, ducking behind it and waving for the others to follow. There was a thin line of trees just to the south, making the ground right behind the structure a good place to hide.

The building was small, and it was in poor repair, but it was made of solid stone and it looked strongly built. His mind was constantly evaluating the defensiveness of their positions, even though he knew it didn't much matter. Sure, they could hold out for a long time if they got into a firefight, but then they'd never get inside to rescue Ark. Stealth was still their best chance to stay alive, to get the captain back.

Ace motioned for the rest of the party to take cover behind the building, and he slipped around the side and through the small wooden door. He stepped inside and stopped dead. There was something hard pressing against his back. It felt like a knife.

"Shira, if that's you, cut the shit." He turned his head slowly, not wanting to make any sudden moves.

"Can't be too careful, Ace." Shira's voice was raw, hoarse. "I've been dodging farmworkers and guards since I got here." She pulled the blade away from Ace's back.

Ace turned around. Shira looked like hell. She'd been up for three straight days, and her haggard expression showed her fatigue. Her face was drawn and haggard, and she was covered in dirt. "Chrono's dick, Shira, you look like you're about to fall over." He pulled the sack off his back and opened the flap. He rummaged around for a few seconds and pulled out a stack of nutrition bars, handing them over to Shira. "Eat something. You're not going to do us—or Ark—any good if you keel over." He pulled the canteen off his belt and set it down next to her.

"Thanks, Ace." She tore open one of the bars and downed it in two quick bites. "I didn't expect to get dragged halfway across the planet chasing Ark." She grabbed the canteen and took a long gulp.

"Eat them all." He motioned to the two remaining bars.

"We've got more, and you need the strength." He turned and walked back to the door, taking a careful look before he stepped out and waved for the others to come inside. He held the door open as they ducked in, one after the other.

He came back inside and sat down on a large section of pipe. "So, Shira, did you manage to find a way in?"

She nodded, chewing quickly and swallowing the chunk of nutrition bar she'd just bitten. "Yes," she said, her mouth still half full. "I think I found one." She stared at Ace, her eyes grim with determination. "And I think it's high time we got the captain back, don't you?"

Blackhawk stared back at Carano, his face expressionless. He was suspended from the ceiling by his arms, and his bare chest and back were covered with bloody marks where the barbed tips of Carano's whip had torn into his flesh. He refused to scream or beg for mercy. None of it would change anything, and he wouldn't give his tormenter the satisfaction. Arkarin Blackhawk knew he was likely to meet his end in this room, and if that was his fate, he'd resolved to die well. He felt fear of course—no one was immune to fear and pain—but Blackhawk had been ready to face death for a very long time.

Besides, his crew would be safe by now, and Astra on her way back to Celtiboria. At the thought of Astra, a smile crept on his face, pushing through the fear and pain. If he had to die for something, saving Astra was a reason that gave him contentment. *It's a cliché, but there are some things worth dying for.*

"You are a brave man, Blackhawk, I will give you that. But why don't you let all of this end?" There was exhaustion in Carano's voice.

The general shook his head. "If you would just contact your associates and arrange for future weapons shipments to come to my men instead of the revolutionaries, we can stop this unpleasantness right now. You can remain with us as a hostage until the deliveries arrive, under much more comfortable circumstances, and then you will be released."

Blackhawk just silently stared back at Carano. Throughout the hours he'd endured, the captain had yet to make a sound, and the only reactions were the occasional smile. He could tell the merc's bitterness and desire for vengeance were waning, leaving an almost desperate tone to his words.

Blackhawk sighed, but remained silent. He knew Carano wasn't going to believe anything he said.

He turned his head, looking around the room. Carano had been careless a few times, coming close enough for Blackhawk to make a move. The mercenary general had no idea of the physical capabilities Blackhawk's enhanced genetics provided him. But the right moment hadn't come. Killing Carano did no good, not as long as the guards had time to react. Sure, Blackhawk could have wrapped his chained legs around Carano's head more than once, snapping the mercenary's neck in an instant. But he'd never have worked his way out of his chains before the guards took him down with their fire.

Being gunned down in an escape attempt was certainly preferable to staying in place and being tortured to death, but Blackhawk didn't think that way. From his earliest memories, he'd been trained, educated—even conditioned—to fight for survival, for victory. It wasn't in him to give up, not when there was the slightest hope, not even to spare himself from pain and torment.

Carano shook his head again. "Your reputation for stubbornness is well earned, Blackhawk, but it will avail you nothing. You will break eventually, so why stretch this out? Just tell me how I can reach your compatriots, and we can work out the terms of your release."

"Carano, I already told you I did not bring those weapons shipments to Saragossa. That is imperial ordnance, brought here on an imperial spy ship." He stared at Carano, his eyes half-open slits on his swollen face. "You saw that ship. Did it look like the vessel of a Far Stars smuggler?" Blackhawk took a raspy breath. "Do you think I care who wins the war to control this festering shithole? If I was running imperial guns, I'd be happy to sell them to your side, especially since you've probably got more money to pay for them."

Blackhawk paused, taking a deep, labored breath. "Did you think about that? If the revolutionaries are getting those weapons from a smuggler, how are they paying for them? You're a military man. How much are those weapons worth? How did the revolutionaries afford them? With tons of concrete and lengths of steel?

"And if I had a shipment of imperial weaponry to sell, why would I bring it to Saragossa in the first place? There are buyers all over the Far Stars who would pay twenty times what anyone on this godforsaken rock could manage."

Carano was silent, staring back at Blackhawk with an uncertain look on his face. Blackhawk knew he'd gotten his adversary wondering.

"If I were you, Carano, I wouldn't be worried about me. I'd be worried about why the empire was equipping my enemy."

Blackhawk saw his chance. Carano was deep in thought, considering what he had just heard. He was standing just close enough. Even the guards had strange expressions on their faces, probably fear from the sudden realization that their enemies might be backed by the empire itself. There would never be a better opportunity. He sucked in a deep breath and quickly swung his legs up and over Carano's head, pulling the chain tight around the mercenary's neck. The guards were taken by surprise, but they reacted swiftly, rushing forward with guns drawn.

"Stay back," Blackhawk rasped. He pulled his legs back, tightening his grip on Carano. "Or I'll break his neck."

The guards hesitated, uncertain what to do. They were Black Helms soldiers, Carano's men, and they didn't want to take a chance on getting their leader killed.

"Step back." Blackhawk stared at the guards as they ignored his command and stayed put. He pulled his legs up sharply, tightening the grip on Carano's neck. The mercenary general let out a sharp gasp, and his soldiers moved back, obeying Blackhawk's orders.

"Now put your guns down."

The soldiers hesitated for another instant, but then they complied, leaning down and setting their rifles on the floor.

"All your weapons." Blackhawk stared down at them, his eyes moving over their bodies. "Take off your coats, and drop your packs too."

The two men followed Blackhawk's orders, throwing down their packs and the pistols they had strapped under their coats.

"Now, turn around and face the wall." Blackhawk waited a few seconds then added, "Do it! Now!" He pulled his legs hard again, and Carano gasped. The guards turned slowly. "Walk toward the wall."

Blackhawk waited until the two men were standing against

the far wall of the room, facing away from him. Then he pulled himself up hard, twisting his arms and pulling the chains up and over the hook that held him suspended in place. He unhooked his legs from Carano's neck as he fell, spinning around and landing on top of the mercenary.

Carano tried to pull away, but the impact of Blackhawk falling on him pushed him to the floor. The two men scuffled for an instant, but Blackhawk looped his chained hands over Carano's head and pulled his opponent back into a tight hold.

"Back!" he yelled. He had to give the guards credit—they had started to move to intervene as soon as they heard the commotion. They just weren't going to be faster than Blackhawk, which he definitely counted on. "One move, and your boss is a dead man." The two mercs stopped in their tracks, staring intently at Blackhawk, but making no moves toward him. Their eyes darted from Carano to Blackhawk and back again.

"Now go grab two of those sets of shackles." When they didn't move right away, Blackhawk pulled the chain tighter around Carano's neck. "Now!"

The guards turned and walked over to the table, and each one grabbed a pair of the tempered steel shackles. They turned back and looked at Blackhawk. They knew what he was going to order them to do, but they waited to hear it.

"Throw the keys over here." Blackhawk watched as they obeyed his command. He loosened his grip slightly, giving Carano a bit more air. "Now shackle yourselves to that column." Blackhawk moved his head, gesturing toward a heavy masonry support in the middle of the room. The two guards looked at each other then back toward Carano, still held fast in Blackhawk's grip. They moved slowly toward the support, clasping the shackles around their hands and feet and wrapping the chains around the column. When they were done, they looked back at Blackhawk, their expressions miserable, defeated.

"This is insane, Blackhawk." The mercenary general's voice was quiet, raspy. "Where are you going to go? There are guards everywhere."

Blackhawk smiled. "I know that, General." He took a step, reaching for the keys to unlock his chains. "That's why you're coming with me."

CHAPTER 27

"ALL UNITS ARE TO ADVANCE WITHOUT PAUSE." GENERAL PETYA Tellurin stood outside his headquarters watching the lines of fresh troops streaming forward. It had been a bloody day, the most costly since the revolution began seven years before, but First Comrade Talin had been clear. "The orders are attack. Attack, attack, attack."

"Yes, General." Captain Josef Vernisky saluted sharply. Tellurin's aide was disheveled, his uniform torn and covered in mud. He'd been up to the front half a dozen times, scouting for Tellurin and personally delivering important orders. "The batteries are running low on ammunition, sir. They have requested resupply from supreme headquarters several times, but no convoys have arrived."

"Very well, Captain. See to relaying my attack order, and I will check on the supply situation for the artillery units."

Vernisky saluted and ran toward the communications tent. Tellurin watched him go, but he made no move to contact headquarters. He knew why there were no resupply convoys coming. It was because there was no ammunition to bring up. The combat of the past several days had been unexpected, and its intensity unprecedented. The constant savage fighting had burned through the army's entire stockpile of heavy ammunition. Soon, his batteries would fall silent, and his men on the front lines would have to continue their grueling advance without artillery support. Casualties would ramp up from their already catastrophic levels, but there was nothing to be done about that. He had his orders, and they were crystal clear. Attack.

Tens of thousands were dead already, but still the army moved relentlessly forward. There was no point in retreat, nothing to be gained by fleeing. First Comrade Talin had decreed that any who failed in their duty to the revolution would be shot down like dogs, and the elite units of the Red Guards were positioned behind the advancing lines, their emplaced autocannons ready to deal out death to any who faltered. They had carried through on that threat several times, and word swept through the army. The soldiers knew they had two choices, victory or death.

The Revolutionary Army forces were poorly trained and equipped compared to their mercenary adversaries, but Talin had ordered all reserves forward, and they outnumbered the forces of the nobles five or ten to one in many areas. Slowly, with great bloodshed, they pushed forward, driving against the mercenary lines until they were on the verge of collapse.

Tellurin didn't know if his manpower would hold out long

enough to break the enemy position and win the battle, but he knew he had no alternative but to press the attack to the last man. The image of General Varig forced to his knees by Revolutionary Army operatives and shot in the back of the head was still vivid in his mind. He'd been Varig's second in command, and he had numbered the general among his few true friends. But there had been nothing he could do to save Varig, and he knew he'd have faced the same fate or worse if he hadn't followed the first comrade's orders to the letter.

He could hear the sounds of battle from the front lines, and he watched the columns moving silently forward. The soldiers moving up now were practically children; Tellurin would have guessed half of them were fifteen or younger. Talin was sending half-trained recruits up now, struggling to pour more numbers into the battle, whatever it took to break the exhausted and overextended mercenary armies.

He turned and walked back toward the main HQ tent. There were three companies deployed in a small field just behind the headquarters. They were veteran formations, armed with the last of the imperial weapons remaining after the battles against the rebel splinter group. They were Tellurin's reserve, the sharp point to lead the breakthrough that would win the battle. He'd been holding them back, waiting for the right moment, but he knew his army was almost out of strength, his exhausted soldiers driven almost as far as fear could push them.

It was time for the final, all-out assault. He'd studied the map. The heaviest fighting had been along a line from the eastern edge of the field to the center, but the richest areas controlled by the nobles lay to the west. That was where he would attack with the last of his reserves. Along the western edge of the battle line and through to the rich estates beyond.

Blackhawk walked slowly down the corridor, limping badly and gritting his teeth as he pressed forward. His captors had given him quite a working over, and his back hurt like fire. He held a blade to Carano's throat, shoving the captive mercenary in front of him as he stumbled slowly down the damp, stone hallway.

"Be reasonable, Blackhawk." Carano's voice was hoarse, and his stress was obvious. "You'll never get out of here alive like this. But we can still make a deal."

"There is no time for deals, General." *Actually,* he thought, *I've probably got all the time in the world.* There wasn't a doubt in his mind that Sam had gotten the core installed. The *Claw* was on its way back to Celtiboria, and he was stuck on Saragossa. Blackhawk's plan was sorely lacking in sophistication. He intended to get out of the château and find someplace to hide. That was as far as he'd gotten, and he had no idea what his next step would be. He probably had a month to kill . . . or more likely, be killed, since that was a long time to stay alive and out of sight in a war zone, with no supplies or equipment. Still, it would all be moot if he didn't find his way out of this cellar first.

Blackhawk shoved his captive forward and shuffled down the corridor to the next intersection. He was pretty sure none of Carano's men had gotten off any kind of alarm, but he knew there had to be scanning and security devices emplaced in the cellar and, if there were, he was likely to have company soon. He wanted to get as far as he could before that happened. The place looked like an ancient dungeon, but he suspected that was an illusion. He was sure Elisabetta's home and headquarters would be advanced in terms of security, and that would apply doubly to the prisons and torture chambers in the lower levels. Lady Lementov didn't strike Blackhawk as the trusting type.

"Where are my things?" Blackhawk followed up the question with a hard knee to Carano's back.

The mercenary groaned, but he didn't answer until he felt Blackhawk's hand press the blade tighter to his neck. "Around the corner. Second door on the right."

Blackhawk held the knife tightly against Carano's throat, and the mercenary let out a yelp as he twitched slightly and a small trickle of blood dripped over the blade. "Any guards in the room? There's no point in lying. Nothing in that room can take me out before I slit your throat."

"There shouldn't be anyone in there."

"Let's hope you're right." He pushed ahead and peered around the corner before he spun around, shoving Carano in front of him. He walked slowly down the hallway, stopping at the second door. "Open it."

Carano reached out and turned the handle with his shackled wrists, pushing the door forward into the room. Blackhawk peered into the dimly lit chamber, looking and listening for anyone who might be hiding inside. When he was satisfied, he gave Carano another push, and the two slipped through the door.

The room was small, perhaps four meters square, with a single light hanging loosely from the ceiling. There was an old wooden table in the middle of the room, and a series of chests with drawers along the far wall. Blackhawk was about to ask where his things were when he saw the hilt of his sword sticking out from under a pile of items on the table.

He shoved Carano forward, and he grabbed his sword with his free hand. He used the blade to poke through the pile of items, finding his belt and holstered pistol on the bottom. He laid the sword down and pulled the pistol out from its place on his belt. He examined it, checking to make sure it hadn't been unloaded or otherwise tampered with. When he was satisfied, he pulled the blade from Carano's neck and threw the mercenary across the room.

He aimed the pistol at Carano's head. "There, I think that's more comfortable, don't you?" He sat down on the edge of the table and stared at his captive. "Now, you and I are going to take a little walk, General. So if you would be so kind, please describe the quickest way out of this château and we can be on our way."

"Chrono's dick, it stinks in here." Ace was in the lead, crawling through the twenty centimeters of muck pooled along the bottom of the heavy concrete pipe. The conduit was part of the ancient water system for the château, long since replaced with more modern facilities. Modern, by Saragossan standards, at least. He stopped and pulled up one hand, shaking off the slimy residue of fifty years of rotting leaves and rat shit.

"Stop whining. It's a way in with nobody shooting at your precious ass, isn't it?" Shira's voice was stronger than it had been an hour before. The nutrition bars had given her a jolt of energy, and Ace half regretted getting her all jacked up. There were times he suspected an exhausted, half-starved Shira would be preferable, but not when they were going into a fight.

"At least it's not a sewer. You could be crawling through a river of shit right now."

Ace flipped his hand again, sending a spray of black water and dark gray sludge flying into the walls of the pipe. "It stinks just as bad." He took a shallow breath and started forward again.

They had come at least a hundred meters, and Ace figured

they had another fifty to seventy-five to go. None of them knew where the abandoned conduit entered the manor house, but it seemed like the best way in. Even if they had to blast open a sealed-off entrance, at least they'd already be inside when they gave themselves away.

The pipe was only wide enough for one person abreast, so they were in a long line, with Ace in the lead and Shira right behind him. Katarina was next, followed by Doc and then Sarge and his men. The noncom had pushed to take the lead position, but Ace insisted on being in the front. He knew Sarge was going to struggle mightily to crawl so far with his wounded shoulder, and he didn't want him up front in case there was trouble.

Ace had looked back a few times to check on Katarina. It was an involuntary response, one he knew was foolish. She was keeping up, no problem—if anything, he realized, she could run them all into the ground. She looked so much like a pampered noblewoman, it was hard to remember sometimes just what a deadly killer she was. *Of course,* he thought, *that's the point.*

He pushed forward into the covering darkness, only the small light stuck on his shoulder to show the way. The pipe was heading steadily down, into the lower levels beneath the châ-teau. With any luck, they'd come up in some mechanical area in the cellar, and they'd be able to sneak upstairs and begin the search for Blackhawk. Then they would grab him and make a break for it.

They crawled forward for another ten minutes before Ace stopped abruptly. He flipped off the small lantern on his shoulder and stared straight ahead. There was a dim light about twenty meters forward.

"Stay put, all of you," he whispered back to Shira, motioning with his head for her to pass the message back. Ace had no idea where the light was coming from or if anyone was there, but he intended to find out.

Shira stared back for a second, looking like she might argue with him. Ace knew she didn't like staying behind—not after she'd spent so long waiting around outside and especially with Blackhawk's life on the line. *Just trust me, Shira.*

A second later, she nodded and turned to relay the command.

Ace crept forward slowly, trying to be as quiet as he could. The light was getting a little brighter, and he could get a better view. There was a grate ahead covering the pipe, and it looked like a room beyond.

He scrambled the rest of the way. The grate was loose over the end of the pipe, heavily rusted and bent at an angle. He looked through into the room. It was about four meters square, with a rough stone floor, and a small light in the ceiling. It was old and musty, and it felt deserted. There were standing pools of water in low spots on the uneven floor. He stopped and listened carefully, but the only thing he could hear was a steady drip of water streaming down out of the pipe.

He gave the grate a gentle shove. It moved easily, and the top section ripped halfway out of the crumbling masonry of the wall, sending chunks of broken concrete tumbling down into the puddles below.

Ace pulled his arm back abruptly, peering around the room again, satisfying himself it was empty. He turned as far as he could in the tight confines of the pipe and he flipped his small light back on, waving it around, signaling for the others to come forward. He turned back and peered through the grate until he could feel Shira move up behind him.

"The room looks empty." He angled his head and spoke softly. "I think the grate's loose enough for me to knock off, but it's going to make a lot of noise when it hits the floor." He took a deep breath. "Get ready, and be on my heels."

"I'm there, Ace. Ready when you are." Her voice was calm, serious. There was no banter between them now, no rivalry. This was it. They were going in there to get Blackhawk, and nothing else mattered. "Ready when you are."

Ace nodded and turned back to the grate. He gripped it hard with both hands and pushed. It moved easily at first, and two of the corners tore free of their mountings, sending a small avalanche of broken chunks of concrete to the ground. He shoved again, but one corner wouldn't budge. The grate pushed out into the room, but the space wasn't big enough for him to slip through.

He took a deep breath and lunged forward, pushing himself against the grate as hard as he could. He felt it begin to give. He pulled back and lunged forward again. And again. He felt the metal sliding out of its mounting. One more good push . . . He threw himself forward with all the strength he could muster.

The last bolt gave way, and the grate tumbled into the room, Ace following right behind. He threw his arms out in front of him, but he fell hard, landing in a puddle of putrid water about ten centimeters deep. He threw himself into a roll, trying to cushion the shock of the impact. He flipped around, coming back up into a prone position and grabbing the pistol from his belt.

His hands and arms hurt like hell, but he was pretty sure nothing was broken. The grate had hit the ground with a loud crash, though, and Ace's eyes panned around the room, searching for doors. There was only one, and he stared right at it, his weapon ready in case anyone had heard the crash.

Shira was down now too, and Katarina as well. If anybody

came through that door, they were going to have a hell of a
fight on their hands.

"They're coming around both flanks, sir. We've got to pull back
now, or we'll be surrounded." Captain Braden had been hit
twice, and his uniform was covered with blood. He was in front
of Colonel Vulcan, standing as close to attention as his battered
and bleeding body could manage.

Vulcan's forces had fought like demons, but the revolutionaries just kept coming. They were pushing old men and boys
into the lines now, but somehow they kept feeding the bodies
forward. The Tiger Company had killed thousands, and the
Black Helms and other mercenary forces had performed just
as well. But the battle was lost. There were just too many of
the enemy, and they kept coming. The only thing he could do
now was try to extricate the remnants of the mercenary forces
as close to intact as possible. Maybe they could regroup and
launch a counterattack, or at least reestablish a strong defensive
position, but they needed time. If he didn't pull them back now,
there wouldn't be any forces left to continue the fight.

"The Second, Third, and Fourth Squadrons will retreat immediately." Vulcan's voice was raw, his throat parched and scratchy.
He was injured too, but it was just a flesh wound on his shoulder,
nothing bad enough to drive him from the field, especially when
his forces were on the verge of disaster. "Order First Squadron to
find their best position and dig in. I want those tanks hull down
and ready to hold while the rest of the line pulls back."

"Yes, sir." Braden winced in pain as he lifted his arm and
pointed to the east. "There's a strong position half a klick east.
Slowly rising ground, very rugged approach. And good ground
to dig in the tanks."

"Perfect. Send those coordinates to Captain Timmons. And as soon as you relay the orders, get to the field hospital." Vulcan stared at his aide. "You look like you're about to fall over."

"I'm fine, sir. I can . . ."

"If you're fine, obey my orders. Relay my commands, and go get yourself tended to, understood?"

"Yes, sir." The officer nodded and hurried off to the east.

Vulcan sighed, looking around at the chaos of the battle. Oily plumes of smoke rose from the other side of the small ridge to his front. He knew what those black columns meant. Each of them was one of his tanks burning, its crew probably incinerated inside their stricken war machine.

The Tiger Company had been renowned for its armor, and it possessed more tanks than any other mercenary force in the Far Stars. *It had,* Vulcan corrected himself. He had armed and equipped his troops so superbly, they were accustomed to quickly overwhelming the enemies they faced. He'd taken the contract on Saragossa because it seemed like just the sort of job for his Tigers. He'd expected his massive tanks to terrify and overwhelm the rebels, but by the time they arrived, the revolutionaries had taken most of the cities and industry, and they'd managed to put a real army in the field.

When Vulcan received the original contract offer, Saragossa had been dealing with localized peasant rebellions. By the time he arrived, it had become a worldwide revolution, and the peasants he'd expected to sweep away had hundreds of thousands of troops under arms. The fast, profitable war he'd imagined turned into a protracted stalemate, and when the transport guilds redlined the system, his people were trapped. They'd become as dependent on victory as the Saragossan nobles who had hired them.

Still, for all the unexpected difficulties of the campaign, he'd never expected to see his men in wholesale retreat. They had lost many of their precious tanks already, and Vulcan had no idea how he would replace the casualties—either the veteran soldiers themselves or the expensive fighting vehicles. He wasn't even sure the Tiger Company would get off Saragossa at all.

He looked out to the east. His First Squadron would be forming up along the position Braden had scouted, following his orders to dig in and hold. He wondered if they realized he was sacrificing them to save the rest of the forces. There were good men in that unit, loyal soldiers who'd served with him for years. He hated the cold-blooded decision to expend them as if they were some inanimate resource. But if he didn't buy time somehow, the entire army would be flanked and destroyed. In the end, it came down to numbers, as it always seemed to.

He turned away. He could hear the enemy shells hitting the positions over the ridge. With any luck, it would take them a while to finish off the First Squadron. Long enough, he hoped, to get everyone else bugged out.

He turned and headed for the communications tent. Someone had to warn General Carano and Lady Lementov that they had enemy forces breaking through. The château was no longer safe, and they had to pull back immediately. That call was his to make, his duty to his ally and his employer. He just hoped he got to them in time. The revolutionaries would probably just kill Carano if they captured him, but Elisabetta Lementov faced a far worse end, especially once they realized who she was.

Ace took a deep breath. He'd been staring at the door for at least a minute, and he realized he'd been holding his breath. Shira and Katarina were standing next to him, their weapons ready, but no one came. Finally he walked across the room and put his ear to the door. It was thick wood, and he wasn't sure he'd hear anything even if someone was out there. Still, the silence was reassuring.

Everyone was out of the pipe now, and Sarge and his boys had their rifles ready, standing at near attention in the center of the room. Katarina was right behind Ace, silently observing, and Shira was next to him, her face an image of pure determination. Doc was leaning against the wall, looking a bit under the weather for the ordeal.

Ace shook his arm hard again, sending a spray of muck and water flying into the wall. "Well, that was a fun route in, but maybe we can do better on the way out." He shot Shira a quick grin, but he didn't say anything more. After all, she had gotten them inside, apparently undetected.

He turned to face the rest of the group. "Let's get out of here. Remember, stay quiet, and let's see how far we can get before we end up in a fight and wake up the entire place."

He walked over to the door, giving it an experimental push. It was heavy and the hinges were covered with a thick coating of rust, but it moved a few centimeters. He took a deep breath and put his shoulder into it, and it pushed open, snapping off one of the hinges and falling sideways into the hall with a loud crash.

Ace leaped out, rifle in hand, scanning both ways as he did. He held his arm up, signaling the others to wait while he listened. The only sound was the hum of distant machinery, probably the mechanical systems for the château, he thought.

He took a few steps down the hall, motioning for the others to follow. He strapped his rifle across his back and pulled a heavy combat knife from its sheath. "Katarina, Shira, up here with me. Let's try to keep things quiet if we can."

They both stepped forward. Shira pulled out her own blade. It was longer and thinner than Ace's knife, and they'd all seen her use it with deadly effectiveness.

Katarina didn't have a weapon drawn, but Ace was familiar with her throwing knives and the incredible skill with which she used them. He had long suspected she could take out an insect buzzing by with one of them, though she'd never indulged him by putting it to the test. The assassin followed a strict code. Weapons were for training and killing only. They were to be revered, cared for, treated with the utmost respect, but never used for frivolous purposes.

Nothing frivolous about what we're doing now.

"Sarge, you and your boys be ready. If quiet doesn't work, noisy is a hell of a lot better than dead."

"We're ready, sir. We're always ready." The noncom had his assault rifle gripped tightly in his hands, and his expression was deadly serious. His men were virtual copies of him, ready for whatever was about to happen.

Ace nodded to them all and started down the corridor. He flipped a coin mentally and decided to go to the left. The floor and walls were concrete, ancient and crumbling in places. The hall continued for about fifty meters before opening into a large room. There had been a door at one time, but the only sign of it was a broken piece of hinge hanging from the frame. The room was mostly empty, but there were a few machines along the far wall, old and covered with dust. From the look of them, Ace guessed they were furnaces that had once been part of the château's heating system.

"This must be an old wing. It doesn't look like this stuff's been used for a century. Maybe more."

Shira nodded. "Wherever we are, no one comes down here

very often," she said, pointing at the thick dust that covered the floor. Her eyes moved to the far wall. Two corridors led away from the room. "So which way, Ace?"

He was about to answer when a loud crack echoed through the still air.

Ace didn't hesitate toward the hallway on the right. "I'd say there's someone down here after all." He had his pistol in one hand now and the knife still in the other. "Let's go."

"I am not going to kill you, Carano." Blackhawk was pushing his captive forward, his pistol aimed at the mercenary's head as they moved through the basement tunnels. "Not unless you make me. That was nasty business on Mycenia, I'll admit, but it was just that. Business.

"Just lead me out of here and when we're away from the château, I'll let you go. I'm not part of this fight here. I have no stake either way. I'm just stuck here."

Carano stumbled forward, leading Blackhawk into the older sections of the basement. Blackhawk didn't know if he was getting anywhere with his prisoner, but he thought he might be. At least a little.

"I don't know these passageways very well, Blackhawk. This is Elisabetta's château, not mine. I don't spend a lot of time in the basement catacombs."

"Well, you know them better than I do, so just . . ." Blackhawk stopped abruptly. His ears caught the sound of boots on the hard stone floor, getting closer.

"What is . . ." Carano started to speak, but Blackhawk grabbed the mercenary and put his hand over his mouth. They were in a long hallway. Blackhawk's head snapped back and forth, scanning the situation. There was a door a few meters forward, and he rushed toward it. He reached out and opened the door, shoving Carano inside just as he saw a shadow coming around the corner. He ducked back as the guard turned into the hallway and fired.

Blackhawk threw Carano to the ground. "Sorry, Vladimir," he muttered as he whipped around the door frame and fired back. One of the guards was halfway down the hall, and Blackhawk's shot took him right in the head. He fell hard, and his companion jumped back around the corner.

Blackhawk ducked back in the room, turning to check on the prisoner. "I don't want to kill any more of your people, Vladimir, so call them off now."

Carano pulled himself to his feet. "None of my people would be down here."

Blackhawk stared at his captive, trying to decide whether to believe him or not. "Light gray uniform, black beret . . ."

"Those are Elisa's men." Carano brushed himself off. "Her household guard."

Half her private army will be down here in a few minutes. He peered outside the door, ducking back as another shot rang out. "We're trapped."

"I told you we'd never get out." Carano's voice had a strange tone. The hatred toward Blackhawk was gone, replaced by a vague curiosity.

Blackhawk raced toward the door, checking the hall. He heard more footsteps, from the other way this time. An instant later he heard a shot. There was a pause, no more than a second or two, and then a full-scale firefight erupted. The footsteps became quicker, louder, and they were coming his way. He flashed a look back at Carano. The prisoner was standing quietly, but showed no signs of making a move. Blackhawk peered around the door frame, toward the guard who had retreated. There was no trace of him. *Maybe he ran for help,* Blackhawk thought. *Or just ran.*

He spun around, bringing his pistol to bear facing the other direction. He could hear the footsteps getting closer. They were louder, faster. Whoever was coming his way, they were running now. There was still gunfire, but it was more sporadic now. There was something familiar about the pitch of some of the fire.

There are R-111 assault rifles in that mix of fire.

The guns he'd bought for his crew. State-of-the-art military weapons, at least by the standards of the Far Stars. Who the hell would have those here?

No. It can't be . . .

Just then he saw Ace swing around the corner and race down the hallway, with Shira right behind. His rifle was out in front of him, and the right side of his face was covered with blood.

"In here!" Blackhawk screamed, waving his arms from the doorway.

Ace stared at him in shock and ran into the room. Blackhawk stepped aside, letting them run in one after the other. Shira, Katarina, Sarge and his men. He slammed the door shut and turned to stare at them all. His stomach had clenched when he saw the blood all over Ace's head, but now he could see it was just a flesh wound, a close call that came a couple centimeters from finishing him off.

His concern quickly turned to anger. "What the hell are you doing here? Where is Astra? Is she okay?" There was concern in his voice, fear.

"She's fine, Ark." Ace pulled up a section of his shirt and wiped the blood from his eyes. "She's on her way to Celtiboria, just the way you wanted." He inhaled hard, trying to catch his breath. "Lucas, Sam, and the Twins are with her."

Relief flooded Blackhawk. "Thank you, Ace. But you should all be there, too. I'm pretty sure I ordered you to leave. Now you're all stuck down here with me."

"To be fair, what you ordered . . ."

"I know what I said, Ace, and you knew what I meant."

Ace hung his head, as did the others. Blackhawk wasn't one to berate his crew, and even now, his voice wasn't angry. But he knew the disappointment was apparent. The crew of the *Claw* were all fuckups in their own ways, and all he asked was that they try their best in whatever he asked of them. They rarely let him down. Hell, even now they had done something he would have thought impossible on this war-ravaged planet: sneak across hundreds of kilometers and infiltrate a heavily fortified position. It was impressive. And it wasn't that he wasn't grateful they were here—he truly was—but he had sent them away for their safety. They were all still in deep shit, and the thought that they might have just showed up so they could all die together was too much to bear.

Fortunately, Elisabetta's men weren't going to let him dwell on it. He could hear the sounds of boots in the hall, running back and forth. "Sarge, grab that bench. Let's barricade the door." Blackhawk helped the noncom shove the heavy wooden bench in place. He leaned against the door and shouted. "We've got General Carano in here with us. I want to talk to Lady Lementov. Now!"

He turned toward Carano, an odd look on his face. "I hope you don't mind me using you as bait, Vladimir, but I'm fresh out of other ideas."

CHAPTER 28

"IT APPEARS WE HAVE A STANDOFF, CAPTAIN BLACKHAWK."
Carano was exhausted, and it came through in his tone. "The
way out is blocked. You can kill me, but if you do, you and your
people will never leave this château."

Blackhawk frowned. He knew Carano was right. It had been
ten minutes since Blackhawk had made his demand, and still
nothing had happened. True, they were safe for the moment,
but they were also trapped. And while Carano was a valuable
hostage, it was only a matter of time before someone—possibly
Lady Lementov—decided he wasn't worth it. Then the guards
would force the door, and Blackhawk's crew was outnumbered—
probably a hundred to one once their besiegers called for aid. It

would cost the guards heavily—the door would act as a funnel, a perfect kill zone for the *Claw*'s crew. Until their bullets ran out.

The whole thing was frustrating. He didn't have a stake in Saragossa's war, and he didn't want one. He was disgusted with both sides, the nobles who had kept the peasants under their iron boots for so many generations and the revolutionaries who managed to become as corrupt and brutal as their former masters in a few short years. The thought of his people getting killed in a cesspool like this sickened him. But it still wasn't his fight.

"I'm telling you for the last time, General. I had nothing to do with supplying the rebels with those weapons." His eyes bored into Carano's. "Why would I? Think about it.

"There were three men in the brig, prisoners my people captured when we took the ship. They are imperial intelligence operatives." Blackhawk paused. "I don't know why the empire is involved here, but my people had nothing to do with it." He stared into Carano's eyes. "Order your men to stand down. Let my people go. We are not your enemies."

Ace was standing by the door, listening for any activity in the hallway. "Someone's coming, Ark."

Every member of the crew snapped their weapons around, pointing toward the door, waiting. There was a small knock, then a muffled voice. "I am unarmed. I have a message for General Carano. It is from Colonel Vulcan."

Blackhawk nodded to Ace, and his number two shoved the bench aside, opening the door slowly. "Inside," he said. "Now."

A tall man slipped through the door, clad in the uniform of the Black Helms. Sarge grabbed him and pushed him against the wall, searching for weapons. He turned toward Blackhawk after a few seconds. "He's clean."

Blackhawk just nodded, and Sarge released the rattled mercenary. "You may report to your commander," Blackhawk said softly.

The soldier looked at Carano. The general shrugged and said, "Go ahead. You may speak freely in front of these people."

Blackhawk looked at Carano sharply, but he couldn't find any deceit in the man's eyes. *Maybe I actually got through to him.*

"Sir, Colonel Vulcan reports that the enemy has launched a massive counteroffensive all along the front. His lines are broken in multiple locations, and he is attempting to disengage and withdraw to reform. It is urgent that the château and the surrounding areas be evacuated at once, as he can no longer ensure security."

Carano nodded to the soldier then he turned to face Blackhawk. "Well, Captain Blackhawk, this complicates matters, wouldn't you say?"

Blackhawk looked around the room and took a deep breath. "Well, Carano, I . . ."

There was a loud crash, and the building shook. Chunks of concrete fell from the walls, and dust came down from the ceiling. Another explosion followed a few seconds later, louder, closer.

"I would say the revolutionaries are here, General Carano," Blackhawk said. "So shall we stay here until they dig us out and shoot us all, or should we put aside old grudges and new suspicions and cooperate?" Blackhawk extended his hand.

Another explosion shook the room, and a section of the ceiling collapsed in the corner. Carano had a surprised look on his face. Blackhawk didn't blame him—trained mercs with superior weapons were losing this battle to a bunch of raw soldiers armed with crude tech. Blackhawk looked at him and shrugged. *Of course there are a lot more of the green revolutionaries. A lot more.*

Then another shell hit, and the lights went out.

"Are your forces ready, Captain?" Tellurin was standing behind the moving columns, shouting orders to his aide. Vernisky's battalion was a mixed bag, a cadre of veterans fleshed out with a bunch of old men and kids. But they were in the right place, and the commander of the Revolutionary Army was here himself to lead them.

The enemy was pulling back all across the field, and the exhausted revolutionary armies were close on their heels. He couldn't even guess at the casualties his units had suffered, but he put that out of his mind for now. The losses had been staggering, he knew, but now they were on the verge of making all the sacrifice meaningful.

Vernisky's troops were moving on a large manor house, supported by the last of the heavy artillery ordnance. The château was the home and headquarters of Elisabetta Lementov, the effective leader of the noble cause. If she was killed or captured, the nobles would be dealt a fatal blow. She, as much as anyone, was responsible for preventing the revolution from achieving victory the past seven years, and her loss following right after the defeat of the mercenary forces would be a body blow to her compatriots.

Tellurin watched his soldiers moving forward, heading toward the great house in the distance. It was almost dark, but the shelling had set parts of the massive building on fire, and the flames glowed eerily in the fading dusk. Hope rose in General Tellurin. Lementov was his enemy, a member of the noble caste that had kept the rest of the population in virtual slavery for centuries. He'd hated her kind his entire life, and now he was on the verge of destroying her and achieving total victory.

Still, he'd seen enough revenge and brutality to last a lifetime, and he found himself hoping she would die in the fighting, rather than surrender. He had no desire to see her dragged before Talin, gang-raped by soldiers, and finally tortured to death before a bloodthirsty mob. Once, perhaps, he might have, when the abuse of his noble taskmasters had been fresher on his mind, his scars and empty belly feeding his hatred. But he'd seen too many die on both sides since he'd worked in the factories and, unlike Talin, his bloodlust was long sated. He wished for nothing more than a time when the guns stopped firing.

The general looked out at the shells impacting around the château. At least three had hit the massive building, and a section of one wing had collapsed. Troops were streaming out, taking up defensive positions all around the property. Tellurin stood and watched, waiting for the artillery fire to cease. He had released the last of the ammunition to bombard the château, and he knew the batteries had to be down to their last shots. When they were done, he would send in Vernisky's people. He had reinforcements on the way, and other battalions moving around both flanks, maneuvering to cut off any retreat. The trap was set, the final battle about to begin.

He looked around, realizing the shellfire had stopped. It was time. He walked toward Vernisky. "Captain, you may begin your attack."

"What the hell is going on down there?" Lucas was staring at his scope, watching the scanner results go crazy. The *Claw* had just entered the upper atmosphere, and Lucas had done a routine scanner sweep.

"What is it?" Astra was sitting in Blackhawk's chair, staring intently at the *Claw*'s pilot. She'd put the pistol away, but she still held the stun gun in her hand. She stared at him suspiciously. "Don't try anything, Lucas."

"I'm not, Astra. A real damned war has erupted down there." He paused. "I hope the skipper and the others aren't in the middle of that."

She stood up, moving cautiously toward Lucas's station. The *Claw* was streamlined for atmospheric flight, but it was still a rough ride. She was still suspicious of the pilot, but he sounded sincere enough, and she decided to see for herself.

She looked down at his station. There were intersecting red circles everywhere, explosions across a forty-kilometer front south of the capital city. She glanced at the energy readings scrolling down the side of the map and gasped. It was nothing less than total war going on down there, a massive battle along a broad front. It looked like the two sides had begun the climactic struggle—and if she knew Blackhawk, he was in the thick of it.

"We have to get to them, Lucas. We can't leave them down there with all that fighting going on." Her voice had been firm, in command, but now he could hear the fear creeping into her tone. She was scared for Blackhawk, and she was desperate to go to his aid.

"We're on the way, Astra. But it's not that simple. It's a complete fucking mess down there. I could use your help. I need you to let the Twins out. We need them in the turrets, because it looks like we might have some fighting to do. Please, just trust me. I'm with you, Astra. We've got to get them out of there. But I need you at Ace's station. And I need the Twins in the turrets." He stared at her, his eyes pleading for her trust. "No tricks, Astra. My word."

She hesitated for a few seconds, then put the stun gun in her pocket. She turned and walked back to Ace's station, sitting down hard on the plush leather chair. She slid Blackhawk's keycard in the slot and punched a series of keys. "I unlocked the hatches. The Twins and Sam are free." She looked over at him, and he could see the worry in her eyes. She was no stranger to war, nor its cost. She knew Blackhawk could die here—all of them could die. "What do you want me to do, Lucas?"

He leaned forward and activated his comm. "Tarq, Tarnan, I need you in the turrets. Now!" He turned back toward Astra. "You know how to use the comm?"

"Yes."

"We'll be in range in about a minute. I need you to contact Blackhawk, Ace—anybody you can reach. Find out where they are."

"Got it."

Lucas grabbed the throttle, twisting it hard to the side. She struggled to stay in the chair as *Wolf's Claw* banked hard. "And strap in. I'm going to get us down there fast."

Lucas flipped the channel. "Sam, I need all the power you can get me. Now."

"Get your men deployed in those outbuildings. A squad in each, with at least one autocannon." Blackhawk crouched in the makeshift trench, shouting out commands to Lementov retainers and Carano's mercenaries alike. They didn't have enough troops to face the attackers in a conventional battle line, so Blackhawk was directing the defenders to scattered strong points. The revolutionaries weren't well trained, but there were a lot of them. He hoped his dispersed defense would break up their formations and disorder their attack.

As he gave the orders, that familiar calm came over him. There was something in his voice and his presence on the battlefield, a confidence and authority that commanded respect. He was in total charge, as if he'd been born to lead armies. He just started issuing directives, and the confused and terrified soldiers obeyed. They now had a leader who didn't just command respect—he demanded respect.

He could see the enemy forces advancing. There was at least a battalion to the front, and he knew more troops would be coming around the flanks. The defenders would make the revolutionaries pay, but in the end Blackhawk was fairly certain they were doomed. Carano had contacted Vulcan, but the rest of the mercenary forces had pulled back farther to the east. They were trying to push a relief column through, but Blackhawk knew they were too far away. By the time they got to the château—if they got there at all—there would be nothing left to do but bury the dead.

"Back in the shit, hey, Ark?" Ace was standing next to his leader, holding his assault rifle. Doc had managed to get a quick dressing on his head wound, but there was still half-dried blood all over his face. The injury wasn't serious, but he looked like an image of death itself.

"Get yourself some good cover, Ace." Blackhawk's voice was cold, distant. He turned toward Ace and there was a strange fire in his eyes, as if some mysterious force had taken him.

Blackhawk's voice was different too, his tone almost daring anyone to disobey his commands. It was a sound of pure confidence, even arrogance, and no one on the field—not crew, not mercenary, not house retainer—no one—disobeyed his orders.

Blackhawk turned and walked back toward a low stone wall. Carano and about twenty of his men were crouched behind.

"You see that line of burned-out trees, Carano?" Blackhawk didn't wait for an answer. "As soon as the enemy reaches that, I want you to open fire. Not before. Understood?"

"Yes." No questions, no hesitation. Just obedience. The jaded mercenary leader was following Blackhawk's orders like a lieutenant fresh out of some military academy.

"Good." Blackhawk estimated the tree line was five hundred meters away, well below the minimum range of the Black Helms's assault rifles.

491 meters.

That's what he wanted: to wait until the enemy was in the true killing zone, and then hit them with everything all at once. They were mostly green troops, levies conscripted by the Revolutionary Council. Blackhawk could tell from the way they were advancing: disordered, clumped together. He wanted to hit them hard and break their morale before they could bring their numbers to bear. He knew it was ultimately futile. He could see more formations moving up behind the front rank. He doubted Carano or any of his men had been able to make out the distant figures in the near darkness, so he didn't bother to tell them. Better they focused on one threat at a time.

He pulled back from Carano's position, ducking behind the shattered remains of an old storage shed. He crouched down in cover, observing the field from a new angle. He was on a small rise, and his location gave him the best visibility available on the night-shrouded field.

He watched the revolutionaries approach. He suspected the early rebel armies had been driven by revolutionary ardor and hatred for the nobility, but those days were long gone. He had no doubt the force approaching him was sustained as much by fear of its own leaders as it was by foolish dreams of freedom.

The men and women—*and children,* he thought grimly—now moving forward were pawns, caught up in the power struggles of others. They would do most of the dying, as they had throughout history, little more than slaves. Blackhawk would normally pity them, but he was focused on the battle, and old impulses rose up from the depths of his mind, where he'd kept them long suppressed. His pity turned to a merciless drive to destroy those who opposed him, without hesitation, without even a second thought. War was war, and he was in command. It was victory or death, and if it was to be death, he would make his enemies pay dearly for it.

He heard Carano's line open up, and his head snapped around, looking toward the tree line, watching the attackers fall in bunches as they ran into the deadly fire. The stunned enemy staggered, but they regrouped and pushed forward, driven, Blackhawk suspected, by kill squads positioned behind them.

The revolutionaries ran toward the stone wall, right into the withering fire of Carano's twenty troopers. Their lines rippled with disorder, and some sections stopped to return fire, while others continued forward, further disordering their already mangled formation.

They passed by a series of small buildings and piles of ruins, and as they reached each of them, the troops Blackhawk had positioned there sprang out and blasted their flanks with deadly fire. The formation was reduced to a disorganized mob, and the soldiers paused—the worst thing they could do, Blackhawk thought, with the grim anticipation of a carnasoid eyeing its next meal.

He felt the excitement, the satisfaction at crushing the first attack so brutally. At least three hundred were down, well over half the men who'd come past the tree line. Now, the survivors were panicking, and his men were raking them with fire from three sides. Barely one hundred were left standing when they raced back the way they had come. Blackhawk knew there was no escape for them back there, as their own brutal masters would cut them down for fleeing.

Across the field, the defenders were cheering, raising their rifles in the air and taunting the retreating enemy troops. They had shattered the attack, suffering only a dozen casualties in the process.

Blackhawk could hear them chanting his name, but he stood stone still, staring out at the field. He felt alive, his mind given over totally to the fight. He was like an addict fallen from a long recovery, savoring the first taste of his drug after a long abstinence. He remembered the feelings, the exhilaration of the battlefield, and his mind drifted back across the years. He recalled the glory of battle now, not the cost that had so long haunted his dreams. Right now his nightmares were forgotten, and images of victory passed through his mind, of broken enemies kneeling before him, of cheering soldiers screaming his name. *Let them celebrate. Let them shout my name. They'll all be dead soon enough, and me along with them.*

"Anyone who retreats will be shot!" Tellurin was shouting to the surging mass of soldiers. "Today the revolution achieves victory. Today the long struggle ends." He'd sent three waves to attack the château, each one larger than the one before. By all accounts, he was facing fewer than two hundred men, but they had shattered every unit he sent against them. They seemed to anticipate his every move, and they were always positioned perfectly.

He'd faced the mercenary generals and the commanders of the noble troops before. Some of them were capable leaders, but this was something different. He had a feeling, in his gut as much as his head, that he was up against someone new, a military genius of a sort he'd never encountered before.

He knew the enemy troops were better trained and equipped than his levies, and he was rational enough to understand that the enemy commander, whoever it was, outclassed him in every way. Every way but one.

Numbers.

He'd massed ten thousand troops here, and he was going to send them on one giant wave, pushed forward by Red Guard kill squads positioned to shoot down any who retreated. This time he would take the château, and his army would drive through, flanking the retreating mercenary forces and destroying them before they could regroup.

Today the revolution would see its greatest victory, and the total destruction of its enemies. He turned to his aide, and spoke a single word. "Attack."

Blackhawk knew it was over. He'd seen the shadowy formations in the distant darkness, moving forward, massing behind the trees. The next attack would begin any moment, and it would be the last. He shifted uncomfortably, trying to move his leg somewhere it gave him less pain. He'd caught a round in his thigh in the last attack. Doc had put a field dressing on it, but it still hurt like hell.

His makeshift army had fought hard, driving back three attacks and killing thousands of the enemy. But they'd lost a

332 — JAY ALLAN

quarter of their numbers, and they were running low on ammunition. Leadership, morale, training, technology—they were all crucial to success in war, but at some point, the brutality of mathematics asserted itself. His one hundred fifty exhausted soldiers had no chance against the thousands he saw formed up and ready to attack. They would fight bravely, and they would take down hundreds more of their enemies. But they would die, all of them.

Blackhawk could feel his second in command come up to his side.

"Well, Ace, we did the best we could, but there are just too many of them." There was an aching sadness in Blackhawk's voice. It wasn't for himself. Once more faced with death, he realized he didn't fear it. Not really. In many ways, he suspected it would be a release for him. But the thought of his crew dying here tore at his insides. They were good friends, loyal and true, and they deserved a better end. "You should have left, Ace. All of you."

Ace smiled. "We're a team, Ark. A family. There's nowhere else I would be right now except standing here at your side. And Shira and Sarge and the boys all feel the same way. You know that, right? You pulled every one of us out of one shitstorm or another. Do you think we'd ever leave you to face anything like this alone?"

Blackhawk stared back at Ace, his eyes locked onto his friend's. He opened his mouth, but no words came. He just nodded. *At least Astra is safe,* he thought. *And Sam and Lucas and the Twins.*

"They're coming." It was Carano, standing just to the side of the shattered building that Blackhawk had made his command post. "It's time."

"You fought well today, Vladimir," he said softly. "You and all your men. You've done an admirable job training them. You should be proud."

The mercenary looked back, an odd expression on his face. Blackhawk realized the dominating commander with frozen blood in his veins was gone, replaced by the grim adventurer he'd been before.

"Thank you, Blackhawk. I never thought I'd say this, but it's been an honor."

"For me too, Vladimir." Blackhawk extended his hand. "If we must die, let us die as friends."

The mercenary grasped Blackhawk's hand and repeated the oath. "If we must die, let us die as friends." He nodded and turned to run back to his men.

"Well, Ace . . ."

Ace's comm unit crackled to life. "This is *Wolf's Claw* calling to any crew member. This is *Wolf's Claw,* calling to any crew member. Ark? Ace? Shira?"

Blackhawk's head snapped around. He knew that voice.

What the hell was she doing here?

Ace grabbed the unit from his belt and raised it to his lips. "Astra? What the hell is going on?"

"We're saving your ass, Ace, that's what's going on. And that arrogant SOB you work for too." Her voice was cocky—and one of the most beautiful sounds Blackhawk had ever heard. "And now that we have your coordinates, we'll be there in a flash.

"Don't get shot in the next minute or two."

"My God," Lucas muttered as he moved the throttle, putting the *Claw* on a course for the coordinates of Ace's comm unit. "You were right, Astra: they're right in the middle of a shitstorm."

He flipped the comm to the shipwide frequency. "Tarq, Tarnan—get those turrets warmed up and ready. We've definitely got some fighting to do." He turned toward Astra. "Ace's station has the cluster bomb controls. The AI will help you get them activated." His voice became almost feral. "Let's give those fuckers on the ground a demonstration of what the *Claw* can do."

Astra smiled. "I'm on it, Lucas." She stared at the scanner. "There must be ten thousand troops concentrated right there. And more coming in from both sides." She flashed a glance back to Lucas. "They sure managed to step in some neck-deep crap, didn't they?"

"It wouldn't be a wolf's claw if it wasn't covered in blood and dirt," he said. "Hang on, we don't have any time to lose." He turned toward the comm. "Sam, that extra power we talked about. Now would be a good time . . ."

The *Claw* ripped through the atmosphere, her engines flaming yellow and red in the dark night sky as she raced for the battlefield. Lucas was pushing her as hard as he could, throwing caution to the wind. He knew the *Claw,* and he took her to the edge of the ship's endurance . . . and then kept going, watching gauges and feeling the controls, but never once doubting the *Claw* would do whatever he asked of her.

She always did . . .

Lucas swung the ship around and dove, dropping from five kilometers to a bare one hundred meters off the ground. He could see the scene ahead, the fires and explosions of battle lighting up the blackness of night. He looked down at the masses of enemy soldiers, thousands of them, pushing forward toward the château and its outbuildings. He angled the throttle again, bringing the ship around for an attack run along the enemy line.

"All right, guys, get ready. Tarq, Tarnan, you have full power for the lasers." He stared at the display, adjusting the course, cutting straight across the widest swath of enemy soldiers. "Astra, let's make those cluster bombs count. We don't have many, but they are nasty as hell."

He couldn't see the frigid expression on her face as she stared into the firing scope. If he had, he wouldn't have worried.

"Lucas, my man!" Ace thrust his arm into the air. Blackhawk almost did the same thing. They were standing behind the pockmarked stone wall of a partially collapsed building, watching the *Claw* tear across the night sky. The ship looked like some nightmare from mythology, a fiery dragon swooping down on the masses of confused and terrified soldiers. *God, I love that ship,* Blackhawk thought. Blinding bursts of deadly light flared out from her laser turrets, ripping through whole rows of men, obliterating their burned bodies and leaving piles of dead in their wake.

But it was the cluster bombs that ripped the heart out of the enemy formation—in many cases, quite literally. The fuel air explosives dropped from the *Claw*'s belly, and the big thousand-kilo shells burst open, scattering small incendiary units across a path five hundred meters wide.

The entire field erupted into billowing flames, lighting the whole area like day. Inside those plumes, hundreds died gruesome deaths, their bodies incinerated by the raging fires or suffocated as oxygen was sucked into the whirling firestorm.

The survivors of the *Claw*'s attack turned and fled for their lives, trampling the autocannon teams positioned to prevent their retreat. The revolutionaries were shattered, their morale utterly destroyed. Even their officers joined the rout, abandoning their rally points and chasing after their terrified soldiers.

Blackhawk stepped out from his command post and watched the enemy fleeing the flaming nightmare of the battlefield. He still didn't understand what the hell the *Claw* was doing on Saragossa, but he couldn't argue the timely intervention had saved the day.

He looked back away from the battlefield to the south. Lucas was landing the ship just behind the château, and Blackhawk made his way over, Ace and Shira falling in behind him.

They walked around the manor to the open field beyond, staring up at the looming bulk of *Wolf's Claw*. The ship had just landed, and they could feel the heat radiating off her hull. The airlock opened, and the ladder slowly extended down, settling in the soft dirt. A few seconds later, Lucas poked his head out and climbed down, with Astra just behind.

Blackhawk walked forward. "What the hell do you think you were doing, taking a risk like that, Lucas? You should have been on your way back to Celtiboria." There was anger in his voice, tempered with gratitude, but mostly he felt relief. Astra and the rest of his people were safe.

"Ahh . . . well . . ." Lucas was trying to think of something to say, when Astra pushed him aside and walked up to Blackhawk.

"Don't blame Lucas. I forced him back at gunpoint."

Blackhawk stared back at Lucas, a puzzled look on his face. "At gunpoint?"

Lucas nodded. "I'm afraid so, Skipper." He glanced over at Astra. "She's quite a handful."

Blackhawk nodded. "She certainly is."

"I told you I wasn't staying behind the next time there was a fight, Arkarin Blackhawk. Maybe next time you'll listen to me, you pompous ass. We saved your life, so just say thank you and shut the hell up."

He stared back, astonished, but before he could answer she grabbed his shirt and pulled him to her, kissing him with enough heat to consume even his anger.

"Bring those crates over here, boys." Blackhawk stood just behind the *Claw*'s cargo hatch, shouting to the Twins. He'd sent the brothers to get the crates of weapons they'd taken from the imperial ship. There hadn't been much time, and his people had only taken four of the big boxes. Now he was having three of them unloaded. "Set them down here." He pointed to a spot near the château.

It was dawn, and the early light was coming up across the fields. The battlefield was a vision of hell itself, a scorched plain covered with the dead and the charred remains of those consumed by the fires. A hazy cloud of smoke drifted across the gruesome scene, and in a few places, the remnants of buildings still smoldered.

"I want to thank you again, Ark." Carano walked up behind Blackhawk. Emotions were warring on his face, and Blackhawk could guess what was going through Carano's mind. He'd gone from a sworn enemy, torturing a captive Blackhawk for information, to a timid follower, to a soldier leaping to carry out the commands of the great war leader. Blackhawk too felt conflicted—it's hard to forget a man who whipped you for hours. But at this moment, it occurred to him perhaps he was just speaking to a friend.

Maybe not that—not yet. But you share a foxhole with a man, and you certainly can't call him an adversary anymore. Maybe someday . . .

"Let's call it even," Blackhawk said with a smile on his face.

"We survived the night, and we gave the revolutionaries something to think about before they come back and try to attack here again. Your forces should have time to regroup and get back in the fight." He stared at the pensive mercenary. "That's enough to make up for a shoulder wound, wouldn't you say? Even with ten years' interest accrued."

"More than enough. My anger and thirst for revenge nearly cost me far too much." He extended his arm.

Blackhawk grasped the mercenary's hand firmly. "Just to make sure we're even . . ." He gestured over to where the Twins were stacking the large crates. "We grabbed a few of these when we stole the core from the imperial ship, but one is all we really can use. I figured you need the rest more than I do."

Carano stared back, a stunned expression on his face. "But, Ark, even those few cases are priceless. I can't pay you anything close to what they're worth, not while I'm stuck here at least."

"They're a gift. Put them to good use, and maybe someday our paths will cross again." He smiled. "If they do, I'll have a friend next time instead of an enemy."

"You will indeed." Carano returned the smile. "And thank you again. The weapons will be enormously useful to us."

"I will ask one thing of you in return, General." Blackhawk paused. "Use the weapons to defeat the extremists, but then broker a peace between the remaining rebels and the nobles. This war is pointless. Neither side can function without the other, so some sort of settlement should be possible." Blackhawk was uncomfortable siding with the nobles to begin with, but he had no choice. The empire was backing the other side, and that meant their victory would be a worse calamity than anything Elisabetta's people might do. He hoped the two sides would find a way to coexist, but he'd back the devil himself to thwart whatever imperial scheme was afoot.

"I will do that, Arkarin Blackhawk. You have my word." Carano paused and took a deep breath. Then he added, "Besides—I need this war to end or the guilds will never drop their embargo. And I don't relish the thought of spending the rest of my life here."

"If I had any influence with the guilds, I'd try to help you arrange transport off this shithole, but I'm afraid my word wouldn't carry much weight there." He paused and forced back a grin. "In fact, if you do manage to contact them, I wouldn't mention my name." Blackhawk left it at that. It was a long story, best told another time.

"I'll make sure not to. Good-bye, Arkarin Blackhawk. Fortune go with you."

"And you, Vladimir."

Blackhawk turned and walked toward the château. Elisabetta was standing there, staring out over the fields, a thoughtful look on her face.

"Lady Lementov." He walked up and took her hand, kissing it gently. "I'm sorry we didn't have a chance to explore the friendship you spoke of in such intriguing terms."

She smiled. "You are indeed a gentleman, Captain Blackhawk, and a man of many talents. I will regret not having the chance to learn more of your . . . ah . . . skills." She glanced over toward *Wolf's Claw,* and Blackhawk followed her gaze. Astra was standing near the airlock, pretending she wasn't watching the exchange, but not doing a very good job of it. "But I see now why my charms failed so utterly. She is beautiful, Captain, and I suspect there is far more there than just a pretty face."

Blackhawk nodded. "There is much more, Lady Lementov, but Astra and I are only friends."

Elisabetta smiled. "Of course, Captain. Whatever you say." She stepped back and bowed her head, the native farewell for an honored guest. "My thanks again, Captain Blackhawk, for saving my life and those of my retainers. My best wishes, wherever your travels take you."

"Farewell, Lady Lementov." He smiled again and turned, walking back to the *Claw*. It was time to get the hell off Saragossa.

CHAPTER 29

"I'M PICKING UP A CONTACT IN ORBIT, SKIPPER." LUCAS WAS staring into his scope, the *Claw* tearing through Saragossa's heavy atmosphere.

Blackhawk's head snapped around. He felt his stomach clench. A ship in Saragossa orbit had to be bad news. "Any specifics yet?"

"Not yet, Skip."

Blackhawk flipped on the intraship comm. "We've got an unidentified ship in Saragossa orbit. Let's not take any chances. Ace, Shira—let's get the turrets ready just in case." He paused. "Sarge, get your boys and the Twins ready for damage control."

He turned back toward Lucas. "Anything yet?"

"Wild guess, Skip, but she looks like one of the pirates from Kalishar." His face was pressed against the scope. "Similar mass and energy readings. If I had to guess, I'd say it followed us here."

Blackhawk's face twisted into a frown. If a ship from Kalishar had come after them, it wouldn't be alone. "Ace, Shira, you guys in place yet?"

"Just climbing in now, Cap." He could hear the sound of the hatch slamming shut through Ace's comm. "All set."

"I'm ready, Captain." Shira's voice was clear and calm, as usual. "Precombat diagnostics in progress."

Blackhawk gave himself a brief smile. The rivalry between Ace and Shira was always amusing, and it was usually a positive force that drove each of them to better performance. Shira won the honors this time, at least so far. She was already in place and checking her equipment while Ace was just climbing into his turret. No matter which of them managed to edge the other out, though, Blackhawk knew he had two of the best gunners in space ready for whatever fight they were up against.

"All right, guys. As soon as we get a positive ID, I want to blast that ship to dust. If there's one, there'll be more too, and we need to pick off whatever we can before they can gang up on us."

He glanced over toward Lucas. "Positive ID yet?"

"Not yet, Sk— Wait. I'm picking up transmissions. Skip, they're powering up their systems!"

Close enough, Blackhawk thought. "Ark, Shira . . . fire!"

Lucas was staring into the scope. "Two hits, Skip One was a grazing shot, but the other a solid hit amidships. Looks like significant damage. I'm reading gas and fluids escaping from the hull." His tone deflated a bit. "No secondary explosions."

"Good shooting, guys. Keep it up." Blackhawk was about to

ask Lucas for another update when he heard someone climbing up the ladder. He spun his head around to see. "Astra, what are you . . ."

"I'm going to man Ace's station while he's in the turret, Ark." She glanced over at Lucas and gave him a wink. "Lucas and I make a good team on this bridge. Besides, I can man the scope, so he can concentrate on flying this tub."

Blackhawk sighed, but he didn't argue. She was right. Lucas might have some fancy flying to do if they were going to get out of this mess. "Fine, but make sure you're strapped in."

"Wooo! That's the way we do it, baby!" Ace's voice reverberated on the shipwide comm. His shot had been perfect, a point-blank hit on the reactor. The enemy ship lost containment, and an instant later it disappeared in a massive fusion explosion.

"Nice shooting, Ace." It was Shira. Rivalry or no, Blackhawk knew she appreciated excellence, and she showed it.

"Ark, I've got multiple inbound targets," Astra said. "Three—no four ships coming in from 315/160. Possible additional contacts at 280/140."

Here we go. "It's probably the whole damned Kalishari fleet." He flipped on the comm. "Sam, how long to power up the core?"

"At least twenty minutes, Captain. This thing is way beyond our wiring and infrastructure. I can't even believe I've got it working, but if I let it draw power too quickly, I'll burn out every system on the ship. Figured you'd want a little something for the guns."

"You figured right, Sam. Do the best you can." He turned to Lucas. "Looks like we're going to have to fight. Let's head for the asteroid belt, Lucas."

"Just what I was thinking, Skip." The pilot punched at his keyboard. "Everybody get ready for acceleration." He pulled the throttle, feeding more reaction mass into the engines. He flipped the force dampeners on full power, but it still felt like close to 3g in the *Claw*.

"Estimated entry into asteroid belt: eight minutes," Astra called from her station. "Projected interception by enemy forces nine point five minutes. That's cutting it pretty close."

"That's what we do here, Astra," Blackhawk said. Lucas was pushing the throttle forward, feeding even more reaction mass to the engines, going past 100 percent capacity to 105 percent then 110 percent. It was dangerous, but then they had Sam Sparks down there holding things together, and he'd never seen the day she couldn't coax a 10 percent overload out of her engines.

"Because that's what we do," he muttered.

"We're getting energy readings, General." The officer turned toward Wilhelm. "It appears some kind of battle is in progress."

Wilhelm felt a rush of excitement. Saragossa was redlined. If there were ships fighting here, maybe Tarn Belgaren's people had found *Wolf's Claw* after all. He'd come to investigate what had happened to Agent Sand, but if the ka'al's fleet managed to capture *Wolf's Claw,* he could take Astra right back to Galvanus Prime. The fate of Saragossa was insignificant compared to securing the Lucerne girl.

"Full thrust." He turned to face the pilot. "Get us into that combat zone now." He strapped himself into his chair.

"Yes, sir." The officer was hunched over his station, punching in course codes. "It appears the fighting is in the system's asteroid belt, General."

Of course it is—I wouldn't expect anything less from Blackhawk. "I want all weapons systems activated." *It has to be* Wolf's Claw, he thought. Wilhelm could feel his heart pounding in his ears. *Who else would be fighting off a dozen ships in Saragossa's embargoed system?* "And advise all gunners, I want that ship disabled, not destroyed. I will personally space anyone who destroys that vessel."

"Plot another pass!" Admiral Kharn was sitting on *Red Viper*'s bridge, screaming into his fleetwide comm. "We are the scourge of half the Far Stars, and we cannot score a crippling hit on a single ship!"

"Admiral, I have never seen a vessel piloted like that one. Whoever is at the controls is like a sorcerer. He seems to read our very thoughts, and he maneuvers around these asteroids like nothing I have ever seen." The pilot was sweating, working at his controls, trying to bring the ship around for another attack run.

"Perhaps I should make him an offer, Grindle." He glared at his pilot. "But that would make you expendable, wouldn't it?"

The pilot didn't respond. He'd served Kharn for years, and the admiral knew he was an excellent pilot. But whoever was behind the controls of *Wolf's Claw* had him completely outclassed.

They had scored half a dozen hits on the enemy ship, but most of those were grazing shots. Still, even a great beast could be brought down by enough small wounds. Grindle gripped the throttle and pushed it forward, driving *Red Viper*'s straining engines harder as he vectored toward the fleeing *Claw*.

"Talon reports a hit, Admiral." Jacen Nimbus turned toward Kharn. "It appears they have damaged or destroyed one of the target's engines."

Kharn slammed his fist down on the arm of his chair. "Now that's what we need." He looked straight ahead, his eyes focused on the viewscreen. If they could destroy the *Claw*'s engines, they could take the ship and recapture Astra Lucerne. "They're damaged, Grindle, crippled. That should slow down their hot-shot pilot. Now, get us in firing position."

"Nice shooting, Shira." Blackhawk was watching his screen when the enemy ship just vanished. That was three kills now, plus the one in orbit. But at least ten other ships were hunting the *Claw*, and that last dead pirate had managed to score a hit before Shira took him out. The *Claw*'s engines were down to 60 percent, even with Sam's best efforts at damage control. She was a wizard with ship's systems, but even she couldn't do anything about metal parts that were melted and fused together—or blown completely off. Not in the middle of a fight, at least.

"How is the core, Sam?" They needed to get the hell out as soon as possible—sooner if possible. They were schooling these pirates in ship-to-ship combat, but ship-to-ships was a different story. Eventually the pirates would get enough ships on them at once. And that would be the end.

"Four minutes, Captain." He could hear the stress in her voice. She was powering up the core, working damage control, and trying to keep the battered engines online. For the millionth time, Blackhawk was thankful he'd found Sam and added her to his team. She'd saved their lives more times than he could count, and she'd kept a battered *Claw* functioning when Blackhawk knew he had no right to expect more from his ship.

I know I ask a lot of you, but I need that magic one more time, Sam.

"We've got three ships coming in on an attack run." Astra had six screens going, monitoring projected plots and vectors for the enemy ships. "Sending targeting data to the turrets."

Blackhawk was pleasantly surprised how well Astra blended in and worked seamlessly with the crew. He knew she was more than capable—he'd observed her erratic brilliance on numerous occasions—but this was her first firefight, and she didn't skip a beat.

Still, even as he focused on the battle, he couldn't help but feel a touch of sadness. He would love nothing more than to have her at his side, on the *Claw* and in his life. But she had a far greater destiny than wandering the Far Stars with a pack of moderately disrespectable adventurers, and even if he hadn't had his other concerns, he would never allow her to leave that behind to be with him. *You shouldn't have to be great at space combat. You deserve so much more . . .*

"Another kill!" A rush of excitement flared in Astra's otherwise businesslike tone. "Ace this time."

The ship shook hard and pitched to the starboard. Blackhawk's mind snapped back to the battle, and he scolded himself for being distracted with nonsense when his people were fighting for their lives. He could smell the burnt machinery, and he knew immediately the news wasn't going to be good. "Damage report."

"It's bad, Captain." Sam's voice was harried. He could hear her spraying fire retardant in the background as she spoke. "We're below 50 percent power on the engines for sure, and maybe worse. Probably worse . . . definitely worse. We've got power losses all over the ship, including the lower turret." *Meaning Ace is out of the fight.* "But the reactor's still online, and the core seems functional." She coughed. "I've got smoke down here, but it's clearing. The ventilation systems are still working, at least partially." She paused. "One more hit, Cap, and we're not going anywhere. I'm showing two minutes, ten seconds left on the hyperdrive sequence, but we're going to have to risk an early jump. I'll overload the reactor and hit the jump system with a power spike. It's risky, but I think I can make it work."

That was enough for Blackhawk. "Do it, Sam." He slapped his hand on the comm button. "All crew, prepare for immediate jump to hyperspace." He turned toward the pilot's station. "It's you and Sam now, Lucas. Get us the hell out of here."

"We are reading a power spike from the enemy ship, General." The officer turned and stared at Wilhelm. "They're jumping."

Fuck! "Get a tracer on them. Now!" *We can't lose that ship,* he thought. *If they slip away, we'll never find them again.* He stared at the tactical plot. The pirates had lost heavily in the battle, but they'd inflicted serious damage on *Wolf's Claw* too. The combat was almost over, victory at hand.

Unless Blackhawk and his people managed to escape into hyperspace.

"Got the trace, sir."

"Send a transmission to all Kalishari vessels. They are to hook into our data net and prepare to jump. We're going after that ship, wherever it goes."

CHAPTER 30

"ENTERING NORMAL SPACE NOW." BLACKHAWK COULD TELL THAT Lucas had ignored the hyperspace plot, managing the last few seconds before reemergence by his gut. Anyone else, and that would have scared the crap out of the captain. But he'd seen Lucas do it before—too many times—and trusted his pilot. They had caught the signal of a tracer right before they jumped, and he knew the pirates were right on their tail. If Lucas needed to get creative to shake them, Blackhawk was all for it.

The fact was, their only chance was coming out of hyperspace close enough to Celtiboria to make a run for it, and no AI-assisted hyperspace plot was going to drop a ship that near a planetary body. Gravity played havoc with jumps in and out of hyperspace, and executing an insertion or extraction too close to a planet or sun was extraordinarily dangerous. That kind of thing took a natural pilot, one with a sixth sense for space travel and a streak of insanity. Lucas fit the bill on both qualifications.

The ship shook hard and the viewscreen came back on, displaying the starry background of normal space. They all stared down at their stations, waiting for the systems to reboot. It only took a minute for the navcom to reactivate, but it seemed like an eternity.

"Yes—that's how we do it!" Lucas shouted when the screens came back on. He was staring at the plot.

Blackhawk looked down at the map. The pilot had managed to bring them within half a light minute of the planet. "Nicely done, Lucas. That's threading the needle by anyone's measure." He turned toward Astra. "Any pursuers?"

Astra bent down over her scope, looking for signs of vessels emerging from hyperspace. "I don't see anything yet . . . wait . . ." Her head snapped up, and she looked over at Blackhawk. "Multiple contacts emerging." She turned back to the scope. "They're about a light minute back, Ark." That was close. The pirates hadn't been able to match Lucas's piloting skill, but they'd done a damned good job themselves.

"Lucas, can we get to Celtiboria before they engage us?" He knew the answer before he even asked.

"Afraid not, Skip. Not unless Sam can get me a lot more power."

Which was almost certainly out of the question. The *Claw* was limping along on one-quarter reactor output, and she only managed that because of Sam's wizardry. The jump had taken a lot out of the ship, and he doubted Sam could do much more in the time they had . . .

I didn't survive Kalishar and Saragossa just to give up now. Not when we're so close.

Blackhawk punched a code in his comm unit. "Attention all Celtiborian authorities: this is Arkarin Blackhawk on the vessel *Wolf's Claw*. We are returning from a mission for Marshal Lucerne, and we have heavy damage. We are being pursued by hostiles, pirate vessels from Kalishar, and we request immediate assistance."

The bridge was silent, as they all waited to see if any Celtiborian ships were close enough to intervene. The seconds ticked by, as their transmission went out in all directions at lightspeed. Blackhawk felt his hopes start to sink as the seconds turned into a minute, and he looked over at Astra. "We better get ready to put up whatever fight we . . ."

"*Wolf's Claw*, this is Commodore Rochfort, commanding the Third Cruiser Squadron. We have received your communication and located your pursuers. We are moving to intercept. Marshal Lucerne has the whole fleet out looking for you. Welcome back to Celtiboria."

Blackhawk pumped his fist and let out a yell. "Yes!" Astra and Lucas were cheering too, and he could hear the rest of the crew all the way from the lower level. Rochfort's cruisers would make short work of any Kalishari pirate ships that stayed to tangle with them. Blackhawk let out a long sigh.

We made it.

He turned toward his pilot. "Lucas, if you would be so kind, please plot a course for Celtiboria."

Lucas looked down at his board, a broad smile creeping across his face. "My pleasure, Skip."

———

"I never thanked you for saving me, Ark." Astra stood next to the door of his cabin, smiling warmly. She'd been borrowing Shira's clothing since they'd snatched her back from her kidnappers on Saragossa, but now she was wearing something different, as beautiful and elegant a dress as Blackhawk had ever seen. It was made from shimmering blue Delphian silk, and Blackhawk could tell it had cost a king's ransom. He wondered where she'd gotten it until he realized Katarina must have lent it to her. She looked beautiful, her golden blond hair flowing loosely around her bare shoulders.

"I knew you'd come for me, no matter where they took me." She walked across the small room, stopping in front of Blackhawk. "I never doubted you, not for an instant." He was sitting on the edge of his bed, wearing a pair of breeches, his shirt cast aside. The welts on his chest and back were painful, and the rough material of the shirt was too uncomfortable. He was resting his leg, propping it up on a small stool. Doc had cleaned the wound and dressed it properly, but it was still painful.

She ran her hand softly across his savaged back, and he shivered at her touch. "I'm so sorry you were hurt so badly, Ark. More than you can know."

He looked up at her. *I know, Astra. I know.*

There were so many things he wanted to say, but he stopped himself. He loved her, and he knew she loved him, but that wasn't enough. There were too many problems for them to overcome, old secrets and new battles to be fought. It was a place he wouldn't let her go. He had nothing to offer her but pain, and he loved her too much to share his nightmares with her. Any doubts he might have had, any delusions he'd entertained of living a normal life with her had been stripped from him on the field of battle at the Lementov château. It was all still there inside him, the monster, trapped again now in its cage, but waiting always for the chance to break free, to turn him into something dark and loathsome.

If he ever lost control again, became what he had been, he hoped a bullet would find him and end his pain. He could face death, but the thought that terrified him most was Astra seeing him that way, as he had been long ago. He knew he could never share her life and her love, and the image of her looking back at him with fear and revulsion in her eyes wasn't something he ever wanted to see.

"Astra, I don't think . . ."

"Shh . . ." She put her finger over his lips. "No, don't say anything." She sat down next to him, and she leaned her head against his. "I know everything you're going to say. You're older, we have different responsibilities . . . there are a thousand reasons we can't be together. You have suffered, my love, I know. Your past causes you terrible pain. Do you think I'm blind? A fool?" She moved her hands up, taking hold of his face gently and turning him toward her. "I know it all, Ark, and I don't care. Not about any of it."

He started to open his mouth, but she covered it with her hand. "No, my love, no reasons, no arguments, no speeches." Her voice was soft, almost hypnotic. "We'll be on Celtiboria in a couple hours, and then you can argue with me and tell me all the reasons we can't be together." She leaned in and softly kissed his neck. "I don't care what happens when we land, or next week or next year. All I care about is now, and for these few fleeting moments, you are mine."

He closed his eyes, trying to summon the strength to get up, to push her away, but it just wasn't in him. He knew it was the right thing to do, that he shouldn't let her become more attached to him than she already was, but he couldn't. He'd loved her for so long, and more each time he saw her. The softness of her skin, the scent of her hair, it was all too much, and his resistance crumbled.

He felt her hand on his face, her lips on his. He took her in his arms and laid her down on the bed, staring into her eyes. *Just this once,* he thought, shoving the doubts and fear and even good sense out of his mind. *Just this once.*

CHAPTER 31

"I DON'T KNOW HOW TO THANK YOU, ARK." AUGUSTIN LUCERNE
was looking at his friend, his eyes conveying his gratitude. He
looked rejuvenated from the last time Blackhawk had seen him,
when the marshal had asked the captain in a broken voice to
find his daughter.

The two men were alone, sitting in front of a roaring fire in
one of the many reception rooms in Celtiboria City's massive
palace. The ancient dwelling place of the planet's kings had
been unused for centuries. The city itself had been controlled
by more than one of the planet's warlords in that time, but the
old palace was too vulnerable to serve as a home base for any of
Celtiboria's old warrior elite. Lucerne had ordered it reopened
to serve as a symbol that the planet's leaders had no need to

lock themselves up in great fortresses for fear of the people. Much of the work of governing a planet was conducted in the building's lavish halls and offices, but Lucerne himself lived as frugally as ever, commandeering a small suite of rooms that had long ago housed servants.

"You have thanked me already, several times." Blackhawk leaned back in the chair, enjoying the plush softness. He healed very quickly, but he'd been battered pretty badly on this mission, and he was still sore just about everywhere. "And there was no need, even the first time. I would go through the fires of Hephaseus to save Astra."

"And I would reward you more richly if you would allow it. Anything, Ark. Just name it." Lucerne's voice was sincere. He had wanted to shower his friend with titles and riches, but Blackhawk had refused.

"Seeing Astra safe and home is reward enough." Blackhawk's voice was soft, quiet. Lucerne's efforts to reward him were making him uncomfortable. The thought of taking money—or anything else—for saving Astra's life was unthinkable to him.

Lucerne had promised the *Claw*'s crew an enormous price if they found and returned his daughter, and he'd been true to his word. Blackhawk allowed the grateful ruler to indulge his people. They had worked and fought hard, and they deserved every bit of reward and praise Lucerne offered. But he would take nothing for himself, not a single imperial crown. He gave his share of the reward to aid the poor and displaced of Celtiboria, the victims of its long wars of unification. He didn't want thanks or public acclaim. The knowledge that Astra was safe was enough reward.

The two sat quietly for a few minutes, enjoying the warmth of the fire. They had been friends for a long time, and Lucerne was the closest thing Blackhawk had to a confidant. He'd discussed many things with Lucerne over the years, but he wasn't ready to share his thoughts now.

"Stay, Ark." Lucerne's voice was uncharacteristically emotional. "Stay with us on Celtiboria. Help me build the Far Stars Confederation."

Blackhawk shifted uncomfortably in his seat and stared back at his friend. "You know I can't, Augustin." Lucerne was the only person in the Far Stars who knew the truth about Blackhawk's past, about the enormity of his crimes.

"It has been a long time, Ark, and you have proven your worthiness since then. Whatever sins you committed years ago, you have become a good man. You have conquered what you once were." He paused, reaching out and putting his hand on his friend's arm. "I trust you, Ark. I trust you with my life. It's time to let your old demons go."

Blackhawk gazed down at the floor. He smiled briefly, but the sadness was still heavy on his face. "Your trust is one of my most prized possessions, Augustin, and I can never tell you how grateful I am for that. It means more to me than I can ever explain." He turned and looked into the fire, remembering how he'd felt on the battlefield on Saragossa, the thoughts and urges that raced through his head. "But I haven't conquered anything, my friend. Some things stay with you forever, and all you can do is remain vigilant."

He paused and, for a fleeting second, he thought about Lucerne's words. He wanted nothing more than to help Celtiboria's new ruler fulfill his goal, to help make the Far Stars safe from the brutality of the empire. He, more than anyone, knew what imperial rule would mean to this sector so used to its independence. He believed in Lucerne, and he would have been honored to follow the man wherever his standard marched. But he had long ago put aside such ambitions. "I trust you, Augustin, but I don't trust me." He looked up at Lucerne, but all he could see was a parade of old memories passing before his eyes, fire and war and death. "I can't do it. I can't lead armies again." He took a deep breath. "I'm sorry, but I just can't."

Lucerne nodded slowly, and he sat silently for a few minutes. "What about Astra?" he finally said, turning to face Blackhawk as he did.

Blackhawk tensed, and he felt a knot begin to grow in his stomach. His mind was suddenly filled with thoughts of Lucerne's daughter, arguing with him, ignoring every command he tried to give her. The feel of her skin against his, the sweet smell of her hair. "What . . . what do you mean? She is safe now. She's home."

Lucerne's eyes bored into Blackhawk's. "I mean she loves you, Ark. Do you think I'm blind to my own daughter?"

Blackhawk sat speechless for a few seconds. "I . . . ah . . ."

"And you love her, too." Lucerne's stare was unrelenting. "Do you think I'm blind to you, Ark? That I cannot see what is plain as day?" His chiseled expression morphed slowly into a smile. "Neither of you is as subtle as you think."

Blackhawk fidgeted uncomfortably. "Augustin, I . . ."

"I know you have tried to suppress your feelings, but there is no need. I appreciate the loyalty, Ark, but I want my daughter to be happy, and I trust her to decide what she wants. Astra is a . . . ah . . . spirited girl, as you know, but she is smart too, and willful. No one tells her what she wants or thinks. No one who wants to walk away still standing, that is."

"Augustin, no one regards Astra more highly than I do, but I don't think of her like that." He was lying to his friend, and trying to convince himself as he spoke. "She's just infatuated with me because my people and I rescued her. When she calms down, she'll come to her senses."

"Ark, I never thought you'd lie to me," he chided. "Astra doesn't get infatuated. She's been stone cold since she was a little girl. She grew up on the battlefield. And she doesn't need to calm down. Did she seem scared when she was with you? For that matter, have you ever seen her afraid?"

"No," Blackhawk said, grinning as he thought of Astra in action on the *Claw*. "The girl's cool under fire, that's for sure."

Blackhawk's passing grin faded. "It doesn't matter how she feels, Augustin. And it doesn't make any difference how I feel either. I'm much older than she is. I know I don't look like it, but I am. I'm tired and used up in a way she couldn't understand. If she has some feelings, they're for an image in her mind, something that doesn't really exist."

"Ark, you may be older, but you're different from most people, and you know it. Your genetics are extraordinary. Astra may be twenty-five years younger than you, but you will probably outlive her. No one knows what your lifespan will be, but you'll live long after most men would be in their graves. And with all Astra has seen, the death and destruction of war, is she really so much younger than you in spirit?"

Blackhawk didn't answer immediately. He wanted Astra—he wanted to go to her now, to tell her how he felt. But the discipline was still there, and it clamped down hard. The pain was sharp, and it cut deep, but his resolve was strong. "It's more than age, Augustin, and you know it." His voice became sadder, quieter. "You know the life I have to lead, the reasons I can't join you and help build the confederation. You, of all people, should understand. I'm a monster caged, but still a monster. Everything I did, all the horrible crimes I committed—I cannot take a chance to allow that side of me to come out again. As much as I want to join you, to fight at your side, that can never be."

He took a deep breath. "What life could I offer Astra? To fly around the Far Stars on *Wolf's Claw*, to live the rest of her days as a mercenary surviving on the fringe of human society?" He stared at Lucerne, and the pain in his eyes was there for his friend to see.

"I won't do that to her, Augustin, I just won't. Without me she will stay here. She will stand at your side as you build a new order, as you secure the freedom of the Far Stars for generations to come." Another pause, longer this time. "I am the one stained with guilt, and I must live my penance. But I will not drag Astra into it. Even if she loves me. Even if I love her. I will not steal her chance of greatness from her."

He stood up, feeling edgy. "I've got to go, Augustin. I need to check on the repairs to the *Claw*."

"Ark . . ." But the words wouldn't come.

It didn't matter; Blackhawk knew what he was going to say. In a way, he was glad Augustin didn't say them—if anyone could convince him he was being a fool, it would be his friend. And maybe Augustin would be right. But he had convinced himself for so long that this was the only way, he wasn't prepared for a world where this wasn't his reality.

I've faced death countless times. Been tortured and inflicted horrors. And I'm nothing but a coward.

"I think I'm going to stay on the ship, Augustin." Lucerne had arranged plush accommodations at the palace for the entire crew, but Blackhawk needed to get as far away from it all as possible. "I need to be alone for a while. I—I do want to thank you, though, for putting the crew up in such style, Augustin. If it's okay with you, they'll stay here a few extra weeks. It was a hard time. They need some R&R. They deserve a break, and we're not likely to be someplace as civilized as Celtiboria anytime soon."

"Are you sure, Ark?" Lucerne spoke softly. "I can make sure you're not disturbed here."

I don't think there's anywhere in the Far Stars I won't be disturbed, he thought. But he simply said, "Thanks, Augustin, but I think I'll be better off in my own quarters. Besides, Sam can probably use some help supervising the repairs." He reached out his hand to his friend. "I'll see you again before I leave—I promise."

Lucerne grasped Blackhawk's hand, and the two shook warmly. "And I intend to hold you to that, Ark. I don't see you nearly often enough, and we're going to have dinner and kill a bottle of Antillean brandy before I let you go."

Blackhawk took his leave, hurrying to get past the servants and courtiers to the solitude he needed. Augustin had seen right through him—just as his daughter had—and for all his wounds, it was his soul that was giving him the most pain right now. He knew his friend wouldn't stop trying to convince him of his place in the galaxy—fighting at the marshal's side, embraced by the love of Astra.

And he knew that he just might let him.

Just not yet.

EPILOGUE

"GREETINGS, LORD GOVERNOR." VILLEROI SET AN ORNATE BOX on the floor and knelt before Vos. "Your orders have been carried out to the letter on Kalishar, and I am pleased to report complete success."

Vos sat on his chair, looking down at the operative. "I am gratified to see you have returned so quickly, Lord Villeroi. Your efficiency and competence is greatly appreciated, as always."

The governor looked up and gazed out across the hall. Guards were lined up along each wall, and two stood at each side of his own chair, all dressed in ornate white-and-gold dress uniforms. He gestured toward one of them, pointing to the box Villeroi had set down on the floor.

The soldier snapped to attention at the governor's gesture and stepped forward, leaning down and opening the box. He reached inside and pulled out a severed head, holding it firmly by strands of sparse, stringy hair. He stood and held it aloft before Vos.

The governor stared at the severed head of the ka'al. The former leader of Kalishar had taken the governor's gold, and he had failed him badly—and repeatedly. Now he had paid the price, and his head would hang outside the Capitol, its slowly rotting remains a warning to others that Kergen Vos demanded success and competency from his minions.

This pristine city and its pampered people would know what the rest of the Far Stars was about to learn: that ugliness could come to them, too.

Vos nodded toward the prone agent. "Rise, Lord Villeroi, and accept my compliments on a job well done." He'd always known the bastard noble was a capable agent, but he'd been concerned the man's sadistic tendencies might affect his performance in the field. Vos himself was never hesitant to resort to cruelty or inflict pain, but he did it in furtherance of his strategies. Villeroi enjoyed it.

Vos was pleased to see that Villeroi had executed his instructions perfectly and with complete success. He had kept his own impulses in check with admirable discipline, and he followed his orders with ruthless efficiency.

Though I'd bet the ka'al's end had not been pleasant.

Rax Florin was Kalishar's new ruler, and the coup that gave him the throne had been achieved quickly and almost bloodlessly, thanks to the vast quantities of imperial gold in his coffers. Florin's allegiance had not come cheaply, and Vos was stunned when he first heard what Villeroi had promised. But the new ka'al was a vastly abler man than the old, one who promised to be a far more reliable ally than his predecessor. Nevertheless, even with stable leadership from Florin, it would be some time until Kalishar regained its strength. Half its ships had been destroyed in battles with *Wolf's Claw* and the Celtiborian navy, and those losses would only be replaced slowly and at great cost.

Villeroi rose and stood at attention before Vos. "My thanks to you, Lord Governor, and my loyal service, always." He bowed and turned, marching toward the massive entry doors, his boots echoing loudly on the polished stone of the floor.

But pleasure is so often tempered . . .

Vos turned to the left, focusing on Mak Wilhelm. The general had returned from Celtiboria's system a few days before. His ship had fled before the Celtiborian navy blasted the Kalishari ships to plasma. He hadn't abandoned the pirates out of cowardice, but he couldn't risk his ship being captured or even identified. Pirates invading Celtiborian space was one thing, an imperial vessel was quite another.

"Out!" Vos roared. "All of you." He waved his arms toward the guards and other functionaries. "I wish to speak with General Wilhelm alone."

There was an instant of stunned surprise, followed by a rush to the door. Vos walked back to his chair and sat down while the last of the guards stepped out of the room, the big double doors closing behind them. He looked down at Wilhelm. "Speak, General."

"I'm afraid Saragossa may well be lost, Excellency. The revolutionaries launched an offensive and appeared to be on the brink of success, but they were checked at the point of victory.

Reports suggest a spaceship of some kind launched a devastating ground attack and routed their forces after inflicting enormous casualties. The forces of the nobility have apparently regrouped and launched a counterattack. Intelligence is sketchy, but it appears they have inflicted a serious defeat on the revolutionaries and are now threatening to retake the capital."

"A spaceship of some kind?" Vos's eyes narrowed. "Care to venture a guess as to what vessel that was?" Vos knew what Wilhelm was going to say, but he wanted to hear it from his general's lips.

"I have little hard data from the ground, but I can only assume it was *Wolf's Claw* before . . ."

"Before it took off and blasted its way through the entire Kalishari fleet and then delivered Astra Lucerne back to her father?"

"Yes, Excellency. That is correct." Wilhelm stood at attention, obviously ready to accept blame for the debacle. "I offer you my sincere apologies, Lord Governor, and my sword if you wish it." He knelt before Vos's chair.

Vos let him stay in that position for a moment before saying, "Get up, you fool. This setback is not your fault. Indeed, I knew I should have replaced that imbecile the ka'al long before I did. Without his incompetence none of this would have happened. We would have Astra Lucerne, and Saragossa would be in the hands of the revolutionaries." He sighed. "Still, we have made some progress. The Far Stars Bank has played right into our hands, and they have no idea of our true intentions. We have made inroads into the transport guilds as well, progress that will accelerate as we consolidate control over the bank. Our plans on other worlds are also moving along quite well, and we have strong prospects for success on many of them."

His expression hardened. "We still have problems, though, and we must formulate plans to deal with them. Marshal Lucerne has successfully consolidated power on Celtiboria, and worse, he has come close to concluding an alliance with Antilles. We must develop another plan to contain or defeat Lucerne, and even more urgently, we must prevent his Antillean alliance from becoming a reality."

Wilhelm had stood up. "I agree, Excellency. Marshal Lucerne is a more dangerous problem than ever, and we must prevent him from extending his authority and influence."

Vos leaned back in his chair, silent for a few seconds. "And this Blackhawk and his crew. They are extremely capable and far too dangerous to ignore. We must find a way to rid ourselves of them once and for all.

"We need a plan to kill Arkarin Blackhawk."

Captain Blackhawk and the crew of the *Wolf's Claw* continue their adventures in *Enemy in the Dark*, Book 2 of Jay Allan's Far Stars series!

"I'll see your thousand and raise you . . . five thousand."

Ace stared across the table, through the dim light and swirling haze of cigar smoke. His opponent wasn't half the poker player he fancied himself, and Ace would have been licking his chops anywhere else, ready to pounce. A pompous fool, whose arrogance greatly exceeded his skill, was tailor-made for a shark like Ace Graythorn. But today he had a job to do, and that was to keep the sucker at the table—something he would hardly accomplish by cleaning him out early.

Ace looked at his cards for the third time, part of his carefully orchestrated act, and he exhaled loudly. Finally, he pushed his cards facedown into the center of the table with a groan that was only half playacting. Granted, he was sighing because he was laying down a winning hand—he figured his kings were a 90 percent favorite to win—but the sigh went over well. No matter what, the mission came first.

The mission always came first.

Alejandro Jose de Cordoba reached out and pulled the chips across the table with pudgy hands festooned with gaudy rings. He wore the elaborate dress of a Castillan nobleman, though Ace knew there was nothing but peasant blood coursing through his veins. Cordoba had earned his position the old-fashioned way. He'd killed for it.

"Ah, Lord Suvarov, now you find yourself in a real game. One hopes you are not easily intimidated." Cordoba's voice was pleasant enough, despite the slightly mocking tone, but there was something else there, a menace only another killer would have noticed. Cordoba was a loud and boisterous man, but just like Ace, it was all an act. He was definitely not a man to be trifled with.

"Indeed no, Lord Cordoba. I find the challenge . . . stimulating."

Ace had been gambling almost around the clock for five days, waiting for Cordoba to notice him and invite him to a game. Cordoba was well known at the Grand Palais as a high-stakes gambler . . . and more important, as the top henchman of Lord Aragona, the venerable establishment's notorious owner.

It was easy enough to play the buffoon, but much more difficult to strike the balance Ace had managed most of the last week: that of a reasonably capable player, but one with inadequate control over his emotions. Just the sort of opponent an arrogant shark like Cordoba would seek. Strong enough to feed his ego, but weak enough to fleece.

Ace had vacillated between winning and losing, managing to stay about even despite making some wild and foolish bets. Of course, that was exactly his job, but it still hurt the gambler inside to give it all away just to play a role. And it wasn't easy, either. He wanted to appear as a gambler who was reckless, but he wasn't looking to actually lose money. Anything he left at the tables would just ramp up the costs of the mission, and that would come right off the bottom line.

"I am delighted to hear that, Lord Suvarov." Cordoba stared across the table, looking into Ace's eyes.

He's trying to get a read on me, Ace thought, *see how far he can push me. Good luck with that, you arrogant ass. It will take a better man than you.*

"Perhaps you'd care to up the stakes, Lord Cordoba?" Ace slipped his hand under the table and pulled a large purse from his belt. He dumped it on the table, and an avalanche of platinum coins poured out. "I need a chance to win my money back, and I am prepared to wager my imperial crowns against your Castillan florins. Shall we say fifty crowns to the florin?"

Ace knew it was an attractive trade for Cordoba. Imperial coinage was illegal for use on Castilla, and although the official exchange rate at the planet's central bank was twenty-five to one, that was a ludicrous example of wishful thinking that only supported a flourishing underground economy where a crown could fetch at least sixty florins, and often eighty or more.

"Very well, Lord Suvarov." Cordoba nodded, his eyes barely betraying him. *He's good,* Ace admitted.

Just not better than me.

He'd put it about fifty-fifty Cordoba would try and bargain him down, but he'd picked just the right number, an attractive deal that wouldn't look suspicious. "Then, by all means, Lord Cordoba . . . deal." Ace looked out over the table. He was down about fifteen hundred florins, nothing he couldn't manage. And the big pile of platinum crowns was occupying Cordoba's attention.

Ace wondered how the others were doing. His "wife," Katarina, would be in the restaurant, hopefully making a fool out of him by now. And Blackhawk and Sarge would be approaching the target location soon. In another few hours, the crew of *Wolf's Claw* would be blasting off Castilla after another successful mission—or they'd be in deep shit.

Just like every other mission, he thought.

"Lady Suvarov, what a delight to see you again." Arragonzo Francisco de Aragona stood next to the table, smiling. He wore a magnificent suit, perfectly tailored and trimmed in gold and silver lace. His neatly arranged hair was pulled back and fastened behind his head with a jeweled clasp.

Unlike Cordoba, Aragona was a Castillan nobleman. He was also a renowned ladies' man, one who preferred his women as beautiful—and married—as possible. His noble pedigree was modest, something that would normally have placed a ceiling on how high a Castillan could rise. But Aragona was smart. And ruthless. His willingness to use whatever means were necessary to clear rivals from his way had taken him far, and now he was one of the Oligarchs Council, twenty men who ruled the planet.

His interests included most of the hotels and all the gambling on Castilla and, less formally, almost the entirety of the planet's underworld. He was the most junior member of the council by lineage, but he'd made up for that with fear. The other oligarchs, members of proud and ancient families, held their arrogance in check around Aragona. It was well known how he'd dealt with his rivals on his rise and, while he'd never made a hostile move against any in the highest ranks of the nobility, none of them wanted to risk being the first.

"Lord Aragona, what a delight to see you." Her voice was

haughty, but there was something else there too for anyone truly listening, a hint of seduction. Katarina Venturi had played many roles, and she slipped effortlessly into the guise of an exiled Saragossan noblewoman. She glanced up with a smile. "Won't you join me for dinner? I'm afraid my husband's attention is consumed by the gaming tables." She sighed, a passing hint of sadness on her face.

Aragona bowed slightly. "By all means, Lady Suvarov. It would be my great pleasure. If I may say, your husband is a fool."

Katarina's smile broadened, and she looked across the table to her dining companion. "Natasha, do get up and make room for Lord Aragona. You may retire." She glanced back at Aragona, a playful glint in her eye. "I don't believe I will be needing you any further this evening.

Sam Sparks stood up and bowed her head toward Katarina. "As you wish, my lady." Samantha was doing her best to look comfortable in the elaborate dress she was wearing, but Katarina could see how much difficulty she was having trying to keep the long skirts in place.

"Lord Aragona." Sam bowed again, but Aragona didn't acknowledge her. *I'm not surprised, given the neckline of this dress,* Katarina thought. Indeed, his attention was focused on Katarina, who was leaning forward slightly, giving him a better view. Sam turned and quietly slipped out of the restaurant.

"Now, won't you keep me company?" Katarina smiled again, more mischievous this time, turning up the seduction just a bit.

Aragona glided around the table and slid into Sam's chair. "This is an unexpected pleasure." He raised his hand, just a few centimeters above the table. The waiter rushed over, clearly trying to hide his nervousness. "Yes, Lord Aragona? What can I get for you?"

"Have you ordered yet?" He glanced over at Katarina.

"No, Lord Aragona. I have not."

"May I?" He smiled across the table.

"Of course."

Aragona turned his head slightly. "Bring us a bottle of the Antillean Black Château. And we'll start with the chilled Paru melon, followed by the fire-roasted dragonfish."

Katarina suppressed a grin. She was an expert in aphrodisiacs, and she knew most of them were either frauds or only marginally effective, Castillan Paru melons among them. She had a few truly effective elixirs in her own bag of tricks, but she was confident she wouldn't need them. Aragona's mind was already where she wanted it.

"I have heard much of the legendary Castillan dragonfish, Lord Aragona, though I have never had the pleasure." The large fish was from the extreme arctic regions of the planet, and it was considered one of the finest—and most expensive— delicacies in the Far Stars.

"I am certain you will enjoy it." He looked across the table and smiled. "And please, no more Lord Aragona, I beg you. I am Arra."

Katarina returned the stare with a smoldering sensuality. "And I am Irina."

Arkarin Blackhawk crept through the thickets on the outskirts of the estate, knee deep in the warm waters of the estuary. Aragona's home was a vast compound, built along the sandy lowlands just south of Madrassa. The lights of the city were visible in the distance, along the ridge behind the great château.

Blackhawk held his hand up behind him, a reminder to Sarge to move slowly, cautiously. Aragona's residence looked like the opulent seaside home of a wealthy nobleman and, indeed, it was that. But it was much more, and Blackhawk knew it. Arragonzo Aragona was more than a businessman and a politician. He was the undisputed leader of most of the Castillan underworld. Blackhawk didn't have the kind of scouting data on the compound he'd have liked, but he was sure the place was a veritable fortress.

But every fortress has its weakness . . . and sometimes that's someone inside.

He was confident Katarina would manage to do the job. He almost pitied any man who was the target of her seductions. No, it wasn't getting her in that worried him. It was getting her out with the prisoner that gave him the cold sweat on his palms.

Blackhawk suspected Aragona was neck deep in a wide variety of unsavory enterprises, but the Castillan mastermind had made one crucial mistake. He'd included the Far Stars Bank among the targets of his frauds, defaulting on a loan for more than ten million crowns. The bank was not an entity to accept such a loss without consequences, and it had hired Blackhawk and his people to capture Aragona and bring him to its headquarters on Vanderon.

It's so easy to see power on one world as being universal. Aragona probably thought he was secure in his little fiefdom.

Blackhawk knew better. *There is always someone more powerful.*

He reached his hand out again, about to signal to Sarge to move forward, but then he froze. He heard something, far away, his ears picking up the dull roar long before Sarge knew anything was going on. Then, a few seconds later, he saw the lights, moving down the road from the east.

It was some kind of convoy, and it was heading right for the compound. He stared into the darkness, trying to focus on the oncoming vehicles. There was something about them, something troubling, familiar.

> **The convoy consists of imperial Raider-class ground assault vehicles. Probability 93 percent.**

The artificial intelligence implanted in Blackhawk's brain was limited to the same sensory input as his own mind, but it was often able to make more effective use of the data.

> **Imperial Raiders are armed with dual particle accelerator cannons and can carry up to ten . . .**

I am well aware of the specifications of imperial Raiders. There was an edge to the thought, directed toward the AI. Blackhawk had an odd relationship with the computer presence in his mind. He couldn't dispute the fact that the AI had been incredibly valuable on many occasions, but there was still some part of him that resented the intrusion. Despite the indisputable usefulness of the intelligence, he frequently found himself sparring with it . . . pointlessly, he realized, but he did it anyway.

What the hell are imperial fighting vehicles doing on Castilla? More to the point, what are they doing on the way to Aragona's estate?

He wondered for a few minutes if Aragona's château was about to be attacked by his enemies, but as soon as the lead vehicle reached the gate it was apparent they were expected.

He stood stone still, watching the scene unfold. His grip tightened around his assault rifle, but that was pure reflex. He knew fighting wasn't going to solve his problem, especially not a suicidal assault on Aragona's villa.

Blackhawk had no idea what was going on, but this was the second time in six months he'd run into imperial involvement in the affairs of backwater worlds, and he didn't like it one bit. He wasn't a great believer in coincidence.

There's no time to worry about that now, he thought, setting the topic aside. He knew immediately he had to change the plan. Katarina was planning to seduce Aragona and lure him back to his estate, where Blackhawk and Sarge's crew were positioned to get them both out. But the château was going to look like an armed camp in a few minutes. There was no way they'd manage to sneak anyone in or out.

"We're going to have to go with the backup plan, Sarge." That meant getting back into the city—fast. And he'd have to break communications silence, at least briefly, to let Katarina know. Hopefully, he'd get to her before she and Aragona were on their way to the compound.

He reached into his pocket and pulled out a small controller, pushing one of the buttons with his index finger. The communication was short, just a microburst to a small receiver in Katarina's ring. She wouldn't get any details, just a prearranged signal telling her to move to the backup plan.

Just let it be in time . . .

"Let's go, Sarge," Blackhawk whispered. "We need to round up your boys and get back to Madrassa." He took one last look at the château. The convoy was still coming, with no end in sight to the line of armored vehicles. *That's trouble. Big trouble.*

"C'mon, Sarge. We're already late."

Continue reading *Enemy in the Dark* in trade paperback and eBook, on sale December 2015.

ABOUT THE AUTHOR

Jay Allan currently lives in New York City and has been reading science fiction and fantasy for just about as long as he's been reading. His tastes are fairly varied and eclectic, but favorites include military and dystopian science fiction, space opera, and epic fantasy—all usually a little bit gritty.

He writes a lot of science fiction with military themes, but also other SF and some fantasy as well. He likes complex characters and lots of backstory and action, but in the end believes world-building is the heart of science fiction and fantasy.

Before becoming a professional writer, Jay has been an investor and real estate developer. When not writing, he enjoys traveling, running, hiking, and—of course—reading.

He also loves hearing from readers and always answers e-mails. You can reach him at jay@jayallanbooks.com, and join his mailing list at http://www.crimsonworlds.com for updates on new releases.

Among other things, he is the author of the bestselling Crimson Worlds series.